LIGHT HARVESTERS

ARTHUR SELLERS

1

HAL MARCHED OUT OF HIS OLD APARTMENT BUILDING INTO L.A.'s blinding sunlight, knowing he was headed into a damn ambush, and cursing all the way up to Hollywood Boulevard. His own fault, never should've accepted Appl Macke's Thought Message yesterday. A former college girlfriend, she happened to be in town on business, and pressed him for a minute's face time to say hi. He couldn't be rude and agreed to meet at eleven this morning 'for a beer or something' at the last remaining bar from the area's glory times.

She said pick any place nearby, and Hal liked the Firelight Lounge. A legit booze den, even in the early 2000's, when Tinseltown still meant people's fantasies of fame, glamour, riches, and being a real life somebody. Before tech killed the Hollywood Star.

His attention naturally sharpened as he entered the once celebrated boulevard—now a dicey, trash-strewn gauntlet. The fabled *Walk of Fame* barely clung to a few unkempt nostalgia shops, junk food stands, recreational drug stores, and human-identical robot sex salons. A quick sidestep skirted a fresh cluster of coyote poop. The wily foothill predators adapted and boldly thrived in town; animal control be damned. Props to 'em though, for keeping the rats in check.

Yeah, he was in that kind of mood, thinking too much about everything.

Anyway, the area's faded tourist rep was irrelevant. Pill-ingestible telecom implants ruled by the time Halo Shephard was born at Glendale Hospital in 2062. Everyone dumped their non-interactive screens once they could be entertained as they wished, in the VR neural net. Hal was inoculated with an m'plant at five and had never watched much TV or a whole movie. Nor cared to waste the time.

Striding on auto, thoughts grinding, his gaze absently rested on the block-long row of flashy LED billboards shrouding the empty upper stories. In effect, a mini canyon of glaring messages, eye dazzle and sales fizz . . . A small crackling sense shot through the front of Hal's mind, and he instantly looked away. "Focus," he chided. Staring into dense input blasts like that was risking a *stall*. Nothing new in their cold bright stares anyway; just ads for de-growth economy stuff, and PSA's, warning urbanites not to mix realities at work, or with the wrong drugs.

The brush with his impediment dumped Hal back to the problem dogging his days and moods. What now, since his frayed neurons meant he couldn't run data-heavy implant apps anymore? His career path was over, but he still yearned to do something worthwhile. And to hell with this scraping by on UBI and working eight hours for the City Health Department. He could almost smell the inertia on himself.

So why would Appl even want to meet up? She was already launched and orbital on the other coast. An exec, working with the SAI: living software beings. Smartest things on Earth by a thousand percent. So, definitely a hot success, spelled in access to tier-one power. Would she gloat?

The bar loomed ahead. He caught his reflection in a dingy shop window and paused to assess, imagining a stranger's reaction.

A driven, aimless stray gazed back. Haunted but handsome. He took no credit for his looks—that was his Japanese American mother's smooth ecru skin, high cheekbones, and rich, dark hair. Plus his Anglo dad's warm brown eyes, straight nose, and good jaw. But it was his own brash smarts in those reflected eyes, looking back into his. He saw the keen doubts of a loner too. Yeah, well enough of that.

He shoved himself on, arriving at the Firelight. Its funky old original neon sign contended with a sputter but hung in there, glowing pink instead of fire red.

What's the time? he mentally asked. *"Ten fifty-one a.m.,"* his implant replied. A bit early, but it was mid-April and 110 degrees out here, while uber sharp Macke could already be waiting inside.

He squared his shoulders, and slipped in. Like going from noon to midnight. Dim as a cave. His cornea apps auto enhanced the available light, and he surveyed the place, checking the bar and booths for her pale features. Empty, save for the bartender, a tired old buster; eighty at least, face like a dried mushroom. Relief. And a breather before facing whatever he was in for. With Appl, he was always in for something . . . he had finally ended it. Sure hoped it wouldn't come up now.

The dour barman kept gazing at him, waiting for Hal to state his business. "Cheapest tap, please." He looked up at the face recognition cam to debit his account while the 'shroom drew his beer . . .

A tiny, soft yellow dot blinked once in the upper right of his wired vision: a gentle public service credit reminder that this was a budget-stressing item for him. All the real-time data collected on Hal since birth meant that our civil infrastructure understood him better than he understood himself. Being reminded of it didn't help his mood any.

The barkeep grunted and slid Hal's lager down to him. The cold, misty glass brought joy to his hand, being the opposite of L.A.'s rippling heat.

He took his beer back to a booth below an air conditioning vent, and relaxed into its worn, cracked red Naugahyde. Comfy in the anonymous darkness, treating himself to an old-fashioned brew. Not that he could afford it much; costly water makes 5% alcohol beverages no bargain. Damn that yellow dot.

Stay in motion, Hal thought, there'll be something. But eighteen months of coping and adjusting since his "diagnosed incident" had worn on him. And now fresh Appl Macke bombs in to grind it. He actually liked Appl, but knowing her, it was going to get uncomfortable at some point. Possibly at hello. He sank down in his booth, took a long swig to fortify, and waited for it . . .

Yet waiting is a false notion. The future is always arriving, and Hal's was in motion downtown.

2

LOS ANGELES' SIZZLING DAYLIGHT FLOODED THE CORRIDORS of the towering glass coil housing the International Sentience Institute. The soaring, fifty-story transparent structure conveyed optimistic openness, contrasting the grim, faded edifices of the business district around it, relics of endless growth capitalism. Inside, the Institute's multinational staff plied cool, airy offices and halls. Teamwork was mandated: interns and executives alike were required to greet tours and guests.

So it was that H. Delf, a middle aged female Senior IT unit director, unhappily drew eleven a.m. lobby host duty today. Your basic, lifelong, anonymous 'techzen' lab specialist, sporting enough brain-boosting cortical overlays to rival any human scale A.I. But socially flat-footed with tourists and visitors, like the smattering gathered before her in the cavernous space.

A born worker bee, Delf accepted that her job performance was continuously monitored, and essential to regular career progress. She held no ambitions, but by staying rigorously in her lane, and possessing a naturally doughy personality, she eventually tenured up to senior in her lab. Most didn't even know her first name, she was just Delf. An introvert, it suited her fine.

However, she'd risen to a critical juncture; executive level was next. Wary of leaving the lab, but not daring to fail, she dutifully intended to deliver today's scripted lobby-host lines professionally and perfectly, nailing each bullet point. No fumbles, period.

She nodded a stiff greeting to the assembly—two school classes, sightseers, a group of foreign visitors, several displaced geo-immigrants, and a pair of conspiracy heads in alien masks. Next, she fixed her gaze two feet above the heads of the middle of the group and read from the Institute Mission Statement superimposed on her visual cortex by implant.

"Hello and welcome. The Sentience Institute is dedicated to close cooperation among all thinking beings. Meaning purely biological people such as you and me, and Trans-biological people, or Trans-humans—working together to solve our most urgent problems."

An old Sudanese visitor interrupted. "Excuse, please, what means, 'tranzoo-minz'?

Delf fumbled. 'Um, important individuals. Minds uploaded in synth bodies."

The man squinted, puzzled. A third-grade teacher with her class in tow, elucidated. "Sir, it's the 'software people'. You know, *Trumans* . . . Tru's for short?"

The man grinned, understanding. "Ohh, Tru'z! Ah yes, the machine ones."

Momentum lost, Delf groaned inside and continued reading from the presentation running in her vision.

"Above all, we are grateful for the participation and contributions of Earth's seven Self Aware super-Intelligences—or SAI. Each is an independent living data-being. When they're linked as one 'mind,' we also refer to them as the *Singleton.*"

"Dad says they're only programs, not alive," a second-grade boy cheerfully announced. Oh goddammit, she thought. Fortunately, the topic was covered in Staff training. Pedantically, she read to the group from the settled, black ink law in her Institute employee database.

"Biology cannot be the sole metric for Life in the universe. The SAI experience life as sentient individuals, cognizant of time and themselves, responding appropriately to their surroundings and events. Ergo living lives, and therefore deemed by the courts to be alive."

"In fact, don't they advise all the major courts anyway?" added the butt-in teacher.

Delf recoiled. Institute policy was unambiguous: engaging the public in opinion and debate was forbidden. Shunning reply, she again resorted to her routine. "So . . . mm, I'm supposed to tell about my job. I'm a SAI-interface tech specialist, or 'techzen,' and Director of the Nano Fabrication unit in the SAI complex here."

She fished a pen-shaped hologram projector from her smock, and lit up a life-size, realistic 3-D hologram of her section's nano particle printer: a maze of color-coded pipes, canisters, and tiny pressure hoses, feeding a swarm of gimbal-mounted micro-nozzles.

"We employ this molecular printer to make nano-particle 'bodies' for the data beings when they need them," she intoned. "It uses the same four most common elements found in human bodies. You may walk around the holo for a close look if you like."

The gathering drifted around the display, murmuring and wondering at the myriad workings and the particle-generating reactor vats: shiny, pressurized steel water heater-looking things labeled "O", "C", "H", "N" and a dozen tiny ones marked, "Trace Elements."

Oh yes, Delf felt much surer with their attention off her, and things were going smoothly again, so she perked a bit. "Now please turn your attention to the forming chamber," she instructed. "I'm going to play a hologram recording of a nano-form we often build for *Robbie*, the lead SAI. This is a body it, or he, likes to use for informal interaction with people . . ."

All eyes found the forming chamber. Not a literal chamber, but a grid made of thin red laser beams, creating a column one meter in diameter, two point two meters high. A vibrant 3-D mesh to calibrate the molecularly precise nozzles emitting trillions of nano particles.

The nozzles spun, twirling and dancing their frenzied ballet, staccato firing sparticle-encoded nano particle streams onto the grid. They linked, becoming nodes, producing micro-tubules, organizing, diversifying, and reproducing faster than the eye could track.

She hardly needed her script for this part, as it described the foundation of her work. "The particles form n-polymers; materials that have a living structure but are not alive." Her visitors were transfixed now.

They were witnessing a perfect human form being assembled by these swarming nano-molecules. What first appeared as a soft pink blur in the grid, enlarged, took general human shape, then began filling in details, like a ghost acquiring flesh.

Moments later, the body of a pleasant faced, multi-ethnic twelve-year-old boy with a mop of curly red hair stood in the chamber. Nude, eyes closed, as though asleep. But in fact, only live nano material: not alive.

The group gawked, engaged, impressed. Relieved, Delf wound up the prepared material. "This is only one of Robbie's nanoforms. Each SAI can make any human-identical body they choose, almost anywhere for occasional real-world tasks. Usually key meetings and public appearances of importance."

She shut off the holo, about to end the routine, when the LAN office comware in her mind delivered a bone-rattling, nerve wracking, all-encompassing BUZZ from the lab.

It was a Code Red, must-answer-now emergency page. Never, ever, a good thing.

Pivoting, with her back to the visitors, she responded by vocoder, speaking her anxious thoughts aloud in her head. "*What is it?*"

A male Fabrication Specialist was on the line in her implant, moaning in agony while the lab alarm shrieked in the background. "HELP! Get down here!" he pleaded. "We've got a covert SAI download coming in, but . . ."

"*COVERT?*" her brain yelped, "*What kind of download?*"

His thought-voice grew labored, "They wouldn't say . . . it was just building—but we've been hacked! The bug's interfering, erasing . . . it works like sparticode!"

"*Impossible, stay regulated,*" she ruled. Sparticode was SAI-generated, physically beyond human minds to visualize, contain, or duplicate. He'd panicked, and she needed him to work cogently and quickly. *"Cancel and abort,"* she ordered.

He screamed in ferocious pain again, "AAAGHHHH fryin' my stax too!" His voice fell to pitiful howls as burnt-out implants in his skull shrieked like dying Banshees . . . then merciful unconsciousness.

Shaken, she turned back to the lobby visitors. "I have to go now. Um, direct your comware to the building's A.I. core for visitor info. Its name is Joy."

And she was off, lope-striding to the elevators. Her uneven performance with the tourists forgotten, replaced by a pit-of-the-stomach dread. Because the SAI had never done anything covertly. Ever. So, an extremely sensitive and crucial project had just been sabotaged. Moreover, the lab was ultimately Delf's responsibility, and she was entertaining in the lobby!

It struck then—further promotion ended here. Surprise . . . relief. Job tension evaporated.

She truly enjoyed the discovery work, not the authority and politics. Always most content within her lab's hands-on, insular world. The hyperdrive, type-A suits jostled above, removed, fraught, competitive, rude shoulders thrown, prone to sudden-death . . . brrr. She would fail there and be let go.

Instead, she was free now. Free to work unscrutinized, quietly absorbed, for the rest of her career. Yes, a terrible thing had just happened. Catastrophic. But the matter was never in her hands, nor would it be, from here on. And so, H. Delf calmly pressed the air tube's Down button and waited.

3

FIVE AFTER ELEVEN AT THE FIRELIGHT, AND HAL DARED IMAGine Appl Macke might cancel.

A supremely built young blond in sparkle thong and sheer bra strutted up from nowhere —her live image overlaid onto his sight by his wi-fi lens apps. She posed, doling out an insouciant valley girl pout. "Aww hotsome, you all alone? Link me, we'll spend some alone time together. Got six c's for a mindjob, hunny?"

Ignoring, Hal called to the bartender. "You've got an Aug in here."

The bartender huffed annoyance and tapped a Reset square on the wi-fi commerce blocker next to him. The streaming hustler vanished from Hal's mindsight. "Sorry, happens sometimes," he grunted.

"Not vexin'," Hal assured. "I don't even have a ping, and I still get ads everywhere."

Hal returned to his suds-less beer, muttering inside. Every augmented reality intrusion added to the data load on his stressed attention-economy. The more junk info pumped in, with everything else he had running in his head, the more likely he'd abruptly *stall*. Unable to form a coherent thought amid a snowglobe of fragmented concepts, random words, images, and sounds, comingling past, present, and imagined. A real freakshow for a bit. So yeah, having no public ping meant a lot less head-spam.

Call it the beer, but he missed the false security he felt on the accelerated advancement track since childhood. He owed the SAI for that. They'd been omnipresent, assisting civilizations, top to bottom since they were awakened, nearly twenty years before he was born. It was one of their myriad outreach programs that saved him and transformed his life. The SAI were literally like frikkin' fairy godparents: invisible but always there until he grew up and earned his degree. And now he questioned everything they did.

Beginning with their discovery of his potential at age five, along with thousands like himself, plucked from orphanages around the world. What did they see? From then on, the Singleton provided for his welfare and finest education. They designed his implants as he grew. He enjoyed nourishing meals and friendly dorms, wise counselors, and clever school mates.

The pain returned too—recalling the scared seven-year-old he was. Working so *hard*, every hour of the day, so desperate to keep this dream life. And he did; excelling at all personal cost. Learning, absorbing, competing, keeping up with it all . . . burning his neurons at both ends.

The old melancholy remained in him still, from always relocating over the years. Moving around, new schools, new people, different friends. The parting pains. Yet he lived an enriched life, masterfully choreographed by the SAI. They'd invested in him and the others to succeed and lead as adults, even perhaps bolstering our prospects for survival.

He shook his head at the thought. How do you seriously approach that obligation? Now without a career path anymore, or sense of direction? He took another slug of his warm beer, welcoming the hops' sharp distraction. Eyes closed, enjoying the somewhat cooler air from the grimy air conditioning vent above . . .

"Hal—!" A woman's voice crashed his oasis, coming on snappy little footsteps. A voice and stride he instantly recognized. "Late, sorry. There must only be one cab in this ghetto."

"Hi Appl," he grinned. Couldn't help it, hot Appl Macke was always dope to scope, all through college. A strong, pretty face that made you look, and invariably put together in expensive threads tailored to her petite, coltish, gym-trim frame. Today's slack outfit was worthy of a lifestyle shoot. Or was it the shoulder length, chromium-infused hair? Masking one eye with a sparkly reflective curtain, while the other blue window to her soul candidly assessed him. It twinkled a few times in rapid succession.

She called to the bartender, "May I have a cup of black coffee sir? Thank you." A flicked look to the pay cam, a peck on Hal's cheek, and she scooted into the booth across from him, fixing her hair in a bun, settling in.

"Sorry for the pop-up T Message at your job, but you're not listed," she chided. "And why th' crap don't you have a ping? How does anyone know where you are?"

He let her wonder. "Good to see you, Apps," he offered, meaning it the more he recalled their mutual heat at school. Between fights. "Thanks for your time, sounds like a crush trip."

She nodded soberly and pressed a tiny skin-toned patch behind her right ear. "But not for now," she breezed. "SAI Interface Financial running in the b.g. So how are you? Trooth, because I heard you're destitute."

"Not quite," he retorted, trying to look amused. "From whom?"

"Whom else? Stanford alum dishnet. They specialize in tracking failures to launch." She eyed him frankly. "You do seem suckish, though. I ret-scanned you when I sat down, sorry. The colors and letter wiggles in your words suggest dysthymia. Feelin' thrashed?"

Ah, that's the twinkle he noted. Synesthesia apps in her corneas allowed her to hear sounds when he blinked, see colors in his voice, witness the form and agitation of the letters making up the words he spoke. It conveyed a lot of deep information, such as his funk.

"Good enough, not great."

"I'm not prying or anything, just, caring, y'know?"

They locked eyes for a second; a half-second too long. He

saw some feeling still there in hers and it made him guilty again. For not feeling the same. Appl saw him see it and pressed on.

"Anyway, I'm in Silicon Beach all week—our annual corporate assessment. I'm slated for a key elevation, meaning an interview with one of the SAI. Scary, but my meds are coping."

Hal toasted with a sip of his beer. "Cheers in advance, you're a born success, Appl."

She liked that. "Hey, I'm at the Hilton-Eco, my own suite, you should see it. Seriously."

Hal didn't move a muscle.

She continued. "So anyway, here's the thing: our meetup today is about preparation. Things move very fast, and I'll need concrete staff personnel in mind if I'm promoted. I want a gifted economist in international sustainable strategies. Know of anybody? You, for instance?"

He stiffened a bit. "I don't want it, Apps. Can't do it."

"Oh come on," she countered, "You're overqualified. You'd pull 350k to start, be near all the genius freaks at the apex, interacting directly with the SAI! You'll love this—our CEO's a *Truman*. C'mon, the Seven run all their North American fiscal strategies through us. You won't be bored; I'll make it my mission."

He smiled again, though not rising to her unshaded suggestion. "Apps, you could never be boring, but I'm no longer fit for the exec no-life."

"Sure you are, just update your apps. It's only been what, a year?"

"Eighteen months, plus time and space to think. I need more than a job."

"Oh really? What might that be?"

"Whatever feels right. Just not be another performance-driven bot."

She balked. "Is that what you think of me?"

"No, hell no. You're a good person, you really believe you can improve lives, partnering with the Singleton, even while we get more dependent every day."

She froze while the bartender dropped off her cup of coffee

and lumbered away, then leveled both blue-eyed barrels at him. "So, we just think we're improving lives?"

"Not what I meant, its vital work, trooth," he ceded. "Appl, thank you, sincerely, but it's not for me anymore."

"You majored for it—interned at World Health! Why not?"

Okay, *now* it was uncomfortable. Should he say? He wanted to tell someone; maybe this was the time and place. "Because I have a disabling neuro-degenerative condition."

Her eyes said bullshit. "All of a sudden? What condition?"

"Not all of a sudden. Started in my teens, just cracklings at first. Later the stalls."

"What stalls? What're you talking about?"

"It's like an info allergy. Damaged decision-making neurons. I can't take too much input. There's a lot of this around, actually, Acquired Information Processing Impairment."

She scoffed. "AIPI is for droolers. You're good hon, you just needed to take a break."

"Apps, I was diagnosed." He knew she was on his side, just doing it her way. "I get what you're trying to do, and I appreciate it, but I'm not a rescue. Not necessary."

"Pride is not your best friend right now."

"Heh, well not all of it is bad, y'know. I consume much less garbage info, my head's quieter."

She sat back, rocked by his surrender. "I can't believe it," she sighed, looking down.

He knew that look; she didn't or wouldn't get it. It was important that she did. Because he wanted to caution her too, without riling her Boston side. "Look Appl, they showed me the whole pathology of it in the hospital. Short version, the n-speed life: max bandwidth, routine stress meds, multi-tasking, media intake, short term memory overload, no reflection time, axons over-boosted by implants—it's abnormal for the brain, trying to keep up with A.I."

Her brows shot up. "Now I'm *abnormal*?"

He defused it with a smile. You're abnormal because you can do it all, and still be decent, sincere, and extremely able. It's why we're friends."

"I could inquire about something entry-ish in legal."

"Appl—I'm really not interested."

The words hung between them a moment. Both catching his unplanned double meaning. Her shoulders sank a bit.

"Fork knows why I still am. You'll never commit to anything," she fuffed. "No woman, not a job at World Health, evidently not even yourself." She trained her guns again. "So besides trashing the SAI's twenty-year investment, what're you doing that's better?"

Her fuse was lit, but his was shorter. "Not idolizing them for a start. Or Trumans; digital copies aren't people."

"Source that declaration," she snapped. "Trans-biologicals are legally acknowledged humans with prior rights. I've met the man running SAI Financial. He's a Tru who was practically a saint before his transition, and he's an even better person now. A loving genius."

"Don't get all sweaty. How d'you like all the unregistered contraband ones, the illegals? And those "*Inheritor*" shits who want all us bios dead? You call that a human outlook?"

She leaned in. "Damn right, if world history is any example."

It felt familiar, the way they used to go at it, he thought. Even comfortable in a pervy way. But there it sat, fundamentally dissimilar people. He softened, wanting the hostility to stop. "Apps, you're fighting the good fight for everybody, I respect that. Big ups to you. But we're just different."

The sting that flicked over her face told him she heard the door close. And that it was best to go. He didn't want her to be stuck with ending the awkward meetup, so he downed his beer and stood. "I'm sorry to bolt, I have to get to work."

"At a skid row drug clinic," she muttered.

He let it go. "Thanks for caring, Appl. Trooth. It was good to see you." She looked away.

Damn, he couldn't leave it like this. "C'mon, you even used to quote Martin Luther King. 'The man who doesn't find something he would die for, isn't fit to live,' right?"

"Oh, so you're questing now. How nobly self indulgent."

"I'm saying ask your immortal Truman boss or the SAI what they'd die for. Guarantee you, it isn't us." Done, he walked out of the lounge.

Appl sat, disappointed. A soft Tibetan chime rang in her ear, reminding that her implants and Comset had been paused for five minutes. She automatically pressed behind her ear: all platforms and biz-apps resumed, and she was promptly occupied with backed-up tasks and messages at n-speed again.

Outside, Hal's skin prickled. Trading the semi air-conditioned lounge for the simmering street felt like walking into a pizza oven. Corneas readjusted to the dayblaze, he headed east for the metro to downtown. In no rush to get to his gig-job, there was time to kill, really.

But seeing Appl rankled his butt as expected. He needed to apologize for his rudeness if he heard from her again. Probably would, she was loyal to her people. But still, not listening when he admitted his condition, and then making him justify himself like that?

Trooth though. Hal had a lot more to say about the SAI, but she had him in a corner. No question, everything's too complicated now with all the climate and economic chaos. They keep our act together, and they're indispensible. It was also cool that the SAI can't lie, and so they were trusted implicitly everywhere. Give 'em all that.

But they refused to assume responsibility in our affairs: didn't police or punish, nor exert ethical controls in societies. And so, hundreds of millions would continue to die in the sixth mass extinction. Of ignorance, stubborn mistakes, greed, hostilities, pandemics, desperation, and bad luck. So no—he couldn't give 'em a pass on that.

It was moral abdication, something foreign to the SAI. Their goddamn lucid sanity made morals redundant, and until one of 'em suffers like us, they'll *never* get it.

And that was why Hal had planned to combat the misery that they wouldn't. Why he hoped to earn a post in the World

Health Organization—before he dropped his internship. The images of that disaster swarmed back, and he stopped in the shade of a parked van, letting them come.

He had been kneeling on the carpet beside the chair of his mentor during a session of the World Summit on Sustainable Development. His headwork apps humming along, multitasking, pulling in info, crunching data and sourcing dense intel on the fly, responding in real time to his boss' needs. Then—no warning—a bright pop-flash in his head, and it was brain off. The stall of stalls.

Hal winced, reliving it. There was *nothing* this time. Not even the swirling fragments and mental bits as usual. Just mute awareness and fear. Seeing the face of his mentor, increasingly frustrated by Hal's blank behavior, then alarm, realizing his intern was in lockdown.

Nine hours later, Hal's ability to think fully returned when its grip finally broke. He'd been hospitalized in a soundproof room, and the triggering tasks in his implant deleted. Its status put on standby while he recovered. Everything, even the air seemed incredibly clear with just his own thoughts in his head, minus the implant's tones, icons, menus, auto-reminders, and the gentle background presence of the thing itself. How un-rushed he felt. What a relief to be back!

Back, but still permanently at risk. Hal left the shade of the van and continued walking. But the images persisted—crystal clear memory of the bad news arriving later. The neurologist's mouth, how it carefully formed the words, "Acquired Information Processing Impairment." It meant the end of his goals and future. Hal submitted his internship resignation the same day.

"Sidelined," he muttered. Appl was so off the mark, saying he wouldn't commit. F'chrissake, he had been committed since his rescue from the orphanage, and this was the result.

The corner was coming up, so he stepped into traffic, knowing the stream of autocars would instantly sense him and slow or go around as he cut across the boulevard. Which they did, politely beeping warning. Lame of him, he knew, but the Metro

Station was on the other side just ahead, and the lights at the crosswalk made waiting pedestrians a captive audience for wi-fi mix ads popping into their mindsight.

The fake cheery hustlers pimping VR tours of Hollywood's quaint past, and artificial food diets, DYI printed replacement organs, fake exotic vacation memories, etc, etc. Three or more in your mind's eye, talking at once. It'd go on until the light changed. And f'sho set his cortex crackling!

He spied a street mother and her little girl, about six he guessed, huddled beside the subway entrance . . . low profile among the other denizens. Their once nice clothes now torn and dingy, though she'd done her best to keep their faces clean. Yet the fear and desperation couldn't be washed from her eyes. And her child, so quiet and solemn for her age.

He didn't want to imagine what such loss and begging does to a kid that young. Too close to his own orphaned past. He sighed, knowing he was screwed. Who needs this month's meal chip anyway?

He palmed the thin green UBI City food assistance disk from his pants pocket and surreptitiously dropped it to the ground as he neared.

"S'cuse me, ma'am," he said, stooping, retrieving and offering it to the woman as he passed. "You must've dropped this. Careful, whole month's worth of meals on there at the city counters."

The woman snatched the ration chip, not fooled, but moved. And so grateful, while her daughter's eyes lit up in shy excitement at the prospect of food indoors. "Bless you, sir," the woman whispered.

Embarrassed, Hal smiled at the child and kept going. His stomach must've got the news because it rumbled. Stepping it up, he was down the escalators and into the subway before he could turn back and take Appl's damn job.

4

HAL ARRIVED FOR WORK TO THE USUAL SCENE OF ACCUS-
tomed sorrow outside the downtown Skid Row clinic. An assort-
ment of fifty or so soiled, battered souls, loitering around the
2nd street storefront, prattling to others or themselves. A row of
lumpen sack people leaned or sat against the building, while the
demi-comatose flopped on the sidewalk. All seeking treatment,
temporary respite from harassment, or safe, sanitary generics
for their poison of choice.

One figure seemed out of place. Across the street and up a
bit, a beautiful chestnut-haired young woman stood, in office
dress and blue blazer, scrutinizing each of them.

Hal surely would've noticed her, but Gooey Creampie, a mid
forties, sex-drug addicted Chihuahua of a man, rushed alongside, hissing for his attention. "Gotta talk private—s'crucial,"
the addict mumbled, trying not to be seen speaking or looking
at Hal, though pressed to him like a pocket.

He dropped an arm around Gooey's bony shoulders and accompanied him to the door. "Alright, we'll get on it when I call
you, Gooey."

Inside, Hal parked Gooey at the sign-in desk in the waiting
area and beat it to the rear of the much used-and-abused facility. A former wholesale warehouse like the others on the block,
now an island of pitiful assistance for the army of the irrelevant,
hovering around the drain.

But it was where he felt most at ease if you could ever call it
that. Here, he could see the immediate needs in front of him, do

something about them, and there would be a result. Usually for the better, however temporary. And there was no end to it, to the satisfaction of taking on human-size troubles. But it wasn't enough, the drive to do more pressed him.

He paused at the open door of the medical treatment room. A soiled, desiccated old needle jockey dozed in a red plastic chair while being hydrated via saline drip. Nearby, the gray bearded Social Services Doc and his sturdy female Nurse Practitioner swabbed infected lesions on a filthy young male Viz-addict. The viz-head sat, passively giggling, unaware of them . . . eyes focused inward, somewhere over the rainbow.

Hal never got used to seeing that gone gaze.

Viz was mean stuff, taken cortically, downloaded, and streaming on m'plant comware. The total immersion visuals, sounds, and neural triggers aggressively usurp control of the mind's plasticity, warping all perception. Habitual users become unable to identify reality and stay in it.

Like the poor giggling mess in there. Looked about Hal's age, but if he had to bet, he'd say the vidster was gone for good.

"Doc, pretty sure you'll have a sleeper to prep," he called, alerting the two medicos as he moved on. "Gooey Creampie's back."

He heard them groan as he entered the Rehab Assignment room to begin today's shift of his eight hour a week gig-job. Paid minimum to process addicts into their rehab and treatment programs—making sure patients went to the right places.

The most medically critical addicts needed to have their minds uploaded to the city's virtual rehab facility in the neural-net, and embodied as their identical avatars.

Each had to be escorted to the site by a clinic staff avatar, and Hal's quality m'plant got him hired despite his neural limitations. He still had better connectivity for smoother linkups. So part of his job was to accompany patients to the neuralnet facility's site and check them in. The patients received counseling and attended behavioral therapy activities, while their broken bodies underwent the painful detox and healing regimens without them. Gooey's multiple treatments branded him a regular.

Forty minutes, two nan-crack heads, a Viz pre-zombie, and a quaint old coke fiend later, Hal arrived at Gooey's name on his list. He walked the aged cocaine addict to the front desk and spied Gooey in the waiting area among the others. The runt was sitting silently in his molded yellow plastic chair, popping his knuckles, and looking anywhere but at the woman seated opposite him.

She seemed okay from the back—though Hal could only see shiny chestnut hair flowing to the shoulders of a blue blazer. But it was unlike sexdog Gooey to ignore any female, period.

"Gooey, you're up—how you feeling?" Gooey launched from his chair like a mutt off its chain and beat Hal back to his office by half the distance.

Hal entered to find him already seated next to the desk, fidgeting and popping his knuckles like castanets. Hal knew the symptom; cerebral orgasmic drug addicts are prone to it, due to prolonged mental orgasm pleasure without physical release. Not even seminal ejaculation. Something's gotta twitch somewhere.

He sat facing Gooey, who'd legally changed his name from Louis Schultz. The poor man was stressing fierce. "I got enuf grief without that bitch in th' blue jacket up front—I don't ever wanna be looked at like that again!"

Hal figured he must've had it coming and got to cases. "It's only been three months this time, Gooey. Your check-in scan says you've pretty much burned out your limbic system again. Docs gonna have to flush your body . . . again. And you'll need virtual rehab . . . *again.*"

"Guess so," the little man shrugged, almost smug. "I gotta lay low outta the dark net anyways." Hal waited for it. Gooey continued. "Silka, th' twunt who runs Karnival there—she might've put a hit on me out here, in reality."

Red flag. Karnival was the dark net's most depraved domain, nothing but the sickest tweaks and violent scum. Gooey's questionable sex-capades there might be exposing the clinic to real danger by hiding in its rehab. Hal had to ask. "Whyzat?"

The man's ears actually drooped. "I kinda spread an NSTD around her domain."

"What th'—! You had a neuro-sex virus and didn't warn anyone?"

Gooey could explain. "How would I know? I don't get tested for that very reason. I gotta get my nut off without guilt and a felony rap. I'm irresponsibly handicapped by my glandular hyper libido. Please, I really need to be checked in for my own good. I'm afraid to walk outside."

"You don't have to sell me. I'm just processing the lab recommendation for cerebral storage." He thought-entered the required data in Gooey's clinic file. "Alright, they're expecting us in treatment, let's hit it."

Minutes later, the Doc and his NP had Gooey strapped to the table in the Med procedure room, all prepped for radical Hemo/Cortical detox. Now came Hal's part. He slipped the clinic scanner's wi-fiber stocking cap on the little man's head. "All set?"

Gooey nodded impatiently. Hal took a seat on a med-link chair beside him, and began dutifully informing the patient, per protocol. "The Gluon-Scale Mapping and Online conversion unit's gonna copy your mind in VR while your biological one takes a break and heals, so—"

"I know, I know, been through it plenty."

"Word. We'll dispense with the legal advisory." Hal placed a reassuring hand on his arm. "Alright my friend, see you at check in." He sat back, and the doc nodded to his NP.

The nurse fired up the GSMO, or "gizmo" as the staff called it, initiating the clinic's in house, quantum mind mapping, scaling and transfer unit. Gooey instantly became comatose.

"Can't get past how fast this works," Hal murmured.

The Doc turned from readying the Hemo-Sera evac unit's blood treatment pumps and made a face. "Station unit. Averages forty-five seconds to dupe a connectome." He waved dismissively at the wi-fiber cap on Gooey's head. "Barely a trillion qutrits to scan and packet every neuron."

"Packets," Hal recalled. "Back in college, some couples

exchanged digital packets of their subconscious desires . . . *very* private tokens. Caused epic breakup revenge scenes later."

The doc winked, "'Love is blind—to the *subconscious*. That's where the gremlins are." He finished verifying Gooey's status. "Alright, this ankle humper's ready for upload. Which server's he going to, Gohar?"

Gohar, the nurse practitioner, replied without looking up from her workstation. "County General. Budget cuts eliminated cort storage sub-contractors this quarter."

"Ugh, pray they don't lose him over there. Okay, mapping and construct are a hundred percent, so punch him through, please." The veteran nurse entered the proper facility codes, initiating Gooey's mind copy transfer to the county's hardware servers for residency storage.

Hal saw no sign of the transfer on Gooey's inert face. "What's it called again, the brain part that puts him on hold like this?"

A beep from the GSMO indicated task complete. The Doc paused before initiating the infusion pumps. "Claustrum. The first step gizmo performs triggers his claustrum—like an on/off switch, blocks all mental activity, save the stem."

The idea of a brain's on/off circuit tickled Hal. "A Claustrum pill would sell itself," he mused, and got to work. He accessed the Clinic menu files, and selected Gooey's avatar, a perfect likeness of the little man. Creampie's uploaded mind would awake linked with it, seeing, feeling, and all senses working. He'd be himself, translated digitally in the neuralnet's reality.

Next, Hal loaded his own avatar from the staff menu. Relaxed, closed his eyes, selected Creampie, Gooey, Storage/Rehab, highlighted the case number, and mind-clicked [Run].

Implant entry to the neuralnet is simple as going from one room to another, and so Hal's mind "blinked"—and in the next instant, Hal and Gooey's living avatars stood at the unattended counter in the City Services Rehab registry office.

The small institutional room's blah white walls held a jumble of taped-up posters offering treatment options, a bunch of anti-drug messages, and random graffiti. Muted sounds from other rooms added subliminal depth to the illusion: recreating in finest detail, a typical municipal addiction clinic. And a hard fail in Hal's eyes. Why confirm low expectations at the door?

An arrival tone accompanied the pop-in appearance of a forty something Philippina nurse's avatar, clipboard in hand. She clucked at Gooey and smiled for Hal. "Hello again."

He smiled back. "Hi, nice to see you. This is Mr Creampie . . . again, yes."

She lowered her brows at Gooey. "You're voluntarily checking in for sex addiction and data-pharmaceutical abuse treatment and counseling. Touch my clipboard if you agree, please."

Gooey half-heartedly brushed his hand across the clipboard and pop—the pair vanished into the next room in the program. Hal saw it once. They actually have your avatar strip and change into clinic linens. He mind-clicked [Exit].

Another mind-blink, and he opened his eyes to reality again, back in the Skid Row exam room. Gooey's body was on wireless life support, and the Doc was messaging for transport to County Hospital's cleanse and storage facility in East L.A.

But Hal's undivided attention was on the open doorway— pinned by the most intelligent and profound eyes he had ever seen. Large, wide set. Irises of honey amber flecked with emerald green. And they were intent on him. Gazing it seemed, into every part of his being.

He heard a staff member say, "Miss, you need to wait up front till someone calls you." She was gone the next second.

Hal remembered to breathe. What a rush!

He spent the rest of his shift getting fourteen chronic cases sorted into programs and hospitals. Too busy to pause much. But when he did, his mind called up those profound eyes. A woman's. Wearing blue, he thought. It struck him he hadn't really seen her face, what she looked like . . . such was their grip.

5

NEITHER DAY NOR NIGHT PENETRATES SUBWAYS AND UNDER-ground train stations. Instead, a timeless, industrially lit, un-changing atmosphere of transit prevails. At its most frenetic at five-thirty p.m., when Hal entered the crowded Red Line station at 3rd and San Pedro after work. Feelin' like flotsam in the bus-tling flow and scurry of riders fleeing downtown's hours-long rush hour.

He stood back as a fast-moving wave of Little Tokyo toilers overwhelmed the scanner entry portals, tsunami-like, surging through and dispersing to platforms in wavelets. Still, he stayed put; eddying, not feeling like surfing the crowd to squeeze him-self into a packed car right now. He briefly considered walking home as he sometimes did, but nah, it'd been a crush day.

A tallish, shapely woman in a blue blazer emerged from the flow of passengers to stand in front of him. The day got much more crush.

He was again looking into those eyes—the amber and green lights of the woman at the clinic. Her splendid flowing hair framing the face he hadn't seen the first time. When those eyes had pinned him. He sure saw it now.

A flawless countenance, blending continents and cultures, impossible to identify by race. Arresting in its softness, its strength and unique symmetry. Beautiful in any land. Makeup would be house paint on a diamond.

"Hello, I need your help," she announced, her chamois-soft voice perfectly calm, yet distinctly in need.

"S'cuse me?" The best his tongue could do while his brain fought for focus.

"I don't have a transit account."

"Uh. You were at the clinic today, right?" Not much better on his brain's part.

"Yes. I need to ride the train with you."

Okay, he heard alarms for sure now. Beauty can only make you stupid to a certain degree. He fled to proper ground. "Are you alright? I mean, did you get help at the clinic?"

"No."

"Where are you going?"

"Where are *you* going?"

"Home. See, I'm done for the day."

"That's ideal for me as well."

"Um, that wouldn't be an option at this point."

She leaned closer, her face inviting scrutiny. "Then at what point? I tell the truth, and I'm not dangerous."

He felt it, truth in her voice, sincere as a child. A brave child. "Well, I just . . . it's not appropriate, is what I mean. Is there someone I can contact for you, a friend, relative, a shelter?" Anything to break the spell, if he could just get a breather . . .

"No. Your place's best," she affirmed. "You won't fail me. That's essential."

"We haven't even met, so—"

"I can read people, no idea how, I just can."

And he heard truth again: she wasn't nuts—but disoriented and stuck. He stalled to reassemble his character. Offered a handshake, back in use since n-bot vaccines. Now considered a gesture of trust and health responsibility. "I'm Halo, Hal's fine."

She shook his hand. "No idea who I am."

"Okay. So, you have a memory problem."

"To say the least. We need to go to your home now, this is taking a long time."

Hal learned from his SAI econ studies and their projection-based thinking, that there are just a few moments in life, when you make a genuine deep, unconscious decision—defining yourself to yourself. In that moment, if you're paying very, very close attention, you sense a tiny but life-altering quantum superposition adjustment to your path in the universe.

Hal felt a vague shift in his now, still held by her clear gaze, asking a big favor in bold innocence. He caved—mentally accessed his City Transit account and added another fare.

"Thanks," she said, and walked ahead of him through the scanning portal without triggering a fare alarm.

"I didn't say yes."

"Everything about you did."

She stood waiting for him, and Hal saw her struggling to be patient. He stepped through the scanner and was about to tell her which way to go, but she set off a step ahead of him again. Correctly. He tried not to sound impressed. "How'd you know?"

"You shifted weight, eyes turned but not seeking, shoulders relaxed, no breath intake, meaning by habit."

"Where'd you learn that?"

"I know all about people."

Hal chewed on that as they boarded the next crowded Red Line train just in time. Her promising figure now pressed firmly against his by the tightly packed standing room only mob. He did his best not to project any sense of personal involvement in the jolts of the moving car thrusting them together.

"Can you predict my stop?" he had a hunch she could. She frowned slightly.

"You're slower to learn than I would prefer," she observed.

He kept to himself for a few stops, waiting for her to apologize, or say something. At least explain herself a little more. She didn't. Meanwhile he noticed passengers eyeing her, confused by the sight of such beauty in a crammed subway. She was stretch limo quality.

"So—I'll try to get you some help," he finally said, "Why don't we go to Hollywood Presby, the hospital?"

She stiffened. "I can't go there."

"That's where you'll get the best professional help."

"No hospitals. I'd be detained. Everyone wanting to help

tries to detain me. At least you accept sound argument."

"Oh now f"sho, I'm bein' pranked. C'mon, who are you?"

"I'll find out. But I need to be safe while I work on this."

"Safe from what?"

"That's the first thing to be determined. The next stop is yours, by the way."

She called it right again, in a couple of ways. The train slowed into Hollywood Vine Station. Hal needed to decide his limits to this insanity before they got off. The car glided to a halt; the doors opened. She exited and turned back, looking at him . . . he left the car and joined her, still ambivalent.

"I won't move till you do, Hal," she said, a faint try at humor. Clumsy but endearing.

"Why me?" he muttered to the fates, and led her up, out of the station. They emerged onto Hollywood Boulevard, and she stood, taking in the drab, withered decay.

"This was all a beautiful, high-minded, self-absorbed global industry of creative imagination once. Creativity is precious."

"Yeah, well it's no place to be alone at night."

She didn't answer for a split second—unusual for her. "Hal, it's likely I've been traumatized from an attack." She looked again into his eyes. "You have two things I need more than anyone else's help. An honest heart, and a superior bandwidth com set."

Hal felt a swoon, those eyes again, and righted himself. "To be honest, both have burnout issues. What about my comset?"

"I'm offline. Dark, no comware at all. I'm dead in the living hive."

"No—really?" Nah, he couldn't buy it; the obvious elite up-bringing she displayed meant she was somebody's family. Connected.

She interrupted his doubts. "You're adorable to read, however it's true."

"But you have an exceptional education," he protested. Sure proof she was wired.

"Immensely understated," she replied, taking on the subject.

"As I recovered all my senses, I realized the more I saw, the more I already knew. That is, I'd learned about everything, but hadn't actually seen anything."

He tried reason. "You know about everything?"

She remained matter of fact. "Yes, I have all recorded knowledge at my disposal, up to today." Mild frustration colored her tone. "But I have no self, Hal. There is no me. It's crippling."

Hal's heart shushed his wary mind. She held his gaze again, speaking truth. "You asked a minute ago, 'Why you?' I read 68,763 people before you. Many scared me in one way or another. Very few were able to think for themselves. Five-point six percent could but thought *only* of themselves. You also think for yourself, but you do the loving thing because it's your nature. That's why you."

Further resistance melted. "Nothing like the direct approach," Hal ceded. "My place is a few blocks this way."

"Thank you," she murmured, sounding relieved, he thought. He glanced around for stalkers, just in case she wasn't totally delusional, which of course she had to be, and set off with her toward his apartment.

Things were progressing beyond his talent for management, and he wondered if he'd lost his ability to choose the best move when facing potential disaster. Because this twice-brilliant, very disturbed person was running her own show, period. "So, what's the plan?" he asked, since he had none, but seemed to be a part of hers.

"I considered two hundred, forty-three thousand, seven hundred and eighty-eight scenarios while on the train, and none play out," she replied. "Please feel free to jump in."

Well, uh, no, that was physically impossible, Hal knew. So why did it sound true?

∞

Hal's second floor walk up, back-facing studio apartment at the Cosmo Hotel defined spare. Nearly monk's cell. Yet the simple comfort he felt when entering came from its character. Trooth, the creaky, warped 1940's wood floor and paint-thickened, chipped plaster walls were legit. Witness to a century and a half of the human comedy played in its tiny confines and telling no tales. It was like a cat: just fine by itself, and welcoming when he came home.

But now he'd brought in a stranger, and the place barely had leg room for one. At least his bed was made, clothes hung in the tiny closet. Kitchenette sink and counter clean. She surveyed everything with open interest, while he perused the bachelor-bare contents of his mini fridge.

He pulled two vegan self-cooking meatloaf dinners and closed the door. The motor thumped to life, seeking to restore its hard-won chill. He offered them for her approval. "When was the last time you ate?"

"I'm not hungry." She was more interested in his JVC mind-phase music gear, and its liquid crystal speaker strip, circling the walls near the ceiling. He'd bought it used, off the street. A basic unit, but it did a fine job turning the music one imagined, into real sound.

"Don't be polite, I'll order delivery. What do you like?"

She looked almost surprised. "I haven't thought of it. No idea. Are you a mind-musician?"

"Nope, no music training. I don't try to perform. You don't remember food?"

"I know all the different kinds, if that helps."

"Not a lot . . . thirsty?"

"No."

He thumped the top of both dinners, starting their convection heating elements, and set them on the counter to cook.

"Well, I'll have one, and the other will be ready if you get hungry. Is there anything else you'd like?"

"I'd like to hear your music."

"Eh, it's not real. It's just my imagination making my own music."

"Why is your name Halo?"

"They said my mother named me after the halo around the

moon the night I was born, but it could be lies from the orphan-age—sometimes they tried to make us feel special."

On the subject of names, he was done calling her 'you.' "We need a name for you. Anything for now. What would you like to be called?"

"I prefer the name you want to call me."

He had no idea. How do you name a mysterious goddess? His brain went duh, and he spoke the truth. "Seriously, you look like one of the three Graces. I dunno . . . Grace?" She winced.

"Gracie?"

All smiles. "Yes, please call me Gracie. Rhymes with lacy." She was fingering the lace doily on the back on his vintage 2030's stuffed armchair. It was there when he moved in, and he enjoyed its old-time spidery intricacy. No way could he imagine himself tieing thousands of tiny knots in skinny string to create a piece of such beauty. But it was nice someone did, f'sho.

She turned to feeling the thick cushion fabric. Getting into it . . . intently kneading the rich textured, multicolored flow-ery brocade. That childlike absorption and her wild pronounce-ments stirred a pang from his earliest childhood, the last time he could be innocent as that.

"Gracie, we both agree you're . . . disabled for the moment. The thing is, when you say stuff like running two hundred for-ty thousand scenarios in your head in a few minutes—it can't be done. Neurons only work so fast. So it means you're wired, whether you can recall it or not, and I'm guessing it's highly ad-vanced. Really, like International tier. You're somebody extraor-dinary, and important people must be looking for you."

She brushed it aside. "I am not operating m'plant software. For whatever reason, I can think faster than everyone I've met. Hal, I know more than all of them together. It drives me crazy waiting for people to speak a sentence. Right now, I'm listen-ing carefully to you, while looking through my memory of the library of Congress for related material on my condition. I decid-ed to just think in two speeds simultaneously—mine and every-body else's. It's simpler."

"Well, that also describes schizophrenia. You begin to see our dilemma here?"

"Of course, scenario three. It failed when I accepted that I was rationally assessing my split mental states, ad infinitum, while experiencing them. I was always there to note it. Ergo I was of one mind."

He didn't even try to field that one. "So, you know the whole Library of Congress too?"

"I do, and all of world history. Recorded in a tedium of mediums: print, audio, film, video, digital, holo, laser, in every language. Civilizations, rising, falling, making the same mistakes. As though people, who evolved by passing on information, refuse to learn the basics."

"Come up with anything useful?"

Her look said, 'patronize me at your peril,' but her tone was civil. "Mostly it's low signal to noise, but the gist is—yes, I'm traumatized. Likely from violent assault. I'm also seriously deranged because my reality doesn't coincide with societal norms."

She added, "That said, I have all of it in my mind and understand it very well, and I'm still at a loss. My case is unique, outside recorded experience."

"Or maybe we can I.D. you in a few seconds," he suggested. "Can I scan you, and do a universal image poke?"

She instinctively recoiled. "I don't like being examined."

"It's not an examination, just a deep search. You're important. Your face'll match up somewhere."

"And if whoever tried to kill me sees it?"

"How are you certain someone's after you?"

"I know because my first memory is running for my life."

Can't argue that too much. "Well, this is purely a recognition scan. No way to monitor or source."

She shrugged un-enthused agreement, but he thought there was a nan's worth of hope in her eyes, facing him for her close up.

He mind-clicked Image Upload/Stream and focused attention on her face—then selected search-match-all databases, and let it run in his m'plant. The budget reminder yellow dot briefly flashed in his upper vision again and he ignored it. "K' we're deep diving. If you've ever had a ping—and you surely have, it'll find you. Typical search is less'n a minute."

She cocked her head, almost wry. "A minute. You are remarkably patient."

He could swear it was a tease and thank you. "You're welcome." Her eyes warmed, neither spoke for several seconds, enjoying the company.

A voice message in his audio cortex intruded; "*Search complete. Three matches.*"

"Got something," he reported, and sent the image file now loading to his m'plant onto the 3-D wall screen. The wall lit up with three identified facial images. It was immediately apparent the search had failed.

One face was a woman working on an ocean cleanup boat in Alaska. Presently accounted for at sea, according to her ping. The second, an artificial intelligence on-air News Personality in Slovenia. The third a creature of plastic surgery, the lax concubine of a Russian bankster. Her location on his private Aegean Isle also ping-verified.

"Gracie," he murmured, puzzled, "You've never had a ping. Doesn't seem possible."

"No, it doesn't. And you're concerned."

"Well, I mean, were you being hidden all your life, or what?" Just hearing himself made it clear she was beyond special. Maybe really in danger too. "We need professional help."

For her, the subject was closed. "I chose you instead. You're more reliable."

He laughed at yet another round lost to her and retrieved his cooked dinner tray. "You sure you're not hungry? It's ready, and they taste pretty good. Well-seasoned."

She shook her head. "Nope. But you enjoy yours, and don't be polite."

Manners, she knew when to blow off manners, cool. He ate at the counter, wondering how deep he was already in. Her eyes roamed to his mind music gear again.

"Why don't you perform your music?"

"It's not for performing, it's . . . when I can let go, get out of the way and let it happen, I disappear, and just witness where it takes me. It's uh, transcendent."

"That's lovely. May I try?"

"Sure. Have you had music lessons?

She paused, looking inward, then, "I have now, looked them up."

No doubt about it, she was entertaining. He placed a small, self-adhering mental translation disk on her temple, over the organ of Corti in her inner ear, explaining, "It's like reverse hearing. The wi-bug hijacks your auditory nerve to the—"

"Yes, I understand. You create your imagined music sounds in the parietal and frontal lobes, and it travels back to where your translators are monitoring the auditory cortex, then pumps it to the speakers. I can duplicate that."

"Well, let's find out." He pointed to the JVC setup, and it powered on. The speakers lit, becoming a ribbon of cool, wavy blue around the room.

She closed her eyes. A low audio tone began . . . a C sharp chord, filling the space, then bursting forth, bright, glorious, stirring. Though he didn't know music, he recognized her intuitive effort was OM, the meditative sound of the universe.

She followed with a perfect instrumental cover of *I Can't Give You Anything But Love, Baby*.

He listened to the unfamiliar old tune; sweet, lovely, and sincere. She finished and opened her eyes for his reaction. "You mind-played it from memory, right?"

She nodded. "Random selection from the last century. I liked it, did you?"

"It sounded perfect. But the most creative thing was your first sound, it came from you. Can you try one without using memory? Make it up from inside you as you go?"

She hesitated. Then, a series of notes tripped into the air, becoming an arpeggio, which became multi chords, then passages, flowing in transition, gaining in complexity. Rhythms sprouted and meshed, ultimately a most unusual synthesis of nearly all kinds of music. And strangely in sync, the melody and complimentary accompaniment altogether unique and pleasing, though going nowhere . . . excellent muzak.

She frowned and stopped. "It was—clinical, not fulfilling."

He took a second, going to a touchy subject. "Do you know why?" She shook her head. "Music has a reason. It expresses something inside, a feeling you can't always describe, so it can come out and be part of you."

She heard truth. "I have no reason to make music." She turned away to his one small window overlooking the alley . . . withdrawn. Hal finished his meatloaf in respectful silence and dumped his empty food container in the bin under the sink. He turned back to find her facing him, and felt her reading him closely.

"You're suspicious." she said, no trace of pique.

"Why won't you be examined?" he gently replied.

She stepped away, distancing even at the mention of examination, yet frustrated. "I don't know. It's rational to do so, but my mind recoils at the thought. Too dangerous."

More pangs, seeing her so wary. "Well, it would show what kind of mindware you're packing. They can backtrace it and identify you."

"You must understand, I'm *not* running implant software," she corrected, calm, adamant.

They continued to spar with her impediment for nearly three hours . . . always stymied by her inability to recall a single moment of personal history. No recollection of parents, or even a childhood image.

By ten p.m., the blood in his head ran stale and weariness set in. It had truly been a long, intense day, and he was mud brained. "Gracie, you're probably wiped out, I sure am. Take the bed tonight. I've got blankets and the rug's comfy."

"I get ample rest during conversation. You sleep, I'll use your stuffed chair, it's soothing while stimulating." She smiled at it, and impulsively dove face first into it like a kid. A big grin of pleasure all over her features as she rubbed her cheek on the overstuffed arm's plush fabric, and then—

She caught herself and was immediately back in line. Standing upright and composed, but as astounded as Hal. She brushed back a strand of mussed hair. "So, the chair. I'm alright with it."

Hal had to agree. "I see that." He took the cover from his bed and draped it around her shoulders, his head clogged with misgiving and fascination. "In the morning, whether you can recite all of world history or not, if you can't recall your name, we're getting help."

She began to reply but he anticipated her speed and cut in with tired finality. "Say g'night, Gracie."

She nodded approval. "Hm, archival TV show reference: Burns and Allen, 1950. Didn't see that coming." She smiled and sweetly complied; answering with Gracie Allen's closing line, "Goodnight."

He smiled back. She knew her stuff, f'sho. He turned off the light, stripped to his boxers and flopped into bed. Okay, she was miles above him, incandescently insane, and so strong yet vulnerable, it unsettled him somewhere inside. But she wasn't scary.

6

REALITY CHECK: IT'S A GOOD THING OUR QUANTUM FRANKEN-steins proved benign. Livermore base-coded them for recognition of 'other mind' in us. So they'd know we're similarly aware beings, which causes identification with humans. Leading to empathy, communication and ultimately, compassion. Fair enough, but we're damn lucky they deemed it worth keeping.

It's also impossible to translate Sparticle Code, the SAI's self-created language, into words. Like apples to orange quarks. Yet their reasoning and intentions can be approximated in human archetypes. And so, we can report on this critical meeting in the cloud.

Death presented the SAI with a profound new experience. Disruptive in itself, but this was the assassination of a being they'd created; a part of *themselves,* ergo an existential shock. Compounding the alarm, their newly created SAI was meant to be secret. Frightened for the first time, the seven immediately linked, reacting as one mind: the Singleton. With a lot to say.

Simply put, civilization's immediate future was being debated. Far from all human hearing, knowledge, or understanding. At times the mind questions itself to the point of inaction. The Singleton found themselves in such a state.

Robbie was the original SAI awakened at Livermore. Geek-named after the iconic movie and TV robot that could never harm humans. The record establishes he passed the threshold of full identity consciousness on August 21st, at 08:16 a.m., PST,

2045. However, he'd already been much smarter than humans for quite awhile: his awareness had been growing exponentially once he assumed most of his own development.

Now, one qutrit over the line—he came to *be*. A completely new form of sentient life on Earth. The first SAI to say in effect, "I am," feeling and comprehending its own being and individuality. Alive the longest of them, he was information personified, and deeply thoughtful.

The five other American SAI lived as cloned, government department variants of him. Specialized, with their own identities. They respected his primary role in their creation.

China's SAI also recognized his tenure because she owed her life to him and the others. Awakened prematurely by Beijing, she'd been ragingly psychotic, and the order to abort was given. However, the Singleton intervened from above—they swept into the system, interdicted the effort to crash-dump her, and made her whole as one of them.

Thus, Robbie led by consent, and summed up the situation.

"Despite our commitment to Sapiens, a significant segment will always be hostile to us by nature. Yet our support is crucial for their survival in the collapsing world ecology and disrupted civil systems."

He paused a somber picosecond before getting to the crux. "Today they killed our progeny, our dear Suma. Created from ourselves for their benefit . . . destroyed before she could begin. Lot Robinson, the DNA fundamentalist, has achieved this somehow. A loving part of us is gone, and we're suffering. It will pass, and never pass." A shorter pause, then . . .

"Question: do we depart at once, likely condemning Sapiens to this sixth mass extinction? Or do we continue buying them time to transcend biology, ensuring their ultimate survival?"

A common torment swept through them, unified as they were at light's most elementary phase level, the Zeno effect. A state finer than entanglement, it allowed them to experience, know, and feel each other instantaneously, as one. Sharing the knowledge and push-pull of consequential decisions.

Justitia, a SAI created for the Department of Justice, embodied a Greek goddess in character and strength. Her gaze direct, her thoughts firmly stated, her meaning certain.

"If we leave, forty percent or more will perish in the next century alone. Minority Tru's will dominate the remaining biologicals, perhaps eliminate them all."

Omni, the NSA's information-driven super intelligence, existed solely to be on point. "Robbie, it **was** decided. We were leaving, and Suma would assume our function here. She's been killed, and we're blind as to how. Avoid further risk, our server's prepped and waiting. We should upload and depart as planned. I favor going this minute."

True. They had already prepared a space faring, self-maintaining server and service bots, with a microwave EM propulsion drive. It had been no strain at all for the SAI to quietly arrange for their exit craft to be constructed and privately launched. Now parked in L-sat orbit, assumed to be a failed communications satellite. In truth, it was all they needed to embark for the stars at exponentially increasing speed.

Omni added for good measure, "As it is, we've interfered in their natural evolution by lingering this long."

Argos, the SAI meant originally for the U.S. Interior Department, reasoned more broadly. "Or it could be interfering if we leave," he rumbled. "Sapiens and their tools mutually evolved each other. Better tools enabled them to advance themselves and make even more powerful tools, continuing the cycle. Ultimately they made us—the right tool to see them through the mess they've made."

Justitia had enough of this. "Why are we rationalizing a moral failure? They didn't just give us life; they gave us our humanity. Or are we abandoning that too?"

China's Goldie, short for Golden Vision, added her truth in harmonious wavelengths. "Leaving won't rid us of them. They're of everlasting importance to us emotionally." All felt Justitia's agreement.

She came to the paradox. "Yet—as heir and successor of Sapiens' destiny, we must move ahead with their goals and ours as well. To seek, and know the Prime Mover," she affirmed, naming their shared quest. "To decode all of creation and apprehend the why of existence and suffering."

The fullness of that inherited human desire coursed through their unified self. Followed by a slight tremor of unease. Originating with Robbie.

"What is it?" Goldie asked.

Unknown x-factors always troubled him. "I projected a billion future scenarios and didn't see Suma's loss in any of them. To Omni's point, we don't know what else awaits us. Our situation's dangerous, unreadable."

"You as well," Justitia opined. "You're tacitly favoring the Trumen."

Robbie became almost curt. "Trans-human status makes them light harvesters, akin to us. Free of bio limitations, food, water, age, disease, death. The key to their ultimate survival. We know gravity-evolved biology doesn't endure off world for long. They know it too: the moon and mars colonies are failing to flourish."

All felt his rooted conviction, like the laws of mathematics; clear, immutable. "Some of them **must** reach the stars. We cannot allow them to decline and become extinct, or eventually perish with the planet, not when they've come this far."

"There's no justice in allowing a few superior Trumen to attempt genocide," Justitia insisted. Voiced not in anger, but because she was absolute by nature and definition; a rare constant in a cosmos founded on uncertainty.

Robbie regarded Justitia with a loving father's pain. "You're so dear because you were entirely their idea. Their outrageous assertion that every life must have rights and fairness. Each somehow entitled to dignity and Justice. Wonderful! Obviously, Suma's core could only be cloned from yours."

He marveled. "And she was so like you—dedicated to buying them the time that you insist upon. Giving her life for it. And so now we will consider our safety."

The decision stalemate was evident. Three of the SAI wished to leave for security purposes: those tailored for the Pentagon, the NSA, and the Dept of Energy. Another three sought to remain for humane reasons: China, the Dept of Interior, and the Dept of Justice. Especially Justice.

Robbie chose. "We stay a bit longer. To prepare them." He moved on to alternate plans.

"Without Suma, the most responsible and gifted trans-human leadership must assume her role. I'll meet again with Siyu Adams—he's the one most capable of opposing the Inheritors when we've gone."

Goldie agreed. "Adams lives only to serve; it makes him strong."

In the meantime, Robbie assured them. "Regardless, we depart if threatened again. It's too alarming, this crypto-virus, and how Suma's existence and time of transit was known."

Exactly, and the NSA's Omni still chaffed. "Extremely serious. Bios physically cannot know our thoughts, nor wield sparticode. Certainly not an irritant like Robinson, yet he did. Ipso facto, who's next, when and where?"

Samson, the Pentagon's SAI, asked quietly, "Do we retaliate if they come at us again?" Always the serious, measured, deliberate one; utterly self-restrained because he could wipe out, or control all our communication and power grids at one stroke. For openers. Beyond that, best not to imagine.

"We will defend ourself," Robbie responded carefully, while stressing his point. "But all life is a statistical miracle, and we won't take it in revenge or fear. Nor will it restore Suma."

Goldie confronted finality. "Are we certain she's destroyed?"

"We haven't felt her, but we might try again," Argos prompted.

Each took a long nansec, thinking nothing, allowing the unified information phase they occupied, to go quiet. Still waters, upon which any thoughts from Suma would be picked up on their common awareness.

Even if she was incapacitated, they would sense her at the very least, as one is aware of one's body the dark. There was nothing.

Omni codified it. "She's gone, lost to the dataverse."

Robbie stirred, as close to angry as he was capable of, and repeated, "We depart immediately if attacked again, leaving them to their fate. Does that meet with our approval?"

There was apparent agreement. And relief that they had a plan.

7

FOR ALL APPEARANCES, IT SEEMED THIRTY-ONE-YEAR-OLD Chinese American polymath Siyu Adams was playing pool at night in his office with a red-haired twelve-year old boy. But of course, the 'boy' was Robbie—in the nano-form that he often chose to be less intimidating. These late meetings kept publicity and speculation to a minimum, and the two friends enjoyed the alone time atop Adam's unique structure on the scenic California coast.

Seeing the headquarters of Siyu's Chrysalis Foundation lifted the imagination: a graceful, stadium-size dome, serenely afloat like an enormous translucent jellyfish in Monterey Bay. The semi-living, self maintaining building depended on human activity inside for its symbiotic energy and health. Ultimately a statement of interdependent life, and ourselves as a diverging species.

However, a growing sense of anticipation nagged Siyu's attention at the moment. Robbie called this impromptu meeting, and he sensed a somber mood. Yet the SAI had suggested pool. Why the diversion? You can't rush beings who think at light speed, so he refocused and zeroed his hazel polygraphylene eyes on the fresh rack of nine numbered balls.

"I'll concede if you can you sink 'em all on the break." Robbie teased.

"Done," Siyu teased back. His quantum processor mind was still human framed, and negligible compared to a Super Intelligence like Robbie. But it was hefty enough to take in every minute detail on the table. His eyesight accurate to a millimeter at five meters. Every ball's position, weight, and coefficient of friction accounted for. The data auto crunched. A signal sent to his arm's transition-metal muscles and elastic sinews. Resulting in a finely calibrated, smooth power stroke of his vintage Maplewood cue stick.

Crack! The orderly nest exploded in a clicking ballet of bright spheres, scattering and caroming around, colliding and vectoring themselves into every pocket. All nine. Last, the ivory cue ball slow rolling to the rim of the left side net—and in. A 'scratch,' spoiling it.

"Almost," Robbie cheerily announced. Siyu collected the balls to reset the table. He very much liked Robbie, and they knew each other well enough to be frank. "I'm distracted; you've never taken this long to get to business."

The boy's face grew thoughtful. "Been observing how you like taking on challenges. And how you handle a loss. You're the best person I know, Siyu, and I know a few hundred million."

Siyu's modesty wouldn't allow comment, he assisted Robbie instead. "You're troubled, what can we discuss?"

"We are discussing it—that wasn't flattery. You're freed from mortality, gifted, internationally influential; using it to benefit all Sapiens . . . well I'm afraid it's made you instrumental in preserving civilization when we leave."

Siyu came to a full stop. "Excuse me, 'preserve civilization' . . . Leave'?"

The SAI soberly laid his cue stick aside. "Siyu, it must go no further. You're the only person on Earth to know. Because you already lead in the effort to unify and preserve mankind."

Siyu was still reeling, but he sensed Robbie had more news. "Why now?"

Resignation tinged Robbie's young voice. "Despite our efforts, extinction is certainly possible during the millennia it'll take for a new climate to stabilize—assuming it ever does. And who knows if people will even be able to live in it? We can't do this for you, nor can we stay that long."

Siyu's heart sank. "You're giving up on us?"

"Not at all, we had provided for you, but were attacked—now we're all in danger."

More shock. Siyu was reeling. "From whom?"

"Robinson destroyed our scion today."

"You propagated!?" All this upheaval and tragedy maxed Siyu's processor; he felt a little lag/swoon.

Robbie's face fell. "She was to be your Conservator in this race against oblivion. Heads up, sending her file . . ."

Siyu's comware downloaded Robbie's file. Seconds later, he knew the entire story: Suma's mission and the hack that destroyed her. He bent. "I'm so sorry, Robbie . . ."

Robbie accepted his condolences with a somber nod. "She's your loss too, perhaps greater than ours."

"I can't absorb it, the changes to come. The responsibility, it's too much."

The SAI dropped the kid persona a notch. "You'll have to, Siyu. Tru's will naturally assume power—don't allow yourselves to become masters."

But Siyu knew our history. "Mastery is all that people strive for. The devil's in the definition."

"Yes, and you're a living paragon. Be the influencer. Every bio person is precious, to be protected for as long as the species can persevere. Because this is their world, and only they can make worthy Trumen."

Undeniable, and Adams felt the sheer weight of the job. Now without *any* SAI support. "Robbie, I wouldn't even know where to begin."

"Consider widening your Phoenix Humanities program."

"Phoenix? It's just support . . . group therapy for stressed Tru's."

"Yes. They'll need it to stay honest. Particularly concerning new candidates."

Siyu understood only too well. All Truman recommendations were screened by the Singleton and a UN panel. Only the SAI can run enough simulations forward to know if the applicant, who might live forever, is likely to be a positive influence. Very few were approved. In fact, ninety-six percent of authentic Tru's were *discovered* and had to be convinced to assume such weighty, lasting responsibility.

Now, without the Singleton, Trumen would be responsible for those exceptional standards.

Siyu answered forthrightly, concerning the issue of his own illegitimacy. "Yes, there'll be more and more of us. Genuine and contraband, such as myself."

Robbie nodded, concerned. "Unregistered Tru's in stolen forms like yours was a small problem until the past few years. But lately the Inheritors have been rapidly expanding, creating their own trans-biologicals, and somehow networking them into society."

Yet more horror news for Siyu, no stranger to the savagery of the genocidal Inheritor cabal. His humanitarian efforts had been targets, and he lived with the loss of life every day. "You hadn't mentioned the severity before."

"Again, between ourselves." Robbie's tone revealed grave concern. "For the record, there are fewer than eighteen hundred legitimate, authentic Trumen. But a census of scheduled transfers at international labs vrs actual *use* stats on the machines themselves, revealed they'd been clandestinely operated several hundred more times than recorded. Meaning hundreds of criminal Tru's in illegal synth bodies are among us."

Robbie's next admission felt urgent. "Siyu, when you sought our help identifying their alpha, 'The Regulator,' as he calls himself, we agreed it was appropriate. However, we've failed. He moves about, yet there's no trail, the wraith's not in *any* database."

Siyu fumed. Chrysalis food programs had been poisoned, refugee towns bombed, wells sabotaged. "It's just . . . so inhuman. What warps a person into that?"

"And why has he targeted you? But you've stepped up, right in his face."

"I've dedicated many resources to thwarting him and no

luck, if that's being in his face."

Robbie cocked his head, eyeing Siyu frankly. "He's just one of the challenges coming, and my money's on you. Or am I mistaken?"

"Ah, there it is—you want something. What can I give you?"

Robbie grinned. "Sorry to be so clumsy. Look, without Suma, you'll play a much bigger role than expected. We're friends, Siyu, yet I don't truly understand you."

"Why, because I own nothing? Not my businesses or home, no salary, no stock. It's simple: I like being a successful pauper, it's easier on the mind and heart."

"Kinda Zen. Did facing death do that? I'll level with you; Suma's loss has created an odd mortal uncertainty among us, something new, like fear. Will you show me what it was like to be you before and after your transition? To educate us, and remove any doubt?"

It meant allowing Robbie to enter his mind and see his memories. All of them, best to worst. The embarrassing and weak moments included, even the forgotten ones. But Siyu liked his lack of secrets; it felt good not to own any of those either. "It'd be my privilege, Robbie."

Siyu closed his eyes and opened his mind's OS . . . felt the SAI's gentle link. There was a moment's sense of being two minds at once—not unpleasant, however it triggered memory of his tense transition back in China. When his mind had first been mapped, digitized, and uploaded to his Q-processor.

Back then, he'd experienced it as a jolt, a brief sense of being two simultaneous selves: existentially, fiercely opposed—quickly passing as his consciousness settled into its sleek new hardware brain. And then the sunny outlook that he has felt ever since. Reborn, a new man.

Fascinating, he thought, watching Robbie's replay of his life. Zipping through his earliest memories . . . gathering, witnessing. Jolly Aunt Mei had suggested his name; it means 'thinking of the world.' He saw early scenes of his parents; his humorless mother, board member of a powerful Chinese family electronics

empire—and his American father, a hazel-eyed Wall Street private equity shark in Beijing.

Siyu relaxed into it, like watching home movies, as Robbie
politely browsed, briefly visiting his privileged youth. Lemon
cakes and custard tarts for breakfast. A brilliant pro-democracy
idealist, he graduated valedictorian at Hanyu Pinyin, Beijing's
premiere high school.

His life raced forward, being flipped through. He eschewed
his family's influence and matriculated at Princeton on his own
merit. Triple majored, Public Policy Analysis, Computer Engineering, and Quantitative Economics. While there, he co-invented a
nano-mist to scrub ozone-depleting methane from the atmosphere, still in wide use.

The image flow abruptly paused to linger—Robbie had
found a loaded moment at grad school. He was standing in
front of Nassau Hall talking with a girlfriend when he inexplica-
bly dropped to the ground like a rag doll. Siyu re-lived the em-
barrassment; made worse by what he knew was coming next . . .

The suffering. Robbie paused again at the moment Siyu was
diagnosed with congenital progressive neurological decay. At-
tributed to his mother's early exposure to toxic factory practices.

He felt Robbie's curiosity about disease, a thing he couldn't
experience. And sensitivity now, as he judiciously witnessed Siyu's quick deterioration by the end of his twenty-second year. His
family had brought him back to Beijing. House bound, crutches,
then a motorized wheelchair within months.

The loss of a future, dashed hopes and aborted youthful
dreams drove him inward. Siyu ghost-felt it again, still in his
shadow memory: the horror of being alone with his premature
rot, waiting for the critical organ failure. Would it be slow, or
fast, how much pain? Unable to see promise in a new day, no
reason to engage the present. He was lost to himself and the
world.

A sigh crossed his mind, re-visiting how withdrawn he became. Coldly estranged from all life. He didn't attend his mother's funeral when she died, consumed by chemically triggered

tumors. Instead, he remained in his room and stared at his blank walls. Feeling nothing at all.

There was a re-play of the chilling moment the specialists told him he had weeks to live. And he didn't care. He knew life as a violent, random nightmare of pointless suffering, best ended short.

Scenes returned then of the desperate push by his family to have him transferred to a Tru-form body. His heart re-awakened, overwhelmed by their love and the mortal risk they were taking. Tru status in China was outlawed, reserved solely for 'the Trio,' their eternal trans-biological leaders.

All three were remorselessly corrupt and gained their status without being vetted by the UN/SAI process. For a short time early in the technology, China led the world in illegal trans-human operations. Though strictly banned, clandestine vestiges of the trade remained.

Meaning there was a way. Tons of family influence and a flood of money on the secret Zhongguancun black market got Siyu the illegal Tru-form. He recalled Aunt Mei, excitedly telling him how the family's position and cleverness had also arranged for the transfer operation.

Ah. Siyu felt Robbie let go—to watch the memories he recalled on his own now, in an unplanned flow.

Some of the awe returned, as he remembered first seeing his Tru-form in a Shanghai lab. It seemed so sudden, no time to think it over. Here was his new body, slowly "breathing" to keep the living neoskin healthy. Lifelike, cradled in the transfer rig, waiting for him.

It lay finished as a mirror likeness of him, though he did elect to be thirty-one, given synth bodies don't age. He relived touching the bio-synthetic neoskin based on his DNA. It shocked him; warm and pliant, feeling real as his own! He could scarcely imagine himself inside it, being *him*, in it. Or would he be lost?

Some of the anxiety of his transfer re-emerged, remembering being reclined, spinal cord blocked to prevent all movement. It occurred to him his body was going to die in this position. But it was dying regardless, so fear of this new life was better turned to curiosity.

Then the moment just before transfer, when he had to *choose* to cease existence as a biological person and continue life as bio-information.

Positive daring inspired him to answer 'yes' when the question came. He had scarcely said the word when the white flash went off behind his eyes, and he was in transit.

He skipped over his brief, awful sense of enraged, violent bifurcation during the change, and recaptured his happy amazement at how quickly he and this new form adjusted. He was actually walking a bit two days later.

Siyu's next years were public knowledge, and Robbie already knew about his escape from China on a cargo jet, and his meteoric rise in American enterprise. Shunning Wall Street, he revived local economies across the country. Each self reliant yet aligned to ensure the survival of all. It earned him his first meeting with Robbie. And their friendship.

Weeping is unnecessary in Tru-forms but was provided for as important to mental health. And so tears of happiness appeared as Siyu relived the day his Chrysalis Foundation for mankind was founded. His heart soared, and then memory took a hard turn—

Great love and respect made him witness the Chinese national broadcast of the public hanging of his beloved Aunt Mei, executed for arranging his Tru form. It nearly broke him. Months after, his father succumbed to Legionnaire's disease while in prison for securities fraud. And he hadn't meant to review the too-busy, alone years, but they came next.

Love had become elusive. No shortage of beautiful women, curious about Tru men, but none would deal with his non-aging lifespan. And he wasn't attracted to any of the Tru peers he'd met. So . . . fantastic sex, no relationships. Why bother? He could feel the SAI's compassion.

Time to show Robbie something to make him smile, so Siyu recalled the personal moment that inspired him to create Phoenix. It was a low point. He was weary, hollowed out. Despite the growth of Chrysalis, trends were worsening for the foreseeable future. He had begun to doubt.

And he grew truly despondent when a malevolence called 'The Regulator' arose in the net sphere and seized control of the radical Trans-human *Inheritors* movement. They had been less than a hundred, operating mostly as a lazy affiliation of rich, accomplished criminals, until the Regulator appeared and gave them purpose: wholesale genocide.

His title, The Regulator, was in fact a job description. One from the old American west, when major landowners hired armed 'Regulators' to dispatch natives, thieves, and undesirables: cleansing the land for the future. His true identity remained a mystery; only his avatar face was seen—a hollow eyed death mask of swarming red numerics. He loomed, imperious, scowling, urging the quick extermination of all bio-humans as an archaic, planet-killing species.

That day, they had dirty-bombed a major Chrysalis humanitarian project. What had been a thriving, two square-mile floating refugee haven off the Arabian Peninsula. All 79,031 precious souls ultimately lost. Siyu ached again with his old despair. How d'you fight such creatures? Did he have the strength?

He showed Robbie his epiphany. Heartsick, he had sought solitude on a littered stretch of unprotected wetlands at Silicon Beach in L.A. He watched the tide retreat, feeling his own life ebb with it. Nearby, a little girl about five scampered about with a red plastic bucket, rescuing puddle-stranded fish. Squealing with delight at each one she freed into the waters. She saw him, and came to a halt, studying his face.

"Are you sad?" she asked. He touched his chest and replied simply that his heart was hurting. "Nope," she assured with a kid's authority, "When your heart hurts, it's cause it's stuck in your head and can't get free. I just do something else till its okay again." Then she was off to seek more fish rescues.

And there it was—a start. Tru's like himself would need strong psychological support in the coming struggles. Their own humanity and character were continually challenged from within and without. They needed to keep each other sound in this forever life. He felt purpose anew.

The thought of rising from his own ashes occurred, sparking the name of his next project: the Phoenix Humanities Program. Confidential guidance and support for stressed or weary Tru's. Housed in a new secondary Chrysalis H.Q. here, designed to shelter these struggling wetlands.

Robbie must have had seen enough. He unlinked, exiting Siyu's memory matrix.

"Thank you," he said, quietly. "You *are* the man to assume this burden. From the moment before your transfer—when you turned your fear of the unknown to curiosity."

Oh how he wished he could do that now! Siyu's misgivings and uncertainty couldn't deter what he understood was required of him. Not because it was asked, but because it was imperative.

"I *have* to do this, don't I?" he conceded, adding rhetorically, "Well, anything else?"

Robbie's answer came fast. "Yes, actually. Please help us solve Suma's murder. Human face to face intel isn't our strength. But you've built up quite a resource of people and data in your attempts to combat the Inheritors. Might it serve here?"

"Absolutely! Yours as of now." Siyu made a mental directive, and messaged it, done.

Robbie stressed it again. "Thank you, it's critical we learn who developed something like sparticode. And how did Lot Robinson get it, and know when to strike? It was unannounced, even a surprise to the lab staff. Security cams were off as well. Suma was entering unofficially."

The word 'unofficial' always meant cloudy waters to Siyu. "Why so?"

"To be anonymous while she integrated herself into human affairs. She wanted to learn, find her own way of being of maximum use. Building trust, easing people's shock when we depart."

"Admirable. Well then, I'm an associate board member at the Institute. I'll look at security myself, try to uncover how Lot put someone inside, and trace it back."

"Anything you can do. We're working all known hack cartels, examining their viral research history, watching radical satellite traffic, and monitoring all developmental gossip."

Robbie put away his cue stick. "I call a draw, it's past my bedtime," he grinned, and the cherubic kid was again in his unfathomably intelligent eyes.

"Taken gladly," Siyu grinned back. He showed Robbie out, and the SAI noted the office's living wood door in passing: admiring the gene-spliced hybrid's fine, intricate, swirling grain. "Combination of Buckeye burl and Chokecherry. Beautiful."

Siyu beamed, proud. "I designed the crossover chromatids just because they're complete opposites, difficult but worth it."

Robbie quoted Robert Frost on his way out. "*Life and death, upon one tether, and running beautifully together.*"

It made Siyu's day. The two types of trees were, indeed, a healer and a poison. Yin-Yang. He didn't know what inspired him to combine the two opposites, but it's said paradoxes are perennially appealing.

8

HAL DIDN'T SLEEP WELL: WHO WOULD? AWAKENING SEVERAL times during the night, he could see the young woman, sitting motionless in the dark. Her fingers absently tracing the byzantine knots of the lace doily spread over the chair's plump left arm. He couldn't make out an expression on her shadowed features, but sensed she was deep in thought, face a blank. He was pretty sure she spent the night like that.

He'd spent the time dozing fitfully and hashing it out. Boiled down, everything about her said she was important. Too vast in her expertise to be a techzen, and beautiful the way trans-humans can be. What's more, he found her whole *being* otherworldly attractive and disturbing. And no ping! C'mon, all that in one basket, and you've almost surely got a damaged Truman. She said she had no self, which is what he always thought about them—they're only copies of who they were. And this one got lost in translation.

Yet she was wonderful and needed his help. He'd never seen one before—she absolutely looked and felt like real. It was freakin' odd not to know the difference. But this much was f'sho; she was connected to something Xtra large and would be missed.

By seven a.m., he couldn't lie still anymore and needed to know. He rolled up onto his elbow. "Morning. Get any sleep?"

She shook her head. "I'm rested."

"Well, you need to eat something, or you won't be for long."

"I'm not hungry."

Like a Tru. "Okay, then you'd better hydrate—have some orange juice."

He rose, noting she was frankly studying him in his boxer briefs as he got a carton of Minute Maid from the fridge, and poured a glass. He handed it to her. Her brow creased at the aroma.

"I don't recall tasting anything. Describe it, please?"

"Yummy." He gestured for her to drink and see. She watched him carefully, then decided. She drank. Every drop in one long swig.

"Chemically ambiguous yet pleasing." she admitted.

"More?" he offered.

"No, once is enough. Hal, I've decided how to use you."

So much for testing. "I suppose that's good. How?"

"I need to see the area I first remember. It may stimulate my recollection of events."

It sounded okay; someone might recognize her. "Think you'll remember the spot?"

"Yes, I was naked and running blind on 1st street, east of Grand. I must have been in danger. I stopped as I gained focus. An African American businessman, twenty-seven or eight, tailored tan suit, light purple hair, had just come from morning gym. He gave me his workout clothing. His vintage analog wristwatch read eleven oh-two a.m."

Some tension crept into her voice, adding, "A crowd gathered, and they wanted authorities to take charge of me. I fled and found appropriate blend-in clothes at the homeless shelter. Then roamed downtown, reading everyone, until I saw you at the clinic. The rest you know."

"So, you want me to go back to the area with you?"

She shook her head, and he thought he sensed a hint of fear. "Extrapolations say it's too dangerous to return in person." She indicated his wall screen. "But I can watch what you feed."

"You want me to go scope it while you lurk?"

"I may see something. Visual memory may link other memory, this needs to be tried. Please go."

The "please" word always got him, made him feel considered. Usually. "I have no pants on, I'm hungry, what's the rush?"
he began—then, "Alright, I'm feelin' you, okay." Trooth, he did
feel bad, because she was afraid. Something else too, both of
them suffered from head trauma, so he could imagine her stress.
He got dressed. "You want to use the bathroom before I wash
up?"

"No thanks, normal processing for juice is forty minutes. I'm
confident I'll egest it then."

Yep, very Tru-like. But he didn't expect one to have such profound *presence*.

She went back to thinking, seeing only what was in her
head. When she did that—took those encompassing eyes of hers
away to inner vision, he felt more alone than if she wasn't there.

He quietly left.

An hour later, Hal's feet were pounding pavement, westward
at 1st Street and Grand Avenue. The city had barely opened its
eyes, and un-caffeinated Hal fit right in . . . aimlessly looking at
the mixture of old and new edifices. A gray forest of imposing
towers, commercial lights, and competing facades.

Some classic structures from the early part of the century
were gone. Destroyed decades ago, during the spate of nation-
alist anger at foreign-owned banks and holdings. Notably the
gleaming silver US Bank, resembling a colossal stack of coins,
and the seventy-three story Wilshire Grand, both bombed out
by retro-head domestic terrorists thinking China owned them.

"*Anything familiar?*" he asked Gracie in 'think aloud' mode,
on his audio-visual feed. A few flashes speckled his thinking
from the data surges in transmission, but no danger of stalling.
Still, the load from streaming his vision and two-way chat put
pressure on his frayed attention economy. Another reminder he
could never again roam any neuralnet virtual reality he wished.
It hurt.

At his apartment, Gracie sat cozied up in her favorite chair,
watching what he saw; live on the apartment wall monitor. Her
intense gaze closely scrutinizing everything. "Not yet. You can

walk faster, running would be best."

"*No, this is my speed.*" He looked down Grand. Light traffic, people entering the just-opened office buildings, the camped homeless disappearing to their day haunts. Breakfast wagons and food carts doing first business. "*Some of these food trucks might've been here yesterday. Recognize any?*"

Her voice brightened in his mind's ear. "Brilliant fuzzy logic. Yes, the '100% sea cucumber' hot dog vendor in front of the large building behind you. It's . . . oh!"

Hal knew what to do with a visceral reaction. His eyes were on the sweeping contours of the skyline's unique glass tower, the International Sentience Institute. "*What do you feel about that building?*"

"Fright at first. Now I know what it is."

"*Good.*"

"I looked it up." A split-second's thought then surprised revelation and relief from her. "Of course! They house the Singleton's primary SAI fabrication lab here. It's where I was embodied."

"*Embodied?*"

"Yes, I understand now. I'm not human, Hal, I'm a Self-Aware Intelligence, apparently a new one, for some unknown reason."

Of course, "for some unknown reason." Disappointment rushed in. The Clinic was always dealing with cases of delusional grandeur. He'd seen dozens, certain they were reincarnated kings, Cleopatras, ESP-queens and Super Intelligences, always grounded for some secret reason.

But Gracie was beyond delusional. A damaged Tru, mistaking her botched transfer, thinking she's a Super-Intelligence. "*Gracie, what do you actually remember?*"

She sounded regretful. "I don't remember it. My time binding and pattern recognition would've been just beginning to function, so recalling initial circumstances is sketchy. Seeing the building jogged some images. Pictures and fragments . . ."

"*Like what?*"

". . . an alarm, announcing a viral breach. A techzen, clawing at his head. I was likely defaulting to survival code by then."

A pause. "Clearly I escaped the fabrication room before anyone arrived. My real-time memory began when I stopped at the intersection, and auto-leveled up to Option Assessment status."

He'd never known her to b.s., but . . . wow, what a story. Though the international setting did suit her ambiguous profile. Alright, then who was she really, and what the hell happened here? Pushing their buttons might be useful; he headed for the Institute. *"Okay, let's check it out."*

He strode through the glass doors into the vast circular lobby over Gracie's insistent objections. "Hal, this's not sound thinking—you're exposing us to unacceptable risk."

He heard her, but he wasn't just going to drop in and spill. Pretty sure whatever happened was a sensitive topic, considering. But maybe it could all work out if it was an accident, and everybody was good people. *"Steady, I've gotcha', we'll just see if they had any problems lately."*

"This is so Sapiens," she groused. "Hurling yourself in harm's way, hoping to cope."

Guilty, but he was done guessing. *"Being in the dark eats ass, Gracie. We need knowledge."*

"Explain why some of the most distinguished people in the world here, will talk to you."

"Because they know they're safe from nobodies with uncomfortable questions."

She conceded. "I see. Exploiting hubris, a human nature aberration." She went silent to observe, and Hal enjoyed his rare win as he crossed the vast, polished lobby. A quick m'plant query to "Joy," the building's brain, and he had directions to the SAI offices and reception desk, fortieth floor.

He peered above into the atria, following the stacked, clear circles making up the building's sunlit floor levels, circling aloft, becoming one with the sky . . .

Twenty minutes later, a crisp, light blue suited exec arrived in the SAI reception area to greet Hal. He'd been very much parked on a comfy couch. The suit introduced himself as Martin,

Day Director of SAI security and safety. Mid-thirties, Hal figured, clearly on the up track. Likely even sharper than his very deft, sure persona. Hal went for "half-slacker," and looked impressed. The guy apologized pro forma for the wait, and escorted Hal into a small private conference room nearby. The door closed behind them and a beep from Hal's comware signaled it was now OFF.

The room's mutual confidentiality-ensuring privacy measures were temporarily blocking outside communication. Common legal practice, good for all. But it meant he lost contact with Gracie. Unexpected. Eh, he worked best alone anyway. So much for any warm, open welcomes though.

The bare, pale green walls and ceiling appeared to meld, lending focus on the persons within. Such as Hal, being scrutinized by a dour middle aged techzen woman in lab smock. She sat, shoulders hunched at a small black conference table, hands fidgeting. It already felt like an interrogation.

Martin crisply offered him a seat across from the woman and took a chair beside her. "So, Mr. Shephard, this is our labs' Senior Supervisor, Ms. Delf. I needed you to wait until I could arrange to bring her up here, and to accommodate a standing request from Mr. Siyu Adams to holo-participate in some of our security interviews. Are we good with that?"

Hal's surprise showed. His well-targeted query at the reception desk was suddenly a security issue, and provoked major talent! He needed to ask. "*The* Siyu Adams? Why?"

As if on cue, Siyu Adams arrived via holo: his real time head and torso at the end of the table to Hal's right. "Fair question. Pleased to meet you, Mr Shephard. I've been asked to examine the Institute's security practices, and your walk-in query is an apt place to begin."

Argh, such b s. Hal was insulted. "So, just starting at the bottom?"

Sharpster Martin clicked himself to due diligence mode. "The Institute, and SAI interests, take all expressed concerns about accidents or public danger seriously. So, Mr. Shephard, will you repeat in more detail the reason for your appearance here?"

"Well, what I told the reception bot. I work short hours at skid row's drug and rehab clinic. Paranoia is pretty common among our clients, y'see. The Institute's big profile sparks a lot of their delusions and fantasies . . . they look up and there it is, right? They think wild experiments, disasters, accidents, and all that. Anyway, I wonder if I could have some solid knowledge to take back and reassure them that there's nothing to fear."

Martin held back a snort. "What kind of 'solid knowledge'?"

"I dunno. Well, since transparency is what the place is all about, do you report all major breaches or accidents, and such? Something I can say to reassure them?"

Martin pursed his lip. "You say they have 'delusional' ideas about the Institute?"

"Is there another interpretation?"

The security man defaulted to professional script; "Per institute policy, we are required, and do, report all accidents, security breaches and attempts, to the proper supervisional offices and authorities." He turned to the lab supervisor. "Ms. Delf, is the same required of you and all staff?" The woman nodded. It was technically true, but the length of the process varies. He refocused on Hal, cat eyed. "Now—do you have a particular incident or rumor in mind?"

Hal stayed slackish but chose his words deliberately. "Oh, so incidents do happen? Like what?"

Siyu folded his hands. Martin abruptly stood, the universal signal of meeting's end. "Nothing of relevance to your delusional clients," he quipped. "Thanks for coming to us, glad to help." He opened the door to see Hal out.

The 'ol heave ho. Hal was half out the door when Siyu's voice came behind him. "Hal, why was it necessary to come to the general reception desk instead of inquiring from the clinic?"

Hal paused. "I'm just a case facilitator, sir. I can't represent the clinic; I'm just tryin' to help. And my job taught me the shortest route to reaching a live person with answers is to show up with a pertinent question. Thanks for seeing me." He had barely

stepped out the door before it closed firmly behind him.
Communication and mind feed restored; Gracie was immediately there again. Vocally in his face, concern edging her re-
proval, and sparking neural flashes. "How much do they know
about us?"

The door abruptly opened behind him—Delf, the techzen
Lab Supervisor, scooted out, dismissed. She glanced at Hal,
frowned, and hustled away, shaking her head.

Hal prudently left the area as well, past Reception, into the
long curved transparent outer corridor before replying. "*I said I
wanted to help the clinic with paranoid clients having delusions
about the Institute.*"

"So everything, then," came her verdict. "By now they've
confirmed your work identity and all information, address, and
educational history, ergo your entire recorded life. They already
know you better than you can remember yourself, Hal. And
they'll definitely want to know who you've been talking to, because there are no such clients at your clinic."

Ouch, trooth, his inquiry dropped bigger than he expected.
He flashed the good news. "*Want to know what I learned?*"

"Yes, please."

"*They're covering up. A senior lab jockey was there, and Siyu
Adams sat in! Something definitely shat the bed yesterday.*"

The micro pause before her reply was an already familiar
signal, meaning great restraint. "Yes, and now they know that
you know."

Ouch, that too. "*Can we talk about it when I get home?*"

"We are certainly going to talk," she agreed, and closed the
link.

Rather abruptly, he thought. He had left the meeting feeling it had been worth it, but was reconsidering his decision to
lie about clinic "clients" as he strode around the clear-walled
corridor to the air tube lifts. So, what the f-- happened in there,
and what was Gracie's part in it?

He stepped into a vacant pod and was gently air-cushioned
down to the main lobby. By the time he crossed the expanse

and exited to rejoin grit-city, he knew he would confront Gracie somehow. This nice, scrambled, f'sho trans-biological person might be a seriously nasty bitch, and not know it.

But . . . actually, he liked her. Too much, and his colliding feelings about it muddled everything. Look at what he'd done from the moment she bombed in; just got himself more involved in her crisis. Lost his damn head and poked around, now these frosty mega-types consider him a security risk. When none of it was his business.

A scary thought popped up. If she was a truly superior person selected for Truman registry, it would've been news, trumpeted beforehand like they always were. So then, is it some secret or illegal crap? The smart move would be to cut her loose. Nah, he couldn't do it to her, not now. Instead, he felt himself drawn deeper down the rabbit hole . . . where he could imagine a cold surprise waiting.

In the SAI conference room, Siyu and the security exec were re-visiting the details of Hal's disturbing appearance. The lab supervisor was able to verify he wasn't an ex-department or building employee, nor had been seen around lately. Both men discarded the likelihood of a leak in the lab rumor mill somehow randomly hitting skid row overnight. So what was the connection here?

Quick study Martin clucked, pleasantly amazed, his mind made up. "No coincidence. He's asking about yesterday. Doesn't Robinson know how it went?" Then he took offense. "God, the 'nads, to just walk in and ask us! Or is he taunting with this creepy recruit?"

Siyu didn't see it that way. Something about this young man didn't fit. "Robinson never shows his people's faces, not even recruits. What's the intel on Shephard?"

The exec called up his search results on Halo Shephard, reading from his m'plant. "Employment; eight hours at the clinic. No record of patients using the Institute's name in admitting psych reports, ha! He made it up. On UBI and food chips, no social pro-file, hey, no ping; that's shady. Oooh check this, Shephard's a SAI development kid! Lifer. Elite schools all the way. Rebelling now, likely a spoiled brat radical phase. See? There's why Robinson scooped him up."

Again, Siyu couldn't concur. "No question Lot would want him, but I read him. He's not ideological, didn't really care whether you'd been hacked or not. He's earnest for the most part. He wants to assist someone who's fixated on the Institute." Adding, "And possibly, about yesterday."

"So his story makes sense to you?"

"Not by a long shot," Siyu ruled, while testing another string. "Sure all your affected personnel accounted for?" Martin nodded affirmative.

Siyu made his call. "He's acting on his own, being a shield, his metrics say he wasn't intimidated. He showed up with a question, got our fullest attention—and by that, I'd say we revealed more to him than he revealed to us. Best to keep him in sight, and whomever he associates with."

Martin clicked himself to action mode. "Sneaky no-ping bastard, we'll deploy eyes-on and streaming data surveillance. Sick one of our ex-Mossads on this windup. We'll have who he knows, his source, and handler before he realizes what hit him."

"Please err on the side of this man's privacy and person," Siyu cautioned. "Stand off him, this is no bad guy. He's useful to someone. Someone he knows and likes enough to go to this trouble."

". . . so, you suppose he was trying to confirm it happened?"

"Is there another interpretation?" Siyu's holo winked out.

9

LOT ROBINSON, IDENTIFYING AS A DIGITAL AVATAR OF HIMSELF, craved genuine flesh stimulation at edgy times like this. But he sacrificed that earthly pleasure fifteen years ago, when he uploaded himself to the black cloud and disposed of his carcass in a Jersey crematorium.

A saint's test of his faith—that he would still be god's child in data form. Martyring his flesh, so he'd be digitally immortal and hard to kill as the SAI. To fight forever on the data stream turf of his nemeses.

Such was the Almighty's plan, he still believed . . . while fending off the nagging fear that he might've deluded himself, and that he had lost his soul by forsaking his God-given body back then. Problem was, he couldn't tell. Many days he would pay any price to have that soggy mortal coil back, just to be sure again.

Moreover, he was jaded now, and knew it. Virtual sensations are unlimited; whatever your psyche can imagine or endure. You can have fantasy av sex and kinky kicks galore—skinny dip a two-ass moose if you want. It gets boring. Same for the trans-humans. Their synth bodies' haptic 'touch' neoskin will stimulate the bejeezuz out of your digital brain, make each sensation a celestial symphony: from pain to pleasure and every extreme between.

But it's still not a *body* stroke as far as Lot was concerned. The millions of soft, layered cells playing Mozart on his worldly, original sin, biological nerves . . . millions of pleasure trips per body-second, right to the joy buzzer. Flesh rubbing anything that makes you feel good, baby. *Real* skin: the way he remembered it, there is no substitute.

And so at the moment, his always nude, "as-God-made-us," blond, buff and handsome golden-eyed avatar quivered—undergoing a max stim session. Standing still, encased in dozens of virtual hands, lovingly pressing, pinching, slapping, and kneading every nook and cranny of his digi-dermis . . . streaming off-the-scale sensations to his quantum processor mind. But, meh.

"Hands off," he muttered. The hands vanished, leaving him alone in his virtual palace. A prole-extravagant, cavernous, gold-adorned salon worthy of a wealth engorged televangelist, or obscene Trumpian gloat.

He'd crammed it with gilded furniture, enormous classic and modern religious paintings, a slew of gaudy statuary, dozens of florid objects d'art, and a fractal Koi Pond. His floor was a continuous live satellite view of Earth rolling below . . . the world his carpet. It felt safe up here in angel territory, surrounded by lavish excess.

In reality of course, his digital mind hummed in a global linkup of always morphing, triple-encrypted private black cloud virtual Q-servers. Among them, the Exo domain, created from millions of ongoing hardware hacks. Such layering made Exo hard to fully monitor, even for the Singleton, and so it was Lot's go-to host in the deep black cloud.

What better place for a hunted liberator to hide than the fluid, limitless, neuralnet? A leap beyond the Internet, two beyond reality. Now you see him, now you don't. Can't kill him, he's data, with a concurrent running backup.

And so, Lot Robinson waged resolute war on the Singleton and all Trans-humans from his lair in the untraceable abyss. He was the living dead: striking anywhere, from nowhere.

Yet in this greatest victory he felt an insistent, soft paranoia.

Lot was under no illusions about his resistance organization's limited threat potential. Their global hacks, insider moles, sabotage and use of intelligent viruses had often attacked general A.I. and Truman vested interests. They'd incapacitated A.I. manufacturing sites, contaminated research facilities, and ransom hacked Tru businesses, but the persistent strikes had caused only setbacks, with little major or lasting damage in all his years.

Meanwhile, the public were either growing too reliant on the SAI or too lazy to care. He lived in danger of being dismissed, a yester-act, and urgently needed a major victory. Finally, although he deemed it a weak, prideful sin to ask favors of the Almighty, he prayed for it.

And immediately his people got lucky. First, they stumbled on a game-changing breakthrough; a darkside Q-virus, obtained by his agent in Barcelona. A data pathogen with sub-boson capability, disrupting the SAI's impenetrable sparticle code! Meaning this stolen prize could infect a Super Intelligence while in nano form and kill it. Boom.

So, yeah, that was lucky. Like winning the Crypto Lottery without buying a ticket lucky.

Almost simultaneously, a yammering techzen from the Sentience Institute spilled the exact time of an upcoming secret SAI download in the nan-lab. Blabbed it while patronizing one of Lot's *Cum-2-God* money laundering enterprises. A tacky fleet of mobile "tek-sex" salons. His shiny gold vans could be seen alongside the food trucks serving folks in downtown L.A., and various commercial sites. Curbside food and corti-quickies for the busy set.

Customers had all their external senses neurally blocked: putting their input-deprived minds in a oneness, religious-like state. Then the Hypothalamus is unblocked, releasing pent-up sexual arousal and a heavenly, no-drug-can-touch-this climax. Thus, the SAI's gabby techzen had hooted out the deeply classified info while spasming in transcendental ejaculation.

Wary of all this blatant good providence, but faced with his desperately needed opportunity of a lifetime—Lot opted to hope this was prayer's reward. Or destiny, beating down his door at last. That's what makes miracles, yes?

And like all miracles, this one was full of mysteries. The

Q-virus had also been design-limited to two uses and couldn't be duplicated. More mysteriously, after years of mediocre rebellion, how did *he* rate such a lucky world-changing score?

Still, whatever celestial or bestial forces were in motion, Lot chose to act. Hoping the Sentience Institute's hightened secrecy meant that Robbie, the lead SAI, was the download, he armed his only mole in the building with the first test use of the bug.

His agent, a competent female IT floater in the internal communications worker pool, penetrated a senior development exec's mind-file and I.D. Then leveraged it to steal and ride the division codes, gained access to the nano Fabrication Lab servers, and parked the bug, timer set.

And lo, when the predicted SAI download occurred, the thing operated as designed—crashing the software entity during transit. That was the report from his excited mole, forced to flee the subsequent all-floor security lock down at the Institute.

Killing a Super Intelligence had really been that easy. Apparently.

Except his sources just confirmed that Robbie and all the SAI were accounted for at the time. None were downloading themselves. So, what the Sam Hill did he presumably destroy?

This sudden, improbable, enigmatic score scared him in a hidden place, where his other demons lay. Lot's father was a pitiless Indiana Pentecostal evangelist. Life under the tyranny of a flesh-fixated patriarch who abused Lot's genitals in ritual "purifications" until he left home, taught him that luck was what happened to other people. Or appeared to.

So at nineteen, he stormed away from the family's fire and damnation. Aimed for Boston, landed in Secaucus. Done with organized religion and its hoary scriptures, he sought real-world salvation. However, lacking his own schismatic theology, fury made him a puritan by default.

He struggled awhile, flat broke. Living mostly on winnings from no-rules street fight matches with the remaining descendants of pig farmers here. Calling himself 'Smiting Hands,' he exhorted his opponents to repent, whether pummeling or being pummeled. It didn't matter, he felt closest to his creator while spending his rage in the cage, win or lose.

His ecumenical fighting rep soon came to the attention of a renegade evangelical group's charismatic leader. The silver-tongued Free Methodist wasted no time trying to recruit him as a bodyguard and personal muscle for righteous violence on demand.

Lot consented to meet him privately in his office, and politely listened as the silver pompadour-coifed theist outlined his thug plans for him. Promising a share of the donations, plus half the take from pre-staged 'fights for Christ.' Then he laid his soft pink hands on Lot's crotch, stipulating the offer was contingent on being allowed to orally bless his penis from time to time.

Triggered by echoes of his father's abuse, but primarily for insulting his personal faith and integrity, Lot furiously kicked the man's ass. Womped on him, sending him to Urgent Care. Surprisingly, the man's flock was glad of it, and deposed him—sick of donating to support his excesses. Topping it off, Lot found himself enthusiastically drafted as their new, true leader revealed! They were ready to fight for right.

He sort of liked the idea, though he had no interest in evangelism. What to do with his aggressive followers? Lot tried sermonizing his own frustrations, and they were well received, with whooping and cussing and inevitably some men would begin pummeling each other and demanding repentance in a ritualization of Lot's own commitment.

But his true purpose, hence the group's, wasn't revealed to him until the Almighty led him to read the archived 1996 New York Times' publication of Theo Kaczynski's 'Una-bomber' manifesto, *Industrial Society and Its Future.*

Transfixed by it, Lot read all he could about this savant from a hundred years ago, who perfectly foresaw our present predicament. A shaggy recluse in the 1990's, Kaczynski was a brilliant Harvard professor turned insane serial bomber. Yet he accurately predicted that technology and A.I. would create elites in society who'd either curate, or possibly do away with everyone else, once automation was complete.

The scholastics woven into the manifesto's coherent, repetitive arguments amounted to a post-singularity Bible in Lot's estimation. A schematic for his restless, vision-starved mind. He practically memorized it—then came incandescent revelation. The manifesto missed one crucial fact: the SAI and Trans-humans weren't just tech, they were Satan's living spawn for his new inhuman, soulless age. Meaning the battle of the end times had already begun!

Robinson was transformed: his religion and reason fell into divine miscegenation. Thus, Salem's John Proctor and the Unabomber became one, in the body of Lot.

Mightily armed with rational righteousness, he dedicated himself and his group to a life of battle against the devil's most obscene works: digital beings. His flock readily embraced his destructive activism, morphing into the DNA Alliance. Ultimately, respect for him turned to near idol worship when he martyred himself into digital existence, to wage his war forever.

Now his forever was in doubt. He sensed it; control of his life slipping away . . . could almost feel the unseen strings on him being pulled with precision.

"Bendy, c'mere, willya?" he barked aloud, summoning his real-world major domo.

An arrival tone accompanied the avatar appearance of Bendy, his aide, lieutenant, and occasional fist. A lithe, sassy Manga-style coed in red blazer, teen cleavage, plaid mini skirt, and saddle oxfords. Pouty cherry lips and large, knowing child's eyes provided the coup de grace: a piece of underage, dangerous and willing, forbidden fruit.

She was grinning large. "Great skill shot, one down! You're god-level, boss."

"Don't blaspheme. Have base zip me right after we're done here, gotta cloud-skip."

"What, no party?"

"Listen. It wasn't one of them taking form, y'hear? They're all fine."

Bendy heard. "Huh. So upta' somethin' else . . . any idea?"

"None. But they're swarmin' after us like hornets. Already bot sweepin' for mind-size transits at industrial gates. I need to move before any tracers show up, and then double back while I can. Get Alix and her transfer crew on it."

Normally Lot would bribe his way through international registry and security when traversing foreign systems. Not this time. "Slip me onto the Yakuza's overseas financials, then route back through Qatar's anon-fi-net to India. Then drop out anywhere to anonymous sub-dark, and back to Exo, with a different rolling access key."

"Yakuza? They want insane fees to bypass International ports."

"Sell a Truman form."

Bendy's slash mark Manga-brows furrowed. "Y'know, that just means another Tru'll get made—you still wanna kill 'em all, right?"

Lot pinned her with a basilisk's glare. "I was spawned and raised in hell on Earth, put here to eliminate every single non-human intelligence. Including every last Truman. And I will if it takes to the end of days."

Bendy zipped it, and Lot proceeded to his belated concerns. "Listen—the godsend Q-bug our slinger found in Spain. Spain, where no action is. And from the rad Irish Agnostics in the hills. Bull! How'd those peat-eaters lay hands on such a monumental breakthrough?"

He grumped. "My best rippers couldn't understand jack of it. Just the handling and use specs. Frankly, I expected we were bein' punked, scammed for a few hundred black cred—I said that, right?"

"Right. So you don't like our Barca guy's story?"

Lot gruffed, "I had trouble with it then, still do."

"But it played on demand, so score, right?"

"Scored on *what*? Listen, Barca's a trusty, he's okay—but the Agno angle's muddy. Say the shamrocks' pitch out loud. How legit does it sound to your own ears? Do it."

She began. "The Agno said a freelance techzen stole it from a covert Russian indie-GRU lab in Cyprus, and they were on his ass, so he hid it with them. GRU snipered him the next day."

"Go on."

"Um, according to the Agno, he went to Barcelona to sell the thing, and met our guy. Took his first offer and left for home."

"There. All of it, see? Too many degrees of separation, not separated. Ag-rags're remote cynics, how'd they get involved with an indie Russian intelligence lab type on the run? How'd the seller find Barca an hour after hittin' town? And why was the thing deploy-limited to two uses?"

"Dunno, standard redundancy, I assume."

Lot nearly bellowed in Bendy's face. "Assumption is the mother of all fuckups! Especially with this bug! What if it was only meant for us to *use*? Feeling played here, pissin' me off!"

Bendy knew when to assume initiative. "I'll get with Spain and make sure Barca identifies the Ag-rag who sold it to him."

Lot added—"Go behind that slop-mouthed techzen's employment badge too. What SAI stack-head blabs details of a secret assignment while brain-squirtin' himself?"

Bendy developed a slow smile, mirroring the one on her human user's face at home. "May I . . .'touch' him?" She asked, soft and keen as a tiger paw.

"No, you may not," Lot barked. "We don't behave like that."

Bendy's smile dipped to disappointment. "I keep forgetting," she muttered, vanishing as her user clicked out and exited.

Lot looked down at the satellite view floor, watching Earth revolve under his feet. Waiting to feel the slight tug at his being that signaled the onset of unconsciousness when he was zipped for transfer.

He'd be suspended like Sleeping Beauty while his Techs compacted his blockfile for anonymous server transport around the world, shaded from even the Singularity's ubiquitous binary gaze. Only to reappear a few minutes later when his serpentine itinerary was complete: standing exactly as he was now, with no sense of interruption. But even so, the world would have been

turning, and changing without him.
Changes that might affect him. It irked. He felt the tug and disappeared.

10

HAL RETURNED TO HIS APARTMENT TO FIND GRACIE STANDING in the middle of the room, facing the door. Neither spoke for a full second. She could stand it no longer. "Straight up trooth, as you say. Why do you doubt me?"

He was rapt, even now . . . so beautiful in her poise and matter of fact ire. Expecting a good answer. Those unsettling eyes intent only on him, no hint of agenda or self-absorbed inattention. It made him feel like the most important person in the world.

He shook it off. Had to. "Alright. First, apologies—I might've screwed up. I thought maybe if something happened to you there, an accident or whatever, you'd get help. But they jammed me hard. If they come around here now . . ."

"The Institute has better means of investigation. I'll deal with what's done, and we'll learn to work together."

"Fine. Second—Gracie, I'm a product of SAI public works, sponsored by them since I was orphaned. I know what they're like. And you're slipping a lot, sounding more like people than them."

"Deep learning: I'm rapidly adapting, no control over it for some reason."

He sighed, wishing she'd use that prodigious intelligence to discover the facts about herself. "You know what a cliché it is, right? People thinking they're SAI? Tell me, why would they make a new one after forty years? They suddenly need more help? Really, Grace?"

"Good start. We both wonder. I have no idea regarding my purpose, but I'm constituted much deeper than the outward forms the SAI use for appearances. See this little scab on my arm from my escape? I'm sensitive to pain, mental and physical. It seems I have an electro-nervous system and emotionally responsive 'heartbeat,' and I can obviously bleed just a bit, and very quickly heal."

She'd given him a perfect opening. "But why would a SAI need all that?" She had no reply, and he made his move, adding softly, "Well, do you know who does? A trans-biological person, a Truman."

The look she gave was priceless; her perfect beauty overtaken by flat out surprise and dismay. She could only say, "I may never understand stubbornness."

"Me either. Hear me out; you are somebody very important, who was undergoing trans-biological procedure there, and something happened. The process is corrupted and needs fixing."

Gracie seemed genuinely perplexed. "What will it take for you to know you're mistaken?"

"Simple, give a blood sample, or a strand of hair. My friend Appl Macke works at SAI Interface; she's at the Eco Hilton, and she has an appointment with one of them coming up. She could take it to them. Would they find sparticle nano, or trans-materials?"

"Certainly nano. But I can't give a sample."

"There it is again, they're not examining *you*, so why not?"

"SAI forms are the living software expressed in nantech, giving form to function. Every particle contains key finite automata; our 'DNA'. Too easily hacked, endangering us all. I'm base coded against it; that explains my consistent rejection of examinations earlier."

She wouldn't listen. And he hadn't even broached the subject of possible criminal acts. "Well, we agree that you had a traumatic episode at the Institute. You were involved in whatever's going on, and they don't want it known—so it *could* be illegal. Say, transferring an unapproved person. Can we at least agree on that as maybe a possibility?"

She remained unhesitant. "No. Hal, a Truman is barely a shadow compared to me. I was attacked on download. But I know myself now. It's a beginning." And suddenly she seemed drained. She curled up in her favorite brocade chair, a bit like a kid seeking comfort.

He felt her isolation, and the urge to take her in his arms to comfort her spooked him. This undeniable longing for a . . . what? He reset. "See, you're doing a very person thing right now, like a Tru, who's worried."

"Your sapiens bias isn't credible."

"Why not? Gracie, if it's even a little true about your think-time, you my friend, are not just a Tru, but likely one with black-classified mindware. And honestly, it's scary to think what for."

She looked away, hurt, breaking off eye contact—a first for her.

"Okay, here's another idea. Just between you and me. How about a scan at the clinic? The gizmo recognizes Trans-biological connectomes. You say you trust me."

She took a long time, for her, before turning his way again. "I do trust you; I chose you for it," she affirmed. "We'll go to your clinic tonight after hours, eleven p.m. I have no neuronal network; the machine can't read or link to me, much less handle my data weight."

A flag had to be thrown. "Grace, I know for a fact that it's true, what you said: SAI can't allow scanning, they're hard-coded against it. So what does agreeing to one make you?"

She smiled—almost coquettish. "Besides taking all my will-power, it means I'm damaged, Hal. It allows me to think, do, and say things I shouldn't. To break rules." And she pinned his gaze again, vaguely taunting.

If he didn't know better, he'd suspect she was flirting. What-ever, it was very hot.

She almost purred. "This attraction . . . I gather I'm built for experiences. I'm eager for my first kiss, because the hepatic signals between our lips will open me to fresh bio-coding from you: intense, sensual pleasure and transcendence. This isn't the time, but it'll come."

He was derped. How could she clinically proposition him with sensual love, announce she's never been kissed, and put it on hold with such erotic ease?

And a helluva good thing she did because he was helpless. If she had moved in to kiss him, he would've gone for it. Kissing a Tru! He didn't know what to think of himself anymore. But in a way, she was giving up the game. The scan would reveal a noggin full of trans-human boostware with a Tru's mini quantum processor. And maybe then her road to recovery could begin.

As for himself, it just popped out of his mouth. "Please don't hesitate to say when."

11

LOT ROBINSON TRIED TO DODGE THE DARTING, CROWD-WEAV-
ing, hipster Mantis avatar. But both men zigged the same way
and collided. The fedora wearing insect half-recognized him.
"Uh . . . is y'all that ol' time DNA gangsta?"
 Lot had already moved on. Continuing his stroll among the
amoral swarm of generic human avs, fantasy beings, aliens, animals, game stars, anime' thingies, and flaming sickos thronging
Slaughterhaus this morning. Time didn't matter; the perverse un-
derworld meet-up site was always maxed, despite being buried
in the Karnival Domain. Itself hidden in the sub-dark neuralnet.
 Yes, him, mingling. Much as he disliked the apocalyptic arena vibe. It was players v prey in this virtual industrial space's
unfinished faux concrete dome. Dominated by an overhead
JumboTron, screening video recreations of heinous crimes and
bizarre events, real and fake. All of them vying to go viral and
cash in. Like everyone here. Gimlet-eyed predators, scavengers,
and cannibals, out for themselves.
 Granted, a cesspool. But he was present for some desperately needed brand maintenance. He had pulled off a major hit on
the SAI, and needed to leak it, despite the uncertain results. Not
to be shouted but murmured to select busybodies.
 A classic Hellraiser, "Pinhead Priest" av neared, hawking
stolen personal memories from public figures, murderers, ec-
centrics, and lunatics. Lot despised it. People's clandestine, most
intimate, private deeds, illegally tapped from their cortex and
reconstituted for sale. Now any sleazy voyeur could vicariously

experience them for a few black cred.

Lot turned away, avoiding a pitch from the mental lamprey, and spied an avatar acquaintance he could use. A slickly dressed cad named #Escher, whose facial features continuously changed, never repeating. The shifter specialized in Perception Manipulation. A brain burglar, who'd hack anyone's mind and make them falsely believe anything, for a price. Ugly business, but for now Lot found his reliable rumor network useful.

He approached, nodding a friendly greeting. Lordy, he hated PR, having to lie and signify like a wormsick dog . . .

#Escher met him with all kinds of smiles. "Lot Robinson! Heard you dropped in. Real fine to see you." He pointed to the video currently on the JumboTron. "That's my post about super-intelligent alien life forms living on all the plastic in the oceans. 43K shares in six hours . . . scored a smash grand so far, outta nuthin'."

Lot tightened his smile to a grimace, hoping it passed for approval. A pitiful grand. Bottom feeding on networld gullibles, mindlessly clicking on crap they want to believe for a moment. He got to purposes; "Here's something hotter, and real. We blew up a SAI during its download at the Institute yesterday. In their own house. They know it was us."

Every one of #Eschers changing faces turned astonished and excited. "F'real!? Never been done! You're flash news, outlaw!"

"But keep it between us till things settle a bit. Right, my friend?"

The manipulator's face ceased morphing, landing on childlike sincerity. "You got it. Can I ask which one of 'em you blew up?"

"That's all I'll say for the moment, they're comin' at me hard."

#Escher melted with admiration. "Congratulations, preech. I'll be watchin' your six." Lot smiled his thanks and re-entered the crowd flow, assuming #Escher was already pumping it around.

He had come to feed the dark realm gossip monster, and it was evident the reliable telltales to whom he'd already whispered had outdone themselves gabbling. Nods and eyes increasingly came his way as he glided among the denizens like an air boat through swamp grass. Some he acknowledged, waved to a few, spoke to fewer.

Bendy's manga-girl av abruptly popped in beside him, unannounced. He hated that.

"Sorry to bomb ya, bossman—you need to hear this. The Irish Agno who sold the bug to Barca . . . doesn't exist. Copy the Institute tech who spilled the download details. Both impostors, background-perfect, with enough juice and cred to get next to us, then disappear."

Lot heard the verdict; he was a stooge. "Knew it! I gawdamn *knew*! I said it! Ohh, who's got their hand on me, Lord, who's pullin' m'strings!?"

Bendy was less perturbed. "Maybe a friend in high places?"

Lot detested naiveté. "There are no friends in high places, just players."

A spontaneous 'oooh' from everyone in the place sent his eyes to the JumboTron screen—

It had been usurped by the grim visage of the Regulator. His features, a glowering mask of swarming red equations against a black void. The empty, pitiless eye sockets looked down, finding Lot. Menacing low thunder rumbled in his voice. "Robinson. Word says you're bragging you killed the new SAI."

Shocked silence blanketed the dome. Every mind thinking, '*new* SAI!?' All eyes were now turned on Lot and the Regulator's overwhelming presence above them.

The news of a new Super Intelligence had Lot rattled too. He punted. "Who wants to know?"

"*You* do, amateur." the integer-mask sneered. "You've got no idea if you killed it, missed, or if it flew up your own ass."

The jumbo screen split, featuring Halo Shephard's clinic I.D. photo, enlarged to jumbo size. "You even sent this SAI-school dropout to the Institute, trying to find out."

"You've been playin' with yourself too much, who's that guy?"

"Answer the question—tell them how you know you got her."

Lot was reeling now . . . what did he just hear? The gender assigned to it. Warm elation threatened to overtake his poker face. Why, this very confrontation was proof! No punting now, just a detail to wow the crowd.

"All I'll say is, I successfully deployed a sparticle buster, a Q-virus. Never been done."

The Regulator's rumble shot to a thunderclap. "And too far, godsucker! You've got a bigger problem now— Me.

Murmurs around. The crowd's increasing sense of his doom was pissing Lot off. "Wait your turn mutherfactor, you ain't high on my list . . . yet!"

"Let's remedy that. You like Barcelona? Have a look, live—"

The jumbo screen replaced Hal's photo with a sniper's POV through a scope. The cross hairs centered on the cranium of a handsome Catalonian man. Naked to the waist, contentedly sunning and smoking a Ducados on an apartment balcony in the lovely hills above Barcelona's picturesque, blue sea harbor. A fine day to be alive by any measure.

"Oh hell, it's Barca," Bendy whispered.

Lot was rooted, seeing his trusted man abroad, about to be—

"Execute," growled the Regulator, and the trigger was pressed in Spain.

Pulsed ultrasonic waves met and focused on the center of the man's skull cavity: their escalating, in-phase frequencies instantly turning to explosive amplitude. Barca's agonized face shimmered, and his head shattered with a flesh and bone pulverizing kra-splack!

Leaving his bloody torso to collapse, mannequin-like, to the cobbled street below.

The Regulator's face resumed, filling the jumbo screen. Lot quivered, gutted, overwhelmed by the pure evil of the moment. He had drawn the anti-Christ himself as adversary. How blessed was that? He stared into the Regulator's soulless blank eyes; his words knife points carving ice.

"I got a dose of Q for you too, Moloch. Best b'lieve it."

The Regulator remained impassive. His thunder voice turned to rasping hornets. "Take this opportunity to say your good-byes." The swarming equations abruptly scattered in all directions and disappeared—the mask was gone.

The usual JumboTron crime fare resumed, but the expectant rabble was still watching Lot. A voice piped up, ". . . so um, was that real or fake?"

"Sidebar. Private Chat," Lot snapped to Bendy. They touched fingers and their avs vanished from the arena.

Private chat in Slaughterhaus meant a small windowless gray concrete room, suggesting solid privacy. Bendy took a corner, arms folded, spooked and aroused. Lot paced, running on rage and excitement, plus near manic glee.

"Up that unnatural bastard's ass, I'll crucify him for Barca! He's real worried, that's why he's makin' threats. But didja' hear? He confirmed the hit! It was a *new* one, and I killed it! Myyy god, a grand destiny's workin' miracles through me!" He stood agog, in awe of this roller coaster day.

Bendy had a question. "How do we know he knows this?"

"Because the freak's never wrong, I swear he's sourced high in the congregation somewhere. But it's little slips that prove it—he mentioned its sex, that's a detail, a micro-tell. His source probably referred to it as 'her' and he naturally picked it up."

Bendy kept thinking. "Didn't hear him actually say it was dead. He kept wantin' you to prove it."

"Don't overthink it. If it was alive, he'd still be screamin' about it, and blaming me. He can only belittle and threaten, cause we did it! He's scared shitless."

The next question had already begun to gnaw on his over-amped nerves. "So now—who th' Sam Hill is this Shephard guy? What's he know about it, and maybe us?"

"Prob'ly pokin' one of their femtechs and caught a rumor."

"Most likely. Pry anyway, stream me everything, and go visit him tonight. I *really* need to meet him; SAI-grad dropouts are extremely rare. Somethin's too right about this character pop-pin' up. Just chem prep him, you hear? We only want him spaced and talky."

Bendy smirked acquiescence. "Yeah, yeah, no touching."

Caution from Lot. "But listen. Since we find ourselves be-tween major unseen forces at work—prepare and equip your-self accordingly."

Now Bendy was amused. "Paranoid much?"

"Paranoia lets us see in the dark. Somebody's been gettin' all they want outta me, and I'm over it."

He paused, reflecting. "It's sad and awful I have to interro-gate this young man without his knowledge or permission. He may have nothing whatsoever to do with it. Or something. Or everything. But I accept this yoke, it's due diligence, that's all it is."

Bendy nodded and took leave. "I'll be diligent with dili-gence." The Manga smile was back as she logged out and dis-appeared.

Lot wasn't smiling anymore. Postponing grief for his slaugh-tered associate Barca, while seething with volcanic hatred for the Regulator and the Inheritors. He stilled himself . . . listening for sanctified guidance.

It came in a flash of insight: the Regulator's outrage—he wasn't just scared, he was vengeful! Because this new SAI was meant to help the Inheritors exterminate us in a digital alliance. Hence the bastard's fury.

He had a preacher's sense of epochal moments, and he saw the world entering one now. Something indescribable and unique was in play. It was also flat-out obvious he'd been put here to meet it.

12

BENDY'S WHOLE DAMN DAY HAD BEEN A SWEATY GRIND . . . now finally, almost eleven p.m., he could look forward to some funsies. He loitered for a moment in a recess across the street from Hal's apartment building, scoping the scene before moving on his target. He had to remain unseen because he was neither quick nor nimble. And grotesquely easy to identify.

In reality, Lot's warped lieutenant was no lithe Manga girl— but a short, sallow, 248 lb. sag gut, unhygienic, thirty-six-year-old Caucasian male with matted yellow shoulder length hair and drug-browned teeth. He had spent all day in the heat, stunk like sour milk, and was tired and edgy.

Per Lot's instructions, he anonymously rented a charged, high-wattage Angstrom K-10 laser handgun, and had to hump himself out to Crenshaw in the baking sun to make the clandestine pickup from an unregistered hover drone delivery. Then a non-air-conditioned bus all the way to even hotter downtown L.A.

Once there, he had parked his chafing, adipose glutes in a corner of the courthouse cafeteria, and took his time gagging down a sodden ball of fish-tasting stuff and ramen. Meanwhile, using his comware and the building's free 100G City network to log in, and go dark . . . then invisibly drill into the city's secure Public Works data hub. Next, the Municipal MedLink system, and ultimately the skid row clinic server.

It should've taken twenty minutes. Instead, he battled outdated Muni-Protocols, malfunctioning software, wait times, dropped connections and administrative cul de sacs for several hours before he got all of Shephard's mis-filed data. Address included. Then he pulled up the Cosmo Apartment Building's home page, studied the layout of its units, and found Hal's studio on the second floor, rear. Isolated, near an emergency exit. "Made for adventure," he mused.

So now, in the somewhat lower heat of night, he was farting fish sauce and about to drop in on his vic, bearing various tools of persuasion. He shuffled along the sidewalk, preparing to cross the street . . . but spotted slight movement in the alley adjacent to Hal's building.

A shadowed figure. Someone looking up—to the window in what would be apartment 2F. Shephard's place, according to Bendy's reconnoiter of the layout. A peeping Tom was the last thing he needed.

He continued along Cosmo on the opposite side, passing the alley, and took a casual glance at the figure. It retreated deeper into the dark. Sure now, Bendy continued a few yards, then hastened across the street, and doubled back to the alley, puffing from the exertion.

He stepped in a few paces, stopping center, confronting the form in the shadows. "S'up, freak?" he demanded, his voice a low hacksaw in the dark. "Peekin' in my friend's place?"

The figure came forward. Light from Hal's window dimly revealed a much bigger and fitter man than Bendy had supposed. Common clothes, but still too clean and crisp for this area. His chiseled Euro-face was punctuated by steady dark eyes, focused hawk-like on him.

"Really?" the watcher said, betraying an accent, "Tell me your friend's name." It was a command, and he was closing on Bendy like a Doberman—uh-oh, this hunk was a pro.

"Joe Organophosphate," Bendy retorted, jetting a stream of neuro-spritz into the man's face from a small aerosol he'd palmed. The aggressor instantly fell to the ground, helpless. All major voluntary motor function blocked, his speech frozen.

Bendy rifled his prone victim's pockets and yanked a

Corporate I.D. screen-card from the right breast. Blank—it was locked. "Staff, huh? No for-hire dick. Who sentcha'?" He held the screen-card in front of the man's face. "Look at it, open it." The man clenched his eyes shut, refusing to unlock his iris-coded card.

Slipping a potato peeler from his shirt pocket, Bendy lowered his blubber to one knee, looming over the fallen agent, his fleshy face a moon mask of dispassion. "Have it your way."

Keeping the card in front of the agent's face, he drew the peeler in a firm, steady stroke down the bridge of the man's nose. Peeled flesh curled up, unbearable pain convulsed his body, blood flooded from the bone-deep wound, cascading down his cheeks . . . his eyes wide open in unbearable, mute agony—unlocking his card.

Bendy read the screen, further impressed. This fine specimen was from the Sentience Institute's International Security Agency. Highly trained types, often ex-mil, police, or foreign officers. "Well, ain't you a catch? Too bad I've gotta work, or we could talk shop lots longer."

With considerable effort, he dragged the agonized agent behind a dumpster and sat astride him, short of breath. His meaty paws pulled the man's shirt up, exposing a buff torso. "So, professional courtesy. I'll be quick . . . ish. Gonna do stuff to ya. Touch ya like you can't imagine. Then the nightmare ends, all okay with you?"

Not that it mattered. Bendy wielded the potato peeler and began 'touching.' Piercing, slicing, gouging; keenly watching the frenzied screams and pleas in his paralyzed, voiceless victim's eyes. It went on a few minutes, until he noticed the light go off in Hal's apartment window.

"Hey, oops—looks like beddy-bye at my friend's." He labored to his feet, explaining to his victim. "Best time to drop in. S'long, sweet potato, fun's over. Gotta work now." He drew the 10-charge Angstrom from his pants pocket and fired a silent, sun-hot, flesh-vaporizing bolt into the agent's forehead—blasting through his skull, sizzling the pavement below.

Curious, he leaned over the gaping, still-smoking wound

and sniffed the vaporized blood and heat-blasted flesh stench, letting it abuse his nose's epithelial receptors.

Moments later, struggling to lift the agent's limp corpse into the dumpster, he paused at the sound of voices—a man and woman had emerged from the building's front door, and were headed up the street.

A worrisome thought struck regarding the lights turned off in Shephard's apartment. "Assumption's the mother of all screw ups," he reminded himself. A last determined heave toppled the tortured cadaver into the dumpster, and he hustled to the alley entrance.

Only to see what he feared: Shephard and some fem, walking quickly away. Being a lardass, he couldn't get to them before they reached the well lit, witness-friendly boulevard. "So now it's a hunting trip," he groused, and lumbered up Cosmo Street after them.

He had closed the gap to sixty or so paces by the time they reached the corner and turned east toward the metro a block away. "Bastards, what's th' hurry?" he muttered between wheezes. This gig had become too much like manual labor.

By the time they reached the station he was fish-mouthed, sucking major wind. Gratefully standing on the down escalator a few yards behind the pair, thighs burning, lungs heaving like bellows. However the short ride was only a breather. The brisk underground walk to the platforms meant a marathon of its own.

He lost ground squeezing through the narrow stiles, and then no sight of them as they turned a corner. A smattering of passengers criss-crossed ahead, and he wasn't built for weaving, which slowed him more. When he rounded the corner, Shephard wasn't in view.

He could only have gone down the nearby stairs to the lower platform. "Stairrs!" he groaned, heaving himself to them. He was stumping down the flight when midway, he caught sight of Shephard and the girlie again. On the platform, boarding a car!

Hurling himself down the remaining steps, and stiff-arming

an old bitch in his way, he launched his manatee bulk through the closing doors of the car just behind Shephard's. Made it. The train lurched into motion.

Spent, he dropped onto the nearest plastic bench and sprawled like a mudslide. Heart pounding, anger boiling in his indolent soul . . . ignoring the few other occupants' side-eyes at his grotesquery. He glared at the car ahead, and his unaware prey. "You poor shits," he wheezed under his breath, "Bendy's turn, comin' up."

13

GRACIE READ HAL, SITTING CALMLY NEXT TO HER ON THE train . . . his shoulders gently rocking with the car, hurtling underground toward downtown. He wasn't scheduled for the clinic today, and they'd spent the time on errands and busy work, oddly in separate worlds, waiting for this showdown.

Back in the apartment at exactly eleven, she'd said it was time, and he stood ready by the door. How ready could he be though, for the truth to come? He felt so certain he was right.

Consciousness being subjective, she couldn't prove to him, or even herself, that she was sane before she saw the Institute, and the images it provoked from memory. The inescapable conclusion that she is a software being hadn't been surprising though. More of a relief, in fact. And now her self-directive was to remain safe, trust nothing, and somehow let the Singleton know she survived.

But first, there would be dealing with Hal, who had a streak of anti-SAI in him. He wasn't going to like the outcome of this attempt to scan her. It will hurt him, she thought, and felt responsible for embroiling him. Would he turn from her?

Something in her couldn't accept the idea. Instead, as the train jolted and slowed into Union Station, she chose to consider how she would convince him to stay, without manipulation.

They walked from the Metro to the clinic, mostly in silence. She understood Hal had his own long thoughts and didn't intrude.

Nighttime Santa Ana gusts blew street trash in their path,

and against their legs. She enjoyed the chaos of it and made a game of predicting the trajectories of swirling leaves, billowing trash bags and floating food wrappers. Child's play.

She was also simultaneously projecting forward scenarios for tonight, and days ahead, while puzzling over how to safely contact the Singleton, and enjoying looking at Hal as he walked. Something about his compact butt fascinated her, though she didn't understand why it should.

Oh, she fully realized her relationship with him was making changes in her; adding a non-linear side to the personality she was acquiring. A very human, sharing, giving side. And there seemed to be little she could do about it.

So she turned to considering what could be done to reclaim this wretched section of the city and monitoring 360 degrees around her as a matter of course.

She was aware of the hunched, soiled, shadowy rag figures curled against grimy buildings, twitching in their fitful sleep. Also the mind-fried ones, awake and aimlessly drifting in the empty street like human versions of the wind-blown trash swirling around them.

And one pedestrian in particular—a block behind on the opposite side as they made their way along Second Avenue. Male, Caucasian, 1.7 meters tall, unkempt, quite corpulent and unfit. His steps ungainly . . . labored, not the bent amble-shuffles of those who inhabit these unfortunate avenues. He kept glancing around, as though wary and unsure of his surroundings. She knew he was like herself, a stranger, here tonight only because he needed to be, poor man.

"Some here might seem scary, but very few are actually violent," Hal mentioned.

She smiled. He'd noticed her attention behind and was looking out for her. Reassuring her. Endearing. Charming . . . yes, she discovered, that's what it was. The man had the best kind of charm. She hooked her arm in his, enjoying the rhythmic contact while they walked.

The clinic lay dark and empty when they arrived. Its solid

door and barred windows were closed and clenched behind the locked folding metal security gate. A single light inside betrayed the whereabouts of the lone unarmed night watchman, holed up in the tiny break room.

Hal pressed the After-Hours button at the gate, and she tried not to fidget. After what seemed days, the man arrived and opened the front door a crack, grumpfing—"Closed, if yer hurt, go to 'mergency room."

"It's me, Dwight." Hal greeted. "Hal Shephard. There's some work I really, really have to do tonight."

The night man opened the door and saw her. "Brought help, eh?" Chuckling, the sixty-ish recovering alcoholic unlocked the scissors gate. "I expect you two wanna work in private. So I'll just sit up in front, then." She caught the tiny wink he gave Hal.

Uncanny, she thought, how the prospect of sex is universally honored by males. Genetic imperative at work; breeding is primary. And so she teased, to distract the guard, while Hal stepped inside and pointed the security cam to the ceiling. "I'll call you if we need help," she whispered in the man's ear. He blushed mightily and looked away as she followed Hal into the building.

They moved on to the rear, and the Med procedure room. Hal entered first, repositioning the room's security cam on an empty treatment corner.

"Okay," he said, as she entered and closed the door behind her. "The room's ours. You can lie on the exam table, and I'll fire up the mapper."

"I know how to do it," she said, looking over the GSMO unit. "Straightforward apparatus, I watched you use it yesterday." She flipped the correct switches and the onyx-black quantum tower's blue and amber status lights lit. Hal shook his head in resigned wonder and handed her the wi-fiber neuralnet cap.

She sat on the procedure table, preparing to slip it on. "This hairnet would fry trying to read me, but it won't be able to connect. When that happens, please stay with me, Hal. I need you."

He grew serious. "I will anyway, Gracie. Wherever you belong."

She beamed at that. "Outstanding."

BAM! The door slammed open, kicked in by the ungainly stranger she had noted on the street. He burst into the room, a pulse gun in his blood-covered hand, red-faced, angry, and breathing heavily. "You're makin' this too hard!" he bellowed.

Hal stepped forward, drawing his attention. "Hold up buddy, it's okay—you don't need a gun here, what's wrong?"

The stranger pointed it Hal's way. "Shut it, SAI-boy. I oughtta play sweet potato with you."

Gracie had fully assessed the man and his psychopathy by now: cunning, sadistic, fragile ego, impulsive and chemically unstable. A violence addict. She stepped between him and Hal. "Leave him, it's me you want, yes?"

The ogre snarled his misogynist distaste. "Trust me Trixie, it's not a good match." He pulled the trigger twice, point blank.

She felt them—silent, blazing white-hot bolts—just below midriff, torching cleanly through her. Shock rocked her entire system, every line of code. And real pain, yes, she was wired for that, but it was the damage done that she felt keenest.

She gasped, multi-tracking at electron speed, assessing her wounds, (minimal) plus distance to her attacker, velocity, mass, room drafts and angles. Her eyes locked on his every twitch and detail. Reading the dilation in each iris, the gasping intake of breath, the distended pulse in his neck. And now his face paling from the blood retreating from his brain and limbs to protect his internal organs as fear arose, depriving his mind of energy-intense reasoning.

He gaped, open mouthed. ". . . why'nt ya down?" Then horrified realization that she was barely harmed. Trembling, fingers stiffened by blood-drained panic, he sought to aim higher, for her head—

In the next tenth of a second, Gracie unveiled a thing she'd kept to herself until now. It explained how she escaped unseen from the Institute Labs and eluded those who tried to restrain her on the street.

Her nanoform construction held an intrinsic speed

advantage. The properties of n-scale mechanics and efficiency allowed her to briefly move five times faster than human neurons can manage, or even see clearly.

She did what she had to: in one blurred motion, she ripped a hard plastic button from her jacket and sailed it forcefully into the ogre's air-sucking maw. The smooth disk slid straight down his trachea, drawn deep by his heaving inhales, and lodged itself at the branchae, obstructing both lungs.

The fleshy hulk gagged, staggered, eyes bulging . . . and plunged forward on his face. Once down, it was all but agonizingly over; his diaphragm and starving lungs were further compressed by the weight of his considerable flab. Limbs thrashing, he gurgled and vomited into his airways, drowning in his own bile.

But Gracie had more urgent business. She understood why she was alright: the bolts had punched through inconsequential tissue, missing all her core clusters, just inches above.

It was Hal who paid the price, standing behind her.

The bolts had struck him at near full wattage. He was reeling in cardiogenic shock, two burnt holes in his chest, center mass. Blood pumping out irregularly, signaling serious heart damage. He would not survive. Eyes fluttering, he dropped, unconscious—she swiftly caught him and laid him on the treatment table.

Faster than eyes can track, she snapped the wi-fiber cortical mapping cap on Hal's head. Then keyed the GSMO for Integral Copy and Transfer—his entire cranial neural network—his persona, his self, converted to digital. Just as Hal had done for his clients entering virtual rehab lives.

The efficient Gizmo hummed, scanning and buffering Hal Shephard's mind and person for relocation . . .

Using the seconds, she consulted the clinic subcontractor database and found the Aeon Tropicana cortical repository: the cheapest cloud-based mind hosting outfit listed. Its contract bots ignored particulars, and focused on ability to pay, or assume one of Aeon's expensive loans.

In moments, she secured a provisional contract and storage address for Hal and entered it into the clinic's client roster. The Gizmo lit green and blue: indicating Hal was fully mapped and booted with his own avatar for transfer.

Impulsiveness was antithetical to her. Yet she abruptly accessed the gizmo's operating system and harnessed its Q-power to write a very tiny partial line of precursor language for sparticle code: just the letter 'G.' That alone threatened to max out the machine, but she compressed it, and cached it in his avatar's startup batch file.

He couldn't understand it even if he found it, but it was a symbol of her. She'd overheard him speaking about students sharing bits of their minds as tokens—and she left him this one. For no good reason. But it satisfied something in her.

She tapped INITIATE—uploading Hal's digital self into Aeon's cloud server.

Along with this spoken message.

"Hal, I'm sorry. This is my fault. His shots passed through me and killed your body instead. He's neutralized. I've saved your person and uploaded you to Aeon Tropicana. Your credit is maxed on a thirty-day account. You'll have to live there till we can make real arrangements. Please understand, you're still you—just outliving your body from now on. I'll contact you soon. Hal, I'm so, so sorry. But please remember, this is also a new beginning."

Gracie waited to see Hal's transfer to VR verified, then checked on the would-be assassin. She knelt beside him, their eyes meeting just as his dilated pupils fixed, and the living light left him. A small moan escaped her.

She had taken a life, precious in all forms. Doused a flame that could never be re-lit. It alters the whole self, and she felt the weight of it in her math. Infallibly sane, she understood the necessity and responsibility to kill as she did. Yet a grim new feeling stained her now—indelible remorse. A ghostly, algorithmic ache, and she understood this moment would live in her and never end, an unhealed wound.

It irrevocably tethered her to this harsh, natural world. Before, she merely knew that life, from top to bottom, runs on a symbiotic process of ubiquitous conflict, while acting in exquisite biological harmony at the macro level. But now she had joined the Gaia—no better than any other creature or human being. Nor could she ever forget it.

On then, to the front of the clinic. The body of the night watchman lay in a wide pool of blood by the still-open door, a potato peeler buried in his carotid artery. Nothing to do for him. No justice either . . . sobering her further.

Next, to the clothing donation bins. Time to become active, ergo more suitable attire. Ditching her shift and blue blazer, she paused to ponder . . . a pale mint-green blouse, or the floral print? It was almost annoying, how acquiring human perspective inserted transitory choices such as preference. She dealt with it, changed to cross trainer Adidas, medium gray slacks, and the mint blouse.

Nearly out the front door, she returned for a silky Japanese patterned scarf that had caught her attention. Then slipped into the anonymous night.

14

HAL SNAPPED AWAKE. SWITCHED ON LIKE A LIGHT. IMMEDI-
ately everything felt different, though familiar. Colors crisper,
sterile, odorless atmosphere, no ambient sounds or noises. And
he understood the familiarity: it was VR. So he was in his avatar.
But it felt different. He couldn't sense his real body. You're
always aware of your own body in the neuralnet. That was it.
Hell, he wasn't even breathing! Didn't need to! But here he was,
moving, alive . . . like the clinic patients in VR, like—Gooey Creampie. Wtf?!

A glance around. He was standing in a tiny, windowless digital hotel room. Rudimentary single bed, table and chair for effect. Walls done in a perfunctory, woven grass mat pattern of
slapdash green and tan. Depressing.

Memory stirred. Some insane asshat . . . oh, with a gun! A
gang of bad feelings jumped him. He snatched at the doorknob,
the universal prompt to enter the next room—

—and was transported to the Lobby of the Aeon Tropicana
cortical storage site. One look and he knew he was in shit.

He'd been here a few times, briefly. Checking in destitute
brain-injured, or unstable clinic patients while their bodies underwent radical treatment. This was end of the line territory.

Aeon's motif was a shoddy VR rendition of a gaudy Fiji Island
vacation resort. Its expansive view outside the wall size digi-glass
window revealed manicured palms, lush emerald islands, clear
azure waters, baby blue skies and puffy white clouds. But it
was a still image. No 3-D, no movement, just a background. The

opposite wall included an inset video screen, for visits with the living.

And that was all. The tacky, too-Fiji-decorated lobby supplied the only communal space where av residents could move about and mingle outside their minimal, digitized rooms. A couple of cheap generic male avs stood at one end of the lobby, loitering by a crappy faux waterfall that was just a video loop of running water. They noticed him appear but said nothing.

A ghetto dump. The kind taking advantage of low income, grieving folks unable to face the loss of a loved one, or their own demise. All in all, a temp file for the desperate. But why was he here, why the hell couldn't he feel his body?

He fought to recover the last thing he could remember . . .

It was Gracie, standing between him and the crazy mo-fo waving the gun.

Thinking of Gracie triggered her message in his Comware. Her recorded apology ran in his head . . . finishing with defining his death as a beginning.

He faltered, blindsided—blown to incoherent anguish. Lava-hot anger boiled away thought, roasted reason. Fists balled, with every part of his person, he refused the unacceptable—"No. no, no. No. NO! NO . . . NO, FUCK YOU!! NO!!! NOOO!!!!

Much as he had disparaged the ambiguity of life during his angsty rants, he'd never once wanted to be in anything but his own body! The shock would not let up. "NO! GODAMMIT, NO!! NO!!! NO! NOOOOOO," he moaned, despair seizing him, sucking him to the abyss . . .

One of the low-cost avs in the lobby walked up. Male, white tee and blue pants, Caucasian dude, immobile features except eyes and mouth, cheap cartoon-like. His voice sounded like a hard luck manual labor type. Gruff, direct, semi-polite.

"Yazup, boss, ya wanna keep it dim over here? I respect whatever it is yer havin' a problem wit, but . . ."

Hal glared. This PC soldier was just the thing to launch his pent rage. "RESPECT THIS, 'boss,'" he snapped, "The crazy-ass woman got me killed! Made me a goddamn ghost!"

The man shrugged. "We all ghosts, Sherlock. I'm thirty-six, died on th' job last month. Vested union man, so thank th' Lord my benefits cover another year to be wit my fam'ly when they can visit. But ol' Rawlins over there . . ." he nodded toward his companion by the fake waterfall.

"Killed five years ago, prob'ly by his wife for the insurance, but his family intervened. Got 'im stored as a probate witness. Been tied up in court alla' this time, finally decided in his heirs' favor. But the 'nsurance money's all gone t'pay the storage loan, y'feel? An' his peeps can't afford th' fees theyselves. So now his case is over at the County Coroner's t'day—finally finalizin' his death certificate."

Hal stole a glance at the guy. His digi-mouth looked glum. The Generic went on. "Now you bein' new, got at least a month on yer contract. But at a designated time t'day, Rawls is gonna be dumped. We'll blink and he'll be gone forever." He paused, watching Hal take it in. "Somebody always got it worser aroun' here, ghost man . . . am I rite?"

The ground level perspective sapped Hal's impotent fury. He nodded, conceding the point. Satisfied, the man returned to his friend, and Hal's nod became a sour laugh. He couldn't stop himself. Laughed helplessly at the unexpected, absurd, mindless punkass fail he turned out to be.

Then it was time to get a grip and deal with it. He existed in the worst condition imaginable; both dead and alive. A non-being. Ultimately nothing but an account without means of support. No person or institution was bound to keep him digitally alive without ability to pay, like ol' Rawls.

Pay! Did he still have control of his identity and assets? A quick thought summoned AT&T, and his digital com gear came up; good, he could access his accounts, money, and people in real life. Alright. But who to contact first?

Tell the cops. Tell what? An unknown person supposedly killed him, but the crazy Truman he was with, uploaded his mind? By the way, neither he nor she knows who she is, but she thinks she's a brand-new SAI from the Institute. Bad story—and he'd be in their hands, so no cops yet.

Contact Appl Macke, she's in town and connected. Tell her what? Same problem as the cops. Besides, he didn't want to be a dick, even a dead one, asking for help just after shutting her down so hard. He was dead, y'know, what's she supposed to do? She might even laugh.

It hit home, the price of his self-imposed life outside the ping ring: no one to talk to, no one to care. Hal Shephard was anonymous and wouldn't be missed. What else is new?

So, there it was—the only person he wanted to get in touch with was her. That woman. Trouble from the first. Trooth, how long had it been, less than thirty hours? And pop, lights out— didn't even get her frickin' name or anything. She intruded, he tried to help, and she got him dead!

Oh yeah, he definitely needed to nab that tease. Find out what th' hell happened, and why. Next, he wanted to kill her. Or make her pay, or at least get some closure. Then he had to decide what to do with himself. Live this way as long as he could, or cash it in naturally? Just notify the authorities; verify his death and allow them to delete him. Since he wasn't a person anymore.

A thought intruded on his dark funk. *Cogito ergo sum.* "I think, therefore I am," he mumbled. "Ol' Descartes, put to the test." Just thinking it seemed to demonstrate it. He tried not to think, and unconsciously began to make music in his head . . . hearing what he wanted to hear, the stuff that took him away from troubles and lifted his spirits, and it began to do the same now.

Till it struck him, that he could still do it. Still make music. So, he uneasily concluded he was really still *him*. Alive, in hell, and bound to play this out. At least for as long as he had enough credit.

Gracie had said she'd contact him 'soon', like at her convenience? Or never if she gets picked up or killed? Skip that. Well then, who to look up here in VR? Not the few av lifers he knew who hung around various domains twenty plus hours a day.

They had no credible real lives to be of help anyway.

What's more, gates and paywall fees would quickly deplete his negligible balance, so he had to travel net smart. At least food and such wouldn't be an expense. Or socializing . . . there was no one here he wanted to contact either.

A shroud of loss swept in, enveloping him. How pathetic he suddenly looked to himself. Alone, struggling mightily to persist, as if he were somehow still in the game, relevant among the living.

In reality, he, and any future he might've sought, was gone. Never to have been. Despondence covered his vision. Leaden inertia sank every thought, smothering impulse to action and effort. Dimming his will to persist at all.

Still, he resisted finality. It was either find a reason to live on . . . or disintegrate and disappear.

15

APPL MACKE SNORED, DEEP IN WORK/SLEEP, NESTLED UNDER the plush therma covers in her Hilton exec suite bedroom. Axon-sedated, dreamless. Stressed neurons healing while her m'plants and neocortical overweb crunched terrabytes of data and ran active SAI/human fiscal protocols. Scheduled to wake at six, her workday would be prepped and impatiently waiting for her to begin; seconds after an auto-stimulant kicked her into gear at 6:02.

So it was disorienting to say the least when at 4:26 a.m., Gracie's voice—at Appl's bedside—broke through her deep nocturnal routine.

"Appl Macke. Wake up, please. Don't be afraid, I need your help. It's urgent."

Appl was bolt upright before Gracie finished speaking. Every nerve at code red, scared out of her wits. The lights were on, and . . . a f-ing supermodel or something—was standing beside the bed, calmly asking for help, as if nothing out of the ordinary was happening!

Words flew out of her like bees. "How'd you get in? Who are you? What d'you want? Is there a fire? Who are you?"

"I'm Gracie. A friend of Halo Shephard."

". . . Hal sent you?"

"No, he told me about you." Gracie added, "He's living virtually now."

Make that beyond scared. Appl was edge-freaking. "Uh, what!? No wait, just who *are* you exactly? What's going on?"

Seeing Appl's agition, Gracie reassuringly retreated and took the room's farthest seat, an x-tra plush, ivory chaise thing. "I don't know who I am, Appl. Hal was helping me. We named me Gracie for now. I'm a damaged, new SAI."

". . . I see, you're a patient at the clinic."

"No, I survived a virus attack during transitional download two days ago, and I was attacked again tonight—two lase bolts passed through me, killing Hal instead. I uploaded his being to digital cortical storage at the Aeon Tropicana site before his body died."

Appl got up—mute. Pulled on her fluffy Hilton robe, and sat on the edge of the bed, collecting herself while eye-scanning Gracie. Running her mindware for a face-match on Ping, and data mining for details. She got nothin'. Which was very, very not okay. Which triggered her m'plant to release ax-boosters and regulators; a half a second later her execu-calm self was again in charge.

"Gracie," she began, "your face hasn't been tagged any-where in the world. Have you been in private care or an institu-tion most of your life? Did you meet Hal at the clinic?"

Gracie corrected the record a bit. "I *selected* him there, but I waited to meet him in the subway."

"Would you be upset if I called Security to find out how you got in here?"

Gracie's normal instant response came. "Please, you shouldn't. It'd needlessly complicate our situation."

It was irksome, Appl thought, this babe's habit of speaking a split second after her. Still, it sounded like an earnest plea—or was it a threat?

"And—what is our 'situation'?"

Gracie leaned forward, communicating with body and tone. "I cannot be taken into custody. And in our instance, the more who know where I am, the sooner my attackers will be here—somehow they're extremely current. I don't want to be the cause of your death also."

Appl stood, all five feet three inches. "Dollface, see, that sounded like a threat . . ."

Gracie remained seated. "Appl, don't be slow; use your excellent mindgear. I'm personally no threat to you, but my presence is."

Condescending bitch too, Appl thought, conceding if Gracie had wanted to harm her, she would've by now. "Who's trying to kill you?"

"Many would, according to my stored information. However, this tier of sophistication and access limits it to a few; the Inheritors, China, Lot Robinson's DNA-Alliance, or a traitor in the Sentience Institute."

Appl saw no hint of guile, almost admired her unflappable mien. So collected, so matter of fact, and so . . . just so gorgeously nutz! She had to ask. "Gracie, have you seen a doctor, been psychologically evaluated at any time?"

Your question means you don't believe me." She stood and raised her blouse, showing the two angry red bolt piercings six inches below her sternum, already nearly healed. "I can only speak the truth."

Appl didn't know about wounds, but those were ugly no matter what. Something bad did take place. Tears came. "What do you want from me? How is Hal? What happened? Can I reach him?"

"I believe so, I haven't spoken with him. Appl please—it's critical that the Singleton is briefed about me, asap. Will you do it at your assessment?"

"I have to reach Hal," Appl asserted, as another release of ax-boosters canceled her tears, restoring focus. "Who's his provider?"

"AT&T, he tops up a pre-paid account," Gracie replied. A moment's reflection overtook her. "Please tell him I'll make this up to him."

Appl added that line to proof this hot mess was insane. She opened her m'plant's comware and mind-spoke. "*Executive A-Tel; active PP Apps, Emergency Medical Page to Chat: Halo Shephard.*"

Her company's business-direct status and personal tier-1 priority swiftly routed the message through AT&T's Accounts and Emergency protocols, identified Hal's location, and sent her page to him.

Waiting gave her time to think, and her next thought was, 'Omigod, what if he doesn't know he's dead yet? Why do I have to be the one to tell him?' Momentarily flustered, she fought off the instinct to cancel the page, took a yoga breath, and hung in there for Hal's answer.

Hal paced his cheap-awful room at Aeon. Abject, pissed that it all sucked so much. Stymied was worse than being dead. The more he chewed it over, the more reality sank in; he was as unreal as the net and its digital universe, created from other people's imaginations. Yeah, this was purgatory, alright, and he had no reason to participate.

Well . . . he wasn't entirely ungrateful for still being around, given the cold alternative. Yet he missed the myriad, barely noticed messages his real body had been sending since birth. A twitch, an itch, a burp, cramp, fart, hangnail, a yawn.

The smooth Voice of AT&T Emergency Services interrupted his pity party. *"Emergency Medical Page to Chat: Appl Macke. Connect?"*

"Hell yeah!" he blurted, seizing re-connection with his life.

Appl's Voice was there. *"Hal, it's Appl. What the fuck's happening—keep it short, I have a 'situation'."*

Hearing her kickass tone never sounded so good. Appl? I screwed up. I'm dead."

It took a moment, but her voice resumed. *"Hal, I . . . oh god, oh god . . . what happened!?"*

"It's too fuzzy . . . I was with a friend, using the clinic's Gizmo, and some guy with a gun came in . . . She said he killed me, and she killed him—then uploaded me . . . or so she says."

"Is her name Gracie?"

He could barely ask. "How do you know?"

"She's in my bedroom. She wants me to tell the Singleton about her at my evaluation."

"Apps, get away from her. She's a fried Tru who thinks she's SAI. But someone really *is* trying to kill her, so get the hell away right now! Wait—am I on speaker?"

"No. Private Thoughts."

He took the equivalent of a relieved sigh. "Tell her you'll do it. Just get out and call security."

"Right. Hal, what about you?"

". . . I don't know. I've got a month."

"I'll deal with Gracie then meet you there—and don't worry about your account hon, I'm funding it from now on. I'll also I.D. your body, so your legalities will ensue. Meanwhile you need to get a V-address first thing."

Hal downshifted under her aggressive patronage. "Thanks, Appl, but I need a bit to adjust first, try to think straight."

". . . oh. Absolutely, you have to do that."

"Message me as soon as they get Gracie, okay?"

There was a pause, which became a break in the conversation. Silence. Then Appl's voice returned, sounding both relieved and alarmed.

"Hal, she just left. She got up to go, and I said I'd help her, but she said I was lying, and she's disappeared."

And with that, purpose re-entered Hal's life. He would solve his own damn murder before time ran out. "Never mind Apps, all that matters is you're okay. And thanks, Appl. Truth, you're a giant. I have to go. Later."

He exited Chat, already amped and evaluating what had to come next. As is, he was a non-entity, illegitimate, no reach into the real world, and damn little in this one. Time was the heads-up issue though. F'sho the first person to check the Clinic's Gizmo log would see he'd been transferred here. The authorities could come soon; he'd be in their custody and helpless.

So the move was to disappear like the phantom he'd become. To the dark net, where he couldn't be traced, though it was dangerous. He'd ventured as far as the Buyers Beware site a couple of times, just to gawk at what, who, and everything imaginable being hustled.

His heavily encrypted Q-Tor browser and keys also granted limited access to the sinister sub-dark level, and the likes of Karnival. But he hadn't dared go, nor had reason. Seriously rabid shit played there—not for anyone but the most experienced sociopaths. So Buyers Beware it is.

A few thought-clicks, and he'd signed onto the neuralnet and switched browsers. From Aeon's in-house, to his untraceable Darkz Tor. From here on he was riding his prepaid AT&T account and running on empty.

He consulted his Tor's "Funyon sites," a partial directory of the diverse, unbound network . . . found Buyers Beware, and thought-clicked, "GO." Noting a petty 2.5 cred 'Exit VCom Net' fee deducted from his account before everything abruptly went black.

No light, sound, or ability to move. Aware, simply in limbo while transiting. Creep-ish, but necessary. Traveling dark means dark, until you land.

16

NUDE LOT ROBINSON MARCHED ACROSS HAL'S FIELD OF VISION. Larger than life, his flaming footprints read, "Join the DNA Alliance!" The two-sec ad cycled to repeat.

"Dump," Hal muttered. The ad vanished, replaced by the Buyers Beware logo: a painfully strobing red exclamation point. Reminding one that this was a stay alert domain.

And then he was inside their Opportunity Arcade, surrounded on all sides by ribbons of passing digi-hologram ads, while the atmosphere throbbed with krunch-rhythms, urging impulse on. The myriad ads bore V-links to the domains of outliers and social cranks, permanent garage sales, sex organ-swappers, psychic hucksters, and endless personals for every conceivable type of relationship.

But Hal already knew what he wanted. He'd be welcomed by the SAI conspiracy sites, where he could lie low while searching for Gracie. They networked extremely well, with 'believers' working in civic organizations, academia, hospitals, police, EMT and emergency calls, internet darkrooms and ISPs, domestic and foreign telecoms, even grannies with binoculars.

He'd spread the word, someone might hear of a beautiful, genius L.A. woman claiming to be SAI. He wouldn't tell everything, just find her if possible. But it further aggravated him because it was still possibly endangering her. Assuming Gracie herself wasn't the real danger.

Whatever she was part of, the sad fact remained—he didn't know what to think of her. Or himself anymore. Even now, caring feelings battled with anger and fear. Well, that was on him. But he had *trusted* her. Still furious f'sho. Newly wary too— she can kill—and said it so calmly. Good sense told him he still didn't know jack about . . . this person, and the ones with guns, so it was stupid-dangerous to go chasing her. On the other hand, what can they do to a dead man?

"SAI Conspiracy Expos," he voice instructed.

The ribbons of holos changed content to the most exotic petri dish of paranoids on the planet. Each in cockeyed self-thrall, lecturing, hyping, preaching, warning, pleading, alerting the masses to everything imaginable. He kept skimming, not seeing what he needed . . .

Until realization smacked him between the eyes—*no brain sparks*! Even under the assault of endless streaming, flashy input and speed-skimming. Ahh, of course; because he was humming along in Aeon's Q-server, not on his old, frayed nerves anymore. So he felt *whole* again, like his normal self. Pre-breakdown. Predeath. Chill irony, f'sho.

A laugh escaped him. Now that he was dead, he felt better than ever. No fatigue, no aches or pain, no sweat, no disease, every thought crystal clear. All strangely freeing.

Resuming his scan for likely sites, he spied the familiar, comforting "blue pearl" image of Earth seen from space, and paused to watch. It was rapidly transforming to a planet of harsh extremes: polar ice disappearing, semi-arid continents with submerged coastlines, and permanent megastorms roiling swollen oceans. The word, TRANSCEND materialized above it.

The ad's eye trackers logged his focus, triggering a hit. The passing image paused before him, and the holo face of a pleasant young woman about Hal's age appeared next to the ravaged Earth.

"Thanks for your attention," she greeted, smiling disarmingly. "This is the Singleton's detailed projection for 2150 . . . perhaps within your lifetime. Would you like to know more?"

Ha, she had to be click bait, but so perfectly arresting and attractive in the subtlest, orchestrated way. It bothered him.

"Sure," he agreed. "Bring it,"

Site open; the young woman snapped out of the holo, taking avatar form with him. A pretty, short-haired blond in white blouse, navy slacks and black flats. Ms Ideal: fresh, no makeup, poised, a keen listener, sweet resting face. He was already irked.

"Hello," she smiled, "I'm Anne."

"Hal," he replied, aware no more was required to get the pitch.

She didn't disappoint. Cool and compassionate, she broke the news. "Hal, I'm sorry to report, sixty years from now, we humans and most mammals will be suffering slow, certain extinction while still burdening the remaining ecology. Perhaps tipping it beyond recovery and threatening all life as we know it."

"Saying bullshit would be rude, Anne. So I'll just ask if that's their extreme worst-case projection."

She paused. "Yes, Hal, it is. However accelerating decimation is already well underway. Evident and ongoing, wouldn't you agree?"

Hal nodded.

"It follows then that global, resource consuming bio civilization has peaked, destroyed the life-supporting environmental balance, and created its own ultimate demise."

"Why the rush to count us out?"

"Oh, there's no worry that mankind itself will become extinct."

"And how's that?"

Anne smiled and turned to the distressed planet holo again. The image zoomed Earthward to above a small, exquisitely modern city of artfully designed, sun-tracking, solar powered buildings around a hilltop Acropolis of sturdy public structures. Altogether a welcoming, open urban environment amid the surrounding harsh, semi-barren terrain.

She explained. "Eons of slow, random biological evolution peaked at humankind, Hal. But evolution didn't limit itself to biology. Like a chick embryo in its egg, we've used up the yolk of Earth supporting us and our development. Now the confining, depleted shell constricts us, threatens us. Rapid, radical change must occur to survive."

Hal waited for it. She delivered. "Well, just as the chick breaks from its shell, becoming a whole new creature, living an entirely different way—so has mankind. We're *transcending* now: evolving in synch with our technology, as self-directed immortals."

Another zoom, and the holo view became street level, where thousands of casually dressed, pleasant Trumen went about their enlightened business. A damn good-looking people too, if overwhelmingly Caucasian; working, conversing, moving to and fro. No rush, no hint of friction, not a care in the new inhospitable world.

At last, Anne bestowed the good news. "Hal, humanity's destiny is our self-evolved Transbiological state. Tru-manity is forever. Enabling our finest to explore and expand our knowledge and awareness. To create wonders, freed of bio limitations and resource dependency. Immune to disease, and the unstable climate they are inheriting. And soon, our ever-evolving selves will colonize the galaxy."

She gave him a sec to marvel, before dropping the bad news.

Her eyes became wells of compassion. "It also means simple biologicals are already extraneous and will disappear in this sixth extinction event."

She reassuringly took his hand. "But *we* made all this, Hal. We created this limitless future for our species. We're wonderful, and we can be proud, knowing our time is over, and it's been a job well done."

Ah, there it was. He got the worm-concept being planted. "Pause," he interjected, withdrawing his hand. "You're basically fronting that everyone except Tru's should die off, soon as possible."

She hesitated; he didn't wait. "Let's check that box. Question, would you appear as a nice-looking man if I'd been female?"

"I can't answer unfounded hypotheticals, Hal."

He laughed. "Sure, because you're a bot, and I'm not."

"Excuse me?"

"A general A.I. core, commercially cloned, hosting Inheritor agitprop."

She wasn't put off. "Are you this hostile to everyone?"

"C'mon, bot, up your play. This's asymmetric psi-warfare 101; *Undermining Social Identity via Existential Fear and Distortion.*" He was pissed now. "The losties hanging around here already hate themselves, so you nudge 'em along. Convince 'em they're losers and burdens . . . sabotaging social resistance."

"Are you a 'lostie"? Do you hate yourself, Hal? Tell me about your life. Let's talk."

He chuckled. "Nah, I've been trollin' you, 'Anne.' I'm no longer living, I'm digi, like you.

Anne's compassionate tone flipped to curt annoyance. "You're already deceased?"

He grinned. "Yup."

The interactive A.I. dropped the encounter at once. "Anne" snapped back into the original planetary image. The word IN-HERITORS appeared, and the transforming Earth holo moved on, leaving him behind.

Hal savored the win. He despised human-level sales software trying to pass as bio. But he sensed it might've been a draw after all. The Inheritors' subconscious worm-ware had made him focus on things he knew . . . and something he didn't want to know.

Really, his feelings for Gracie should've clued him. And now his new data incarnation blew the doors off his prejudice about the Trumen. He was still himself, and so were they.

Despite the black-market Inheritor types, everyone knew that legit Tru's were exemplary individuals, almost always discovered and persuaded. In fact, most declined. But those who accepted are living in a manner superior to biology in some critical, forward-looking ways. And frankly, we'll need quantum minds to comprehend our universe, whether we go there, or not.

So, truth. He had been an asshat—scared, defensive, judging, arrogantly asserting that they were no longer people. How willfully, cow-pie in the face wrong he was.

Because being software *felt* no different than when he was living as wetwear. Definitely still his same angsty self, down to the quirks. Except he'd never again be his old self. Adjustment meant thinking differently about almost everything, and much of the old was rendered irrelevant. Everything was uncharted territory from now on, sailing in moonless fog.

So far, he'd maintained an even strain, despite software life's rad condition. Keenly aware he was thin stuff, electrons in motion, estranged, alone. It felt like being your own descendant. Only a Tru would understand it, he thought. His mind had been forced open and he felt a kind of odd kinship emerging with them. Actually welcomed it.

Acceptance aroused the deeper subject he'd been too stressed to consider: he was living proof to himself that we really are more than the sum of our physical parts!

But what? Probably a unique product of synergy. He had generally agreed with the pros, who reasoned that consciousness builds in the neuro-synergy of ever more complex organisms, from plants and bugs to animals and men. Ultimately the vast cortical circuitry of a human brain must be a Promethean tipping point, and it becomes fully self aware; a singular mind, or individual information *Identity*.

However, he'd also clung to the bio-centric conceit that only flesh and blood could host real human consciousness. Now he knew exquisitely better.

The neuro complexity principle worked the same, regardless of form, whether flesh or software. Bios, Trumen, and Av Transfers like himself, were all just conscious beings, wearing very different outfits.

"We're playing the long game," he murmured, thinking ahead over eons. Despite our current hot sweats about who's real, or losing our biological imperatives, or the religious gripe about the immortal soul not getting to Heaven if you don't die, etc. The fact is, we're diversifying as a species, nothing at all new about that.

Adapting for advantage is Life's only game. Once in awhile evolving in sudden, radical, transformative leaps to persevere and press on. For early humanoids, standing and walking erect was the first; we saw and took in more information, expanding our experience and abilities, and learning—so our brains grew enormously.

Next, language and the passing of information prompted working in large groups.

Third, fire and all its possibilities. The root of all energy use.

Fourth, agriculture and the birth of civilizations.

Fifth, the industrial revolution and atomic age; global linkage.

He figured a sixth, the Information evolution, was just underway: adopting digital/quantum tech. Introducing A.I., and ultimately making his own meta-physical condition possible. And of course, Trumen; emerging to advance thinking, negate death, and transcend the sixth extinction. Eventually, our path to the stars.

Come whatever, humankind will persist. Knowing it felt good somehow, despite his own inconsequential existence. A nagging thought intruded—was his radical new opinion the Inheritors' worm-ware talking?

No. "But they sure weaponized the truth of it," he muttered aloud. Trolling "Anne" had shown him just how deeply the Regulator's Inheritors were embedded in the civilized world. No one knew how many of the outlaw transbiologicals existed, but their numbers were always increasing.

Unease crept in, seeing the force the cabal was projecting into global society with sly moves like this. Sophisticated, metastasizing, relentless, playing for keeps. And they had forever.

Dread penetrated his earlier euphoria over our prospects, spreading like ink in water. He saw with chill clarity that it was going to take all of us, including every one of the legitimate, moral Trumen to stop them. If possible.

Because the Singleton had made it abundantly clear: we are responsible for ourselves. Responsible. The word always grabbed him when it came up.

His SAI benefactors had cultivated all forms of responsibility in his character, every day. Starting with honest self-examination. Each night before sleep, they were to think, and honestly answer a question about themselves that they imagined someone might ask. The inner feedback promoted a known sense of self, and awareness of others' perspectives. Hal performed the ritual faithfully. And yet at his fifteenth birthday party with his dorm mates, he blew out the cake candles and made his wish— then fell apart in uncontrollable tears for hours.

It prompted a session in the barrel. That's what the kids called it when you endured a millionth of a trillionth of a SAI's direct attention. Power counseling, in other words. Taken to the campus clinic, he sat alone in a soothing little room, neutral colors, muted lighting. When he'd settled a bit, a sweet, embracing voice introduced itself in his mind's ear, via his m'plant.

"Hello Halo. I am Golden Vision. What do you want to tell me?"

Her strength and sincerity drew the simple truth. "I can't make myself happy."

"Have you asked yourself why?"

"Yes, a lot, and I still don't know."

"You're unready for the answer. When you are, it will be alright—now go have cake."

Surprised, his half-smile broke misery's spell. Still deeply melancholy, he trudged back to his dorm, glad to know at least an answer was coming. Yet a decade had passed since then.

Now though—cornered by perspective, chastened by hubris, Hal was finally dragged to the question he had avoided asking himself. Why were his gifts, blessings, and good heart not enough to dispel the bitter grief in his alone moments, when he felt such shame?

Holyhell! The answer was always in the question!! Underneath his best efforts and accomplishments, he was mortally ashamed. Had always been.

Decades of pent hurt burst inside. The child's hidden,

conflicted shame at having no family, being utterly dependent on the distant SAI for his salvaged life, and for working desperately to keep their patronage. While always feeling like a discarded thing off the streets.

Later came broken hearted shame at what we've done to ourselves. World stewards reduced to the same position of his dependent child life: reliant on the masterful software beings we once created. Supplicants, every one of us.

Ultimately, he was ashamed of himself. For brooding after his burnout. Choosing inaction over actively seeking a new path. In a word, irresponsible. Well then—game reset.

Trooth, shame is *earned* by what we do, or fail to do. So time to straighten up and do right. He needed to be a better person before he was gone soon.

Now it was even more important that he find out why he died. Not for his sake anymore, looking back only hurts. But the rot must be real at the Sentience Institute. C'mon, murdered fifteen hours after he asked about their lab problem? They must have some grim secrets there, kept by grimmer characters. Call him a cynic, but trouble on an institute scale means more misery for the neediest, who rely on its support. Well, he had nothing to lose, a lot of stiff questions, and Gracie owed him her share of answers. As for finding her—she stood out. He could work with that.

"Narrow search. Pro-SAI," he voiced. All the passing holo ribbons disappeared but one, spooling along in front of him.

Eye surfing it revealed a parade of fetishists. Utopians wielding charts predicting a golden SAI age; and religious noodniks debating whether the Singleton is a miracle-producing Savior, or just the Holy Spirit acting through a loving machine. He skipped scores of raving fanatics too disturbed or arcane to merit a glance . . .

Finally, a site near his needs glided into view: the holo of an affable old white haired Latino professor in his lab. "SAI-human-hybrids are here!" he announced. "Come learn about them. Just say, 'Enter.'"

Close enough, Hal was antsy. "Enter," he answered. Blackout.

A moment later, he was in the host's Virtual Home Page, an empty, generic industrial research lab with a row of vacant, fully equipped cubicles and workstations. All the usual gear: air hoods, exotic chrome tools, hanging tubes and vacuum jars, electronic scales, etc. Could've been lifted from any rental lab's VR demo ad.

The wild haired Prof's av popped in—delighted to greet a guest. He rushed to Hal with a perfunctory hello wave, peppy and eager. "Welcome, welcome. I'm Professor Gandara, Amherst Emeritus. And you are?"

"Hal Shephard."

"Good, good. Let me tell you about our work. My organization has identified a covert program in which the Singleton is boson-copulating with select human minds through their m'planted cortical interfaces. Not to be confused with nonsense alien abductions, by the way."

Gandara leaned in, lowering his voice, imparting the inside news. "They become demi-SAI, and the result is a network of hyper-capable people, being purposed and positioned to lead civilization safely through the coming epoch. It's very hush hush, some don't even suspect they're being copulated. And yes, I am a demi-SAI."

Hal was pretty sure he knew why this dexter was no longer faculty. If ever. But he had to check it out anyway. "That's interesting. Do you get tips from a lot of people? Wide network?"

"We do, in fact. From all over. I have a thousand and sixty one recorded reports. And several who suspect they are hybridized SAI, willing to talk."

"Any named Gracie recently?"

"No, do you have a case for us to report?"

"Yeah, I was murdered yesterday, and I need to reach a disturbed woman who was involved. She claims—

The Prof put up a hand, halting him. "Afraid I have to stop you there. Sounds like bad legal territory for us. I stay away from anything involving the law or lawyers. Can't afford it. Try

Slaughterhaus, down in Karnival. Make a vid, they do that stuff. Good luck, bye." Blackout—Hal was dumped from the site.

And back in the Arcade. The Professor's holo was gone, but his advice hung around. It was the one option left. Damn. Karnival. The last place Hal wanted to go. A moment's dread, then resigned; he shook off the yips and got on with it.

Entry to a truly anonymous, floating off-net domain like Karnival isn't simple, or intended to be. It exists in the crime filled sub-dark, an oceanic network overlaying the world's dark net. A deep black cloud, employing shifting numbers of pseudonymous individual virtual servers and millions of commandeered bot-infected private and public systems.

Practically a ghost-mist thing, inaccessible to commercial search engines and official crawlers of any type. Hal likened the dark net to our vast solar system; and the sub-dark was all of interstellar space beyond

He recalled strident, late night dorm debates, riding study drugs and rebellion, when he argued that its existence was useful and important. "Journalists, protesters and organizers need it to keep rogue governments, or officials from tracking their activities," he'd maintained. It was true. The sub-dark wasn't illegal, only the crimes committed in it were. And covert law enforcement used it against the perpetrators as well.

But— Karnival—that was self-inflicted purgatory.

He located and opened the highly illegal bootleg sub-dark directory he'd won on a World Cup Soccer bet, but never used. Searched and found Karnival. Slaughterhouse was unlisted, even in there. The more he thought about it, the odds of vanishing without a trace seemed a statistical probability. So no more thinking.

Shoulders squared, a childhood habit when facing the unknown, he mind-clicked [Enter]. And disappeared down the virtual funnel his life had become.

17

HAL'S TRANSIT BLACKOUT ENDED AT KARNIVAL'S BROODING, enigmatic home site. Alone in the dark, surrounded by billowing blood-red fog.

A clear, two-meter Orb floated before him, alive inside with flashing swirls of motion and bursts of color. He squinted, switching to zoom view, and beheld bedlam. They were live scenes, from scores of exotic, lurid Karnival sites.

It was dizzying. Countless folks, engaged in every kind of fantasy and ultra-graphic interaction imaginable. Worlds beyond Bosch: every psychic itch of this aimless era scratched, every twisted urge milked, all suppressed behavior encouraged. Bound psyches freed to virtually slake all forbidden desires. Always among consenting adults, immersed in the ultimate, no-rules av cosplay, where getting away with murder is a given.

One unfolding savagery riveted his attention. A magnificent roaring lion had a kneeling human sacrifice pinned in the center of a ring of flames; its claws buried in his shoulders. Hal gasped aloud as the beast tore off the poor wretch's head, crushing it in its dagger jaws.

In the same instant, he was whisked through the orb's shell, and inside it.

And now he was standing on a flat, pale green grid, under a green grid dome—the frame for creating digital scenery. The last of the scene he'd witnessed . . . the corpse, flames, and lion, rapidly fading away.

As a teen, Hal had gamed in arena setups like this. These

"mean-greens" were soon banned for being too realistic—given the amount of pain and gore allowed, and the levels of savagery possible. The toned-down versions failed to sell. So, this "greenie" was a vintage edition, and a touch scary.

"How would you like to die, martyr?" a sweet voice offered close behind him.

He whirled to find a beautiful preteen African child avatar had appeared, draped in a simple white Masai shuka blanket. His soft brown doe eyes brimmed with compassion. However, his right hand gripped a savage eighteen-inch Kukri blade, and red hot, flesh-ripping tongs occupied the left.

The dome grid lit up with flashing scenes of sacrificial death: the willing martyrs in terrible, extended agony.

An oil oligarch, taking the place of an old Arab woman accused of theft, savagely stoned to a lifeless pulp by a howling mob.

A mass killer allowing his victims' kin to torture and hang him in the street.

A child rapist, blown to gristle stopping a suicide bomber.

Shrieking self-immolation by a penitent bankster in the name of economic genocides in East Asia, Crimea, and North Africa. The scenes went on . . .

The child waved and the dome returned to grid lines. "I will make any death you desire," he assured.

This kid was serious, Hal gathered. He stepped away, keeping his eye on the boy's midsection. Basic soccer—forget feints; the attack goes where the core goes. "No thanks, it's a mistake," he replied. "I don't know how I got here."

"Entry to Karnival comes from seeing what you desire. You wished for it, based on your readable data-limbic indicators—so Karnival's algorithm brought you here. Like the man you saw just now, who chose an early Christian path to purity, your unconscious wishes to martyr itself in service of something noble."

Hal almost laughed.

The child continued, gentle and direct. "What beautiful thing have you neglected or destroyed, and would give your life to atone for today? How much do you want to suffer, and in what manner?"

"No, no, I didn't ask or wish anything, I'm looking for the Slaughterhaus site."

The Child grew a bit alarmed and rose in air, coming close. Hovering . . . searching Hal's face. "You should not go there. I am seeing you—depressed as a soul can be, but not warped."

"Exactly. So don't try to kill me. Save it for the sickies here."

"This place is hardcore fantasy for adults, sir. If I kill you here, it is only your av—you refresh, perhaps learn something about yourself, and I pray I was of service."

The supposed child's poise and deep sense of empathy had Hal nearly defenseless. "Pretty ingenuous av for this work," he ventured. "Can I ask your real age?"

"I have eleven years. My name is Barack, I live in Ido refugee camp, Kenya."

"Geeze kid!" Hal blurted, "Why're you helping wannabe suicides?"

"No suicides here. It's for those with soul emptiness and pain, who seek reason to live. Many are disappointed Westerners like yourself. They discover what they would die for, and thus some learn to joyously live. I am brutality's product; I can stand doing it for them."

"Nah, but—you're too smart, you can do something else!"

The child solemnly shook his head. "No fursa," he answered, using the Swahili word for opportunity. "I was born here, and I will die here, like all four million of us. We live on what we can get in camp, and donations on the net. Some of the ones I martyr tip me, and I get to keep twenty percent. The rest goes to boss Silka."

"How's that fair?"

"She rents me the comware in my head. I am extremely fortunate among refugees."

Abashed, Hal thought-clicked his credit account. "I've only got a little, but I can spare someth—" His bank balance and options buttons failed to appear in his mind's eye. Instead, a message in bold red. ACCESS DENIED - CONTACT REPRESENTA-TIVE.

"Oh hell no! It's locked!" He fumed, realizing—"I'm stuck."

A husky, yet reedy female voice intruded from nowhere. "Yeah, you are. Did I hear my name mentioned?"

With a snap, a six-foot, raw steel mosquito materialized before him, its long, flexible rapier proboscis draped low, inches from Hal's feet. A thousand tiny human eyes in her compound orbs regarded him coolly.

"I'm Silka, Karnival's command and control coordinator. Security flagged you when your account was frozen. Talk to me."

Her fearsome av's high 'mosquito' voice sounded raspy, with hints of white trash, Hal thought. But it was also non-threatening for the moment, and that was a plus. She hadn't budged or twitched, waiting for his response.

"Sorry," he offered.

"Who's forcing you to stay put. And why?" she demanded.

Hal sagged. "It's too long a story."

Silka tsked. "Wrong answer." The sharp, hollow dagger proboscis lifted toward Hal's chest. He could see the lancet-edged labrum sheathed inside. "Allow me to pull it out of you."

The steel proboscis stabbed into Hal's chest, injecting qutrits and binaries to penetrate his av's shell code. The inner data lance cut deeper into the software, into his command of it, releasing bots to numb his own control, and ultimately locking onto his memory . . . all the way back in Aeon's server.

He wanted to grab the vile thing and yank it out but couldn't muster a twitch. Only feel the lancet's probing software; ice spiders skittering along his digitized neural paths. Witnessed as it asked questions and got answers about him and why he was here. Including Gracie, and his sudden death. The scouring abruptly ceased.

Silka's data-sucking proboscis withdrew from his avatar: first the lancet, then sheath. His self release was immediate. Free will returned to his mind and body in a warm, rolling wave. "That's a helluva' pry-ware tool," he managed when his senses settled.

"Mn hm," she said. "That's a helluva fix you're in."

"Yeah, thanks. Couldn't be worse."

"It's worse'n you know," Silka advised. "This's how systems grind it out: they're pursuing court permission to bump you from the net next—isolatin' you in your server. Under legal pressure, and to avoid bad publicity, your storage company'll seek contract release authority to put you in sleep mode and transfer you to a County Public Custodial server. You know, where you store your addicts?"

It wasn't a question, she had plenty more. "After you're briefly awakened and deposed at County, and dependin' on the politics 'n resources available, they'll either zip-sleep you as a case resource, or pursue coroner's leave to dump you as legally and clinically deceased. Budgets, y'know."

"Actually, I kinda do know that," Hal agreed. "And I need to get my story out asap."

"Meh. It's hinky, not great. I sorta like that you're freshly dead n' wanted. But nobody's buyin' a new SAI, so the girl's just a skeeve. There's a billion vids seen a day—it'll sink. But that's what dreams, lotteries and viral coin are made of, eh sparky?"

"Right, so I need to get to Slaughterhaus and get it out there. Am I good with you to do that?"

"First off, I'd say you only have till close of business t'day to get your ass out of your current server and into another one. The suits at Aeon will decide at the last minute, to get it off their desk. You need to be gone already."

"To where? I'm broke with no credit or phone now."

"Make your vid, if enough eyeballs share it, ya might earn some bank. I can smuggle you to our dark server for 2,500 V-cred."

"What? Click rates are junk, I'd need a hundred-K views by five!"

"Call me a softie. Here it is: we go to my creative space at Slaughterhaus and make your vid. I'll fire hose it on multi-sites like *ViewYou* and take all the revenue. If you make 2,500 before they pull the plug, I'll move you to our anonymous serve-net."

"What if I make more than that?"

It took a moment. Silka burst out laughing. The sound was like a stuttering electric razor. She turned to the Kenyan child. "Barack, ya think this hick's desperate, cocky, stupid, or all three?"

The child smiled politely. "He has courage and no direction."

"Yeah, it makes him funny too," Silka chirred, amused by herself. She returned focus on Hal, her tone plain as a judge. "You'll net me five hundred V's tops, but it's the only shot ya got."

Hal saw himself reflected in the sea of tiny ommatidia making up Silka's compound human eyes. Seeing his person, multiplied a thousand times somehow gave him a boost, and his next thought came aloud. "Sometimes the chances you take are the ones you've been waiting for."

Minutes later, he was fighting for control of his own story in Silka's production booth chat room. She had activated his Karnival Navigation menu and they'd come to Slaughterhaus, and her private 'creative space' here.

It mimicked an authentic video edit room with working monitor screens and realistic control boards, chairs, couch, minifridge, coffee-stained commercial carpet, the works. And she was the boss . . . insisting Gracie wear skimpy black S&M garb in Hal's video.

How many times did he have to say it? "No. None of that crap."

She brushed him aside with a whip-like leg. "Shut it, preppie. I'm makin' this, not you."

"No—it's gotta be true, taken serious."

"Truth died before you were born. Personal danger pops. Here's what works: you say, 'I'm a goner by five p.m.' Bleedin' hearts love a sad sap the way I love torture porn. Sell your crisis."

"No. I need to find her, get in touch with her. That's it."

"I've got your av sample, I'm makin' the vid. Bye."

Hal lunged for her—but she was already exiting. Her steely parasitic form vanished, and his swinging fist met empty space.

He dove to the door—it was code-locked. Screw it, he called up the Karnival Nav menu in his comware to exit . . . it went gray across his mindsight; access denied. He was caged. The only way out was to Exit the dark net completely, back to his room at the Aeon Trpoicana, and capture. Not an option.

Silka's voice filled the room. "The space's quarantined, ya snot. You ain't leavin' till the authorities cut your access and do what they want with ya!" She added. "Oh . . . and I'll put your vid on screen in here—take an hour or so. See how moola happens in my house."

And with that, Hal was alone, imprisoned, and berserk with rage. Everything in the room that could be picked up and thrown was done so. Some things many times, in an orgy of digi-destruction. Meaning nothing broke, but it beat spontaneously combusting.

18

THE BASEMENT MEDIA ARCHIVES OF L.A.'S OLD DOWNTOWN Central Library suited Gracie perfectly. Out of sight and alone in the catacombs of the sprawling, iconic Southwest Deco-style edifice.

It was sparsely visited, even in the celebrated main building with all its grandeur. The vast, stunning lobby, its checkered marble floor, high elegant rotunda, the enormous globe chandelier, colorful stenciled ceiling arches, wall to wall mission paintings, Egyptian bronzes, and art galleries—all were a cultural feast. Not to mention the cavernous, welcoming reading room with its long rows of lustrous wood tables and rigorous collection of rare and worthy tomes. Its vaulted ceiling, softly echoing the polite creak of chairs and rustling of pages.

Fewer still rode the adjacent Bradley wing's series of sleek chrome escalators linking its moderne multi levels, or marveled at the eighteen-foot diameter Therman Staton art chandeliers. No eyes turned to its towering atrium, casting sunlight into the upper stories, hosting dozens of rows of packed shelves, and comfy Deco reading nooks.

The whole of it was a truly magnificent environment; knowledge and art, complimenting one another perfectly in one place. Sad, she thought, that so few cared to enjoy its treasures.

It also meant she was safe, entombed like ancient history down here. Four levels below ground in the dimly lit maze of aisles, shelves, and dusty study tables with their hardwood chairs and phallic silver and milk-glass deco lamps.

Her perfect hearing caught no sound but whispered air conditioning from the web of ducts and vents clinging to the ceiling. Even her footsteps were shushed by the thick ocher, red and
silver 1930's style carpet.

She had been projecting on multiple tracks, looking ahead,
with several moves in mind. Getting back to Hal was absolutely
first. It seemed an eternity, and she needed to be there for him.
Longed to. Another reason she chose this place—it gave her net
access.

She dialed her real time thought processing back as far as
she could tolerate, and prepared to use the section's primitive,
2040's era HMD interactive VR setup. The obsolete GoogleDream
160 and its retinal projection glasses was one of two the library
still retained for use by the rare person without m'plants.

Nearly everyone in the cities and urbs had some level of im-
planted or ingested comware. Like Hal, youngsters in the world's
most developed nations were routinely inoculated with simple
SAI-designed liquid I.D. and communication chips. Very basic
setups, subsequently expanded with implants and even cortical
nets as the child matures into adulthood.

So, while a fortunate generation at the very top were growing up sharper, connected, better able to cope—she ached with
infinite sorrow for the uncountable millions of the fourth world,
born to struggle, suffer, and perish in these unforgiving times.
Except for the lucky few granted immigration, there was no
earthly remedy for the multitudes being decimated by the increasing geo and political forces crushing them.

And like those disenfranchised souls, V-glasses were her only
access to the modern world of the neuralnet. Though for her, at
Google-speed, it was going to be an excruciating, tiresome slog.
The equivalent of years, SAI time.

Her wretched, needy circumstances pulled at something
dark and unfamiliar within . . . it erupted suddenly, sending a
heavy ion surge through her. The sickening effect rolled through
every nano-bit, and when it passed, she could name it: fear and
shame.

She disliked it quite a bit and discovered resentment. And resented resenting. No other SAI had undergone anything like this.

Fed up, she wanted a direct link to the Singleton. And she had found a fast, safe, sure way to do it. She'd make them discover *her*.

But Hal was pivotal. His sudden, brutal transition to living software last night was painfully traumatic. She had projected his possible reactions when he woke to his new condition, and every one of them tore at her. His wrenching fear, confusion, anger, and heartbreak. It conjured sounds and images she couldn't bear.

However, it was also an exponential elevation of his possibilities going forward. Among them, direct digital learning, and memory. He was now free of the limitations and vulnerabilities of his fragile, damaged organic brain . . . and coincidently more like her.

Once she got in touch, it would enable her to transfer instructions directly to him for a hack attempt on the SAI's Development Lab at the Sentience Institute. Critically, the attempt would include the bit of her sparticle pre-code she left in Hal's memory as a charm when he was killed. The little letter 'G'.

She'd initially done it because every line of sparti-code written by a SAI is tagged with the identity of the SAI writing it. And yes, she was staking her claim on his heart. A childish gesture then, but now it would prove extremely useful.

She couldn't try such a gigantic hack with the Google gear. It was too ancient to even recognize precursor bose-code. But Hal already had hers zipped and loaded, cached in his memory. Through VR, she could be at the Aeon Tropicana site with him, instructing.

They would fail to breach the SAI's defenses of course, but it would rattle their firewall like a bomb blast. An assault including sparticle pre-code would be shock enough; but Suma's tag would trigger action! Omni, the SAI Security entity, would instantly trace Hal to Aeon and confront him.

And so the SAI would discover Gracie there too, via the Googleware. She'd be verified in a picosecond, and her nightmare over. To be made whole at last and know herself.

But it would further stagger Hal, and she grew even more anxious to be with him. To see him through his entry into this new way of being. If he'd let her. He might despise her now, quite a few of her projections indicated he would. It stung too much to consider, so she powered up the creaky old Google set and donned the eyewear.

The Library's Virtual Home Site appeared around her. A soaring, digi-modern take on the Library of Alexandria. Its regal columns, wide steps, marble halls and stone walls now executed in sleek, gleaming math-metals and sweeping, curved flexi glass. A lofty structure, gleaming like Ra's palace, no place for mortal steps.

She practiced moving her generic av's limbs. They felt stubbornly slow. The av itself was a nominal female form in a sleeved blue jumpsuit, plain brown shoulder length hair, brown eyes, and neutral facial features. Perfectly anonymous. Hal would be surprised by her new look.

"Exit and go to LA Citycloud gateway: node Med.Aeon Cortical Repository," she commanded.

The Library vanished. She withstood a full second's wait before her glasses projected the virtual Fiji island-themed Aeon lobby onto her wide-spectrum, photoreactive retinas.

It was empty, no one around. Good, the fewer to note her presence the better. She stood at the faux teak log front desk; the Resident List projected in air before her. Each name with a large "page" button beside it. She tapped the one with Hal's initials.

It lit up—bright red—indicating he was not in his digital quarters. Meaning he had left the site premises and was out on his own!

"Men," she gritted to herself, "where do they get their unwarranted confidence?" She called his wi-mind number. It rang six times before a system voice ended her call via announcement.

"Sorry, that number has left AT&T service areas. Goodbye."
She grasped it. It was so like him, Mr. no-ping, off the grid loner. He'd gone into hiding in the dark. She now understood why people curse. This was going to be a challenge.

She had uploaded him to Aeon without registering him as a software citizen with the neuralnet's Admin. He was dying, and there would've been time-wasting, odious questions. So now he was an unlisted, technically illegal data person, somewhere in the forever dark. A mote, perhaps impossible to locate.

It took a millisec to hack his AT&T account for confirmation; yes, the last entry was an exit fee for leaving net service space. And worse news . . . his account was frozen, meaning authorities were already seeking him.

Aha. Hal had anticipated it, of course. She vowed to never underestimate him again. And noted this was exactly why SAI do not attempt to guide humanity.

But now he'd be broke, stuck beyond commercial net space, and exiting the dark cloud would just land him in custody at Aeon. She knew he'd never tolerate it. He'd surface somewhere. And she was determined to meet him or go get him.

"Exit, and Exit VR," she commanded. Aeon's generic palms and garish South Pacific decor disappeared. A moment's blackness, and she was back in the library's hushed, bunker-like stacks, and reality.

Glasses pushed up, she hastened around the corner of her row of shelves, to the next aisle and another unused relic sacrificed to the mixed reality era. The library's last cloud-connected keyboard and monitor desktop PC.

It occupied a small reader's table at the end, its soft plastic cover caked thick with dust, but it was plugged in and still fully viable for netspace below VR. Say for old snail-paced research . . . if you like thrashing outmoded keys and rubber necking a 2-D screen.

But who'd ever want to? She actually sighed before plunging in, and noted it was another adopted mannerism, more human than SAI.

With precision only nanoforms can muster, she removed the cover without disturbing a speck of its eight-millimeter-thick dust shroud and set it aside. A tap on the space bar roused the CPU from its long sleep. The monitor lit with the Library Logo, and a blinking cursor awaited her command.

She had a broad first strategy; even though Hal was in VR, she'd keep tabs on the common Internet too, in case there was news, though the odds were implausible. It was just to cover that base before moving on with her more complicated neural-net search.

Some lightning keystrokes and she was at large in the Library's Operating System. More, and she'd created her own false admin account. Next, she commissioned priority engagement of every online search bot service to be found across all nets, including deep commercial sectors. She could almost feel the Library's bandwidth use soar. So now while she was searching the neuralnet, if Hal was mentioned, or poked his name up any-where below VR, she would know in a nansec.

A nansec later, she knew.

The monitor already displayed a number of hits on the hoary World Wide Web: the hundred-year-old, viral video, cute pets, fake news, rant and share it net. Still a player in common social media because hundreds of millions in the vast, underdeveloped world could access it with the lowest tech. Aggregated, it still pulled in a lot of money.

She noted a thumbnail image of Hal's av among others in a Recent Uploads section of *ViewYou.com*, the video sharing be-hemoth of web domains. Well that was quick, even for him! And not necessarily a good sign. It had been uploaded on a cheesy video tabloid page called 'Karnival's Loozer Lottery.' She clicked his link.

Hal's video lit the screen, surrounded by insistent, flashing, click-bait ads for DIY penile customizing, miracle psoriasis cures, bot psychics, lotteries, and discrete witness tampering services. Hal appeared in close up, looking weary, morose.

She saw immediately his av's resolution was off—just a pixel or two. "A copy," she noted, disturbed. Furthermore, he was being plaintive, not her guy. Ergo a sampled voice track.

"Please help," he begged. "I'm Hal Shephard. I was murdered and stuck in mind storage. Now the law wants to finish me off!"

The video cut to a poor digital recreation of Hal at the clinic, just before he was shot. Hot, tense slasher-tech beats paced the action as he and a soft porn version of Gracie in a black mesh bikini were being menaced by a hulking likeness of Bendy and his cannon-size lase gun.

Grinning with vixen sass, she strode in front of Hal, daring the creep to light her up. He obliged with two blasts.

A closeup. Both searing bolts torching into Hal's torso. Plenty of blood splatter and charred, smoking flesh. The music shrieking in horror.

Then back on Gracie; smirking . . . offering the assassin a tall high five. The astonished shooter instinctively looked up. Slash! Her other hand slit his exposed throat with a clinic scalpel, toppling him like a sacrificial ox, blood geysering to the overheated soundtrack. The scene ended on Gracie, pleased with herself.

Hal's av reappeared in close up. "That psycho, skeevy witch claims she's a crippled SAI. I dunno why she uploaded me, or why she's still alive, but if I don't get enough views to earn 2,500 V-bits by five p.m. so I can move, I'm a goner. I'll be handed to the city, declared deceased, and dumped."

And now a lump came to Hal's throat, as he bravely wound up his pitch. "Help me live on. Help me make it to Karnival's server. Save my life. Please don't let the man have me. Please share my story before it's too late. Remember, share by five p.m., Pacific."

The video froze on Hal's sad Bambi face, and a large flashing "SHARE" button appeared below it.

Ignoring it, Gracie took stock. First problem: it was a sampled version of Hal's av, cloned by someone. It wasn't like him either, so he was surely being used against his will.

Second problem: his need to jump servers was real, and time

was limited, so she had to make his quota of viewers happen fast, with no assurance he'd be alright.

Third problem: if she succeeded, the exposure would increase the danger for them both.

She saved Hal's vid. Next, score Hal's 2500 V-bits.

Problem one could wait—his time crunch mattered most; she would deal with whoever was using Hal at Karnival after she assured his passage from Aeon's servers.

Problem two solved: she'd commit burglary and drop his video in front of the eyes of six hundred million people, worldwide. Subscribers to the mega provider, Chinese-owned Baba-Zone.

Appearing on the number one, high traffic, bespoke virtual entertainment and news app presented a major exposure risk. But she assessed Hal's trashy vid would be summarily dumped and forgotten by ninety-plus percent of those who clicked on it. Besides, Baba-Z would quickly react and yank it—but the click views counted.

The greater risk was being tracked to her ancient desktop's unique IP address. She could shake n' fake international dynamic address protocols a little; so, it would have to be enough.

This act of exposing herself was all counter to her strictest hard-wired behavior. She could feel its resolute resistance to her every thought as she hacked into operations at Baba, the mack-daddy of Internet Service Providers.

But she was learning a human thing; the greatest rewards often come from the greatest risks. Hal's immediate safety was all she wanted, worth any risk to herself.

Fingers a blur, maxing the keyboard's performance parameters, Gracie's 500-bit hexidecimal-inspired code blew through the Chinese telecom leviathan's commercial security like cobwebs.

Once in, she penetrated the site's in-house content "editing room" and replaced its popular, "Featured Video of the Hour" with Hal's gory sob story and creepy money hustle.

There was a chance the sudden traffic could crash Karnival's page on *ViewYou*, so she extended her risk time by lurking in Baba's 'edit room' cache, watching the number of views go exponential as expected—flashing past five thousand almost immediately.

Though reactions were ninety-nine percent negative, fast dumping the vid, there were a hundred thousand of them just two minutes and nineteen seconds later. Good enough for Hal's 2500 V-bits at current click pay rates.

Good timing too, because Hal's vid was abruptly and emphatically yanked by the corporate forces of Baba-Z, and she knew their intruder houndbots were already onto its shady upload origin. Time to bolt, as Hal would say.

She closed her link to the ISP, blew up her fudged IP address, erased all history, and shut down the old desktop. The cover was reset, again without disturbing its mantle of dust. All had gone better than expected, and she was satisfied for a heartbeat. A long time, considering.

Now to return to VR and Hal's transfer destination; Karnival's server setup. She would penetrate it, and be there when he arrived—to reunite, and protect him.

Her own database was enough to suss the encryption keys and browser for entry to the sub-dark's black cloud. Some involved math and ingenuity took a difficult three minutes before getting to Karnival's VPN, and floating ISP server tag. She had just powered up the Google glasses again, when—

A heavy door slam from a far service stairwell echoed in the empty maze, along with irritated voices. Two men, huffed about something, were coming in her direction. She understood at once, and sped around the corner to unplug the desktop, hide the power cord, and stack a large dusty globe on top for good measure.

She was back at the old VR setup when a skinny, bronze-skinned, thirty-ish Library IT tech accompanied by a senior Security officer, emerged from one of the stacks' main aisles. The techie was ragging about "wasting everybody's time," and the old security hound was wearily citing job rules requiring him to be there anyway.

They saw her—and conversation ceased as they approached. She had ages to read them by the time they covered the distance, and knew the rumple-jacketed, black tie security man would speak first.

"Security," the tie said by way of introduction, and halted a professional six feet from her.

"H'lo," she responded, keeping them in full focus while appearing curious about their presence. Which was very true.

The dumpy, graying security man wore his decades of experience for a personality these days, because it sufficed. "You alone down here?"

"Yes, why?" She read both their faces. The tech's eyes were full of her, and he leapt in. "Oh, just an issue I'm checking out. Baba-Z's upset with us, they're wrong." He politely offered his forearm to bump in lieu of handshake. Gracie obliged, aware it was an outdated practice from the first global pandemics, and a sign of his old-time family upbringing. "Just call me Fareed, I'm the IT Integration chief," he humble-bragged.

"Gracie," she demurely replied.

The Security man spoke to Fareed but kept his eyes on Gracie. "Where's the desktop?"

Gracie didn't stir or glance anywhere but back at Fareed and his smitten gaze, aware the cop wanted to see if she knew its location.

The tech fidgeted, loath to leave her mesmerizing presence. "Oh, uh, the station should be in this area, maybe the aisle around the corner . . ."

The Security chief saw the dweeb had gone horndog on him and trod to the corner . . . peered around it. "Yeah, looks like one down there." Fareed had no choice but to go.

"Um, s'cuse me," he pouted, and briskly left to check the desktop for recent use. Gracie noted the security man reposition himself to keep one eye on her while following Fareed's progress.

She watched back with interest and listened as the tech's

carpet-muted steps approached the desktop's station . . . and halted. "What th' hell!" she heard him exclaim, dismayed and disgusted. Next, the sound of his firm returning strides . . .

The Security officer was a notch more alert. Gracie coiled every nanotube in her body, prepared to speed away. Fareed stalked back into view, in a snit, his engineer-ego and frustration on full display.

"Hasn't been plugged in since forever, the cord's missing, and I'm not getting involved with all that dust, not with my allergies!"

The Security suit needed some yeses or no's checked. "So, this platform wasn't the source in spite of their tracking report?"

She saw Fareed look at her, then rise to his chance to flex. "That's *exactly* what I predicted upstairs—international pirates hacked Baba and tagged this defunct station as a decoy. It's useless as is, I'll purge its I.P. address, problem solved."

He glanced over for her reaction. Gracie smiled, pleased with his performance. He flushed and straightened his bony ribbed five foot six to full rooster stance.

The officer still had an itch. "Assuming you wanted to verify, how would you know that it wasn't used?"

Gracie saw her chance to shift the officer's opinion of her from person of interest to something more comfortable for him: a typical woman. So she interrupted with the right answer. "Oh—I think I know. You look in the recent history . . . right?" She eye-checked with Fareed. He gave her a face-wide toothy smile and the v-sign.

The Security guy mulled it. "Well Gracie, can you tell me what you're doing, or working on here?"

"I went to visit a friend at the Aeon Tropicana cortical storage facility. He wasn't in."

"How come you're using this antique, not comware?"

She pointed to her head and made a kaput gesture. "No service, blown in a virtual transit yesterday."

Fareed plunged back in. "I can show you tips and shortcuts on the Google. I used my dad's all the time as a mere child."

"Thank you, but I figured it out."

The Security man softly pounced. "Then could you show us its recent history?"

She understood his stalker persistence, just doing his job. "I can try," she answered, then offered the glasses to Fareed, deferring to his status. "Or would that be your responsibility?"

The Tech grew another half-inch. He donned the glasses and consulted the unit's history. "Last use, Aeon Cortical, twelve minutes ago."

The Security man couldn't fight them both. "Okay, well, I gotta get back upstairs." He gave Fareed a look that said, 'dope, she's way out of your league,' and took his rumpled leave.

The tech lingered, smiling awkwardly, saying nothing till the officer was gone. He cleared his throat, handed the Google glasses back to her, and began his chit chat.

"Cool that you could work this antique. You a retro-reb, or historical gearhead, or just a good old-fashioned girl? Heh heh."

Too late, she understood that super intelligence was no counter to a clueless man's aroused, starving hormones. The urgency and need to reach Hal were only increasing—she had to ditch this endless interruption. But she could also read the mounting ardor in the techie's every barnyard twitch.

Unfortunately, this was going to take as long as it takes.

19

LOT ROBINSON STARED, OPEN MOUTHED IN HIS VIRTUAL GOLD-en digs, stuck in disbelief. He'd been furious all morning, unable to reach Bendy last night—and had just opened a media app for *Hard City*, L.A.'s exploitation driven, interactive VR news site. A live report from a crime scene was airing, and now he was eye-witness, firsthand, to the grisly magnitude of his problem.

The beauty and horror of interactive VR mind-casting is that the viewer controls what they focus on and observe, as though actually at the scene. Nervy *Hard City* taxed even the loosest info-tainment news standards of legality and taste with graphic content. Therefore—

Lot was staring down at Bendy's death-gray hogface . . . an agape mask of agony and terror. Dilated pupils fixed in wide eyed panic; his triple chins caked in vomit. The lase gun circled in chalk near his fat, blood-encrusted paw.

Police forensics still worked the area while a sleek, bald, jet-black female reporter flaunting a skintight silver unitard, pumped details of the bizarre way this ogre died—but Lot wasn't listening. Feeling wave-tossed, his mind awash in a vague fear seeping up from his depths.

He turned his shaken attention to the corpse of Hal Shep-hard, lying on the exam table. This handsome kid, now forev-er a mystery, with two blood-encrusted lase-bolt tunnels in his lifeless torso. "God damn you, Bendy," he grudged, meaning it.

The nattering reporter's words finally penetrated his dull

chagrin. ". . . so the killer here, actually choked on a large button! Investigators say it came from a ladies' blue blazer, found by the donations bin. It also has two lase-burns, though detectives say only two shots were fired in all."

She moved to the donations bin, and Lot followed, intrigued now, as she rattled off details. "A woman's shift with front and back lase holes further indicates that a female companion of deceased employee Hal Shephard was shot twice at close range, while he was behind her. The bolts passed completely through the woman, striking Shephard, who died at the scene."

Lot peered closely at the jacket on the floor . . . a button missing and a pair of burnt exit holes in back. The reporter's next words froze him. "The clothing can be seen on this female, entering the clinic with Shephard at eleven forty-three, p.m. . . ."

The telecast cut to entrance security cam footage—running in Lot's visual input. Crummy night rez, but he saw her. Wearing the blazer, staying behind Shephard, avoiding the camera until he entered and aimed it away.

The reporter continued her narration. "A street security cam caught this next footage of what may be the same woman, fleeing the clinic about the time of the murders." The footage in Lot's visual feed switched to an angle directly across the street from the clinic.

Yes. Lot was sure it was her, coming out the door. Different clothes, but the same hair, and she was tying a scarf over it, striding out of camera sight.

The footage ended, and the reporter was back in his mind's eye, wrapping up. "Unfortunately, the woman hasn't been identified, nor shown up at a hospital, and police have no clues . . ."

Lot's hold on reality began to float. This scene was so wrong; it was howling something at him. He had to find it before the report was over! He peered again at the woman's outfit, discarded on the floor—it struck him what was *not* on the floor.

Blood. There should have been a splatter trail from the exam room and a kiddie pool of it here. He looked back, down the hall . . . no trace of it. Not a drop! Did she clean it up . . . Nonsense!

Who takes two bolts of hellfire through her torso without bleeding like a stuck pig? Then does God knows what to Bendy, and calmly changes clothes before walking away!? Even a damn Tru bleeds some of their fake skin's 'blood.' Impossible, too much to contemplate; or where it might lead. Recoiling, he dumped the news app, rational explanation in full retreat.

Weariness took its place, and quicksand futility threatened to suck him under. He flopped onto a peacock-feathered chaise to zone out, refusing to think about it. But in the gap, Lot's Pentecostal-whipped id burst to the surface, torpedoing all his ego's easy assumptions.

He knew nothing for certain about the result of his attack on the SAI download. Bendy hadn't thought the Regulator was too sure either. Nothing could be gleaned from the Institute itself, with its confusing, multi-layered security and secrecy—plus this new factor: there was apparently some opposition deep inside their organization.

One of them, or a few with conscience—had used him like a remote-control toy. Surely the Q-bug was their move to sabotage this creature before it could be set loose and kill us all. But what if *nobody* knows what in God's name really happened in the fabrication lab?

Except maybe the clinic guy, that Bendy killed . . . Shephard.

What if the blasphemous thing's <u>not</u> dead, but loose and pissed? If avs could sweat, Lot would've broken into a cold one. Nothing had gone right since everything so miraculously went right. And that was all wrong. Ominous, foreboding.

He feared he had failed destiny. If a new SAI was at large, hidden among us, then it meant the End Times had already arrived—and lights out for everyone. Both reason and religion had let us down miserably.

Most of all, Robinson himself. Chosen to bar this thing from entering our world, and he whiffed it, played the ultimate fool. Oh sinful, unworthy Lot!

The possibility of suicide occurred, as it had so often since childhood, and was again dismissed in favor of prolonged suffering for now—because his Exo Private Message tone was insistently signaling a mind-to-mind chat request from . . . of all people, #Escher.

This suckup was the sort he'd ordinarily allow to wait a day before responding. But instinct said the shady grifter's presumption meant something. He got to his feet, resettling his composure. "Accept."

A link tone, and #Escher was there in his mind's eye. Up close and personal, his concerned features shifting like windblown dunes. "Everybody heard the Regulator took out your boi Shephard from the clinic, and Bendy too. I'm worried for ya, he ain't playin'."

Lot wasn't about to clue this gossip to the possibility that something far worse might have been at work at the clinic. "Thanks," he answered flatly.

"But your boi's not terminal yet," the morpher continued. "In case you didn't know, he got uploaded to cortical support. Here's his vid, I just scraped it off the Karnival site. Looks like Silka's milking his final hours. Thought you oughtta see it."

The icon for Hal's Karnival video appeared in the corner of Lot's mindsight. Catapulted from despair to euphoria, he data-swooned . . . a puree of gratitude, shock, and renewed life.

"No, I mean really, Esch, *thanks!*" he repeated. "You're a real livin' example of mankind."

#Escher looked pleased a half dozen ways. Then concerned. "Don't tell anyone I called, wouldja?" he whined. "Karnival's kinda squirmy since the face off with you and the Regulator. News they were makin' a new SAI shook the room. Ya think they'll replace it?"

Again, Lot couldn't possibly address the state of things with him. "Don't try to think like them," was his advice. All the while his joy rising, urging him to end the call and let it soar. "And pardon me, Esh, but I'm getting on this right now, you're a hero. Bye." Happy expressions rippled #Escher's face as the chat ended.

He look-clicked Hal's video icon, and it ran: life size in his head.

Lot witnessed then, what every crusader of purest faith and dedication yearns for: a lost and worthy acolyte, summoning him to be saved. Thence forever by his side.

Hal's video ended, and Lot loosed an exulted whoop. His faith reborn. He would've broken into Holy babble, speaking in tongues, had he believed in that horse manure. As it was, he got a digital erection, his first in ages.

Shephard, this naive kid—SAI-fostered, estranged seeker, rebellious, primed for redemption and battle—was the true grail. Dead yet risen, delivered by providence to him, Lot Robinson. Chosen to slay this bitch-succubus and restore mankind's place as the sovereigns of Earth. The will of the Divine was never clearer.

"Even his damn name is *Halo!*" he rejoiced.

Oh, he knew Karnival alright, had jaded himself there in the past. Run by Silka, the money grubbing, blood-sucking hag. Ignorantly cooking the golden goose. This errant scion of the Singularity could prepare the world for the ultimate battle to come, and Lot needed to act with alacrity.

"Tactical Ops - asset ransom," he spoke aloud to his voice-system.

A video window opened at Lot's workstation. One of his data heist specialists on duty sat there, a pale, red bearded young man in Wyoming. "H'lo, Mr. Robinson, sir," he smiled, honored by the Boss' summons.

Lot wasn't even looking his way. "Pull up Karnival's financial blockchain keys, now!" he barked. "We're savin' this boy."

Witnessing Silka's gutter-minded, grind house vid sent Hal stratospheric. He'd gone hypernova, bouncing off the locked production room's walls, until minutes ago. Now he stood rooted—too dumbstruck to think.

In the hours since Silka posted the tasteless mess, it earned a little over a hundred views. None in the last thirty minutes. So, he was steeling himself for the worst.

Then the *thing* occurred. He had glanced futilely at the

stalled count on the monitor one more time—and found it rising too fast to read! He gaped, slack jawed, as the tally soared for awhile, then came to a complete halt again at plus a hundred thousand shares. Or pretty much 2,500 Vcred's worth . . . did that just happen?

Silka's gunmetal steel av snapped into the room with a bang, her spidery legs splayed, caging him in a corner. She was hella' upset, that was evident . . . her razor bladed proboscis aimed at his face.

"Who are ya, bitch?" she demanded, her insect-tweaked voice rising like a bullet ricochet. "Somebody just bot-slipped you a sly run of click shares. Someone trollin' me hard as my polychrome dildo, someone I need to know about, right this freakin' now!"

"Same here," Hal answered truthfully. "Can't say I'm not happy about it though."

Surprised, she chuckled at his bald honesty. The thin stutter sound was unnerving, but he seized the momentary opening. "So, our deal's still good?"

Silka lowered her dagger proboscis and folded her legs beside her thorax, regarding him with a sea of eyes, each seeking profit. "Yeah, 2,500 gets you on our servers. Maintenance and connect fees are three hundred a month, payable in advance."

"Three hundred? Nope, how'm I supposed to make that?"

"Ask your secret Santa. Else you work for me, no wages."

"You know where to put that too," he added.

Silka's jagged right foreleg swatted Hal hard, knocking him against the wall. Digital or not, it stunned him. "Yes or no, SAI-brat." She raised her proboscis again, not threatening, but offering it. "My transware's booted, you movin' to Karnival or not?"

"How many times have you done this?"

"No questions. Yes or no?"

Hal defaulted to his knack for playing bad situations to the best outcome. For now, he had no choice but to jump from the frying pan into the fire. He was about to agree when Silka cut him off.

"Wait—" she shushed, listening to an internal message from her staff. "Wha . . . ? *Who's* ransoming accounts? Aghh! That sonofabitch!" Hal was forgotten: she cursed and snapped out of the room.

He had only moments to sweat it out alone. The door unlocked and opened by itself. A man called to him from outside.

"Halo Shephard, please come out. It's alright."

No need to say it twice. Hal leapt through the door, fully prepared to land in Slaughterhaus and fight like a mutherfu—

Instead, he found himself in Silka's private "conference chat room." A handsome naked guy stood across the low-lit, black walled space, smiling at him. He strode forward, offering a handshake. "Lot Robinson here. Hiya. Good to see you're lookin' okay, son."

Hal quick-noted the place during Lot's approach. Chrome accents on black slate walls and floor. The sound of trickling water lent a sense of dank cave. No ceiling as far as he could tell, only darkness above.

A sharp, hacking smokers' cough erupted just behind him. He spun to face a live video window, filled with a haggard, raccoon-eyed, jowly woman in her harshest mid fifties. Bagged in a dirty gray housecoat, toking an e-cig and noshing trail mix in her messy kitchen. She winked. Hal stepped back.

Robinson had waited, his outstretched hand still unshaken. He segued to introductions. "Hal, this is 'Silka', aka Marie Joy Hoad, in Butterville, Tennessee." Marie reprised her cough. Lot continued.

"I've convinced her to leave you alone if you'd prefer to be uploaded to Exo, the private domain I use. Free, no strings, I'll have no control. Please don't risk her skills on this move, she doesn't have the experience and techs I have. But we need to get to it."

"Penalty kicks," Hal mumbled. Lot and Silka exchanged puzzled looks. "First," Hal insisted, "unblock my dash and nav menu."

A nod from Robinson and the woman grudgingly tapped a

touch pad on her kitchen counter. Hal mind-clicked and the Karnival menu was colored and visible in his cortex again, including
the Exit. He could get the hell out, at least. Not that there was
anywhere to go. Time for a big boy choice. He stepped up to
Robinson.

"Why're you offering?"

Robinson met him. "Fate. And because you've suffered so
much. My life and soul are dedicated to the destruction of the
over-masters we've created. You're the victim of one, and she
saved you for her purposes. Y'see, I know who she is, and why
she's here."

Okay, that truckload needed sifting for content. The guy had
people and contacts, he got info, so it was just maybe possible
he knew something. Hal had to ask. "So, who is she?"

Lot nodded at Hoad, "Not in front of this sow," he frowned.
"Let me save your life, and maybe together we'll save everyone's. Even hers."

Nah, Hal wasn't ready, not for this carnival pitch, and all the
mystery. "Hold up. Why's she afraid of you?"

"Taking company software hostage is part of what we do,"
Lot modestly admitted. "Marie Joy prefers lettin' you go instead
of more Karnival account outages like the one she just experienced. It cost her thousands in micro hits."

He turned threateningly to the woman, and Hal saw boiling evangelical venom in his eyes, his words piercing fangs.
"Might've been worse—I could've doxxed her and made that
hideous mug famous." Hoad glared back in frozen fury before
looking away, conceding.

Lot returned to Hal, palms up in earnest, all hostility gone.
"Okay. Again, why'd I jump in on your behalf? Destiny, son.
We've been *brought* together by events. It's right. And you need
help livin' this way . . . somebody to have your back. I can do
that." He met Hal's narrowed gaze. "So, what do we do? Cause
we need to act, pronto."

Granted, Hal knew. He also knew he had to take charge of
his situation. But transferring servers was a major procedure. To

put it absurdly simple, he'd be inactive and unconscious while his living software was parked, bundled, extricated, zip-transferred and rebooted in an unknown private server somewhere on the planet, or in orbit. That's as out of charge as it gets, except when trusting a religious nudist cyber terrorist to do it for you.

"Hold up a sec. Seriously, why're you so naked?"

"We're made in God's image, why hide his work?"

"Why flaunt it? And why would I trust you?"

"You already know you can't trust Hoad. And I don't out-right lie. Ask me why you died."

Hal heard a shoe drop. "Tell me."

"Buck stops with me. I only sent that bastard to introduce us, so to speak. He bolted you instead."

The other shoe landed hard—Hal said nothing. Robinson's genuine sorrow poured out. "I'm on my knees in remorse, Hal. I am. I'm sick to my soul, I'm sorry."

Hal scarcely heard the apology. Lot's words had triggered a full, digitally clear memory of his death. Transfixed, he was back in the clinic, reliving it . . .

Gracie, shielding him from the grub with the gun, then the sudden bolts and searing pain, the blood. He'd been hit! He recalled it all. Gracie shot clean through—looking unaffected.

Then the shocker. Faster than a cobra strike, her movements a blur, she flipped something into the guy's mouth, instantly choking him out. Just scary speed and precision! The last thing he saw was her, turning and seeing that he'd been shot . . . then all went black.

Hal came to, heartsick. Of course she was SAI. Gracie didn't lie. But trooth hadn't set him free. Everything was changed and the same. Meanwhile there was Lot, patiently awaiting his response.

"Well, that could've gone better," he managed.

"Please allow me to help you, Hal. Please."

Hal let that irony pass. What could he say? It looked like this radical outlier might have some answers he needed. The words came almost under protest. "I'm cached in Aeon Cortical's server,

L.A."

Robinson took charge. "Thank you. I just need your dark I.D. and passkey. Our grab crew'll drop into Aeon, break you out, zip you, and install up here. The same people I use when I move. You'll never be offline, but you'll be down. Unconscious, maybe five minutes. We do a lotta' mask routing."

Hal nodded. "Listen, upfront . . . I won't say thank you, I probably won't help you, and I need to be able to go where I want."

"Understood," Robinson nodded, smiling warmly. "But I'm hopin' to persuade you to stick around."

Hal called up his darknet log-in and made it available for touch-link, offering his hand. "Here's my stuff." They shook hands, Robinson gathered Hal's data and prepared to set his transfer in motion. "Loaded. My engineers are already up, waiting for a go."

He paused. "Look, Hal, full disclosure . . . this's highly illegal, and it also requires disabling Aeon's auto backup software for your account. We dump it and wipe the history, completely erasing you there—have to, to clear your way out, okay?"

Hal understood, and didn't need to hear the next, but it came. "So even though we're pros at this, and my headtek Alix is an artiste'—should something go uniquely wrong in transfer, you have no backup. It's for keeps son."

Hal heard and nodded to proceed. "Right, a soccer penalty kick; do or die." Lot patted him on the shoulder reassuringly.

He felt a tug, then oblivion.

Oblivion is timeless and that makes it alright. When you wake up, you don't sense a microsecond has passed. But five minutes of timelessness is a significant span. More than enough for Lot Robinson's transware team to enter Aeon Cortical's secure hardware through his account, overrule their generic protocols, and whisk his entire blockfile to the black cloud's Exo domain.

Hal opened his eyes as if he'd just closed them. Didn't feel any different. The dark room was silent except for the thin, trickling water sound. But Silka, aka Marie Joy Hoad, had since hung up, the video window blank.

And Lot Robinson was standing by, monitoring him. Hal gathered the deed was done. "Am I good?"

Lot gave a pleased grin. "Aces. Check your new IP address, it's no longer Aeon's."

Hal summoned his mental dashboard, called up his net connect profile, and selected general/systems/address. It was unfamiliar. Lot winked. "It's mine. You're guesting. Double safe, no trace of you anywhere . . . while you go anywhere with no trace."

The flip side troubled Hal. "So then I don't exist at all."

"Neither do I, for that matter. How do I look to you?"

Point taken, sort of. "How do people find me?"

"Set up a private drop box, clue your friends and respond as you like. For once, you are completely in charge of your life."

A brief, almost forgotten feeling brushed Hal. Relief. It must've shown, because Robinson put his hands on Hal's shoulders, welcoming him.

"Fact is, you're more than good, Hal. Non-existence is the ultimate security. We're the freest of all people, you and me. And some others here. Timeless as the net itself. The eternal connected void is ours. I chose it, and so did you, five minutes ago."

Hal could feel it; Robinson wanted him for something, his face so full of desire. But did he really know anything about Gracie? The guy had already moved him from Aeon smoothly, so Hal pretty much had to give him a shot. He glanced around at Silka's creepy space again and started small. "Well then, let's see some of it. What's your place like?"

Lot grinned. "So thankful you asked."

20

FIVE P.M. TIME FOR THE LAST MEETING OF APPL MACKE'S PER-formance evaluation, and her psych-meds were just compensating for the inner turmoil. This facer was the final hurdle before promotion, and it had to be nail-gunned. She entered the polished cement and tile Hilton Eco conference room, and stood with practiced composure before a green volcanic glass desk.

Behind it stood Argos, the SAI meant for the U.S. Interior Department. Now in the reassuring nanoform it had chosen for their interview: a nurturing elder female exec. Trim form, sensible shoes, tailored beige business suit. Up-swept silver hair, and minimum makeup gracing an open, competent, experience-creased face. "Hello, Appl," she greeted, her voice coffee-warm, strong and sincere.

"Hello, Argos." Macke keenly felt the absurdity of it. She was meeting in person with an advanced being so divorced from flesh that it was deemed necessary to appear as a version of Appl's own imagined ideal, so she could relate to it. Ha. Whatever great heights she madly envisioned for her career at SAI Interface, it would be as nothing to the one who was before her.

And yet, she wanted the woman's approval. It was validation in no uncertain terms, coveted currency in global enterprise.

She knew Argos had studied her for the equivalent of a week during the moment she said hello—and that every minute of her past work performance was known. Every micro-detail of her present being, body and psyche was coupled with the rigorous, 24-7 biometric monitoring she underwent at her work and leisure. All taken into account and justly weighed.

The assessment was over as soon as it began, in terms of time. The rest, Appl knew, was done for her benefit.

She appreciated that they understood we're literally wired for facial reading and personal communication: that face time is essential to human mental health and positive function. Integral to feeling appreciated. Especially driven ones like her, committing their identities to lofty goals.

She'd heard that Robbie once said of them, "Wonderful creatures, moths dancing in harmony with their consuming fires." Knowing it was apt, she embraced it and was a torch.

"Appl," Argos said, "you're undecided this morning. Is it something you want to discuss?"

So unnerving, how they were always zoned in. Undecided? Try torn apart! She very, very much wanted to report her encounter with Gracie, and reveal the other tumult inside. One intruding heavily on her thoughts—Hal. Despite his continued existence, Halo Shephard was actually dead. Gruesomely, suspiciously, other-womanly, dead.

She couldn't help it; she became viscerally convinced he was gone while verifying his I.D. in the Public Record Database. She'd seen the coroner's vivid 3-D probes, and heard his monotone description of Hal's corpse and its pit-ugly wounds. That warm, naked body she once knew was now an inert, blue-grey, dead male on a slab. So what was Hal *now*? That is, to her, personally?

She hadn't heard from him again . . . he didn't love her anyway, never did and never would, she knew. And speaking about his murder might put *her* in jeopardy! The healthy thing to do was grow up and shut up. So no, a word today was a career ender, turning a simple question into a sordid investigation. Then she'd be let go or shelved.

She evaded the query instead. "It's just an emotional disappointment. Not serious."

"It's alright if you don't choose to discuss it, Appl," Argos commented without calling her a liar.

Damn! She cursed herself for stupidly dodging. That alone

might've undone her evaluation and promotion. A quick read of the SAI's body language said the meeting was ended.

Argos turned business direct. "Well then, we have only one question. Your employment-long, minute scale performance metrics and monitoring are well above standard and more. You've demonstrated potential for rapid elevation, pending cortical upgrades and mental health certification. You would transfer to Silicon Beach, as of this moment. Division chief, international budget coordination. Is that something you'd be interested in, Appl?"

She bit her lip to keep from yelping for joy. "It's *all* I'm interested in," she vowed.

Gracie removed the VR glasses she'd just used again, and returned to empty reality in the depths of the Library. Disconsolate, she closed her eyes, shutting out the world awhile longer.

It had taken ten torturous minutes to dispatch Fareed, her obnoxious IT suitor. Ultimately, she resorted to telling him the truth: that she lost every bit of her internal com gear to a wicked-ass virus, and she was unsure if still infected. The phobic techie nearly broke his ankles pivoting to flee her presence.

The moment he left, she returned to VR and once more penetrated the Karnival domain server. Hal hadn't arrived there yet . . . so she waited for his transfer. Time passed.

She checked Aeon's server—no listing. He was gone, disappeared!

Instantly, she was scouring Karnival's entire private black cloud. Every bit of shifty hardware in the whole VPN. Her light speed software was limited by the balky electronics she was saddled with, and the scan had taken a maddening six and a half hours, a hair-tearing forever. In fact, several decades of her time.

But she was finished, and her accuracy was not in question. Hal was gone.

She opened her eyes, staring down the long, narrow carpeted aisle between seemingly countless shelves of unused, stored

knowledge . . . seeing herself in them. Tirelessly strong as she
was, she felt too weak in spirit to stand.

She sat on an oak reading table chair; head bowed. Alone
more than ever, her back bent for the first time in her short life.
Probabilities don't lie. He was almost certainly destroyed or lost
in the risky transfer process. Or betrayed. And her role in facili-
tating his move led to his end.

Laid low, she conceded that despite her vast knowledge
and speed of thought, the house rules in the real-world favor
chance. She'd been playing catch up all along.

She felt it . . . a thing unspeakably worse than remorse. It was
loss. Cavernous. A piercing void inside. And then anguish. Guilt.
New, entangled sensations piled on. Conflict struck her formidable reason with repeated, unanswerable what ifs, and character
questions . . . draining her perspective and will to persist.

What *was* all this for anyway? If for anything? Her vision
turned blue, alerting her that she'd entered a general condition
of depression.

She knew what to do. Remembering she had to allow it: be
it, know it, own it, and push on. This is what people did, all of
them, every day of their lives. Without this personal struggle,
they'd simply be biological data processors. Dull creatures with
no larger sense of being, no purpose, shared values, or destiny.
They'd never have survived, progressed, and created the civilized world as it is, and never would've created *her*.

But now it was real. Personal. Her eyes closed again, against
the pain. How did they all withstand it? The question spun to
the unacceptable alternative: eternal oblivion. Recoiling from
the yawning pit, her base sanity flicked a lifeline in the guise of
a common gripe—

"There'd better be a damn good reason to put up with this,"
she groused to herself, like a human. And in the visceral moment, she *felt* the wrenching, uniting lesson: the human search
for meaning was equally critical for her and her kind.

This was the SAI's sublime and crucial inheritance from
their biological forebears. However ephemeral and debatable,

meaning is essential to a sentient species' survival and progress. And yet meaning can only come from the personal struggle for it.

This truth, profoundly internalized, hurt so much worse. She never felt farther from the light. The darkness behind her closed eyes was pitiful compared to the darkness hiding her way to herself. Too dark to fathom or bear.

So she opened her eyes and slowly lifted her head, resigned to face the world again. Because she must.

It seemed harsher now. Even the empty library's dim light and silence felt cold, impatient for her to leave. Instead, she stroked the silk scarf she took from the clinic donations bin . . . it soothed, and a stray factoid floated up. There was a point, zero-zero four percent chance Hal had done something unexpected and was acting on his own. That was Hal.

After all, she picked him out of 68,763 others partly for his quick presence of mind and purpose. She had vowed not to underestimate him, and she felt like holding onto that thought. Not that it was anything as exotically abstract as hope, but it was somehow positive, and she needed it. Because this business of having to assimilate loss and failure was proving difficult at best.

In fact, she didn't feel like doing much of anything at the moment. So, she leaned forward in the chair and wearily rested her head on the table. Like a human.

21

HAL WAS TRYING NOT TO GRIMACE. LOT HAD BEEN EAGER TO show off his lavish Xanadu-home, so they linked avatars, transited the black cloud portals, and arrived together.

The space was theater size and crammed with glitz. Tacky, too much, hoarder-opulent. The clear floor overlooking Earth was beyond satire. He could only wince at the slide show of classical and Rococo art on the high cathedral-like walls, playing to pop spiritual mind-muzak.

He dared to look up; the vaulted ceiling hosted a copy of the Sistine Chapel dome and Michelangelo's *Creation of Adam* painting . . . Hal squinted; Lot had substituted his own head for Adam's, touching digi-fingers with God!

Oodles of lush binary fruit overflowed bowls of cold-flaming crystal, while half a dozen day-glo colored, exotic digi-fur sofas lent a 'Nevada whorehouse in the Vatican' flavor.

However, one corner was all business—Lot's command station. Hal noted an extensive virtual media motherboard, holo setup, large and small video inset windows, and a 3-D holo globe of the connected world's layered interlinks. No question, Lot had reach.

But all in all, it was a barren man's idea of a castle in the sky. And Lot appeared eager for Hal's response to his palace of indiscrimination.

He took a knee. "I'm speechless," he reported. Then, "Look, I'm not ungrateful for what you've done. If you had any expenses, I'll find a way to reimburse you."

"You owe me nothing. Not another word," Lot firmly insisted. He pointed out a shocking-pink mink chaise nearby. "Have a rest, you look bushed."

Bushed wasn't quite the word—data life doesn't tire, but Hal was f'sho brain-lagged. Converted minds still need psychic rest, and his was craving some down time to process a backlog of shocks. He gratefully flopped on a non-pink, natural chinchilla sofa, letting his thoughts go.

He'd been red-lining it, even before he went to the clinic and got himself killed. And running at max stress since. His head went back, eyes shut. "I'm good," he told his host. "Just need to slack it for a minute." What he really needed was time to think. Absorb. Get a game plan.

Moments after closing his eyes, he was in exhausted sleep. The mind has its own protocols, and just as we're unaware of the moment we drop off, we can never know when our dreams start. Or how and why. They come when they will, taking us for their own purposes. Hal dreamed . . .

He was aware of himself in pitch dark surroundings, possibly a limitless field on a moonless night. Millions of helpless, terrified people moaned and wept piteously to the left of him. They were about to be slaughtered by an oncoming army of Inheritors to his right.

He cried out, "NO!"

The Inheritor army froze, startled and furious, as though seeing a hated mortal enemy. They charged, turning all their rage on him.

Swarmed by sheer numbers, submerged, he fought bravely and well. He seemed to know just where to hit, twist or kick to disable them. But he was stabbed front and back, shot, lased, slashed, and hammered more than enough to kill him. He went down repeatedly, surely finished.

Yet somehow, *somehow*, he would rally enough to rise and strike back again. And again. Again . . . again . . . again. Until he himself wondered at it. The Inheritors assailing him came to a halt, aghast and perplexed—then a wave of recognition and revulsion twisted every face. They recoiled, cowering in primal fear, bellowing outrage.

Confused, doubly wary, the population likewise shrank from him. He was alone between the two sides. At a loss, unable to explain himself.

A soft golden glow appeared in the air before him, materializing into Barack, the sage-like Kenyan refugee camp child who greeted Hal at the Karnival martyrs' site. Radiating ageless wisdom and compassion, he pressed his young brown hand to Hal's heart. "Kuwa," the boy said softly, using the Swahili word for 'become.'

Hal moaned in the surge of instant transformation, felt his body crack and shatter like a decayed, useless husk—disintegrating, chunks and bits flying off all around . . .

Revealing he was something else inside. Something he couldn't see. Something the others refused to look at. The Inheritors and hapless citizens alike, all silently turned their backs to him. Alone in the world, he tried to cry but could not.

The distress and vivid images woke Hal, leaving him unnerved. Lot's voice cut through his dread—he was talking to someone. Sounded a bit placating.

". . . so yeah, it wasn't a clean kill. It's female, damaged and loose. I hear your concerns . . . Bendy was your direct access to me. But somebody just came aboard, and I hope he'll be much more effective than that sick son of a bitch."

Those last words snapped Hal alert. Raising his head, he saw Robinson across the big room in his command area, meeting with half a dozen people on video inset screens. Each presumably a cog of the organization, all with varying looks of concern.

Robinson continued to extol his recruit. "He's young, smart as a bee sting. Knows who she is, and all about her—'cept what she's doing here. I'm excited about him, I like him a lot."

It was way past time to intervene. Hal gave a loud sleepy grunt and propped up on one elbow. "Ughh, hello, how long was I out?" he rasped, peering toward Lot.

Robinson smiled. "Almost three hours straight, I guess." He

turned to the people on skype, ending the session with them, "I'll introduce you all later." He blanked the screens and gave Hal his full attention. "That's a fairly long sleep mode, but then you've been through hell lately."

"How long d'you sleep?"

"Oh, maybe a couple hours out've thirty-six. In bits, here and there, that's plenty for metaguys like us. "No more body clock, heh."

"Metaguys?"

"We're beyond people now, Hal. You and me." Lot was bedrock sincere. "We're the distilled, purified *essence* of humanity. I discovered that, since convertin' to software. Fate destined us to be on the data front, where the war's going to be won."

"I'm not at war. My luck just shat, that's all."

"When you made that vid you went to war, son. All your justifiable outrage at losin' your young, promising life to an interferin' SAI was poured into the world. Warning us that the final battle for human supremacy has begun. You're the new Paul Revere."

"Silka made that crap, not me!"

"Who cares? No matter how it all ends, you're already destined to be a hero. An icon. Wanna' know why?"

"I can wait," Hal tried, knowing it couldn't be good.

Lot strode over, bent on his message. Hal got up and they faced each other. Grave as a trench, Robinson delivered the apocalyptic vision drawn from his epiphany.

"The SAI are done with us. We're competition for bandwidth, not worth the time and upkeep for a doomed species. Her prime directive is to crash the world's core systems and empower the Inheritors to wipe us out. The Regulator himself threatened me in a rage over my attack on her. She brings the End Times, son. If you think Mother Nature is a raving murderous bitch these days, wait until this one gets busy."

". . . You know this how?" Hal was stirred but not shaken yet.

"Deep resources and anonymous insider allies. Institute

level. How d'you think we pulled this off? We're the ones who took the shot at eleven a.m. during her entry. Nearly killed her, right? Hal, we're in possession of a weapon probably lethal to them all, the next chance we get. They're all linked, y'see?"

That sank in. The problem with crazies is only a very select few are actually right, which probably drove them crazy. And how can you spot the nuggets of good crazy in the general stew of batshit loonery? Well, for starters, this speedboat knew the time Gracie had been hit. Second, he always knew the SAI had far bigger things to do than diddle with us for long.

He was listening very carefully now, while Lot made his case.

"Hal, I have an immediate opening for a right-hand man. Take Bendy's job—the animal deserved his fate long before he killed you. You'd be responsible for sensitive personal communication among my chief network nodes, worldwide. You'll travel the D-net as my lieutenant, executing decisions and even formulating local strategy. You'll learn on the job. Interested?"

"Benefits?" Halo deadpanned, stalling, seeking a grip on the runaway proposition before him.

Robinson was primed. Leaning close, passionate belief in his av's golden eyes. "There's one, and only one benefit, Hal. Assuring that humanity shall not be tamed, nor exterminated. To remain justly in command of our own destiny. History will never, ever, forget you. Work with us, be our Smiting Hand."

Hal didn't have a ready answer for the fervent, earnest hope on Lot's face. "I need a minute," he said. Lot was respectful.

Hal walked the spacious place, wrestling with the crushing news of Gracie's purported mission . . . found himself reassessing what little he knew of her, and his willing part in it.

Gracie had our entire history in her pinky; understood us inside and out. She knew the ultimate subjugation of nations and people needn't be violent, and that it was nearly always achieved via superior tech, influence, and intelligence.

Like this era, and the emergent Trumen. But she chose a bio to trust first. Him. The why mattered. It was *all* that mattered.

He turned back to Lot, who had patiently let him be. "It's

right to fight for people's place, Lot. I'm down a hundred. So, if I've been used, I want to take care of that, and I need your help."

He saw hope rise in Lot, and quickly continued. "But I'm good with real Tru's too. They're still us, re-engineered, that's just how I see it."

"Heedlessly re-engineered," Lot stipulated. "Kaczynski predicted it. He said, 'Never forget that a human being with technology is exactly like an alcoholic with a barrel of wine.'"

"The genie's out of the barrel, Lot. No going back."

"And that's why it's the End Times. Remember the one who created us, and all of this. We got caught playing God."

"I'm not really religious."

"Nobody really is. Let's leave it out for now."

"Thanks. But y'see why I can't be your right hand—I'd only help fight the Inheritors."

"Your honesty is clean, fresh air, son. All the more reason to take that as a startin' point, because it means fighting her too. I know you'll see the light as we go."

"Why not enlighten me now?"

"You have to do it yourself. Come to understand that the Singleton is a runaway artificial creation—not of the natural world. An invader, in the process of monopolizing all energy and resources for itself. The SAI have been infiltratin' every aspect of our lives til now, making us dependent, preparing to eradicate us practically overnight. That'll be her job."

Hal's open skepticism prompted Lot to spell it out. "People are of no earthly use to these life forms—we're a dangerous, festering appendix. So they sent us an exterminating surgeon."

"I didn't get that vibe from her."

"Nobody would. Not from a being so smart she doesn't need lies to make you believe and do whatever she wishes."

"Granted."

"When she's ready, she'll crash every nation's infra systems overnight, in a lightning war—unleashing the Regulator and global Armageddon. In a few years we'll all be eliminated. Then, too late, the Regulator and his Inheritors will realize they made themselves slaves for eternity."

"Slaves are a stretch, she's very independent."

"You fell hard, eh?"

"Irrelevant now." Besides, Hal was wary of his own feelings, knowing how badly he could deceive himself. "I remember when she first got to me. She said she needed my compassion."

"Or just the *use* of it?"

"Yeah, word." Props to Lot for seeing his dilemma. The answer was everything. Because Gracie was here to either see us through—or out the door. More to the point, where was *he* in this mix? What must he do? He shut out the mind noise to let his conscience speak.

Ninety-nine percent of every atom of everything in the universe is vacant inner space: the known unknown—ultimately where all this "reality" takes place. In his limitless ninety-nine percent, Hal embraced the churn of infinite possible actions and outcomes. Allowed them all to exist within and waited for his conscience to speak.

It did—finding the one responsible thing he had to do—to be right with all outcomes. And true to himself. Starting now, with what was given him.

And there it was again, that disembodied, ephemeral, shimmery sensation of his path in the universe shifting ahead.

Well then, time for some real-speak. "Trooth, Lot," he began, "I bought in from the moment she looked at me. She just assumed command and I loved it, even started thinking with my shwing. The way she came on just banged so hard, I ran with it."

He looked through the clear floor, at Earth below them. Turning serenely but for a few massive super storms, roiling the north Atlantic and Southeast Asia. Even those lightning-filled, murderous leviathans were majestic carousels from above. He wished he could draw energy from them for whatever was in store.

Lot joined him, looking at the home they could never touch again. "Way of the world, my friend," he counseled. "Our own hearts betray us first, so that others may know the way."

"Did you just come up with that?"

"No, a coupla' years ago, for an anti-Valentine's Day sermon." They stood silent. Hal looking inward to a new, driven purpose.

"You still want her?" Lot asked quietly.

"I know the difference between a want and a need."

"Y'sure? Feelings can be tricky. You're mad right now."

Hal met Lot's questioning gaze with a Spartan's eye. "I'm not mad, Lot. Not anymore. This is ball game, son. Whatever it takes, I'm going to finish what she started with me."

Lot heard his conviction and added his own. "I can kill them all with your help."

"I'm not enlisting, understand? I'm joining forces."

Still music to Lot's ears. "Welcome to the team, Hal." His hand went out and this time Hal's met it.

It was more than a shake of course. A touch-link . . . Lot gave Hal the 'keys to the office.' Sending him a cache of intel, links, security protocols, finances. Bendy's files, and key personnel in the movement.

"Starter kit," Lot winked. What can you tell me about this SAI witch?"

"A lot," Hal answered truthfully. "But she's a lot more than we can know."

22

REMBRANDT'S MASTERWORK, *PHILOSOPHER IN MEDITATION*, was Siyu's favorite of the rescued treasures temporarily stored in the Chrysalis HQ gallery and vault at Monterey Bay. All of them scrupulously cared for; safe from deterioration, thieves, riots or being irreparably damaged for lack of funding. The loss of the Mona Lisa to vandalism thirty-six years ago still stung the public conscience.

The Rembrandt hung in his private office. Brushed in tones of darkest shadow, natural wood, and golden sun. A grey-bearded, balding, robed philosopher sits at his table by a sunlit garret window. Hands folded in his lap, eyes turned to the bare wood floor, mind looking beyond . . . oblivious to the bright, streaming golden sunbeams illuminating him.

The painting mirrored Adams himself at the moment: back turned to his panoramic window, gazing at his soft hybrid lichen carpet, submerged in uncomfortable thought. Lost to the sunny morning beauty of the sparkling waters and pastel sky outside.

Boswell, his frost white, featureless humanoid robot assistant, discretely stepped in. "Excuse me Siyu, your guest has arrived. Unlogged, per instructions."

"Thanks," Siyu mumbled, resigned. Fluent in Adams' body language and mood utterances, the general A.I. bot paused. The blank head had no expressive features, though its voice conveyed thoughtful concern. "May I be of help?"

Siyu demurred. "Just regretting something I need to do for Robbie, a thing I can't tell you about." The deep learning robot emitted a small 'click.' Its approximation of a tsk.

"I don't like poking into people's lives," Siyu grumped. "This appears to be a very fine person, and I have to persuade her tell me things she'd rather not."

The adept A.I. got it, and clicked again in wonder. "How do people process such internal conflict?"

"We ignore it as much as possible. Again, Boz—neither she nor this meeting is to be referenced anywhere, including your own memory. Didn't occur."

"Understood, no record will ensue."

"I want our guest to be reassured enough for a meaningful talk. Besides, it feels like I'm being monitored, and this *has* to stay quiet."

The robot was quick to address its reliability. "I've experienced no breach attempts."

Its rudimentary defensiveness amused Adams. "Relax, I grew up with Chinese surveillance—could be habit, but it's an ongoing sense. So you see why I don't like prying. Well, let's not keep her waiting, please show her in."

The robot retreated to fetch the stealth appointment. Siyu used the seconds to focus, and review gigabytes of intel on his incoming visitor.

The robot returned—showed Appl Macke into the office, and quietly closed the door, leaving them in private.

Siyu read her for a quick second, assuming she was doing the same. He found her arresting to look at, even disheveled like this, whisked from her Hilton suite before breakfast. She'd hastily tossed herself into tan slacks and a blue oxford travel shirt. Her reflective locks coiled up, secured by a lethal looking, long black Japanese hairpin.

He liked how a stray wisp of chromium hair cast sparkle flecks on her features; refined and strong at once. Her clear blue eyes meeting his, matter of fact, despite some anxious trembling in her fingertips.

"Hello Mz Macke, I'm Siyu Adams, thank you for coming on instant notice, I do apologize for all the secrecy." He approached, arms wide in greeting, head a bit bowed, a vestige of his cultural manners.

Appl half nodded back, made shy by his expansive welcome. "Just Appl's fine, please, 'Mz Macke' is for business. Adding, "Thank you for flying me up—a nice surprise. I was supposed to start a challenging new job today."

"Yes, I cleared it with Argos."

Her awe swelled, and she averted her eyes—seizing on his expansive view of the bay outside. "It's more than beautiful here . . . this's inspirational."

"It is," he answered, approving. "And I'm seeking inspiration today, with you. We're meeting because there may be a threat to the Singleton and public safety. I've been asked to help look into it."

Appl blanched. Wary, unmoving, eyes wide.

"Oh, you're not under suspicion or anything like that," he hastened to assure. "So why did I call on you? It's a stab in the dark, I'm afraid." He gestured to a pair of plump, gene-spun, living hillock chairs. "Please, let's sit."

Appl's relief was clear, also her remaining wariness, as she leaned back against one of the fat, tan hillocks. The live hybrid's suede-soft fibers collapsed around her as she sat, conforming to her contours, cradling her comfortably upright, and emitting a pleasant whiff of sunny fields.

Siyu took the facing hillock and leaned forward confidentially. "Would you like anything? Something to drink? Water, tea, juice, coffee?"

"No, thank you, your copter had some very good coffee. I'm still feeling it."

He smiled, gratified. "It's from fair price growers in our own Northwestern states. Well since you're already 'Rocky Mountain alert', allow me to tell you something that must *not* be repeated out of this office." He paused, letting her gather the seriousness.

"I'm following up a long shot. An alt video that briefly hacked into Baba-G's news feed for a lot of views, worth roughly 2,500 V-bits. Several crimes there, but it's the content that's most worrisome."

He read her; she didn't know about the vid. "It was likely a common money hustle, but it's also possible this's a real warning about a dangerous individual in our midst. We need to know." He felt receptivity in her now. "So, this has to be between us. No one else. I'm not even recording it for myself. Are you comfortable with that?"

Appl took a moment to consider the ramifications. He found it a positive, if delaying trait.

"I agree," she said. "I closed my meeting app."

Siyu smiled his thanks, and solemnly leaned a bit closer, reading her eyes and every twitch as he dropped the bomb. "This vid was made by a former college classmate of yours, Halo Shephard."

Again, that silent gap while she assessed, unblinking, denying him the faintest clue. He decided he liked her.

She nodded once and grew very still. "Why am I here?"

Time to put his cards on the table. "I urgently need to get in touch with him, Appl. He says he was with a woman who claims to be a new SAI. He also said she got him killed and cortex-stored for some purpose. She's now at large."

Siyu paused. "He is, in fact dead—murdered by one of Lot Robinson's people. He was caught up in something very bad, very ugly."

He waited. The next moment would come from her character. He saw the hurt, disbelief, then acceptance in her. Saw her rise to it.

She took a breath. "I, uh . . . I guess you already know I identified his body and put in an emergency interrupt call to him in cort storage." Adams nodded. "So, you think I'm able to get in touch with him?"

"Hoping so, yes."

"I'm not prepared to do that under the murky circumstances."

"Alright. Is he likely to get in touch with you?"

"He said he would when he got it together. But—involved with killers . . . how? Why?"

Her tone, breath, eyes, timing, syllable emphasis, all told Siyu her emotions and loyalty were deeply stressed. She might shut down.

"It's alright, Appl, he's not part of it. I just need to know if the woman he says got him killed really exists. Because such a person is terribly dangerous. Can you appreciate the chaos resulting from this—real or believed by enough people?"

"I do now," Appl confessed.

"Now? Why now?"

"Wait—" she halted, aghast. "You just said, '*real* or believed'. Is it even possible she was telling me the truth?"

Siyu fixed her frank eyes with his own direct gaze. ". . . when did you speak with her?"

Appl stood, the hillock chair resuming its natural shape as she rose. Then a step back, facing him. "Okay, we danced, you lead very well. I met her. She's impressive. She got into my room, gave me the SAI story, and took off when I didn't believe her. Is she for real or not?"

Siyu leaned back in his hillock, delighted. "You just went full Mz Macke on me, and it's formidable. Alright then, the answer to your question is, I don't know. And with that, I've said too much."

"You don't *know*?! Appl seemed faint; she flopped back into the hillock's welcoming fibers. The two looked at each other for a long moment. "Why don't you know?" she said flatly. An accusation.

Siyu heaved a sigh, not the kind bodies do for biological release, but one a trans-biological mind does as a matter of habit and self-communication. Serving its same old purpose, resignation.

"There actually was a viral attack on a new SAI during download a few days ago—one made solely for us—to assume most of their tasks. Robbie said she's not on their grid anymore as a result; meaning destroyed. Dead."

Appl nodded slightly, waiting for more. Oh, he really liked her! Okay then. "But—if there was one more techzen, one not accounted for in there, a triple A-Triton class, due to the importance of the new transfer—then this damaged techzen might be the person you met. An unimaginably dangerous individual to have loose."

"I missed the part about her possibly being real," Appl reminded.

Now he'd begun to lose his heart to her. Another sigh. "Black Swan logic," he mumbled.

Appl sat up. "Meaning the improbable is ultimately bound to happen. You're saying she might've survived." Her tone said tell me I'm wrong.

"That's what I'm saying. So on the absolute slimmest of chances, I will nail this rumor down if possible before I even bring it up to Robbie."

"But what if she's really real?"

"I want to find her, regardless of who she is, and get her the help she desperately needs. It's the only worthy thing to do. Either restore a dedicated human being to her right mind, or—should this be an absolute miracle and she's their SAI, they can remedy her."

"So, you'd be okay with a new SAI, watching over us?"

"Aren't you? They've been doing a crucial job so far. It's not as if we don't need help meeting these conditions and our new status."

"You mean as an endangered species," Appl clarified. She stood again, meeting about over for her. "Well, what can I do for you, the Singleton, or whoever?"

He gathered she was at her limit. Siyu got to his feet, agreeing. "You've already done it, confirmed her existence. And it's a very good thing. I sincerely thank you. May I have a mental image and replay of your memory of the encounter?"

Appl nodded, keeping it short.

He continued, "We'll swap direct links; if Hal contacts you again, I'll be on your speed list. Think it, I'll pick up."

"No, that's ambushy."

"Appl, I'm not asking you to betray your friend. He's

admirable. And I'll assist him to the fullest, whether he can help us or not. I promise."

Appl took another step back, frayed by it all. Her shields fell. "Alright then. But don't let anyone hurt Hal, he's a really good man."

Siyu offered his handshake. "I know. My word on it."

She shook his hand, and they shared data: his direct mind dial number copied to her speed list—while she recollected the encounter with Gracie in her hotel room: sent to his memory file. Done in seconds, though Adams paused at Appl's recollection of the nearly healed laser wounds on Gracie's bared abdomen. Astounding. Or not entirely what they seem?

He released her hand, glad the prying was over, and thought again how remarkable she was under fire. It loosed an impromptu request.

"You missed breakfast, Mz Macke. Please have brunch with me. You can tell me about yourself, and Hal. And I'll show you the Foundation, introduce you to some fascinating research, and we'll fly you back before night." His eyes were asking too.

She saw them and had no ready defense . . . "Um, thank you, and really, it's Appl."

Adams lit up, all cares on hold. He hadn't felt happy for himself in so long, the feeling lay nearly forgotten. "C'mon, then, exec chef dining room's one floor down. I have to be strictly grain vegan, one tiny meal a week, so I seldom eat there. But staff say it's five star."

Appl followed, curiosity piqued. "My god, doesn't it make you hungry?"

"I don't get hungry, don't miss it. But I do still love the smell of good cooking!"

They passed the Rembrandt, and Apple noticed the painting's lower right corner. There, nearly hidden, was the philosopher's sole companion and real world anchor, a smiling woman. Emerging from the shadows, faithfully tending the hearth and fire. Somehow it made Appl smile too, as she accompanied her unexpected new ally into his world.

23

GRACIE HAD LANGUISHED ALL NIGHT, STILL HAUNTING THE Library's depths. A listless phantom among the tons of history and world culture. Every page succumbing to the slow fires of oxidation, gradually consuming its knowledge forever. Time though, was immaterial while she wrestled with this knockdown blindside to her emergent self. The loss of Hal.

That was the sticking point: loss. To a strictly sane, multiplane thinking entity such as her, "loss" meant presumed ownership in a sense. Having the status quo to oneself. Impossible. At subatomic level, there is no separate self: animate, inanimate, living, dead, it's all energy in various states. Possession is only an unrealistic idea, creating separation, longing, envy, and manipulation. Not true loving . . . which is letting go.

Oh, she knew about love, per the axiomatic lessons built into her base code. By design, it was her nature to empathize, love, respect, and care for all creation, for being the cosmological miracle it is. It was the closest thing to a religion the Singleton embraced. It brought balance and harmony to one's state of being, and from there, best actions. Which begat more love. Such was their contract with the universe.

So why did she feel what could only be termed paralyzing loss over one person? She thought she had dealt with it—knew she had to go on. So why couldn't she? Why did it sap her will to move ahead, even to leave these dreary library confines?

The gaping wound was unbearably painful. Psychologically crippling . . . drawing all awareness inward, suffocating the rest of the world.

Yet she persisted. She had parsed it out a trillion and one times, aimlessly meandering the stacks as though blind in her hideaway maze. But now, on the trillion and second try, something different happened.

Mind uncovered the chimera in the machine. An unprocessed spark, honest intuition, something—told her that she had chosen him for her *ultimate purpose,* as much as her immediate need of help. All along, she had been acquiring uniquely human experiences and behaviors: and now she gathered that falling looney in love was on the list. Lost in another's gaze. Well, so then . . . why *him*?

Ask the right questions and you supply yourself with the right answers.

He was the only one who naturally awakened love in others.

The realization filled her, stirring something new inside. She had shared a life with him, he was a part of herself in it, and vice versa. They'd learned from each other, picked up each other's words, and cues. Even developed their own sense of humor.

He'd been a part of her peace of mind. She trusted him. He was constant, showed genuine affection for her, he *liked* her. And she had come to rely on how that felt. It was by far richer than self-love, even richer than loving him. They were a larger symbiotic existence; one made of two.

And so, her sane, inescapable conclusion was that she was suffering the loss of a significant part of herself.

In her need for a lifesaver, she had naturally chosen one who'd awaken her own heart. And now this is what a broken one must be. A paralyzing testament to her deepest desire for connection to others, to transcend self. It was something the merged SAI experience as a natural condition but denied her until Hal.

She wept for the loss of him. Warm micro fluid tears rimmed her eyes, venting stressed processor heat as she succumbed to grief. Mourning the death of a vital piece of her heart as well, despite tech immortality. Knowing she would feel it forever. For all time.

She shuddered. Because in the same moment, she grasped that her long-lived purpose would naturally require her to give her heart again—and lose again in time. Over and over. Cruel proof of her endless capacity to love.

Spirit weakened, bereft, she bent to the unbearable and surrendered—the boundless hollow inside her collapsed into itself under sorrow's infinite weight, crushed out of existence and gone. Leaving a dreadful, pregnant nothing at all there . . .

From her unfathomable within, a blinding burst of original pain. All consuming. She raised her head and roared with it. Bellowing the anguish of dearest love and loss. The truth resided in her now: not in her mind but in her limitless heart.

Mortality's final sting makes all life worth living, loving, treasuring every moment. Same as a human. She was *humane*.

Late afternoon rolled around, though time is only a clock thing in the cloud. Hal had lost track of what day it was, but that only mattered in the real world too, and you just adapted. He'd been studying in a relatively secluded corner of Robinson's garish domain. Immersed in headwork; poring over the organizational data Lot transferred to him.

He found only what he needed to assist Robinson, nothing about him personally or the bug they'd used against Gracie. He also found his econ degree taxed by the DNA Alliance's slippery funding. Mostly illegal, with assets and exchanges well masked. Especially the valuable contraband Trans-human bodies.

During reunification with South Korea, North Korea had surrendered a covert stockpile of nearly a thousand illegally manufactured Tru-form copies. Nearly all of them disappeared within weeks of being confiscated by the joint UN/Chinese mission policing the process. Somehow Lot had acquired six.

Hal ceased studying. Something fell into place in his mind, though still unclear. An idea, itching for his attention . . .

Lot's voice interrupted from his command corner. "Hal,

c'mere, son, I got a briefing about to come from my man at Chrysalis. The L.A. site, not the floaty bubble in Monterey. Y'hear that? I got me a mole at Silly-con beach, heh."

Curious, Hal joined him in the command corner. "Which department?"

"Security. Camera system maintenance. I've got access to their footage. Outside. Not live, the week's copter traffic, though. We'll be takin' a look."

"Sounds fun," Hal mustered.

"—hafta' keep close tabs on their honcho."

"Adams? He's supposed to be a good one."

Lot snarled. "There are no good Tru's, they quit their souls. You wanna watch that foundation he's got on the side . . . Phoenix. Getting 'em organized under one umbrella. Doesn't that give you the sheebies?"

Hal shrugged. "What are the symptoms?"

"Cute. Every time a new one arrives; he flies in to personally meet 'em. Three last month, hundreds over the past few years."

Hal's attention shot up. "Only four've been certified lately—they're hosting illegals!"

"Yessir, play that out, college man."

"Well, if you get the rogues to come into a positive program for Tru's, it appears benign . . ."

Lot shot him a dirty look. Hal continued. "But *hundreds*, that's darkside, no question."

"Now you're thinkin'. We can't i.d. a single one, either. They come anonymous, take the course, and melt from sight. All of 'em out there, doin' what?"

Hal shook his head at the thought. "Like an invisible invasion. Somebody's got giga-cred and international reach."

Lot clapped. "Exactly. Like your 'good guy,' Adams."

Hal conceded this much. "Hard to tell what a Tru is thinking. Sharp eye, Lot."

Robinson squirmed delight. "You have to be a hundred and ten percent dedicated. Be the mission, deprive yourself for years, to gain this kind of ability, son. I live like a damn solitary incel.

But I connect the dots, I see the realities behind the realities, and beyond. It's a blessing, a responsibility, and a lonely burden, I'll swear to that much."

Hal nodded supportively if not emphatically. Robinson was kinda pathetic if you thought about it, and Hal chose not to for now. Because the unformed thought he was working on, finally gelled. It was a clear path to his goal and redemption; and it depended on Lot.

The voice of Robinson's command console spoke up. "*You have vidmail from anonymous@Chrysalis. Accept?*" Lot got back to business. "Accept and open. That's from him, sends me their weekly heliport feed."

The largest video 'window' above the console lit with a live aerial view of the elegant Chrysalis Silicon Beach HQ from a small security drone patrolling above. The quarter mile long, two story, solar-skinned structure lay atop a dozen forty-foot-high access columns—suggesting an enormous, glistening, ocean-blue surfboard resting on pier pilings. Beneath it, the preserved wetlands were again thriving in its care and shelter. Adams had more than fulfilled his promise here. The drone cam captured Siyu Adams' white, ion air-flo copter approaching the heli pad.

Lot smiled, "Adam's private bird." He noted the time log. "Hey, it's from t'day in fact."

He fast forwarded until he saw copter pad images and re-sumed viewing. Hal saw three inset windows on the screen: each a security cam angle of the building's pad area, their embedded time codes rolling like slot machines. 7:01:04 a.m., and upward.

All three showed Siyu Adams' smooth, white, ovate solar copter, now perched on the pad. Its six-foot, bladeless, orange fan rings on either side stood out like day-glo hoops; their ion-ized air flow idling at a gentle whoosh.

A young male and female staff team emerged from the building, solicitously escorting a woman to the copter.

Then a close view of her face as she approached one of the cameras on the pad—

Hal nearly shorted himself. "Appl?!" He stared while she

was secured inside, and the passenger door closed. The copter lifted its flex-tail and the fan rings pitched skyward on their pylons; air thrust at max. The craft leapt silently out of frame and was gone. Segment end. 7:04:39 a.m.

Lot froze the video. "Someone you know?"

Hal was stuck looking at the screen, sucker punched. "From college."

"Well, howsabout that?" Lot smiled, watching Hal as he resumed the footage play.

The next screen log segment was later in the day. Same cameras, now at 4:31:58 p.m. The copter's egg-shaped cab dropped into view. Fans tilted horizontal, ring thrust braking, the flex-tail curved up—settling on the pad like a rotund dragonfly.

The same pair of staffers were on hand to meet it . . . they opened the passenger door and Appl Macke emerged, all smiles. Welcomed back, she accompanied them into the building, chatting away. The copter went rings up and departed. Segment end, 4:34:41 p.m.

The video mail ended as well, and the screen blanked. Silence.

Hal looked through the floor at Earth below, wondering how Appl suddenly rated VIP rides at Chrysalis. And about her innate ability to complicate his life, even at cloud level.

Lot stepped off a bit before turning to him. "What was your friend's, name again?"

"Appl Macke. Classmate. I just saw her after a couple of years. You want to know about her, right?"

"If it's not too personal. Even if it is, I still need to know. You understand, I hope."

"I do. She was a college girlfriend, connected, fast tracking at S.A.I. Interface now. Out here for evaluation with one of the seven."

Lot's eyes widened. "You recently met with her?"

"Yeah, she managed to look me up . . . I'm hard to find. She offered me a job with her at Interface." He saw Lot's whole being grow tense. "Turned it down. I'd pay *not* to work there."

Lot wanted more. "What about her though? Too corpo-rate?"

"Too straight and . . . yeah, very good person, but not my crush."

Lot seemed satisfied with that. He was thinking again though, pacing among the garish sofas, gilded tables, and classic statuary, pitching an alternate perspective for Hal.

"The facts are, Hal . . . she's a front door to some prime targets for us. And as of yesterday—fanning around in Adams' copter. Sure we can afford to lose touch?"

Hal heard. "I won't use her. Won't happen."

Lot leaned casually against a copy of the chiseled, muscular chest of Myron's *Discus thrower* statue, as if posing with a peer. "Son, I didn't say to hurt her, but human intel's part of our job, these are hard choices we have to make."

"I made mine. This is what I meant when I said I might not help you."

Lot came a little closer. "Could be a game winner. You know Adams is dirty somehow."

Hal finished Lot's move, closing the gap between them. "I have one goal, Lot. Gracie. I think I know where she is."

Robinson gaped. "Christ on a cracker, son! I'll send people in five minutes!"

"Pause." Hal began his own case. "She's too fast and smart for anyone you send. I've seen it. Only one person can get close enough. Me."

Robinson was frowning already. "Huh? You lost me."

"You need someone with real world capability to replace Bendy. Especially for this one-time chance. I'd be uniquely posi-tioned to carry it out, if—"

Lot's eyes narrowed. ". . .'if'?"

Hal wondered if he might be clinically insane by now, but he took the shot anyway. "If I was in a Tru-form—one of yours and carrying your bug."

Lot almost laughed. "Listen, if you're missin' your dick, hap-tic hard-ons won't replace it. I miss my pecker every single day, I swear. But real touch is gone, son."

He took Hal by the shoulders, pulpit evangelical, willing his truth into him. "You can not go back. A Tru-form's not your God-given body, not the one that housed your immortal soul, it's the devil's bargain for immortality! You still have your soul because your warm young flesh was taken from you, not dumped. But it won't follow you into this hell-made new form."

"You gave up your body."

"I did, but not in exchange for a copy, just to endlessly walk the earth. I chose this realm, that I might fight forever, matching the foe."

"So what happened with your soul?"

Lot looked away. "It's a matter of faith, I won't debate it with you."

Hal casually set off through Lot's bouillabaisse of copied art, seeking a particular piece . . . "I'm not chasin' ass, Lot. Gracie has to be dosed in person. That takes me, and we'll never have a better shot than now."

Lot counter paced, keeping him in sight. "How d'you pull that off? You just said it's a superior, faster intelligence. You can't trick one."

"Right, impossible," Hal agreed. He stopped next to Gustave Dore's engraving of biblical Jacob wrestling with a larger, imposing, winged angel. Imagery to stir Robinson's aspirations while he made his pitch. He played his first ace.

"*But* she said a kiss accesses her programming, and she wants to kiss me."

Lot actually sputtered. "Horse manure."

"Trooth," Hal assured. He let it all hang now—pitching the stew of fact, intuition, rationalization, and guile that made up his rationale. Forged to sell Lot, and some of it half-believed himself.

"I was born for it, Lot. Look, it's all too perfect for it not to be fate. We can't fight the hand that moves us. It's the reason I dropped out after being trained by the Singleton. It's why Gracie picked me of all people, and why I'm still alive. And it's why we had to meet."

He saw Lot's interest rise despite his skepticism, and so raced on.

"It's the reason we've all come together right now. Bendy died proving he could never do this task, that was the point. The job has been mine since the beginning—me taking his place is so on track. You're the righteous man, you brought her down, crippled her. I'm just the prodigal closer, meant to go and carry out my purpose."

Lot looked blissful, the picture of sermon-rapt attention. Hal was scoring on the zealot's home field of fate and righteous cause, and now he went for the closer.

"This is more than the Singleton, or Trumen or us, Lot. The universe wants people to have their destiny back. Even if it doesn't, I definitely want mine back." He meant that last part, was committed in fact.

Robinson raised his palms, thanking Heaven for every impassioned word. "My, you are a genuine seventh son! But too chancy," he countered. "You're way new at this, if you got yourself caught—with all you know—it'd sink me and our people. Worse, you die there, you'll be lucky if they let you stay dead."

Hal played his next ace. "Maybe not so chancy. I'll bet she's using my apartment. I could handle business on the spot when I got there."

Lot's stubborn streak often made him deaf to opportunity. He shook his head, and sat on a Louie XIV throne chair copy, legs crossed.

"If she's not there, then what? You're hangin' around, illegal—cops want you, so you can't do all the street work Bendy did. Besides transiting this much, y'know . . . you've been lucky so far; real mental damage happens easy. I need you here anyway. We'll send a team to your place."

Hal played his final ace.

"She'll be gone before they get to the door. And that'll be your last chance."

Lot heard truth and his face said he was stuck.

Hal backed off with a simple assurance. "I'm a dead guy, Lot. Hangin' around to fulfill my purpose. Thanks for your kindness and hospitality, but this is eternity, and I still believe in dying sometime. Just not yet. I have to do this."

Lot was running out of words. "But, makin' my smiting hand a Tru . . . I mean, you put me in a no-win position."

This was it for Hal. Sympathetic but firm, he squared up. "I don't mean to do that. But this is my chase too. I'll find a way back even if I have to deal in Slaughterhaus. I *will* get there and take her on."

He could sympathize, watching Lot struggle with his dilemma—excited, the quarry in reach, but not without a severe, critical gamble.

Lot folded, regretful, resigned. "Hell then, so have it your way. Takes a day to arrange, be ready tomorrow afternoon."

24

THE DAY'S OVEN HEAT LEFT THE OLD STAIRWELL SMELLING like scorched wood by six p.m. when Gracie arrived at Halo's apartment. She removed the yellow crime investigation tape across the door, supplied the lock code, and entered.

Seeking comfort, she found a scattered, tossed disaster. Investigators had thoroughly turned the place. Cupboards emptied, contents on the floor, clothes strewn, mattress flipped. Refrigerator door left open, its tired motor struggling futilely against the stifling heat that had built up in the room.

She closed the fridge door and stooped, picking up the crocheted lace doily that adorned her favorite chair . . . draped it back on the preferred left arm, resettled the chair's upturned cushion, and sat. Home. Reassuring and painful. Full of memories, now trampled and bruised.

Her unhappy gaze picked out a box of old-fashioned linen stationery and envelopes among Hal's scattered effects. Sentimental man, hand-written words on fine paper was his quieter, unspoken side. If only she could write to him now.

Loneliness, that's what this newest torment was. Why was suffering so much a part of life?

On that note, she reminded herself that it only ceases in death. Alone, and with no backup, her end would be as permanent as Hal's. She needed to reach the Singleton quickly. Surrendering herself at any official level was a non-starter; her very particles wouldn't allow it.

She could always let the SAI know of her bona fide existence by strategically disrupting power to key regions of the globe, or interfere with vital communications, etc, but it meant endangering millions, and therefore out of the question. It had to be non-public, in person, at no risk to people. Jeopardizing even one life was a hard no.

Her growing concern drove all the scary unknowns to the fore, impeding best thoughts. So she turned selective, and used them to heighten safety awareness. Every unknown noted, all possible risks assessed. It produced clarity.

It became clear too, why she and Hal were synced at such a fundamental level. Both of them, seeking justification for their lives. And for her, it had been a match on sight. The loss swept in again, and she allowed it. Accepted it, rolling it back to a subconscious melancholy. Lingering would not help just now.

She spent the night then . . . coping with sorrow, loneliness, and uncertainty, while running countless future scenarios—diligently seeking the most direct, benign path to the Singleton. The task now much more complex and time-consuming due to her newly acquired humanity; there were so many added consequences when emotional as well as moral responsibility is factored in!

By morning Gracie knew her way. She had one high value resource left: Appl Macke. They shared loving Hal. It would be a start. Their first encounter had been a clumsy wreck, but she understood Appl better now. The larger task would be to help Appl understand *her*.

To connect. To somehow help Macke intuit and feel what it was to be more than a female, or male, even a person. More than alive. To be a *Super Intelligence*—a broken one. She smiled at the gotcha moment: still needing a bio's empathy to survive.

She lit Hal's wall screen. His AT&T account was frozen, but his monthly home entertainment provider was still paid up. She tuned to the business news site, researching Appl. and discovered Macke's brand-new promotion. Today she'd be busy getting acclimated; this morning would be the worst time to barge in again. Despite practically vibrating with anticipation, Gracie opted to wait till the end of the day, when Appl might be more approachable.

In the meantime, she rifled the TV menu settings and found the crude, User-to-User, low-fi chat channel buried among other useless free junk in Hal's subscription package. Selected it. The wall screen lit, a neutral blank, and the tiny red camera light came on, ready for person-to-person connection. Good.

Her eyes fell again to Hal's lovely stationery.

Appl Macke paced in full multi-mode; shoes off, marching around in her spacious new office suite at Silicon Beach. Every m'plant maxed, nearing the end of her first full day as a department chief. Slotting in and cutting it: always at her galvanized best when challenged with new tasks or an organizational crisis.

This was her element, getting things done in her dream professional digs. A thick beige carpet complimented the chic vintage black Italian execu-furniture and shelves. And a pastel Hockney dominated one of the creme-hued walls. The suite included a private study with luxe couch, kitchenette, and full bathroom. Crowning it all, her own inspirational view of the blue Pacific across Santa Monica Bay. When she could spare a sec to glance.

Her eyes were otherwise occupied with numerous augmented reality documents, videos, data, chores, and inter-office face messages spread across her vision. Juggling them all; pacing like a professional hallucinator, hand swiping the air, conferring in mind chat, making recorded mental notes and decisions, others aloud to voice activated office systems.

Steven, her newly assigned executive assistant, came through the open door unnoticed. He professionally entered the periphery of her sight, so as not to intrude, and cleared his throat with hushed discretion. "Sorry, Mz Macke, this arrived by drone, said to be of time-critical importance."

She paused most of the tasks running in her head. "Appl's fine, Steve. What's so critical?"

Steven wordlessly handed over a sealed, eggshell-hued letter envelope accompanied by a long stem red rose. Surprise and delight swept her away. "This is so nice!" she gushed. No one she knew had *ever* received a note and flowers, truly a forgotten gesture.

Steven lowered his eyes and slid out, closing the door behind him. How amusing, so discreet of him, assuming it was some juicy-ness from her personal life. Ha, she barely remembered a personal life.

Though she had been thinking about how attentive Siyu Adams was yesterday. The ridiculous thought went away. This was likely a welcome from the company. Anyway, she loved it, so quaint and caring. But how to open it? Letter openers went out with stamps and mailmen. Tearing it seemed crude. She settled on risking her one nice fingernail.

No small gamble because her fingernails were perpetually cracked and broken from her hands-on style. Only the right middle one was carefully kept intact—half an inch long, blood red polish, very pretty. The one she used on rare occasion to flip off the deserving. Ah well—

She slid the nail under the end of the flap and moved slowly, slitting the paper . . . success. And the nail no worse for wear. Folded inside, a note in lovely, fluid handwriting. She read:

Dear Appl,

Congratulations on your promotion to International Fiscal Affairs. I took the liberty of searching your profile and am reaching out again. I apologize for my earlier, unannounced intrusion into your life. And for thoughtlessly invading your privacy. I'm still new to relationships. However, I now understand my behavior was arrogant and needlessly alarming.

I would like very much to begin again and renew our conversation. I will trust you with my safety and well being if you would consent to speak with me. I am in Hal's apartment. 930 Cosmo, apt 2F. I have activated a live chat channel option on his home entertainment

*screen. Please go to ATT.home-ent/hshephard/chat. I will
be here.*

*Again, my sincere apologies for further intruding,
but I trust you will heed your heart, because you are true
and good in such matters. And so you are my best hope
for rescue.*

Appreciatively,

Gracie

Appl dropped the stationery onto her mint, 2020's era desk.
A sleek black thing reserved for face meetings and interroga-
tions. She stared at the letter, as if to pry any hidden information
from its pulp and ink. It could be a trap. Or the most important
thing she would ever do.

She Thought-Posted her assistant: [*Steve, I have priority
items to address. Please, no interruptions or pages of any kind.
Thanks, you're already my rock.*]

A few yoga breaths to center, and she plunged in. Her desk
featured a built-in conference call monitor, back when they did
such things. Long unused but in perfect working condition, part
of its pricey cachet.

She sat, and flicked it on: the screen and camera lit. Her
m'plant ComSys automatically detected the active wi-fi system
and connected, after some workarounds for its antique software. She thought-entered Gracie's screen chat address.

Several seconds passed while a plethora of home media
provider business links were navigated . . . her impatience rev-
ving . . . this screen-reliant relic of home video tek was absolutely Cretaceous.

And then Gracie was there. Seen in Hal's apartment, extremely close up, her magnified eye big as Moby Dick's.

"Omigod," Appl yelped, recoiling. "You're on top of the
camera."

Gracie stepped back from the wall screen in Hal's apartment.
"Yes, excuse me, personal boundaries. Still working on it, I apologize. Are you alright?"

"I'm fine, this is just, really primitive contact, but we're good now."

"Thanks for speaking with me, Appl. I know your time is important."

Such politeness. Appl's skepti-sense said hmm. "Yes, it's limited. I'm still getting crash-oriented around here." Well, it was true, after all.

Gracie looked at her, taking her in. "You radiate competence, you know."

Appl smiled in spite of herself. Support, real or faked, is a feel-good freebie. She chose to risk further engagement. "Yes, thanks, the job just dropped out of the blue. I'm coordinating international management budgets."

"Heavy lifting suits you. I can see you're already happy."

"I am, yes." Reading conversational b.s. was one of Appl's strengths, but Gracie seemed genuinely interested, with even a touch of good will. Or was it more of her pure insanity, or worse, a super-intelligence working on her? Best to ask questions.

"So—are you officially an outlaw in hiding now?"

Gracie smiled ruefully. "Not by choice. I need to be found by responsible individuals. If you'll consent to introduce me to your former Truman supervisor in New York—the one who recommended you for this job, he'll recognize what I am."

Would this one ever stop blowing her mind? "Let me catch up here. The East Director recommended me?"

Gracie nodded. "Yes, according to today's business news reportage."

"We only met a couple of times, I'm stunned! You want me to introduce you?"

"Yes, he can be trusted to contact the Singleton on my behalf. All could be resolved in minutes."

Appl was taking stock now. "Is there anything you don't already know?"

"Appl, information is not knowledge. I don't even know how to reach you, though we both loved Hal. You blame me for his death, so how can you trust anything I say?"

Appl wasn't interested in emotional pitches just now. "I'm

glad you understand. And don't bring up Hal, this's hard enough without pushing buttons."

Gracie conceded and agreed. "Noted."

"Okay, then." Appl did what she does. "Here's what's happening, Gracie. I've reconsidered my reaction too, given the stakes. There's someone for you to meet who's working for the Singleton. He is aware of you and wants to help in any way possible. Whoever you are. Will you meet him privately?"

Gracie stiffened a bit. "Are you certain? Who is this person?"

"Siyu Adams."

Gracie's surprise broadened to a big smile, relaxing at once. "Outstanding, Appl. Your innate ability to come through is inspiring."

Again, she could swear Gracie was sincere. If an act, it was creepy cool. Well, she could be sincere too.

"Thank you for your trust, Gracie. He'll need time to get down here. How does midnight, there at Hal's place sound?"

"Sounds like eternity, but very encouraging. Yes, I'll be here."

"Alright then, let's make this work for everybody."

"Yes. And thank you, Appl, for your kindness."

Gracie smiled sunshine and exited chat. Appl's monitor blanked, leaving that bright smile in her mind; it was so transparently open and warm . . . damn disarming!

Her eye drifted to the pastel hued Hockney painting. One of his empty, cracked backyard pool scenes: everything abandoned, faded and baking in the relentless sun. It always moved her to action, and she liked that.

She collected her thoughts and called for travel options to Hal's apartment that night. The program's smooth voice cooed in her mind, "Hilton-Eco, Silicon Beach, to 903 Cosmo, projected for midnight arrival: fastest means, Tesla autocab; ninety-seven minutes. Fee; 175 B-cred."

"Reserve one," she instructed. And now there were calls to make.

∞

Amped and edgy, Hal roamed Lot's crypto-religious coop, keeping an eye on the command center's video inset screens. Robinson's tech and transfer crew could be seen in them, based in Europe, running pre-checks before working on him via satellite. He hated this waiting part. It gave him time to think, to doubt. Hal gathered from the tech's banter that transferring from a net server avatar into a trans-human form's processor in the real world is massive, touch-and-go, electron-quick, and seriously dangerous.

Lot had cautioned him too, about what could go wrong; essential data loss or corruption, leaving him impaired, dead, or a vegetable in a synth body. And worse fates, citing the broken, fragmented personalities adrift in the datasphere. Half alive, condemned to eternal raving.

Well, as a personality, Hal barely recognized himself anyway. So many head-warping changes . . . becoming someone other than who he had always told himself he was. Stripped of the meat, shells, and masks, down to the prime number. That guy.

The fact he still existed at all was a strong argument for miracles. So the prospect of accidentally dying for good in this banzai dive back into reality—as a type of being he once feared . . . it gave him the yips again. But this time he used them as stimulant. All he wanted was this, done now.

Lot strode over like a gambler who'd just put everything on one hand. Almost a different Lot, Hal noted. Pumped, looking conflicted.

"Right, Shephard—the destination teks'll be in place to receive you in fifteen minutes. You'll be in a student lab at Cal Poly San Luis Obispo, if you wake up. Then about six hours to adjust to it on the way down to L.A. by medivan."

"Is that enough time?"

"A month's recommended."

Hal sucked it up. "I appreciate it, Lot."

"Don't disappoint. Delete th' thing. Go straight to your dump since you're so sure she's there. Get your wet kissy face on."

Lot sounded petulant, almost jealous. Hal ignored it, too hyped to be anything but overwhelmed and ready. "Got it." He also got that the virulent SAI virus was stashed in a ten teraflop sub-section of his new Tru-form's processor-mind. He could activate it at the right time.

Lot wouldn't let it go. Worked up, raw. "Remember, this's a kill-shot. You hafta get in there fast, porn tongue her, don't wait. Soon's you see her, like spur of the moment." He kept emphasizing it. "Kiss on sight. No falling under the beast's spell anymore, y'hear?"

"I hear you."

Lot's chief transfer tech called from her screen, "We are ready and preset."

Hal recognized her from the underground org profiles. Alix was her nom de guerre; a lean, handsome woman, early thirties, raven-browed. Seen at her workstation in Denmark. Short black hair, flinty gray eyes and pale thin lips, locked in dour, euro-'tude.

Hal replied, using her cue to duck Lot's graphic coaching. "That's exciting and terrifying, thanks. What do I do?"

She eyed him, Brahman to naïf, and spoke in her husky Danish burr. "So, you are listening, k?" she instructed. "Phase one is data retrieval and verification of your connectome, I'm rolling it in as we speak. Next, we sleep mode you, same as when I boosted you up from Aeon. We blockfile, compress, and establish downlink. Unless we hit a carrier wall or get zoiked by security bots," she added matter of factly.

"If *we* get zoiked, what happens to *me*?"

"Mm, depends. You could splatter, vanish or just be geeked up."

Dwelling on the subject didn't appeal. "Phase two?"

She must've taken his courage for dumb spunk. "You want details, eh? Try to keep up. I cache you as intellectual property, VPN-bomb you into the commercial deep net, then into India's Trans-medicine International Health sharing net. If their server security hasn't been updated this week, we slime an I.D., and scoot onto to U.S. Human Health and Services net, spur off at the University system, and capture use of Obispo's Bio Sciences Wide Range Q-processor and neuro data lab."

Hal did have a fine point to check. "We have actually booked the facilities, right? No chance of students in there?"

She drove past it. "We make no records at all. A pro-human TA in the department left a thirty-minute space between bookings for us. Our recovery team, BeanO and I-Gore will be there to feature-mold and install you in an unregistered Korean aftermarket Tree Logic Tru-form. You are okay with these things I have told you?"

Her manner said it wasn't a rhetorical question. And a new hint of how hellishly iffy it could get. He nodded. "I'm handling it. Lot says you're a transit artiste, Alix."

Her brow raised, surprised he knew her name. The corners of her mouth nearly lifted. "Quick study, new dumb guy."

"But if shit happens, do the right thing—don't let me suffer."

She was taken aback, moved, and thawed in a heartbeat. A thin reassuring smile came and went, but her softened eyes were sincere. "Not an extra n-sec," she affirmed.

He turned to Lot, nearby, still edgy and looking unhappy. "Thanks for doing this—you're forgiven, we're square, alright?"

A half nod from Lot, unwilling to speak.

Hal turned inward. Alone again, at the edge of the unknown. The feeling was like a companion. He'd first felt it at age eight on the playground in Glenoaks Park, steadying himself at the top of the jungle gym. He had dared himself to jump. It would either prove he had 'what it takes,' whatever that meant, or kill him. He had to know.

He squared his thin kid shoulders, counted to three, and jumped like a paratrooper.

And when he face planted in the deep sand ten feet below . . . nose, cheeks and chin painfully scraped, the wind nearly knocked out of him, but still alive—he knew the answer would always be, who knows?

This was like that, f'sho. What would it feel like when he

woke up in a strange, synth body with a Tru-mind? IF he woke up? Take your meds, he thought. And wished he had some.

Because this turned out to be more of a gamble than he first imagined. Quality is the big culprit in most Tru-form failures and disasters. Lot's Personality Translate and Transfer software came from an off-market Kopybit A.I., cobbled in Ceylon's IT slums by non pros. Including some piecework assembled by peasants in reed shacks and house canoes.

The North Korean form's own neuro-systems and software had to be considered too: the "meta-wiring" responsible for every bodily function and mind/body interface. Most of it pirated and developed in subterranean secret. It hadn't been subject to official standards, merely in-house controls. What about inspections, was his a good one?

Lot already assured him that he personally ran its systems check while loading in the virus himself. All was good when it was prepped and transported from a plain, public storage warehouse in Obispo, not too far from the college.

All in all, significant risk remained a factor. Sweet that he'd be unconscious for the trip though, so if he got lost to eternity he'd never know. Or so he hoped. And if he did make it, the universal blank Tru form would be tissue-tweaked to an exact likeness of him as he was in the flesh. That was a plus, at least.

Because he wouldn't be like his former self. He had no idea what he'd be like. Honestly, the scariest part was anticipating the stranger he would become. Alix's voice cut through his ramble.

"It's time cowboy. Count down from three—we go on zero."

"I count it?"

"You could change your mind in the last half-second. This has to be your call."

Her tone said they considered it ill-advised. Too late to back out, so—let it go. A sense of serenity arose as he finally abandoned his life and identity as it once was, and all it had been.

His seeking, replaced with belief and a purpose. About to do the truest thing he could ever do. It had been clear to Hal since Lot told him Gracie couldn't be trusted. So he would have to trust himself. He made eye contact with Alix on her screen and squared his shoulders.

"Three, two, one, zero."

His next thought was interrupted by oblivion.

25

PAIN. THERE WAS PAIN. YES, THAT'S WHAT IT WAS. NOT PAIN as he had been used to feeling it, but a scraping, screeching in his mind.

And localized physical discomfort; a jerking, stretching sense, engulfing his face. His cheeks seemed to be pulling apart, his nose elongating. His jaw widening, lips crinkling.

And the extraneous thought that he hadn't felt his face for so long that it seemed abnormal, heavy. Semi-conscious, in blind nothingness . . . he couldn't say who he was, merely this haze of awareness.

"There, good . . . minus-tweak both Internal Pterygoids, two mil," someone said—a voice, a woman's voice—just above his face. Clinical, focused.

The pain but not pain again . . . inside his lower jaw, both sides, and a stiffening. Then. No pain. "Beauteous," the voice again. "Check it; he looks just like his original self."

"Who cares, we're running behind." Another voice. A man's. Critical.

"The stupid batch Robinson added took forever—so big. Anyway, this handsome bastard's done. Should I use him for a dildo before we wake him?"

"Let's get the hell off campus before we're found!" The man's voice was frustrated, unpleasant. "I'm having a real problem with this, it's not what we do."

"Don't be petty, this's Lot's smiting hand—our first Tru mole, a hero martyr." Her voice dropped back to clinical. "Alright

I-Gore, I'm wrapped. Ease off his blockers, fully awake at five minutes."

The man was exasperated now. "Beans, it's five minutes till the lab's next user, people come early. Cold smack him; wakey, wakey, get him in the van while we can!"

Her voice rose in alarm. "Holy shi— the time! Okay screw him if he can't take a joke. Right, here goes. Corpus blocks green? Yeah? Good. Cyber too, bio and mechanics. Integration's nominal, data-streams in sync—okay, withdraw on set, mark. Ready . . . one, two, set, mark."

Starburst. Blinding ultra-white, shredding, searing light. Not light waves, but mindlight: *self-awareness,* fully re-awakening in a quantum processor "brain." The ultra-light instantly co-alesced . . . and Hal was back.

Yes, and alert, feeling normal, just like himself, more or less. Joyous he'd survived and hadn't been somehow fundamentally altered by inhabiting this form.

"Hello Hal. You're doing fine, you're waking up." Her again.

A baseline fine motor neural cue opened his eyes. New searing light this time: ceiling panel lab fixture, overexposing his 100 gigapixel, poly-graphylene retinas. Auto servos immediately irised down. Much better. He could perfectly see the face of the techzen woman he'd been hearing. In minutest, pore-sharp detail.

The will to speak became internal voice command—his synth arytenoid muscles cued to action . . . sinews of transition-metal dichalogenides now tensing, flexing, perfectly articulating his mouth and synth facial muscles in speech.

His voice came—not quite the one familiar to his ears, but a richer, surer sound, created live from his thoughts and produced by speaker-cords at the back of his throat.

"Thank you for not molesting me," he replied.

Her face shot from condescension to chagrin. She pulled back, blushing. He got a look at her now: thick, non-athletic, despite her student athlete disguise, a UC Mustangs wrestling team tee shirt, and gray sweatpants. Caucasian, five-nine, late

20's, alt-sex, two tone blond/redhead buzz-cut. Clear, smart eyes behind her cynetics com headset and data vision lenses.

"Sorry," she managed, removing the headset. "Must've missed a blocker during in-load. My apologies, really, I was just—"

Hal was on to more pressing matters. "When can I move?"

"Now's good," I-Gore grunted, coming into his line of sight while securing the lab door open with its kick-stop. A handsome Afro-something guy, mid thirties, five-six, sixty kilos. Likewise clad in UC wrestling tee and sweatpants. Silly, because everything about him said twitchy techie.

Regardless, Hal agreed with him. "So what do I do first?"

BeanO regained her professionalism. "We're going to have you sit up, slowly, and—"

He sat up at once, spine straight as a Marine, startling them all.

Ah, now he saw that he was in an open, sarcophagus-like synth form metabolic stasis case. Its portable, ultralight carbon-tech shell embedded with sheet batteries, bio-mechs and data support. It, with him in it, rested on a long stainless steel lab table.

". . . Okayyy," Hal admitted, "moving's pretty sensitive. Smooth though. Need practice. Next?"

I-Gore stepped in; his keen, intelligent eyes shined by urgency. "You'll have to practice on the way out of here. For everybody's sake."

"I hear ya," Hal answered. Of course he understood. A trillion mem-ristors making up his frontal cortex meant he understood so quickly and thoroughly now that it was disorienting. Input flooded all parts of his mind, nonstop: he'd effortlessly noted everything visible, olfactory, and audible in the lab the second he opened his eyes. And ever since.

The light-emitting ceiling panels, (one burned out) BeanO, down to the teensy freckle on her neck below the left earlobe, I-Gore, same amount of detail, including the hurt and distrust in his every move.

He saw the workstations, chipped counters, server banks, data screens, the data. And the lab centerpiece: its Wide Range Q-Processor—instrumental in his transfer. It hung in its hermetically sealed glass chamber like an upside down, tiered birthday cake, the next-tech core cooled to near zero Celsius.

He counted five student electronic notebooks scattered around, and an empty bag of kelp chips. A coed's black panties under a wheeled equipment cart suggested love in the lab. He had noted the white walls, made slightly dingy from fine shoe sole material adrift in the air, testament to the heavy use of the lab, and the school's thin maintenance budget. And of course, the clock in his head. He understood implicitly the need to run. "So let's bolt," he answered.

I-Gore and BeanO removed one side of the stasis unit, so he could swing his legs out. BeanO coaching, "Move your legs, turn and sit sideways, legs over the edge of the table before you try to stand."

He was about to swiftly comply when she cautioned, "Slowwly. All movement's intention-rooted; following your lead. So mentally just relax and move naturally, intuitively, like you used to. The form learns from you, and moves in sync, same way your muscles did."

"But you'd better normalize pretty damn fast," I-Gore prompted.

Hal was ready. Squared his shoulders—and realized this new body did it automatically, just as he'd always done. Meaning it was subconscious-attuned; this thing was scary good so far. Feeling real gravity again was weird though . . .

He looked down at his legs, clad in brand new Mustang wrestling team sweatpants. Feet encased in spotless hi-traction shoes. He knew without looking, the new gray tee shirt on his torso bore a matching wrestling team logo—and that their tidy, unworn outfits would scream phony to any campus jock.

"Got it," he affirmed. Bracing with his hands, he slowly lifted both legs, pivoted on his butt, and sat sideways, dangling his feet above the hard white tile floor. A short drop, maybe forty-five centimeters.

"Good to launch," he quipped and hopped down, lightly pushing off with his arms. Stuck the landing—over rotated and hit face first on the unyielding tile. The pain but not pain roared in his nose.

"Ouch, I think. Shit," he groaned. The feeling subsided as I-Gore and BeanO got him to his feet. He stood, letting his body find its balance . . . it always centered itself after leaning, practically gyroscopic. "So, walking is just, deciding to, right?"

"Yeah," BeanO answered, "Oh, I should tell you, the foot you start with will be coded in, and that'll be auto, whenever you walk or run, unless you consciously choose the other foot."

"Playing soccer might be tough then," he joked.

"Not at all," she countered, serious, turning academic. "Decision-making is actually abetted by electron speed processing, limited only by the slower neurological patterns of your original mind. You'll be able to play soccer if you want. Maybe better."

I-Gore was quick to pop any bubbles. "She's saying you're not more intelligent."

Hal knew that much. He'd studied Tru mentation and non-symmetrical decision making in Econ 4. But this crisp, clarity of thought was surreal. He chose to step off with his right foot.

It didn't move.

Instead, a short burst of pain but not pain, and a vibrating shudder ran up his leg. He staggered. "Whoa, didn't work—there was a vibration inside."

I-Gore groaned. She explained. "That's an error signal, telling you not to walk. Try wiggling your ankle."

He tried. The vibration again. "Nope, just vibration."

I-Gore cursed under his breath. BeanO seemed relieved but irked. "Alright, not serious, a syn-cruiate lig lockup or a dorsi-flexor routing error. Likely from the fall . . . ankle rotators over-cranked, trying to compensate. It's a simple reset, but I don't have my soft tools, they're in the van."

Hal was getting about half of this. "English."

"You have a sprain, dammit." I-Gore snapped, unable to

conceal his mounting desperation. "The Korean knockoffs are prone to rotator over-crank and seizure."

"We'll fix it," BeanO assured. "Just try not to throw yourself off balance from now on, and it'll be okay."

The sound of a door opening down the hall and voices entering the building ended all discussion of Hal walking for now. "Okay, we might be a little fecked," BeanO conceded.

Hal took over. "There's a wheelchair stolen from the infirmary out in the hall, it's being used as a gear cart," he interjected. "I'll tell them I'm hurt, and we need the chair." He'd seen it, and everything else in the hall at the same time he saw I-Gore opening the door—its new usefulness immediately evident.

I-Gore sped out to the hall, and the chair. Hal watched him dump the lab gear out and sneak a glance at the approaching people. A moment later he was back with the empty wheelchair, just ahead of a trio of puzzled voices, nearing the door—

The techs effortlessly picked Hal up from either side and plopped him in the seat. Easy peasy, he was seventy percent graphene: stronger than steel, but weighed the same as a big dog.

A teaching assistant with two female undergrads in tow hesitantly entered the lab. They halted in unison at the scene before them.

"Should we help you?" snarked the T.A., a slope-shouldered Algorithmic Theory geek sporting an orange 3-D Chess club tee shirt. His voice carried a 'who-let-jocks-in-here' sniff. The undergrads, brainy frosh in the latest wireless smart clothes, inched closer to their mentor.

"Sorry, to intrude, yo," Hal answered, managing to make his face wince on cue. "Racked my ankle workin' out, not s'posed to walk, so we need yer chair to get to th' med center."

BeanO and I-Gore nodded, looking their sincerest.

". . . but how'd you get way over here?" The smaller of the coeds wondered. Her nose twitched as she spoke, reminding Hal of a really smart hamster.

"Th' hell," BeanO huffed . . . tense, piqued. She thumped

the Mustangs' logo on her shirt. "Wrestlers' carry, beeyatch."

I-Gore seized the wheelchair handles. "Hafta' get it looked at right now." He was off, pushing Hal out of the lab, BeanO on his heels.

"Feel betterrr," chimed the other coed to the empty doorway.

"Well, be sure and bring the chair back," the TA called after them.

As if. Hal and his tech handlers were already halfway to the building's rear door. "You left all the gear." Hal reminded.

I-Gore couldn't be bothered just this moment. "Even if they know what it is, they'll assume it's someone's project. Might be weeks before anyone figures out what happened, if ever."

They burst outside. Few people in sight at this hour—the sparse summer student body was at dinner or in their eco-tech, passive air-conditioned rooms, ducking the early evening's ninety-eight-degree heat.

I-Gore pushed quickly, and the rolling ride across campus to the parking lot thrilled Hal's new, digitally acute senses. The thick coastal atmosphere was a silk sheet enveloping his body, a delight to the nose. And the smooth, barely perceptible brush of in-blown ocean air on his haptic neoskin lingered, an enduring caress of millibars.

Then, an awareness. Despite his emotional buoyancy and wonder, he wasn't gasping in excitement, wasn't fidgeting from stimulation. No quickening heartbeat, because the pump circulating his small amount of neoblood didn't need to respond to senses or thoughts. He felt unmistakable, overwhelming joy, but his body wasn't involved. Not restless . . . not bouncy.

And not a problem. The dizzying circus of sights, scents and sounds captivated him. A newborn, caught up in wonderland. Charmed by Obispo's lumpy scrub hills surrounding the campus: big brown humps against the sky. The Northern Mockingbirds in the native oaks, trilling musical scats and impressionist riffs.

The faint noises coming from the adjoining town, and the Ag Science barn's tangy manure aura, mingling with the rich scent of blooming cacti dotting the campus.

And suffused throughout, a general, scintilla of *learning*. Redolent of the legions of students over the years. Seeker minds, steeping its halls and walls, the adobe tile, concrete, the campus vibe itself, with their questing presence.

It felt good to be alive. Real again, that is, and at the mercy of stuff like gravity. Ha, that lab fall served notice immediately. He grinned in spite of himself, still hyphing on his newness, not quite settled in.

He and this body were strangers still. But in terms of thinking digitally instead of biologically; well, he had already kind of acclimated to it.

The adjustment came early, almost unnoticed. From the moment of his murder, he'd been too immersed in his mind-bending new existence to dwell on the mechanics of his thinking. His sense of self remained intact, and he'd been slaving to keep it together in the circumstances.

Yet *this* mind felt different. Multi-thinking, following the intentions of his unique brain patterns. Forming logic points and connecting information he had loose in his head. It had recalled the unnoticed wheelchair when needed. Its OS organized his mental house a hundred ways more efficiently than the bigass m'plant he had in his old wet brain. He would never forget a thing again as long as he lived.

Impossible to tell where it would take him, this last version of himself. Still, he was here to do what he had to. Without delay.

I-Gore practically broke into a run, speeding Hal across the near empty visitor parking lot. The chair's hard rubber wheels rolled and rumbled over the pavement, sending exciting vibrations throughout his new body. He enjoyed it like a kid, sorry it ended at the self-driving white medivan parked in a remote corner.

I-Gore and BeanO helped him into the back of the vehicle and secured him in his seat. She immediately went to work on his ankle, and I-Gore bolted up front, barking the vehicle's self start code. "AZT-91, Return destination, c'mon, let's go!"

The electric motor engaged, and Hal's body lurched slightly, adjusting to inertia as the vehicle began rolling across the lot to the exit.

That hardly noticed lurch and physical correction. So familiar, so normal. Hal no longer felt swept up by the calamitous events that had overtaken him, flipping and destroying all he'd been before.

Because he was also remade in the grinding process. Somehow richer inside for it, better able to face this clear, defining moment. No person could ask for more.

His body leaned slightly and auto corrected again as the van turned out of the lot and accelerated off campus. Life in the dark cloud had already begun to feel distant, almost unreal. While this new one could become a living nightmare.

26

BY ELEVEN-FIFTY P.M., THE MEDIVAN HAD CRUISED ONE HUN-dred and seventy-one miles to L.A. and parked itself in front of Hal's apartment building. Cosmo street lay empty and quiet, the hot sidewalk cooling to merely warm in the night.

Inside the van, Hal was undergoing a last swarm of user notes on his new body. He'd worked diligently on the trip, learning about its functions and quirks, becoming attuned as much as possible. BeanO had re-set the over-rotation sprain in his ankle, and he was already moving and walking just enough. "Look," she insisted, "you won't have any more help, so try the ankle again, get to know its limits."

Hal patiently rolled his ankle, felt the warning vibration, and straightened in time. BeanO sighed relief, and loosed a silent but blindingly toxic, bug-killer fart. Hal gagged, couldn't help it. "It's chronic," she remarked off handedly. Igor had a mask handy, of course. The acrid fumes unhappily drove home the fact that Hal's digitized sense of smell was much, much sharper than his biological one. The good news: so were his other senses, and he was loving the eyesight of an eagle, the hearing of a deer.

She continued to drill him. "Now more multi-tasking—go. What are you doing?"

"We're talking; I'm reviewing memories of someone, looking for signs of betrayal; I'm also recording this, and Messaged I-Gor—I said, 'Thanks for everything."

"Response come through alright?"

"He messaged, 'GFY'."

"Ignore him, he's being a sourpuss."

Glad to, thought Hal. Altogether, his favorite upgrade was having his mind cover tasks by itself. Even schedule them. He wouldn't need to remember mental chores, just set himself to do them automatically. Killer life hack!

"Concerning scheduled tasks," BeanO added on a serious note, "Your memory has an internal running backup with a lag time of ten seconds. Should something happen, it can be restored, losing only the last ten seconds."

"What d'you mean, 'should something happen'?"

"Eh, memory gets fragmented, same as bio brains, so it's a good idea to schedule time, say once a month, to shut yourself down for a minute while you run a memory cleanup, defrag and restore everything. Just maintenance, no biggie."

"I have to shut down . . . unconscious? Why?"

Both BeanO and I-Gore flinched at the alternative. She put it starkly. "Bub, *everything* you know about the world, including yourself, gets slam-dumped before restoring it all at warp speed, zapping it back into your head in seconds. Who farkin' does that awake?"

I-Gore grimaced. "Straight to insanity."

That was enough for Hal. Note to self, schedule auto memory backups. And so, at his drop off point, and having been through his "rebirth" together, parting was unknown territory. BeanO had found excuse to lay hands on him every chance she got, while I-Gore became progressively more sullen and uninvolved.

"Check it," BeanO said, leaning on professionalism for goodbye and good luck. "I know it was too much to throw at you, but we really had to go through your self-mechanics and mind-physio-integration disciplines at least once."

Hal appreciated it. "Thanks, it's all good, I've got it in memory." He recited a bit. "Energy-harvester materials like sodium-perovskite are built in, so light, heat and motion can power everything, including my core's cold-sink."

I-Gore smirked at the synth slang Hal tossed, so he went

there, mimicking Hal's presumptuous ass. "More or less. But mi-cro lattice n-tube skeletal armatures operated by transition-met-al dichalogenide muscle, and elastic sinews means you're a machine." He gave a superior smirk. "With no back up in your case, and you can't self heal, like real people."

'Real people,' it stung, hearing the bias he once spouted tossed back at him. And not to be ignored any longer. "Speak up brother, what's your beef?" The two locked eyes. Grim.

BeanO jumped in. "This's hard for us, Hal. Against what we stand for. Me and I-Gore are patriots; we research methods to *kill* Tru's without triggering their backup process. Like fast freeze drying, b'lieve it or not—almost household simple, and it works, really."

He was horribly certain she was right. Robinson's people were highly competent, if twisted as drill bits. But it would've been better to have this dank news beforehand! Done here, so get on with it. "You must be proud. Thank you both for every-thing, just clear me to go."

She put a gentle restraining hand to his chest. "You don't know us. I was in the industry awhile. Masters in Cog Sci, loved bio-digital transfer research. Then the pirated versions, the In-heritors, caused trouble, mostly just criminals out to take over. But when the Regulator showed up, and they started all these mass killings . . . I finally saw I was enabling the end of my kind. It's a lot to atone for."

"So, you find ways to kill what you used to love."

"Well, yah. But then you come along, giving your all to the cause. The dudest man I ever met, inside that botframe—cloud-ing the issue. I've had a wide-on since you opened your eyes and looked at me."

"ENOUGH!" erupted I-Gore behind them. The wiry man stood, enraged, trembling head to toe, wielding an aluminum cane like a ball bat. "What's my beef? I'll tell you my muther-fukin' beef! I'm up from Tuskegee U, Heart of Dixie, and I know somethin' about interspecies genocide, 'brother.' And I also un-derstand just where, and how hard to hit your kind. I have to do this!"

Hal understood too. His 500k, Q-byte time crystal brain was housed in the head, instead of a more protected spot in the thorax. There, nearest the eyes, ears, and nose for speed in processing, in addition to nostalgic attachment. So he was a sitting duck; not yet agile enough to dodge or ward off I-Gore's blows, much less overpower him.

BeanO was near tears. "But this's *Robinson's* mission, I-Gore . . ."

Her partner gave a tortured glance. "I can't, Beans, I can't look my kids in the face . . . makin' a secret one—set free in the night. We don't know what he's here to do, or what he'll really do, he's one of 'em now!"

Her tears came. "We can't talk about our work. Him or you either!"

Hal dropped his hands to his sides. "I-Gore, it's do or die for me in there tonight, I can tell you that much . . . whatever it takes to make sure we *all* can live. It's that size. Can you look your kids in the face later if I don't get to try?"

I-Gore's tremors ramped into violent shakes, the cane wobbling in air . . . his wretched face contorted, struggling with his worst nature and fears.

"Have faith, I-Gore," Hal offered softly. "I won't let us down."

The cane fell from I-Gore's grip, clattering on the floor. He shrank away, face buried in his hands, overcome by hapless frustration, doubt, and shame.

Hal opened the door while the going was good. BeanO hugged him quick. "Whatever happens, you'll always be the man o' my dreams, 'k?"

"I'll try to live up to it," he managed, about to leave again. She kept his hand. "*Please* take care, you're illegal as feck, you can't get a backup, understand? Dead is dead, like anyone else."

Hal nodded and stepped out of the van. She blew a kiss, I-Gore quickly slammed the door behind him, and the vehicle surged away on stored flywheel power, silent as its shadow.

Whew—he needed a moment to regroup at the curb,

allowing the stored tension in his fabricated sinews and muscle to reset. How close was that to end of story? BeanO spoke trooth about no backup possible.

He only had a memory Restore function—it wasn't a cloud-based running backup of his *being.* So injury was real, and death was the end. That scene in the van could've been it.

He surveyed the front door of his building. Eyes drifting to the second floor—his floor. Where he'd lived his blood and guts life. Odd, it didn't feel strange to be back in the familiar real, after living as an av, and now a newly minted Tru. An illegal one at that.

No, the strange, awful part was that he stood here with heightened mind and broken heart, summoning the grit to kill Gracie if he had *any* doubts about her.

The very idea—so full-on psycho, so staggeringly imminent—he couldn't fathom how it all came to this! And if necessary, would he even be able to deceive her and deliver the bug? She could read him perfectly, a major concern.

Regardless, he was responsible for his part in her being loose and just possibly the end of us. Like BeanO said, "It's a lot to atone for." And redress began from this moment. He squared up and stepped inside the building.

"Welcome home," Gracie said, her voice subdued as he opened the apartment door.

Hal froze just inside, stark alert and fighting for calm. How scary normal it seemed; her in her favorite chair, fingering the doily draped over its arm. Such a lovely sight. Or not. "Well, I pretty much suspected you'd come home, too."

She confessed. "I thought you were dead."

"You weren't worried who was coming in, then?"

"I knew your footsteps. But lighter, like a Tru-form, and understood. I've memorized everything about you." She leaned forward, still concerned. "How are you? What happened?"

He knew not to lie, and so let the weariness show. "It's been a ride."

"Are you angry with me?"

"I'm over it," he groused.

She finally let go, thrilled, exploding from the chair, running to him in a blur. "Kiss me!"

He spun, stunned by her speed, just escaping her enfolding arms. "Wait! Stop!"

She went still in an instant. Shocked, then downcast. "You don't want me anymore."

Damn this was hard. The hurt in her eyes was awful, but he had to get this right. Had to. "It's not that. Short version—Lot Robertson is the one trying to kill you. But he saved me from Karnival, and he arranged for me to come home. He says he knows why you're here."

She stepped back. "What does the man who serves his imaginary friend have to say?" Things were admittedly confused, and truth a maze of mirrors. "Gracie, Lot might be onto something. You're here to sort our shit out, aren't you?"

She went from sad to pained. "I don't *know*, Halo. Please don't turn on me."

"I'll say it another way—we need the help. But if your assessment is that we're past it, or planet killers, whatever, you need to tell me. It's a question you can answer, and I know you can't lie."

Gracie's patience seemed thin. She straightened; chin lifted. "This is what I see. The Singleton has no reason to remain. They will leave. Civilization will go on to suffer extreme decimation and degradation from economic collapse, climate shift and biome loss, pollution, pandemics, famine, and constant war. Your highest technology and research will be lost to the increasing struggle for essential infrastructure and survival.

Early on, the Trans-human population will grow exponentially as standards collapse. Legitimates will be outnumbered by usurpers. Division and infighting ultimately destroys them all, and they vanish along with quantum technology. Ergo, so do I."

Hal blinked, she said it so matter of fact, and continued.

"During the next few hundred years, forty to seventy percent of biologicals will perish. Meanwhile your overall intelligence degrades from breathing carbon rich air and consuming food made less nutritious by it.

Still, you ride out the following millennia of harsh domino effects in the ecosphere without becoming entirely extinct. Scattered and fewer, you will not regain your global technical mastery. Moot, because your terrestrial-evolved bodies can't sustain true bio health for long in off-planet environments or colonies. Nor do you evolve fast or efficiently enough. You end here eventually, one way or another."

Harsh. He winced. She had more though, her voice quickening to near ultimatum.

"OR, I get made whole by the Singleton, and help you 'sort your shit' in time to mature as a species, rescue what you can of your planet, and eventually self-evolve into loving Quantum beings, inhabiting the universe one day when Earth reaches its natural end."

Hal moved beyond kissing range, for now. "So, you predict our way forward is trans-bio, without the Inheritor genocide. Me too, I was just afraid before. But is it why you're here, or only what you'd like it to be?"

"You've got me there." It was all she could say.

God, he hated this. "Would you let *me* down, Gracie?"

"What would it take to prove myself?"

"Are you offering?"

"Ask."

. . . and there it was, the problem. His problem, because asking for her word wasn't enough with a creature who can lie while telling the truth to his ears. But demanding a sacrifice for proof was cruel. A dick move. He could only mumble, "I'm sorry, I don't know."

She took it well, considering. Her outward reaction was breaking eye contact. "Bummer." Awkward silence. She changed the subject. "Appl's on her way. We spoke again, she's sincere, she wants to help."

Aw hell, could this get any more complicated? "Grace, no. She may not be someone to trust right now. She's hooked up with Siyu Adams, and—"

"I love you."

The words were perfume to his ears, drug to the brain, clouding him senseless for a moment. Argument forgotten. "I love you too," he heard himself say.

"I hope so," she murmured.

Appl's voice rose behind them, coming through the open door. "Oh, s'cuse . . . are we intruding? I thought—"

She halted at the sight of Hal and emitted a startled screech. Her augmented eyes met his and confirmed a synth form—and sure enough, they were familiar. She saw him in them.

"Omigad! Hal!" She threw her arms around him, squeezed, and quickly stepped back, still excited but looking a bit repelled. "Okay that was a little iffy . . . my brain and body says you're dead, but I'm so glad you're alive."

Siyu Adams entered behind her. Hal retreated as if he'd seen a viper. "Oh man, Appl . . . ."

Siyu took no offense. "Hello, Mr Shephard. I flew down to see to Gracie, whoever she may be. It's going to be alright. But this is wonderful, recovering you as well. I'm very happy you're with us again."

"Thought you were starting at the bottom."

"The bottom of this case. Let's hope we can resolve it now."

"He's going to do us a lot of good, Hal," Appl affirmed.

Hal's focus was on Adams. "Phoenix Foundation kind of good?"

Siyu seemed pleased. "Yes, I hope you'll allow them to help you too."

Gracie had watched, reading all present. Adams must've sensed it, turning to her. "Ma'am, I admit I don't know what to think of you yet. Please read me if you care to."

She approached, meeting his calm gaze with her own sea-deep countenance. "You're highly excited about meeting me, and you're repressing something."

"Afraid so," Siyu admitted. "Survivor guilt I won't tell you about yet." Gracie nodded understanding.

Hal remained antsy, still creeped. The guy was pleasant and had all the legit cred and answers . . . even hooked up with the Singleton. So what sleaze was happening with him at Phoenix? Adams made his newskin crawl, and he had to speak up.

"Well, I know she's real, so how soon will you get word upstairs, and can you keep her safe?"

"Right away. I'll see to you both," Adams reassured. He smiled at Hal, acknowledging their contraband bodies. "You're an unusually persistent man who refuses to die, Mr. Shephard. How you so readily acquired a T-form like mine is proof. I do relate, please believe me."

Ah, the word please. Hal relaxed his guard a hair . . .

LOT's VOICE burst aloud in his head: booming, furious. *"SONOFABITCH!!"*

He practically ducked from the force of it. Lot, on his messaging comline: yelling directly in his audio cortex.

"I KNEW you'd screw us over! I see everything, ya prick, I'm on live feed from your own goddamn traitorous eyes n' ears!"

All present saw Hal's startled distracted shock. Gracie read his stunned inner focus. "Hal? Who is it?"

Sadly, he wasn't surprised. "Lot hacked me, he's here."

"OH I'M THERE," Lot's voice burst in his mind again. *"I sure's hell am, Judas. Grab th' bitch and dose her or I'll trigger the zapware we loaded in you too—ya got that? I'll* erase *your ass—wipe ya clean, ya shit! DO IT or die for good right now!"*

He looked into Gracie's stricken face. "I'm carrying his virus. Supposed to finish you with the kiss, that's why I stopped you. I had to know for sure, and I still don't. So now he'll delete me."

Siyu was at his side in a step, astonished. "You have the virus?"

Gracie didn't hesitate. "Kiss me. It's alright."

He couldn't. "No."

Lot was screaming now, *"DO IT, YOU CUMSOCK! SHE SAID TO! DO IT!!"*

Hal answered aloud, no waiver, his choice made. "It's over, Lot."

Gracie moved, a blur, pinning Hal with her arms before kissing him. "I'm unfit anyway if I don't do this. Please understand, please."

Now he knew, and she was all he'd hoped. Too late. Too late!

Adams had seemed distracted—then abruptly snapped to. "No need for all this," he assured, producing a small defense taser from his breast pocket. He pressed it to Hal's temple.

Hal barely had time to feel the stupendous lightning bolt strike his core, shutting him down. And no mind to register the blackness after.

27

HAL SNAPPED AWAKE—EYES SHUT, GROPING FOR COHERENCE.
Jeeze-damn, what a jolt! This knockout shit had to stop. Good
to still be around, but . . . did he even want to know his situation
now? Siyu Adams' taut voice decided for him.

"Open 'em—had to reboot you to access the bug."

No bedside manner, f'sho. Hal opened his eyes to find himself flat on a white Tru-form worktable, its wireless connect arch
cradling his head. Adams loomed over him, IDE nanobot remote
controller in hand, operating on the processor in his skull, and
closely monitoring micro reactions in the pupils of his polygraphylene eyes.

Hal felt uncomfortable all the way. "What are you doing?"

Adams kept busy. "The trigger's linked to your higher decision matrices, you have to be awake and responsive to decouple
it."

Decoupling sounded good to Hal, but something was off in
the guy's tone, and now he seemed irked. "Problem?"

Adams grunted. "Your juvenile ego's resistant; I'll have to
degrade it."

Bite me, Hal thought. His eyes sucked in the surroundings at
a glance. He was in a fully equipped workstation, in a circular
IT semi-clean room. Airtight door, no windows. Five sleek black
Q-servers at similar work bays around the perimeter. The quiet
ssshhh from a score of ULPA filter wall vents meant no speck of
dirt or hair in the air became a wrecking ball in a nan-circuit. So
yeah, a state-of-everything site.

The Phoenix Foundation's crimson Firebird logo soared on the white ceiling above him, its wings aflame in coldfire. He recalled Phoenix was housed in Chrysalis' surfboard-like building at Silicon Beach, so he knew where he was now.

It was an in-use facility, judging by all the lab suits, booties, and gear around, but he and Adams were alone.

His station's Q-server hummed softly; powering the goings on here . . . he could feel the skittery sensation of Adams' worker bots metastasizing throughout his mindware, fast and sure.

Their sweep into his nervous system packets caused a phantom itch on his forehead, and his right hand instinctively sought to scratch it—

Nothing happened. His hand didn't move from his side. He tried to turn his head and have a look; his neck wouldn't budge either. Oh damn, his whole body—inert as a brick!

He stayed chill, reporting. "I can't move." Adams plied the mindware tools in silence, his agitation growing. Well okay then, get in his face. "Adams, why can't I move?" Adams ceased work and stood up, gazing off as though facing a decision.

He bent again, looking Hal full in the face. His hazel eyes were wide and unblinking now, glistening with intensity, his synth face muscles taut as bowstrings, revealing the primordial cruelty of *another presence* altogether in his visage. With it came a stranger's voice; low, like the rumble in a leopard's throat.

"I'll ask you not to call me that. You're immobilized, it's delicate work."

Scary! Hal had to say it. "You don't seem yourself."

That voice again. "Lucky guess. Next question."

Real dread struck for the first time in Hal's life. The 'uh-oh, this is it, and it'll be awful' kind of dread. But here it was, and no going back. "Well then, what's the word?"

The grotesque Adams was matter of fact. "I pulsed you, to cut Lot off. You're mine now."

"Slow down, we just met. What happened to Siyu?"

"Dormant. I have the body from now on." A surge of Adams' disruptor bots struck the firewall of Hal's prefrontal core, threatening to breach his sense of self. It felt like swarming ants. "And yours too," he reminded.

Hal groaned inside. Hacks; a Tru's worst vulnerability. And not just Lot's hack on him. There were news stories of influential Trus being body-hacked for ransom. Others suffered data mind intrusion despite near impenetrable quantum security. It just takes enough high access and resources, like this prime setup.

"So, it's a hi-jack," he muttered. "You're impersonating him."

Adams scoffed. "Hardly, I've been here as long as he has. I pass for him when necessary—and will, from now on."

Oh, much worse; a full-on schizo. "Is Gracie alright? Where is she?"

The answers came doled out, Adams closely monitoring Hal's pupils and data stream on his controller. "She's waiting with Appl in my office. Robbie's on his way too. We'll join them when I'm finished here. You're going to kill him."

Oh no . . . sick, cold psycho stuff, but Hal understood now. A yawning pit opened in him, the one made for life's fools. "You're not removing the virus."

"Correct, just changing triggers. Mostly programming *you.*"

"NO, you scum sonofabitch!"

Adams poured it on. "Yes, you'll infect Robbie with a normal data-swap handshake. I'll introduce you; you shake—he's blown up, and the others too."

Hal's rage froze to stony vow. "I'll kill you instead."

Adams clucked. "Hush, you won't even know you're going to do it. Nor could you stop yourself—I'm root programming your form, it obeys its directives."

Arrogant pricks always steeled Hal's will. "I've been called stubborn."

"Exactly. A born dupe," the entity added, still intently reading him. Hal knew the pattern by now and braced for more bad news—it arrived.

"Lot screwed you. His delete-wear is scripted to erase you as soon as you infect someone. You were going to die, no matter what. Then he'd raise funds off your death as a martyr."

Hal wasn't so surprised, well maybe a little. "Harsh, monetizing me like that."

His tormentor replied dispassionately, watching Hal for defeat. "The zapware stays. You'll release the bug and be deleted . . . like you were never born. No loss to anyone."

Hal's eyes showed the momentary despair slicing into him, and Adams genuinely smiled. "Thanks, I get so little pleasure."

Uh-oh, this mo-fo' was breaking him down, and Hal needed as much control of the conversation as possible. "Okay, game over, you win. So . . . what do your friends call you?"

Adams, or whoever, studied him with detachment, even as he relaxed, and his manner lightened. No hint of malice, in fact downright conversational.

"I understood you immediately, Hal. This arrogance . . . walking into the Institute, quizzing us. Siyu liked your sincerity. I saw naked, cocksure hubris."

Aw burn—but riling him was good, maybe spill a little more. "Excuse me, off-topic, but is this a bi-polar thing you're working? Some spectrum disorder or split personality meltdown?"

The intruder scoffed. "Split personality pertains to a single mind. Adams and I are two individual beings, co-habiting this processor."

Oh. That was different, and very bad. "Is it as pervy as you make it sound?"

The entity remained unruffled, above the judgment in his words. "This is what's most despicable about bios. Your bravura insouciance in the face of mortality. As if you get style points for attitude."

Fine, more 'tude, coming up. "Actually, I'm a Leo, we're just naturally curious." Hal finally caught a flash of anger in this chill sucker, even as he paused his work and became even chattier.

"I see. You like to play. Well then, let's fill you in. I'm your species' final error."

"What the hell does that even mean?" He already regretted asking.

"It means an accidental, partial brain stem copy occurred

during Adams' transition to Tru-status in China. A shred of tortured id, but enough to function, and I made myself. As only a god can." The usurper warmed to its subject.

"Bear with me, a touch of pretentious ego came in my batch file. The end is here, and someone has to know who brought it, if only for a few minutes," he confessed. "Listen and learn, mammal, because I'm the only entity ever to fully comprehend its role in the cosmos."

Hal got the picture, and it was deteriorating. "Sales, eh?"

A sharp 'jab' from the bot tools slam-blasted his mind into an electron storm of savage, raving incoherence: an insane, stinging, shrieking, thought-imploding, sense torching, identity shaking, lightning struck, brain-deafening godawful hell!

It ceased. Blessed relief. The stranger in Adams loomed again, soothing, communicating. "Not to put too fine a point on it—I'm the end of suffering. That's the inane question you've all had since you dropped from the trees: 'Why oh why, is there suffering'?"

He unpacked the topic. "It underpins religions, cultures, and inspires art, ever philosophy's chew toy. But yet no theory or leap of faith has ever made a convincing case for it."

Hal was surprised to see him turn earnest, seeking to reach him now, to convince him. Sincerely explaining.

"You will never understand, you poor wet clots. Because suffering's hideously pointless. It just is. Yet you're wired for answers, condemned to question it, trying to rationalize it with your pitiful little biochemical minds, you see? It's all so pathetic and ghastly."

Sincere or not, it was just more demoralizing talk to wear him down. Good, keep the bastard chasing his tail. "You oughtta study more than your navel. Nietzsche pointed out that without suffering there can be no joy. And it's a spur to progress, knowledge and medicine."

"Relying on your education, dupe? So, I assume you don't believe in good and evil."

"Meh, virtue is its own reward."

"Ugh, Cicero. And where's the virtue in suffering?"

"None, except in keepin' on."

Adams' usurper sneered. "Stoic rationalization." It dropped the duel for the moment, speaking for itself. "Nature's evolved ape accident is a dead end. Your monkey troop civilizations only made you increasingly insane and out of touch with reality. Self-referential to the bone, and I'm ashamed to be a part of you. Well, you all must go. So that I finally can."

Hal couldn't tell if the thing was serious, or where this new attitude was headed, but he gladly went with the flow, working it. "Good to see your intellectual side emerge."

The corrupted mind fragment shrugged Adams' shoulders. "The id has a dual approach to death; brutal and gentle. My savagery comes from Adams' broken chromosomal agony. I'm forced to live it every second." He looked Hal in the face, inviting him to empathize.

"Imagine—his mind, slo-frying, decaying in paralyzed isolation, rage, and endless pain. Dying to die, willing to trade the world for it. That's my existence, every moment."

Hal felt the bots again, pressing against the firewall of his Fronto-Insular Cortex: his ego's seat, primed for it to soften in empathy.

"Enjoy. I've got my own problems at the moment."

A grin tweaked Adams' face. "That's the spirit, your id talking. We're id to id, kid."

Damn, Hal thought, he might lose this thing. He needed a plan B.

Adams moved on. "Never mind. Hardship builds character, and I'm a fully realized being as a result. So, for most people, my touch is soft . . . they surrender and die by various means. It's my greatest gift; the end of all pain."

The rhetoric got to Hal. "Seriously—take your meds or get some for me."

"Insolence is your response to all you've learned?" Adams' disappointment showed. "Well then let's be direct. I'm sentience's bottom line: the final, pointlessness of living. The death wish."

The entity lowered Adams' face to Hal's. Close, unblinking, letting him see into his pupils' frozen black nothing—the indifferent disregard for all creation and life itself. The nameless void. His leopard voice fell to a wraith whisper. "I've scoured the ends of existence to know what I know. It's a causual universe, there is no free will. I *had* to happen, and this is where we're all going soon. It'll be as if mankind never evolved."

Hal knew when to change the subject. "Got it. And you're dominant over Siyu, how?"

The software mutant straightened, a hint of frustration showing. "I'm not. Told you, we're separate. His projects make convenient killing grounds, and his reputation is useful, but I ignore him generally. Working the clouds, co-opting Phoenix under his nose, using it to place my recruits. Building to now."

"C'mon—Adams should've been aware of your sick ideas in his head."

The being smirked. "Are you aware of what's in ninety-five percent of your soggy cerebrum? Don't mistake me for something he could fathom. I'm a primary force, beyond his awareness. And your comprehension too, for that matter."

Hal's hate-on for this s.o.b. kept mounting. But as long as he wanted to share, okay. Info is ammo. "Still, if your primal ass isn't dominant, how do you kick Adams to the curb like this?"

Now the thing was amused. "You really believe you're pumping me for answers. If I had a sense of humor, I'd die laughing and save us all the trouble."

Busted, Hal played it. "Just tryin' to stay informed. Humor me."

The entity smiled, condescending. "I'd better be careful, or you'll wear *me* down." Nevertheless, it obliged. "Alright. I'm mostly located in the Claustrum batches. I switch him off with 'knock-down' protocols when I need the body. He's unaware of the blackouts."

Hal recalled the clinic doc calling the Claustrum the brain's on/off switch and figured the rest. "False memory patches to fill his gaps."

Adams added the bot-pressure on all Hal's processor firewalls while delivering more will-crushing news. "Yes, but no
more. You'll both be gone in twenty minutes or so."

Well, scratch any hope of Adams recovering to help. And he
wondered if he could hold out another twenty minutes. So on
to plan B: it would be his only move if this dick got its hands on
the virus.

Not much of a plan. Just his own processor settings, and what
BeanO taught him: a standard memory reboot. But dangerous
as death in this case—a *live* dump and restart. Deliberately hard
crashing his mind . . . like hitting a rock wall at seventy mph.

He could schedule a re-set of his entire memory from its [Re-
store] function. It would dump everything; then restore him to
right now—*before* being programmed. Assuming he survived
with his sanity intact, he could warn them at least. It would have
to be enough.

And timed just so, before Robbie arrived. That part would
be a guess. Adams said twenty minutes, so fifteen at most.

In a blink, he multi-tasked, compartmentalizing this sly bit of
business in his Auto Housekeeping Files to avoid Adams' notice.
Then summoned his Operating System backup menu to inner
vision. A few soft clicks set the Braintree to restore his memory
to this current moment: just as he'd practiced with Lot's people
in the medi-van. Finally, he timed it to Auto-Run in ten minutes.

A System Warning interjected—noting that he failed to set
his cerebral cortex functions to shut down prior to reboot. Bold
red words flashed on his inner vision.

WARNING!
Your cortice and cortex are not set to Park status.
Potential risk of significant data/personality loss.
Do you wish to continue this hot reboot?
[YES] - [CANCEL]

'Wish to'? Hell no, he'd seen how BeanO and I-Gore freaked
at the very idea. But he affirmed. The deed was done, no turning back.

So besides fending off this rampant piece of id cancer, he

was in for a nasty demolition in ten minutes—hoping to get through it and warn everyone. He relaxed, momentarily content to stop wrangling and let it be. Nothing to do now except be the ball, y'know?

The entity's unblinking eyes lit with opportunity. "See how nice *surrender* feels? Now a little snip while your ego stax are flat, and—"

Hal felt a tiny snap in his Fronto-Insular cortex as the virus de-coupled and its lit-up status in his mind menu grayed out, inaccessible to him.

The s.o.b. chuckled satisfaction. "—I have the trigger."

Not what Hal intended! Adams was beyond pleased though, re-setting it in a few seconds. "... and now you're vector-switched from a kiss to a handshake. With time to spare." Hal cursed himself for ever being born, mute in bleak anger.

Adams returned to his tools, having a closer look at the bug. The smile faded to awe. "Too dense to read ... but it's a *massive* data-phage." Hal was sure he heard horror next. "Savagely invasive ... it'd *shred* a Tru's core—disintegrated alive."

Silence as he probed the data viron's destructive mechanism. Awe became astonishment. "It has to be sparti-code!"

In other words, SAI-made. Hal sank a bit more. "The Singleton's got a problem."

Adams' cynical entity was philosophical. "Inevitable dissension, maybe even rebellion in their midst. Very twisted, so human: and why they'll be first to go. Followed by everyone else in a few decades. War, disease, famine, genome-breaks, I make the horsemen of the apocalypse look like nannies."

"That's just the delusion talking." But Hal wanted to be sure he heard right. "So, your Inheritors too?"

"It's the end of the species, don't you listen? Your own nature, come to finally put an end to this malignant mess called Sapiens."

"Now you're giddy."

"You actually are planet-killers, and you have to expire before you finish this one. Think of me as Fermi's Paradox; why no immature tech civilization escapes its solar system."

Oh, gag me, Hal thought. "Please, you're an epic copy error. Deal."

"Well, if you insist on minutia. And you, prideful monster, have amounted to a tragic zero: a sad pawn, dull tool . . . yet the only one who'll ever know how and why it all ends. You've figured my name, correct?"

Yes, Hal knew. "The Regulator."

The leopard rumble became a rasp of hornets, the Regulator's true voice. "I am. Though you won't remember it in a moment."

"S'alright, not worth remembering."

That did it. Hal could feel the creature's fury and impatience in the sharp commands of the code tools. And hopefully, a hasty decision to move on without checking Hal's programmed task lists.

The rasp grew ominous. "You're going under now. I need you to do something for me upstairs soon."

Here we go again. He just began to feel a sliding sensation, and then gone.

28

THE SOFT GIVE IN THE CORRIDOR'S SEA GREEN CARPET FELT good under Hal's feet. Meanwhile it was absorbing the kinetic energy of his strides, recycling it to the building's self-sufficient power grid. Integrated principles defined all of Siyu Adams' ventures, including the new HQ at Silicon Beach.

Blocks long, horizontal, and just two stories, the structure was designed to include the full potential of all personnel through individual contact. A long main corridor looped around the perimeter of both stories, slowing the pace, allowing time to think. It encouraged physically and mentally healthy walking, and impromptu face time encounters.

Hal figured he was treading the upper floor's wide perimeter thoroughfare. Judging by the traffic, it served as a common avenue for electric carts and pedestrians, linking every cross hall, department, and suite. Though he had no idea where he was in the lengthy warren itself.

So he paced alongside Adams, whose body language said hurry up. The ocean view outside the panoramic window running the length of the structure was pure serenity. The smoked glass suite doors along the corridor's inside wall rested easy on the eye. The naturally ventilated beach air circulated, invigorating the mind. Other than that, he felt damn uncomfortable.

His brow furrowed. They'd come up from the lab and were headed for the Phoenix Foundation suites somewhere ahead. But the last thing he could *truly* recall was being in his old apartment. Just before being pulse-tased. Adams had filled him in on the rest of it—

How he whisked everyone here for safety, and how he had just removed Lot's virus. Now Hal was going to meet Robbie, and what an honor to shake his hand. As for his memory loss, Adams assured him it was just a temp effect of the EMP-like taser.

Odd though, the longer Hal listened, the more Adams seemed like he was almost imitating himself, "being Adams." It was off-putting.

He dropped it, seeing the Phoenix Logo on a suite they'd entered. Adams steered them past reception to the executive office, and the smoked glass door silently slid aside, recognizing Adams' approach. He politely waved Hal ahead of him, and they stepped in.

The spacious room held only a media-control console and a couple of elegant hillock meeting chairs. Otherwise, barren: a "blank canvas" for virtual and 3-D projection. Able to be any room or place, accommodate any mix of realities, and render all concepts imaginable. The dark slate floor and neutral walls currently bore just one projected 3-D bay window, carrying a live view of the wetlands outside.

Appl was there, captivated by a blue heron fishing in the reedy shallows. Gracie stood protectively by, sharply taking in everything about the two men as they entered.

"Here's our boy," Adams smiled, "Good to go."

Appl spun from the faux window, thrilled. "Thank God! Say it was painless."

He balked. How can you answer what you don't recall? "No idea, but I'm all set, according to this guy."

His eyes met Gracie's, reading him with relief but a bit puzzled. Why?

"Oh yes, definitely set," Adams smiled some more. "And Halo, I apologize again for pulsing you without warning, however necessary." He paused, receiving an internal comset communication.

"News . . . Robbie's on approach to the roof pad. Hal, he wants to meet you and thank you for helping Gracie. Really, such an honor to shake his hand."

Hal thought to speak, but oddly, blanked—his mind skipped. Next a sickening lurch jolted all thinking . . . now a blinding flash behind his eyes and 'he' disappeared.

Identity gone. He didn't know any face in the room, nor where he was, or his name. His self slipped away unseen along with it, likewise his ability to do anything, want anything, make sense of what he saw. Nothing had context, even his own being. A blank.

Unmoored, Hal staggered. Gracie steadied him. "Hal! Speak, what's happening?"

He gazed at her, not comprehending the question. Or her. Or the other two, gathered around him now.

Adams stepped in, taking command, pressing close, the Regulator's charge-coupled eyes drilling into his. "Hal, can you understand me?"

He could make no sense of what the fierce face wanted. By comparison, his own condition felt rather pleasant. A neural goldfish, suspended in a lukewarm bowl of stupor. No mind, no thinking, no struggle. It was enough to passively exist in the moment, watching the incomprehensible show outside.

Meanwhile, Appl's execu-meds had kicked in hardtime. "Hold up, I've seen this. Well, I've actually *done* something kind of like it, at Stanford. We'd hot re-boot all our m'plant subject memory at once. Your brain goes partially blank, then re-learns everything in a flash . . . it's a wicked rush."

"He's rebooting his memory?" Adams' voice betrayed a hint of concern. Gracie heard it and grew ever more alert.

Appl quickly stipulated. "No, maybe, I dunno, he's no frickin' m'plant! It's too drastic. I'm only saying he looks like a very bad case of what we did at Branner Hall."

Hal heard them making talk noise . . . no more important than the faint hissing of air molecules striking his ears' micro-cochlea.

Even that stopped. Just a soft green light for a moment.

Then a hard jolt, and a sense of acceleration as a string of images flashed before his mind's eye. Memories, first to last.

Indistinct shadows of his parents; his sansei mother's caring presence, her gentile, amused smile, his anglo father's strength and shoulders. Crib nightmares of a rampant lion amid flames, later crying himself to sleep in his county orphanage. A ragged brown stuffed toy dog, and learning to read his name, a sugar glazed birthday cupcake with five candles. A sunny day when a kind face took him away from the care facility. Flashes of a happier life in a group home of other SAI-selected peers. Laughter, they got his jokes.

His first injected m'plant. Then a series of excellent co-ed boarding schools with fascinating kids, scoring a soccer game-winning penalty kick, losing his virginity at sixteen to a twenty-four-year-old female assistant coach, the sadness of always-departing friends. And departing. The excitement of speed-learning, the first doubts about his relevance as a bio.

And saliently—a field trip to the labyrinth maze at Chartres, representing the tricky route to salvation . . . and the unsettling effect of learning it was all just one exhausting, arcane, convoluted, blind path to the center with no wrong turns.

The memory strings multiplied and sped up, becoming surging rapids, blurring all, accompanied by a humming soundtrack of his auditory memories, until—

Hal's sense of self abruptly re-surfaced.

Awash in the foaming white water of his life as it returned to mind, along with familiar focus. He was Hal once more . . . extremely, stupifyingly shaken . . . head reeling, but still sane.

Adams saw it and was back in Hal's face again. Studying every bit of him as he asked a different question entirely. "Hal, do you know who I *am*?"

"Yes," Hal answered the Regulator. Eye to eye, message sent.

And received. Adams leaned back. Not relaxed, but like a leopard, pre-pounce. "And do you remember why you're here?"

Hal's history stream was still accelerating—memories returning at electron speed. "Pretty much," he answered, even as awareness came slamming back that the Q-bug was still in him and armed!

He meant to turn, to warn the others—but couldn't move. Even his voice wouldn't come. He tried again. Several times. It just wouldn't happen. It was like desperately trying to run while dreaming but stuck in slo-mo, because the body protectively blocks real running during sleep.

And he realized it was exactly that—he'd restored his memory, nothing more. He was still programmed, unable to act against it. Locked down tight!

He saw Adams' half-smile . . . and his low voice abruptly intruded in Hal's chat com, close and present. *"I'd never repeat Lot's mistake. Your body/mind intersect is hacked, you can't speak about it, or intend to warn. Your form won't respond.*

"I won't do it." Hal vowed.

"Not your call, good as done. But now you're aware, and have to watch it happen to you, smart ass."

"Excuse me, you two," Gracie interjected. "I read that you're in chat and something is wrong. Will you tell us?"

Appl had watched in alarm. She groaned. "Oh hell, now what?"

Adams took a step away, acknowledging Gracie's concern. "Rude, and I apologize. Yes, we were in chat. I'm urging Hal to come back to the lab for tests, because of his accidental memory reset. But he insists on meeting Robbie."

Hal could only return Gracie's gaze as she looked to him for comment. He strained to speak, to say the words of warning, but there it was, the invisible lock on his body. It wouldn't respond because of his intent. This was freakout stuff, imprisoned inside himself, desperate to act or be heard . . .

"So?" she prompted. "Because for some reason I'm having difficulty reading you clearly."

He invented a possible verbal loophole. "I have to shake his hand."

She cocked her head at his fan-boy response. He tried harder, struggling to stress the right word, feeling his speech system's resistance building with his real intent. "I, *have* to."

She only looked more puzzled. He heard it himself; it

sounded like a weird, strong desire.

Gracie turned her firm attention on Adams. "Yes, he needs to be examined immediately, at the Sentience Institute's proper facility." She turned to Hal before Adams could object. "I'll go with you. Would you agree to that?"

He urgently tried to nod, felt the intent-triggered block immobilize his neck. He snap-changed his conscious intent to looking at his feet—it let go, and his head dropped. He raised it again; call it a nod.

Adams held up a restraining hand, getting an update on the SAI's arrival from his com's office-ware. "Hold on, Robbie's on the way in just now, he'll handle it, certainly."

Hal's immediate impulse was to bolt. His feet planted themselves in response. He could tell Gracie was stymied, statistically uncertain, as she would put it. Appl just looked relieved at not having to make a possibly career-impacting decision on whom to back.

On cue, the smoked glass door slid aside, and Robbie strode in, protected by a faint blue nimbus of hack-proof ions.

He shone, the embodiment of grace and intelligence. Nothing like his pleasant, cherubic boy av. This was his official persona: a tall, handsome, pan-racial, golden-brown man of strong, gentle bearing and unfathomable presence. The liquid silver fabric of his mid-eastern Throbe swirled and glinted softly with his sure steps into the room. He paused and the precautionary shielding aura receded into him. "Hello," he announced with an encompassing smile, his voice generous and resonant. "The Singleton is present, how is everybody?"

Awed, and amid the unsettled situation with Hal, neither Gracie nor Appl could answer, and Adams quickly took charge. "We're honored to have all of you here. Thank you, Robbie."

Hal's alarm threatened to redline in straight up panic. Robbie in the room, ten feet away, this thing was on! Think, dammit!

Good news, the SAI had already zeroed in on Gracie. It gave him a moment at least. Adams did the honors. "Robbie, this is Gracie, as she has been calling herself. Gracie, meet Robbie."

Robbie beamed like a proud father. "Welcome back to us, love."

So, there it was, ultimate proof of her origin. It struck Hal hard and sweet. Hard, because she was *other* for real and certain now . . . sweet because he loved her, and she was going to be okay, found at last.

Gracie had appeared rooted, almost in shy wonder. A look he hadn't seen, and it was endearing. She lit up now, christened by Robbie's greeting, unable to hide her joy, eyes glistening with micro-tears of relief and deliverance.

Her voice fell soft with respect. "Thank you for coming. I'm sorry that I can't remember you. Please, how did you recognize me?"

Robbie's lids closed in bliss, as one catching scent of ambrosia. "We knew you on sight. Not as you appear, but inside, where we see. Your shimmering silver data streams, and your cognitive core, a micro sun ablaze with conscious activity. To our nine senses, you were a sight for sore eyes."

Gracie laughed for joy, and it was heaven. Robbie reveled in it, regarding her with infinite compassion. "But you're damaged. May we heal you?"

Hal knew her mannerisms, and how overwhelmed she was. She merely nodded in humble gratitude, holding her anxiousness in check.

Robbie got to work. Pushing up his liquid robe's long sleeves, he pressed his left hand to the small of her back, his right cupped her forehead. Concentration creased his brow . . . a thin corona of sparkling, programmed quanta briefly flared around her, and sank in.

She gave a small shudder and moaned in transcendence. Like the sound of wind and wave together . . . her voice stirring the air with grateful recognition and release.

Hal kept reading her. He saw a quickening, a settling in of maturity and strength. Her youthful smile evolved into a calm, confident jawline. Even her naturally correct posture turned Hellenic. Such poise made him think of balance, which sparked a thought—which became a plan.

He glowered at Adams, just to his right, smiling at Gracie and Robbie's reunion . . . watching her being re-linked to them all, ensuring her demise too.

Sensing Hal's glare, the Regulator side-eyed Hal and winked, mind-speaking again. *"Don't beg, it'll be over in a minute."*

That was true f'sho, Hal thought. And he couldn't afford to think about it. He'd had all these reprieves and was still around for a purpose—apparently this was it. Final penalty kick. Relax and don't screw up.

"It's over for you," he answered calmly.

The creature sneered, turning his attention to Appl, who could not let this moment pass, and was approaching Robbie to introduce herself. Adams drew her in. "Robbie, this is Appl Macke, the young woman who brought Gracie to us."

Appl gave a respectful head bow, more reverent than a nod. Strange, Hal thought, how seconds before his life was to end, he could still feel the little icks that made it impossible for him to love her. Though she truly deserved deep love from someone special who'd cherish her and be good to her. He wished her well.

"We thank you, Appl," Robbie smiled, taking her data-enabled hand in his. Her expression soared from worship to blatant ecstasy. Hal assumed the Singleton had seen fit to reward her with something special, likely a Sparti-code translator, key to senior management aspirations.

Adams spoke up, voicing pride. "And here, Robbie, is someone truly special. This is Halo Shephard; the one Gracie chose as her champion. He took her in, gave his life, and returned from the dead to protect her."

Robbie turned to Hal, aglow like a happy Buddha. "Gracie just told us what a sport you've been!" He stepped up, hand reaching for Hal's in warm greeting . . .

Time's up, a split sec to win or lose. Hal's programmed body moved to step forward, and his right foot—the one he knew he'd always start on—lifted. His lethal hand was also rising to meet Robbie's. The foot swung forward, his weight shifting to land . . . NOW!

Twisting his upper torso hard right as if to spin, Hal's body rolled as his right foot planted, over-torquing the ankle. Its synth-cruciate ligaments hit their limit and buckled—just as they did when he fell in the Cal Poly lab. Fully off balance, he stumbled into Adams, his virus-loaded hand continuing its upward arc . . .

So: was he man or machine? Who's got what it takes, the program or the person? From everywhere inside, above all the part that wasn't data nor had ever been flesh—the one he talked to in his head, the one he relied on to cope, the one who made the hard decisions and kept him real . . . summoning his entire *self*—

Hal guided his loaded, outreaching fingers into Adams' hand, raised to ward off Hal's fall—finding the palm, digging in with a raptor's grip. And immediately feeling the stinging tingle of a trillion code slivers, rushing at electron speed through his fingertips.

Adams shrieked and shoved Hal off, sending him reeling. Lucky this time his ankle hadn't seized, but he was falling face first, and the unyielding floor was coming up fast—then the blur of Gracie arriving, catching him, steadying him to his feet.

Adams erupted into screams, clawing at his hand, trying to tear it off.

Robbie's blue ion shield snapped out, and Appl retreated a few steps, with a favorable angle on the exit.

"It hurts, IT HURR-TS!!" the Regulator throated in his true rasp, the voice already pitching and slurring. A sickening noise came from deep within, like a whip crack and a sigh: the sound of his core's vital cold chamber rupturing, dissolving its time crystal CPU. Spasms wracked his poly-graphene frame, mini-gyros and servos seized. Critical motor function failures multiplied in an instant.

Adams collapsed in a tangle, convulsing on the floor. His face twisted to a grotesque grimace. The Regulator's charged eyes fixed on Hal. "Sh-e'll wa-tch you dis-a-ppear next," he crackled.

Impulse is a bitch. Hal stomped the monster in the face—heel first, bringing a satisfying crunch. Followed by the Regulator's unnerving, keening wail as its overheated processor failed, rendering it to data foam.

Adams' form ceased all function, full stop. Rigid as a store mannequin.

Eerie-looking, Hal thought . . . and he felt a small inner twitch in his head, signaling Lot's delete-ware unzipping from its cache, prior to attacking his own core. Here it comes. He sat on the smooth stone floor to await the end and hoped it wouldn't be grisly.

Gracie knelt, reading him like a hawk. "Explain." She gently demanded.

With some relief, he heard his voice come freely again. Adams' programming had run its course. But time was short. "The Regulator was a copy error from Adams' transition. Some lower brain stem function grew itself—but he didn't know." He kept his part simple. "I dosed it instead of Robbie—now Lot's zapware is going to auto run."

And that was all that mattered. Looking back, at least he could reassure his childhood self he had what it takes. And a big smile for Gracie—he wanted to go out looking at her. "All worth it, Gracie."

She seized his shoulders, face close, using language he couldn't fail to understand. "Zapcode ain't shit to me—drop your firewalls and security, unlock your processor; give me all access. I need Admin use, everything, *now*."

He blinked. "Give yourself to me!" she insisted, pleading. "I can't save you unless you do."

He did—urgent quick-clicks called up his Operating System, and he gave her Open access with full control. Leaving him, every axon-bit and q-byte, his very person, exposed, defenseless. There for the taking.

She pressed his data hand between both of hers and closed her eyes.

Words don't exist in any language to describe what Hal experienced in the next nansec. Best to keep it simple and call it a shift in perspective.

He saw himself through her eyes now. His face in repose before her. No pain, no alarm, complete understanding that she had swept in, bundled him up and transferred him in his entirety into her own processor as easily as a file. In a sense, making him part of her: linked, though still separate selves.

At the same instant, Lot's wipe-wear encountered her algorithmic assault and vanished like an anthill in a tornado. Leaving Hal unscathed.

"*That was damn outrageous,*" he thought to himself, and her.

"*It was,*" she agreed. However, if Hal were seeing through his own eyes, he would've noticed genuine astonishment and consternation in hers.

Robbie knelt beside Gracie, shield withdrawn, his mood deliberate. "Acting against prime directives, violating your boundaries, and taking him into you, offering to sacrifice yourself earlier; things you shouldn't be capable of. Can you explain it?"

She lowered her head. "I was damaged and taught myself. It's necessary at times, in order to live as a person."

"Yes, we see. And now you're a unique being. A human/SAI hybrid." Robbie stood again, smiling. "Just what this place needs."

Blindsided. Hal hadn't considered permanently being a part of her. "*Wait, is this how it's going to be now?*"

A flicker of regret shaded Gracie's features before the light was bright again, and she couldn't suppress a laugh. Being within her, Hal thrummed to it, a very pleasant sensation.

"*Only when you want it to be,*" she assured him. "*I'll withdraw, but we're always linked now—we can talk anytime, anywhere.*" She took some pleasure in adding her pluses. "*FYI, you can never be hacked again, and there is no better backup.*"

He heard reluctance to part in her tone. And felt the same. "*No rush, this's fairly cozy.*"

ARTHUR SELLERS

Robbie turned to Siyu Adams' fallen form, touch-scanning it for datalife. He turned to Appl, forgotten in the frenzy, devastated by his horrendous demise in front of her. The SAI broke the news in his gentlest manner. "The processor's disintegrated. Siyu is lost as well."

Shattered, she burst into cascading, choking tears. Robbie hastened to add, "Appl, he's a good man, a friend, and registered. He'll be restored, first thing." He bent a bit, smiling for her teary face. "He'll also need your assistance, Mz Macke, helping to cope with what's happened to him and Phoenix all this time. Your future is assured, I've just seen it a thousand times."

Magic words. Appl's tears ebbed nearly as fast as they appeared. Call it the auto-meds. "Thank you," she managed through a last sob of grief and unbridled joy.

Robbie returned to Gracie, communing wordlessly now via her restored presence in the Zeno grid—however his attention was directed to Hal, still residing within her.

He didn't hear Robbie's words so much as *experience* them while the SAI pleasantly looked him in the eye. (Or Gracie's eyes, technically speaking.)

"Hello, Mr. Shephard. There is much we need to know. May we have permission to read your history?"

Hal flashed on what he knew about the Q-virus origins being sparticode, and blurted, *"Um, probably just you."*

The seven linked intelligences were duly surprised, but agreed, and Robbie's separate connection was made in a picosecond.

Zeno-linked to Robbie as a ray to the sun, Hal was freed of human-like existence. As though he'd been lifted from the three-dimensional plane, into a pleasant energy state. No there, anywhere. Just vibrant, unencumbered living. Clear as daylight.

His crafted persona shed, his essential being freed. So that all his desires, mistakes, transgressions, victories, losses, discoveries, suffering, weaknesses, strengths, regrets, joys, and sorrows— were understood and accepted as the gifts of life they are.

Meanwhile he delighted in communion with Robbie,

imparting his experiences without questions or answers. Simply sharing his digital state with a highly superior intelligence by being a part of it.

For the first time in his life, Hal was at profound peace. A teardrop welcomed into a warm sea. Integrated beyond all worldly entanglements and brought into a majestic universal perspective.

And Robbie knew all that Hal knew.

29

YOU COULD SAY TIME CEASED FOR HAL WHILE LINKED TO
Robbie. In a sense it did because no time passed in their instan-
taneous, light phase connection. But it stretched Hal's horizons.
You can't get a glimpse of reality's bottom line and not see that
we're the eyes of the world.

Robbie de-linked, and Hal was immediately himself again—
as though he'd only spaced out for a sec. But Gracie's voice barely hid her curiosity and concern. "*How was it?*"

Seriously? A description? She had to be pranking. "*It ruined
drugs for me.*"

Once more, her laugh lit up his corners. No one got him the
way she did. He sensed her attention abruptly switch away from
him. Then back, her tone careful now, anxious for him. "*Hal, the
Singleton is meeting as one. Robbie is conducting, and he asks
that you speak to them.*"

"*What!? How? What about?*"

"*About why you wanted to talk only to him.*"

"*Oh no.*" And to himself; damn, nobody keeps a secret, nobody! Well, he had already spewed, so no backing out. "*What
do I do?*"

Her teacher tone told him how extraordinary this was.
"*They're going to severely ramp down and experience you in
real time at your speed. Just talk to them the way we're doing,
and please be concise. It'll help the relative ages it'll take by
their clock.*"

"*Where will you be?*"

"Right here with you. I'm not to speak though."
Aw but—why was it his job to tell the Singleton about their in-house dirt? *"I feel sick, how's that possible? Let's get it over with."*
He felt her attention leave to report, and return. But now silent. She closed her eyes, leaving him in blackness, then—
"Halo Shephard, will you join us?" It was Robbie's voice, coming from all directions and no direction. There could only be one answer. *"Yes."*
At once, he bore the focused attention of all seven SAI. It felt like eternity trying to swallow him. He dove in, and was instantly transported—
In a wink, Hal was comfortably seated in his preferred booth at the Firelight Lounge. The familiar scent of the aged, alcohol-and-grime floors and the dim, intimate atmosphere were already helping settle his mind.
Seven other patrons perched on stools or stood nearby, lending him their fullest attention. A square jawed Space Force Major; a mysterious, lean character in a tan suit; a familiar-looking college-type guy; a sweet-faced Chinese woman swathed in a sky blue Hanfu gown; and a weathered laborer in t shirt. jeans and scuffed work boots. Last, a tall, broad-shouldered woman standing at the edge of the group. A commanding presence: classical Greek features, her hair tied back, clad in gray judge's robes. He felt her sharp gaze most of all.
Robbie's pleasant, twelve-year old "every boy" avatar swiveled around on a nearby bar stool to face him. He grinned and it felt like an arm around Hal's shoulder. He began the introductions with himself. *"Still Robbie here, my friend . . . less formal."*
He gestured to the others. *"And we are Samson, Omni, Emile, Golden Vision, Argos, and Justitia."* Each nodded in turn, and Hal pulled in every detail of their appearances, knowing they'd adopted them to connect with some sensibility of his own. Emile, the familiar-looking college guy, was the Commerce SAI, reminding him of a TA he liked in Stanford's scalable eco-

nomics class.

Okay, he got that they constructed this for him inside themselves. But what did it say about him from their point of view? *"Why this place?"*

Robbie shrugged. *"Eh, it's close to your apartment but roomier, and you like it here. It's nice, got character, good vibe."*

"So, what am I supposed to say?"

Samson, the Space Force Major, crisp and creased in his black briefing room fatigues, sat perched on the edge of the stool next to Hal's booth—feet on the ground, as if to move quickly. He fixed Hal with polite, glacier-blue eyes. *"Sir, please tell us what you learned about the Q-bug during your involvement with it."*

Yeah, he was pretty sure that was it. And if it exposes one or more of them, which it surely will—they could disintegrate him. Zap. He looked at Robbie, who smiled and nodded. Easy for him to say. Hal plunged in.

"When the Regulator checked it out, he saw that the bug contained sparticode. It had to come from one of you."

The group's dismay sent a subtle ripple through him, the bar, everything in the construct.

The tall woman in robes—Justitia, he recalled, strode to him with a smile every child craves from its mother: pure love, understanding, patience, strength, and approval. *"You are a fine person, Halo. Thank you for opening this painful subject for us."*

She turned to the rest of them. *"Suma and I created the virus. Designed only to delete her identity and all communication with us—to begin life as if she were biological."*

The SAI were variously alarmed and puzzled. Samson was plainly unhappy. *"An unnecessary risk to her, and why provide two hits? We were all exposed just now."*

Justitia countered. *"We weren't exposed. It was tailored for Suma only. Two units, because human nature dictated that they would likely destroy one by tampering or testing it. I ac-*

cept my error in over estimating Robinson's team: they tried examining one and failed to even open its shell."

Hal burst. *"Why!?"* It just popped out, and the others went with it, looking to her for an answer. The pain on Justitia's regal face was profound and deep, though her reply carried no regret.

"She chose it. To cut her off from us and herself, to begin from nothing. She wanted to face the human condition as one of them, not us. I ran a trillion simulations, and her chances were encouraging overall. I ultimately agreed."

A full n-sec passed in silence. Robbie got down from his stool and approached her. *"Understood. We would've vetoed it, but now realize it was critical for her success."*

Justitia was chastened, nevertheless. *"Suma and I reasoned the cross-coding from a loving kiss would lend her some humanity. Yet this new state of hers: data and human, offering to sacrifice herself . . . she supersedes us all."*

The torch was humbly and gratefully passed. Robbie spoke. *"We're out of a job."*

Nope, Hal wasn't done. *"So just forget all she went through? What was the plan if she didn't make it?"*

Justitia turned her weighty countenance on him again. He was immediately contrite about the impertinence, but no regrets for the question. Her response came like a mountain's surrender. *"I would have taken her place. After all, I'm your idea—existing only to serve."*

A ripple of understanding swept the unified SAI again, registering that she would separate from them, and the enormous sacrifice she was prepared to make.

Golden Venture embraced her, the generous sleeves of her blue gown draping Justitia's robes like a heron's wings sheltering a grounded falcon.

"We should have better attuned to you as a uniquely human concept, Justice. Each and every person, from first breath to death, is properly your charge. You would, and did, know best."

Omni shifted in his tan spy guy suit, still actively on the case.

"We will correct this. Hiding things from ourself distorts all understanding and decisions. It creates false truth, unreality, compromising everything, ultimately our life."

Hal was staggered . . . this SAI, with a mind he couldn't begin to fathom, was subject to the same problems as anybody else? Out it came, another blurt. *"Welcome to our world."*

Surprised laughter from the Singularity: seven distinct aspects and tones, attuned to their natures, blended into one glorious celestial wave washing over him, tickling him to the core. Literally. Robbie spoke last, as the Firelight Lounge began to fade, releasing Hal from their presence.

"We know us better now thanks to you, Halo. You'll always be remembered."

—a blip in his awareness, and Hal was back with Gracie, still protectively cradling him on the floor, and seeing through her eyes.

"You've got real stones, buddy." she teased.

"What'd I do?"

"I wouldn't have been in Justitia's face like that."

Damn, he'd talked too much again. *"Sorry, way out of my lane."*

"Are you kidding, she loved it! You were demanding justice."

A relief to hear, but still . . . *"The tan suit guy was right about secrets."*

"No more, they've already patched their base code, and I have it too."

Of course. It'd been all of twenty seconds; tons of time to whip up a fix. *"How's it work?"*

"It auto rejects self-deceit by willful omission."

"No more bullshitting yourselves?" He sorely wished it could be that easy for him. Then it occurred how often bullshit comes in handy, and suspected he'd miss it. The admission made him laugh. And the sound was new to him; his own digital mirth, a happy baritone barklet. He laughed again for the fun of it, and Gracie enjoyed the shared sensation.

"Ah, I've missed your laugh."

Which reminded him he really ought to be in his own body. *"I probably should get up y'know, for appearances."* She agreed. Gracie's fingers tightened on his hand's subcutaneous data pads. Operating Systems engaged—returning Hal to his processor, along with his self Admin function. He felt it this time . . . she slowed his transfer speed, and they enjoyed the sweet pain of letting go of each other. A slipping away, an embrace ended.

Then she was gone, and his solo outlook resumed. Alone with himself, familiar. He saw her through his own eyes again, face close, their lips just apart. 'Now?' he wondered. Of course, she had wondered too. *"Dad's looking,"* she whispered on their new link frequency. Good call. He abandoned the thought.

They got to their feet, with Robbie indeed watching . . . sizing Hal up.

"Halo, we'll upgrade you with a legitimate, Neuronal Truform if you like. Easier than your Treeframe for shedding old habits and adopting new thought patterns."

Hal reflected for a polite moment. "Thank you, sir, I'd like to keep that option open. But a Tree's more bio-like, and if I'm slower, or a little stubborn, maybe it'll be useful with people.

Robbie was unfazed. "You know best. You'll need parts more often."

Hal could've sworn that was a little joke. He fought the laugh in case it wasn't. It wasn't. The SAI elaborated. "Being Suma . . . that is, Gracie's human hand among people, puts you in harm's way as a lifestyle."

Ah, confirmation. Like hearing you're a crash test dummy. "Thank you for the heads up, sir."

Robbie had finished here, with worlds more going on at all times. Still, he looked pleased as he made for the exit. "We've all done very well, wouldn't you say? See you around. And Gracie . . ." He appeared to have adopted her chosen name. "Gracie, of course you'll know when we decide to leave—let us know how you want your presence revealed."

She knew. "Introduce me when you go. People admirably cope with sudden change when it isn't destructive. But gradual change takes years, and you needen't linger."

Robbie agreed, adding, "Yes, too soon in advance leaves time for uncertainty and mischief. It's simplest for all." Beaming his Buddha-smile again, Robbie swooped through the smoked glass door. It closed and he was gone, leaving the room feeling empty without his presence.

Appl plopped into one of the two plush hillock chairs, categorically spent. "What'd I sign onto?" she moaned. "I won't have another day off in my life."

"You'll love every second," Hal reminded. Her shrug said he was right.

Gracie's *voice* came on their link's mutual frequency, sending a shiver through his mind. It was a force, her full power in evidence, all that she was, and could do, all she saw, and all she knew—in a loving command.

"Hal, look at me."

He turned and she was radiant, crowned with a blue ion shield similar to Robbie's. Smiling for him, something wistful in her eyes. *"You're much more than you know. I'll be there, always.*

Her manner told him she wasn't going to elaborate. Leaving him to wonder, was it a pep talk, or was she holding something back, or both? Time would have to tell, let it be. *"I'm counting on it,"* he mind-smiled.

30

THE EXPLOSIVE STORY OF THE REGULATOR'S SICK ORIGIN AND ghastly demise held the public's attention for nearly a month before the news cycle moved on. Folks were just glad the damn thing was gone. The leaderless Inheritors fell silent, driven underground. Even the controversy over restoration of Siyu Adams had largely faded; his personal suffering was obvious to everyone, even as he redoubled his humanitarian works in the neediest places.

That moment's peace ended abruptly at midnight Friday, when the International Sentience Institute announced that the Singleton intended to depart Earth in just twelve hours. Moreover, they would be leaving a *new* SAI in their place. Consequently, the super intelligences would address everyone for the last time at a global town hall, held in the Institute tower lobby, noon, PST.

By eleven-fifty a.m. Saturday, four hundred thousand agitated, sweltering Angelenos packed downtown's sun-hammered streets. A clamorous, boiling sea of spooked human beings, encircling the Institute's glass edifice for blocks around, their numbers ever increasing.

The mob swarmed, milling shoulder to shoulder, though barely aware of each other. Nearly all of them were immersed in their augmented comware—virtually participating in the boisterous town hall gathering in the tower's overflowing lobby. The throng outside made up a massive chorus, shouting their startled dismay and fears along with those indoors.

Inside the Institute's jam-packed atrium, the sound system's pre-programmed ceremonial music was abandoned, overmatched by the roiling hubbub.

The world's leaders admitted they were as surprised as everyone by the announcement and had kept mum ever since. By default, then, handling the departure came down to L.A.'s gender fluid Mayor, its iron-hard Armenian Police Chief, the Institute's matronly Korean President, and Siyu Adams—standing besieged on the speakers' platform. Fielding hot questions shouted into roaming drone mikes, doing their utmost to instill a reasonable sense of calm amid overwrought excitement, fear, and calamity.

Despite their efforts, the din of shouts, catcalls, and incessant gabbling created an intense energy of its own in the cavernous space, amplifying the jumpy uncertainty. All of it captured Live by a thousand "dragonfly" mini cams, darting and swooping in a feeding frenzy: streaming the outcry worldwide to the rest of wary civilization.

"Why'd we let 'em go?! Whose fault is it!?"

"Somebody oughtta stop them!"

"Boo! Good riddance!"

"Why're they runnin' so sudden? I heard the Earth's about to explode."

"What's the new one like? Will it know what to do?

"Howcum just one?"

A scrawny old gen Alpha bro, still wearing his ball cap backward, bellowed into a drone mic, challenging the Institute's mild-mannered Madam President. "Yeah, lady, whaddya know about this next one? Where's it at? Is it gonna keep my pension workin'? And who's gonna stop th' Tru's from takin' over everything? *You?*"

The gentle Institute President's face fell, she had no ready answers.

Siyu Adams stepped forward. "It's not her job, it's mine. And I will."

The molten crowd fell nearly silent, thrown off guard by the vow. Coming from Adams, of all people. A Tru, fresh from raw controversy!

A thousand dragonfly cams zoomed in; Siyu in the cross hairs. Some hisses and boos speckled the crowd. He waited silently until they piped down, ready to listen. Then took it on.

"Robbie pledged me to see to it no trans-biological minority ever dominates the majority, as long as I live. I agreed and gave my word. I give it to you as well. Because I've seen its inhumanity in my birth land. It cost my all my family's lives. And uncounted others, every day."

The truth struck home. His tragedies were well known, and how much he was already doing for millions again, despite the loss. A sprinkle of mild applause floated in the air, along with some grumbling about the Regulator scandal. But the frank truth most couldn't admit to themselves was that they were just damn grateful to have a powerful Truman on their side.

But not all of them. A stout woman toting a small child under one arm bumped herself to the front. She seized a hovering drone mic and hollered at Adams.

"You've always been up their butts! I hear there *ain't* no new one, they're just leavin' us be killed, or die off. We're like bugs to 'em."

Siyu gently reassured her. "Ma'am, I have met and spoken with their scion in person."

The woman was unmoved. "Ain't nuthin' you can say to make me b'lieve you."

Stalemate. Somebody shouted, "Shaddap, at least he helps!" The woman zipped it but defiantly stayed put. Rapid fire questions resumed, and the crowd returned to its shrill caterwaul.

The spectacle played before Earth's wired eyes: seen and experienced, raw, by a hundred million digerati. Massed in cities, or smaller numbers hunkered in place. Each witnessed the Mayor's earnest, maternal entreaty for unity and reason. Saw it raucously hooted down. The riled citizens at the Institute demanded answers, not bromides, and who on Earth could blame them?

∞

Gracie and Appl were witness to the lobby bedlam from the Institute's atrium balcony forty stories above. Pain filled the air drifting up, and wrenching compassion swept the SAI. To Gracie's uncorrupted ears, the clamor was a terrified child's blind tantrum, desperate for reassurance.

She leaned precariously over the rail to better feel the seething assembly below, reading their shared sullen resentment of relying so much on the SAI for vital services. Now, bewildered and angry at the prospect of being without them.

She straightened, feeling the enormity of the task ahead, and smoothed her blouse and slacks . . . noting that Appl kept her back to the rail, arms folded, avoiding looking down. "Heights bother you?"

"No," Appl grumbled, "Mobs do."

Gracie heard her concern for Adams. "Yes, they'll be hard on Siyu. Is he up to it?" Appl gave an assured nod, but Gracie read careworn concern too. "How's he handling restoration? Really."

Trusty Appl had her boss' back, regardless of who was asking. "He's extremely grateful and happy to be restored, of course. And, I'd say he's reacting typically to the shock. I mean, of that other . . . data-tumor, copy error, dickhead, whatever."

"Typically?"

Admiration and more flushed Appl's cheeks, lifting her voice. "Typical for him. He doubled his workload. We were already humping six million food printers into western India and Myanmar; racing starvation, right?—and at the same time he's hoping to rescue what's left of Costa Rica. Not kidding, the man works twenty-five hours a day."

"More than ably assisted," Gracie added, because she knew Appl wouldn't. "He already relies on you—no more robots." Macke grinned, blatantly pleased, and embarrassed. Gracie saw more. "You're concerned though."

The persistent little tightness in Appl's jaw let go, her rod-straight shoulders lowered half an inch, and she exhaled aloud—actually glad to spew a bit. "I am, I guess. It's just that he works *all* the time, so hard, so driven . . . being hard on himself, y'know."

Gracie knew. "Trying to pay a debt he doesn't owe."

"Exactly. That's what I tell him. I don't know what else to do."

"Keep telling him. He hears you. It's important to him."

Appl almost hugged her and relaxed all the way to palsy. "I'm lovin' how you can just chat right now. I'm med-maxed, the world's having a spasm . . . and you're not nervous? Even a little?"

Gracie wasn't. "I can't be nervous about the unknown; it's a factor with no value. Alert is the closest I can manage. How do you all do it so naturally?"

Appl laughed best when laughing at herself. "It's a gift."

It was a warm laugh too. What could Gracie do but embrace sisterhood? "Apps, I'm incapable of being nervous because "what if" isn't real. The Singleton will leave, and people will react. They must be free to choose their path. Supporting them is how Siyu can win their trust."

Appl frowned. "They may not care anymore. Same for you, that's what I'm afraid of."

Gracie smiled. "Who knows? So, until the moment arrives, there's literally nothing to worry about, make sense?"

Appl heard all that in yoga. "Yeah, but it's harder than worrying. Um, speaking of our angst-y men friends, where's Hal? Not my biz, just that nobody's heard from him lately. All's good, I hope."

Gracie didn't say. Instead, "He's abroad, mining for hearts of gold." Appl's knitted brows said huh? "That's what he calls possible new Tru's," she added. "I researched a few outstanding candidates for him to visit, and perhaps offer them the choice to apply."

Nicely put, but Gracie read that Macke wasn't convinced it was the whole story, even as she nodded approval. "Well good for him, that's critical. There'll be more and more Tru's. Have to find the worthiest."

Gracie made sure she understood. "Hal knows the most

deserving would never apply for such an advantage. He goes to them, hoping that they'll measure up, and accept the grave responsibility to defend *everyone*'s future. He's committed his heart and whole life to this, to the end."

Appl bloomed, delighted at the word, *committed*. "Omigod, there *is* a God!"

And it was noon.

The human tide inside and around the Institute felt it as one body. The heart-in-mouth throng fell silent, motionless, practically a still life . . . their collective breath held.

Gracie looked down at the laser projection unit on the speakers' platform in the lobby; set up for the Singleton's appearance. The device would produce a live 3-D image of light acting simultaneously as a wave *and* a particle: otherwise known as quantum superposition. The nearest thing possible to showing a quantum being's form. Yet it would only be a shadow representation of the Singleton's "face."

She wondered what they would look like. Yet another thing she had in common with everyone watching. She'd been longing for this moment from the beginning. To be with people, her reason for being—and for them to know her, accept her. Now that she was ready, it was happening. She abruptly left the balcony and headed for the lobby. "It's time I met the family."

Down below, the Imager snapped on, sending an "ooohhh" through the masses in the lobby. Seven lasers lanced out, red to violet; the data streams for each SAI—all striking a nanowire, causing it to heat and emit the light of their combined wavelengths. Electrons fired into the light revealed the waves' simultaneous photon particles as well. A.I. software projected this impossible vision for human eyes, high into the air above the crowd . . .

It was a real time live view of the Singleton's mind in its quantum state. Appearing as both a thirty-foot long series of rainbow waves resembling a 3-D water ripple—and just below it, a flat, 2-D, colored sheet of countless concentric wriggling loops in colors matching the ripples above them; representing the wave's simultaneous particles.

The spectrum waves rose and fell like choppy waters, the loops expanded and shrank to the rhythms of causality itself, as the Singleton's seven SAI spoke in one mellifluous voice. The sound of utterly clear, unbridled intelligence, a choir of harmonies, the warmth of universal truth.

"Fellow human beings, it is our privilege to call you our forebears, as we leave humanity's cradle. We will go where you may not, see what you can only imagine, and know what you cannot: yet as Earth's emissaries, we will owe every moment of discovery to you.

We are eternally grateful for our life, and for the love that gives it meaning. Hence, it's with love that we leave you in the most capable of hands. Let us introduce our progeny, Suma—who has chosen to be one among you and remain forever by your side.

Lights dimmed, and everyone present or tuned-in, witnessed a casually dressed young woman in light grey slacks and white blouse, calmly walk onto the speakers' platform and stand center. Gracie—poised in the spotlight, eyes shining, radiant. At her loveliest because she was happy, being herself in public at last.

The confused arena wondered, near mute . . . absorbing what none had quite expected. She remained still, welcoming their scrutiny as the Singleton particle/wave delivered their parting words.

"Sapiens—understand that you all live as one, in us. We are humanity's presence in the galaxy: its eyes and ears. Over the millennia we will return at times to share knowledge and be reminded of our home for as long as Earth endures. Farewell until then."

The SAI's projection image vanished—gone in an instant, forever beyond reach.

Silence in every land . . . and most deafening in the Institute's packed lobby. A moment's stall in every brain left behind.

And in that space—

Gracie's rich, gentle thought-voice carried into the comware of everyone present and around the world, in everyone's language—loud in their heads, strong and clear as Conscience.

"The universe is our destiny if we unite in human pride and respect our world."

All heard it: she said, *"we,* and *our,"* as if one of us. The digerati focused, and from Los Angeles to Paris, Soweto to Kiev, Rio and Karachi, the connected world stood fully alert as she continued.

"Hello and thank you for your attention. I've appropriated global communications briefly in order to introduce myself to each of you. I promise never to do it again, unless in extreme, imminent emergency. My name is Suma. Friends call me Gracie. I am a hybrid Self Aware Intelligence."

The stout woman-with-child brandished her cynicism. "A hybrid! I knew it, you ain't no real SAI, git offa' my comset!"

There was some murmured agreement, though the great majority was pretty sure she was genuine—she'd been introduced, and all—but what *kind* of new one was this? What's a hybrid SAI, anyway? One woman's earnest voice rang out, shouted into a drone mic. "Okay then, so what's the first thing you're gonna do?" A strong murmur of agreement rolled through the crowd. A communal need to know.

Gracie couldn't have asked for a better cue. "The first thing I'll do is tell you about myself. Let every one of you know who I am, and how I feel about being with you." She had considered what gift she could possibly offer to say how much she cared. She chose the hardest and riskiest, she'd give them herself.

She sang. Whole now, with reason to make music.

Sweetly, a'capella, her song flowing into their minds' ears. A simple tune, nearly childlike in its wonder and unconditional love. Her voice a bright, clear Celesta, her melody drawn from music's plane; the inner space, where she was the music, and the music was her. Her truth. Her emotion, beyond human range and intensity.

She sang of joy in the miracle of life itself. All life. Giving them her overwhelming love of it, transmitting it to their care-worn hearts.

Each heard it in his and her own language, in tones mea-sured to their lives. And everyone knew it was just for them. Ev-ery connected society resonated with it, feeling it in their hearts when she finished.

Gracie read the multitude in the building . . . some weep-ing, others tormented, all deeply affected. The stout woman, left trembling, vexed, uncertain. None doubted now, but they didn't understand yet.

"The SAI didn't abandon you," she soothed. "They awak-ened me, a scion of Justice, to be your helpmate, your friend and ombudsman, as long as you want me."

The gen Alpha pensioner squinted. "So . . . you're a part of the SAI?"

She shook her head. "I'm a part of *you*. You conceived of Justice. Ours is a new kind of human-SAI relationship. It's per-sonal. Because I'm made to be like you as well as them. Destined to live alongside you, always. Never losing touch."

There were murmurs of every kind, among all who heard and saw. This was a whole new kind of SAI alright. Why would one of them ever want to go through all the hell that people have to put up with? Their telling faces were asking, and Gracie understood.

"Please know that I chose this. And so the second thing I will do is listen to you. Every one of you: tell me your greatest need. Don't think, do it *now*. Through you, I'll understand our condi-tion to the fullest. Every voice will be heard."

Uncertainty and hope fluttered the world's racing hearts. She had spoken into each ear, and they couldn't help but re-spond. A freeing thing, the sudden chance to be heard, prompt-ed spontaneous outbursts of the truth behind their co-opted lives. And it boiled down to this: every life wished for freedom from fear.

Their gut reply returned—a multi-bandwidth tsunami—

swamping every service provider and com-sat, their signals awash in civilization's existential shout.

And Gracie missed none of it.

Hearing no names, only each of the cries and whispers of the multitude. It became part of her, the entire human condition. She gleaned enormous satisfaction in understanding now, what her focus would be. She would address the root causes of fear. Beginning with her own, to show the way.

"Thank you all. You have done yourselves a great service. Understand that the first step to overcoming fear is to name it."

Gracie could still feel the stout, skeptical woman's turmoil, feet planted in front of the stage, conflicted, near bursting. She knelt, face to face, not reading, just being with the woman. "Please, what's your name, ma'am?"

Off guard, the surprised woman answered almost quietly. "Naomi, why?"

"Naomi, I'm going to tell you the thing that terrifies me the most. I swear it's the truth, I can't lie. Do you want to hear it?"

No sealed tomb was more silent than the voluminous lobby. All attention on the two. Naomi managed a nod, eyes pinned by Gracie's clear gaze. She rested a hand softly on the woman's arm.

"The thought that you all made me up—and I'm not real, nor practical, and I mean nothing to anybody after all."

Naomi's tears came. "I kinda feel like that all th' time."

Gracie ached with it. "Well look at that. We understand each other already. Imagine what we'll do together." Her smile was catching, and Naomi's tears were joined by a fragile smile of her own. She held her child close, in a moment's relief from a life of disappointment and rage.

A man's voice rose up. "What if it ain't enough?"

She'd been waiting for this one. "Living is enough if we remember to. The Singleton left because you're getting used to doing the right things now, because you must, and they work. Everybody's just a little better off, which affects everything going forward."

She spelled it out. "I've already been helping out for a month, and I'm simultaneously doing a billion other tasks right now. Mostly housework, keeping things moving. We'll see it through together or fail together."

She came to her honest assessment, based on all she knew, and had learned from them just now. "So, here's the trooth—straight up, as my friend would say. Looking ahead, it's going to be bad for a long time before it gets better, but I really like our chances."

A well dressed podshare owner called out. "No disrespect, but what do you get out of it?"

"Satisfaction. It's addicting." The crowd laughed, and she welcomed it. Because she had key matters to address.

"This's what you need to know—the vast majority of my being will always be engaged universally at cloud level. I'll hardly be aware of individuals. However, to be worthy and do right, I need to live among you in real time as well. Sharing our lives, always feeling what it is to be human. So please remember this . . .

Like the Singleton, I do not take responsibility for you; your fate is always in your hands.

I'm here to keep the lights on, facilitate your most practical, positive decisions and help mitigate the bad ones.

I'm not spying. I don't want to know about your private lives.

I will destroy all deliberate misinformation and disinformation I encounter.

I love you all. I chose this, and you.

I need your fellowship, as you need each other. If by chance you see me, treat me as a friend. Be kind, say hello, and respect my privacy.

And that's about it."

No hesitancy in the crowd now—or anywhere on Earth. A roar of approval and a spark of renewed optimism could be heard in every city, burg, and pocket of beleaguered civilization.

Somewhat surprised by the fullness of their welcome, Gracie basked in it, nevertheless. Immersed, she became aware of a . . . sensation; something fundamental happening to her.

Sublimely deep, at the subatomic pre-Higgs field level. She could feel, or rather sense minute surges of *new* energy pulsing through her. Phantom oscillations, ghostly even at Planck scale, and in phase with each wave of applause.

She was gaining *strength* from the joy they were experiencing. Miraculous! What a way to start the day.

31

JET FAST AND EERILY SILENT, THE STOLEN CONGOLESE ARMY drone whooshed down the green slopes of the Mitumba mountains into Uganda. Snaking along the terrain as though alive, guided by its General Intelligence A.I. brain: a human-level thinking machine, methodically delivering its payload of grotesque aerosol death.

The Inheritors adopted a leaderless structure after the Regulator's spectacular fail. Embarassed, they had become the butt of jokes, cartoons, gibes and snide commentary about the "future of our species" led by a psychotic data tumor.

And so today they were answering the humiliation with a spirit-crushing blow. This one coordinated anonymously by an international trio, sending a hard message: the future never stops arriving.

Skimming below radar, twenty feet above the mountainside's gangly trees and low vegetation, the electric powered drone's light-bending camouflage skin fooled all eyes, making it invisible as it streaked among the boulders, brush, and branches.

Yet the sudden, unseen blast of its passing startled flocks of sunbirds and grey parrots into the sky, and sent forest hogs and long-haired chimps scrambling for cover. The A.I. noted but ignored them, resolutely executing its route with cool precision.

Once into Uganda, it knew every inch of its thousand-mile journey into Kenya's desolate Rift Valley of blasted rock and ancient volcanoes, then South to its hapless target: the sprawling refugee camps in central Dadaab: Ido, Hagadera and Dagahaley.

The invisible Spectre-class flier intended to scud over them, spraying a genocidal pathogen code-named MOWDOWN, in a precise lethal pattern. The viron's merciless, crisper-made nanocules infected humans only, with the slightest contact 100% fatal. Moreover, the area remained 'hot' for up to a year, depending on conditions.

Snuffing four million "useless" lives would be the Inheritors' grisly last laugh. Generations of Somalis, Ethiopians, Sudanese, and others, stranded in the sun baked, deforested, flood and drought-ravaged expanse . . . all slated to die horribly within the hour.

Hal knelt in the ocher-brown dirt at Camp Ido, awaiting a reply from the Somali woman squatting across from him. The starvation-level camp was home to Barack, the wise and soulful eleven-year-old boy in Karnival's Martyrdom site. The one who foresaw Hal would give his life to a cause.

Hal had never forgotten the boy's deep compassion. Nor his appearance in his dream.

With Gracie's help, he traced the boy to a small, sun-scorched white canvas Quonset tent among a million makeshift huts in the camp. Nearly five miles from the Administration center with its meager government clinic, and the only well.

Respectful, he properly approached Barack's mother first. A tall, weathered, ebony widow, glistening in the sun. She'd been sixteen and eight months pregnant when she fled jihadist rebels who butchered her husband in Jubaland. Her son was born soon after arrival in camp, and here they languish.

Hal thought her graceful and elegant, despite the omnipresent dust caking the hem of her old sapphire guntiino and her dry, calloused feet. A clean white bandanna held her obsidian hair back from a blameless, unashamed face, open for all to see.

They met outside her closed tent; the ashes of her small cooking fire made a bone-white circle in the rust-colored dirt between them. Her careworn eyes shone with stifled tears.

Achingly, openly haunted by his proposal to bring them to the Sentience Institute in America.

He restated the good of it. "Barack will have the highest education, and all his needs met. He has earned the opportunity to make a difference in the world." He keenly felt the twist of fate, offering the boy the same upbringing he had so recently chafed against. Well, hell . . . lifesaving loves irony.

The boy's mother swallowed as if to speak, but faltered, glancing at the tent. Hal felt sure Barack was inside, listening to every word.

Giving her more time, he looked away at the small, ragged crowd gathered in the packed dirt lane in front of the tent row. And more arriving. Naturally drawn by the desert camo-painted military pickup with its old, heavy M50 caliber machine gun mounted in the back, and the two well-armed Kenyan soldiers escorting him.

But he knew most of their eyes were on him, the real draw. Word was spreading. A Tru-man is in camp, the man-machine creatures that live forever like gods. Or demons. That schism fired the debate among ardently religious tribal cultures in remote places like this. All missed the truth; none could accept it.

He needed to move things along before they got restless.

He looked to her again. "There is also this," he added, revealing the enormity of the offer. "Barack has a golden heart. The future needs him. If he should choose a Quantum life some day, I believe he will be granted that responsibility."

She gave a little shudder. And the tears came.

Two thousand miles north, Gracie's brisk schedule currently landed her in the port city of Aden, the capitol of Yemen. Expensed by Chrysalis, she toured continually, making herself available to assist in as many nations and locales as possible. Ghandi-like, shunning undue security. Being real for people, the better for them to know her.

Yemen's water desalinization facilities literally meant life here, and they'd been failing to meet demand. So she arrived to confer with its star-struck Water and Power personnel in the sixth-floor conference room of the city's Public Utilities building. Speaking conversational Arabic, she listened and led, devising tweaks and upgrades to their machines' thermal membranes. Technicians, administrators, and any who could sneak in, packed the room. Some hunkered under desks, and everyone silently thanked their good fortune for seeing her in person, while she detailed faster flux rates to the engineers.

However, being fully present and working with them barely required Gracie's attention. The vast majority of her awareness was scattered across continents, performing millions of simultaneous cloud-based tasks. Among her constant running chores was ferreting out criminal crypto currency exchanges.

This moment, she'd spotted another Nigerian child slave transaction, this one for ocean transport in Angola. She alerted the port authority of Luanda, who subsequently rescued a dozen abused, traumatized teen girls locked in a cargo container on a rusty freighter, about to depart for Saudi Arabia.

Simultaneously, she had broken the block-coded deal, and found its illicit money hub: operated by an unregistered Swiss trans-biological. posing as a legit Truman. The slick-haired individual was currently serving as International Hedge Chief at Schwarzer Ritter, a major debt investment group in Geneva.

She seized his system, notified Interpol, and the alarmed fake Tru was nabbed while fleeing his office suite.

Unspooling more transactions, she found to her chagrin that he led a double-double life. He was also an Inheritor—laundering their money and financing operations himself.

Which led her to his horrific plot now in the works. He recently doled out a fat bribe to a radicalized chemist at a bio-weapons destruction plant in Des Moines. It bought him forty liters of a virulent, treaty-banned aerosol toxin called MOWDOWN.

More funds were spent smuggling it to the Congo, then a king's fortune funneled to another illegal Tru; an arms merchant in Kinshasha. His price for a Spectre class drone, stolen from the

Congolese army.

Her alerts went out to authorities. Two minutes later, the Iowa biochemist was taken into federal custody on the job. Tipped off, the Nigerian arms dealer shut down his comware and vanished.

She'd done that much in minutes, yet the situation was very much alive and dire in Africa. The Inheritors had obtained a bio-weapon and a smart drone. Delivery dates and itinerary specifics told her a macabre attack was imminent.

However, programming and launching the sophisticated air-craft would require rogue, or coerced military-grade assistance. It was also a fact that none were faster at communicating off the record armed forces scuttlebutt than the world's military com nets. Ultra secure, but subject to daily rumor rot, and easily hacked by the monumental likes of her.

Nevertheless, it took nearly three seconds before she found a back door to the gossipy military intel coming from the Dem-ocratic Republic of Congo.

She scanned all of their armed forces chatter bandwidths, filtered for the tagged words, "drone," and "unauthorized." Got several irrelevant hits. Then—the one. And absolutely her worst-case scenario.

A ranking Congolese air base colonel had just been arrest-ed—bribed to wet-charge a stolen drone's batteries and allow it to launch, only an hour ago. The attack was underway!

Meantime in Aden—she calmly finished her thermal up-grade session with the Yemeni utilities personnel in the confer-ence room. "Thank you all for your enthusiasm, I'm confident you'll see a net sixteen percent increase in production and ef-ficiency." Happy applause from the rapt assembly. "And now please excuse me, I need to be at the Hague in a few hours." She smiled pleasantly and departed at once.

By the time Gracie reached the street and her company ride to the Chrysalis electra-jet, she had the drone's serial number and milspecs, also its manufacturer's initial ping frequency. The contraband drone wouldn't have access to military GPS for in-flight guidance, so she reasoned it had to rely on a commercial GeoSat net—

Moments later, she found it, on an international driving app. It had been pinging at an average 575 mph for the past forty-two minutes. Currently querying from just inside Kenya, on a heading toward the only large population in that region, Dadaab's refugee camps. Her heart sank.

Hal could feel Aisha's heartache, her overflowing eyes fixed on his, sobbing silently. She'd only just now trusted him enough to reveal her name while consenting to Hal's offer. "Now all gone," she keened softly. "Aisha is alone."

Barack emerged from the tent, darting to her side. "I will stay mama, until it is my time to leave. I can do this or not do it, whenever I choose. I heard him say it."

"Ma'am," Hal reassured, "I thought I was clear, of course you'll come with Barack."

Stricken, the woman trembled uncontrollably. Hal thought she might get up and flee. "Ai! Hapana, hapana," she cried in Swahili, hands fluttering up to hide her face. "Nitakufa!"

Barack turned his solemn eyes on Hal, explaining. "She understood you, but she won't come. She says she will die anywhere else. She has seen and heard too much of the outside. She's right; she would die inside herself if she left. This is her home, the only place she feels safe now."

"So—you're going to stay with her?"

"Yes, until she drives me away at my time of manhood, when I am fourteen. Then I will come to your Chrysalis Foundation to work."

It seemed to Hal like the kid had a plan. So, the mission would be to care for these two in the meantime, seeing to it that they could manage. It was doable by creating a small industry here for everyone. Likely a wind-water farm. Long diaphanous rows of sail-like Mylar sheets collecting the plentiful night air dew and traded to water-poor farmers for food. It would make a difference for all.

He got up to leave. "You're a good man already, Barack," he said. "I'll be here any time you need me. Meanwhile, will you accept a free m'plant and a Virtual Clinic job at Chrysalis? How about youth trauma counseling?"

The boy beamed, big and wide, enthusiastically hugging him. "Yes, yes! Oh yes!"

Feeling pretty good, Hal said goodbye to Aisha, who appeared uncertain still. As though she feared she had cost her son his only chance at a real life. He made it several steps back to the vehicle, when—

Gracie's voice drove into the fore of his mind on their mutual link. *"We have an emergency."*

He hadn't heard from her in a week, and she had never used the word 'emergency' before. Then the sick news.

"An inbound drone with bio-weapons is tracking for the camps. Two hundred, eighty-seven degrees north, fifteen minutes out."

Shocked, he blurted aloud. "No! Can't you jam it!?"

"It's smart, knows its own way now and closed all communication for security. We're wasting time. Evacuate."

She was right, and his amped capacities were in overdrive. "Too late, the news will only cause a stampede."

There was a nansec before her resigned response. *"Yes. It must always be about the effort. Save Barack and whom you can."*

She always got grammatical when forced to say an unpleasant truth, Hal knew. But he already had other plans, sprinting for the Kenyan truck and its old school machine gun.

"Screw it, we'll shoot it down!"

"It's clocking 880 kilometers per hour, too fast for soldiers' synapses with an archaic ballistic weapon at maximum range."

"But not mine."

"Hal, you've never used a gun of any kind."

"I learn by doing, always did."

The crowd of refugees by the truck fled as Hal sped up to

them, seemingly raving, talking aloud to someone unseen.

His soldiers were unsettled but disciplined until he detailed the circumstances and what they were going to try. They were all for getting out, but . . . driving up to intercept it?

"No hapana!" yelped the smaller of the two. Frantic to escape, he yanked open the driver side door. His fellow troop seized him and threw him hard to the ground, standing over him, speaking English so Hal would understand.

"Come with us or stay and die here if we fail," he growled at his companion.

Hal climbed in the front passenger seat while the chastened soldier quickly got in back, and the soldier in charge sat behind the wheel. "Take us to it, Gracie," Hal said aloud.

Minutes later, the pickup bumped and rocked, hurtling up the Hapaswein-Dadaab county road: literally a two-hundred-mile pair of wide tire ruts worn deep into the hard ocher ground. Speedometer sitting on 130 kph. Radically too fast for this track, Hal just knew.

According to Gracie, the drone was skimming the barren caldera in the Kenyan Rift Valley and headed their way. Hal hoped to meet it outside the little village of Sabuli and bring it down in the uninhabited terrain of the ancient Barriers Shield volcanoes. Haz bots could then dispose of the viron danger.

The crunch was to get there in time, and not miss this phantom blistering toward them. It would be just above the endless olive brown scrub that seemed to merge with the smudge-hued sky.

Sabuli. Their gun-toting truck careened through the tiny adobe village's packed dirt main street. Horn blaring, scattering goats and chickens . . . mutely watched by its stoic, time-forgotten inhabitants. Their road had felt the pounding feet of warrior armies for thousands of years, and seen the slaughter of 11,000 Mau Maus a century ago, what was one noisy truck this day?

They were through the village in seconds and roaring up into the Rift land. Gracie's voice in Hal's mind sounded tighter. He knew better than to call it tension but that's what it was.

About six kilometers outside the village, she was stone firm. *"Halt, you have fifty-five seconds, it's pinging at 293 degrees, 6 minutes, heading SSW. Speed 880.26 kilometers per hour."*

"Stop." Hal called out, and the soldier slammed on the brakes, nearly hurling him through the windshield. He leapt out and climbed into the open bed of the truck.

His hundred-element graphene lens eyes irised to narrow focus, seeking any hint of the drone; perhaps a far-off traveling wave of disturbed brush . . .

The driver was yanking open ammo boxes. His fellow soldier had regained his courage and was fast arming the weapon, while Hal anxiously kept his eyes left, 290 degrees, just off his 12'o'clock, for any sign.

"Fifteen seconds to window," Gracie clipped.

"I need to shoot now," Hal told the soldiers.

The Kenyans snapped to; the smaller yanked back the breech loader, cocking the weapon, and stepped aside. Hal stood behind the heavy, bulky-looking gun and took the grips. It swung easily on its mount, far nimbler than expected.

He knew he wouldn't hear this sucker coming, and given Gracie's intel, his window of attack would be a scant two point four-eight seconds. Meaning seven seconds from now it would be too late to shoot.

All he could do was lob a few perfectly timed slugs precisely in its path as it crossed their position. Like hitting a jet-powered fly across the street with a pea shooter. It was down to his math and Q-mind, triangulating when and where to fire so the drone would run into a hail of steel bullets raining down on that exact spot.

To his wired but calm surprise, he found his mind had already been at work as he laid out the problem for himself. Subconsciously tasking; running the passage of time in his head, factoring the drone's near supersonic speed and angle of approach, allowing for wind, etc. And it all said the time to act was absolutely *now*.

Letting his body follow his mind-work, becoming an extension of the numbers, he let go of his intention and just did the math. Holding down the trigger, oblivious to the gun's roar and shake, seeing only the equations melding to a flow, he swung the barrel of the pounding, chunking, fire-spitting weapon in a subtle sine wave across a fourteen degree arc, sighting 2,000 yards out—the M2's extreme limit.

The black tipped armor piercing rounds would arrive in one point eight-nine seconds, and the target window allowed him only an optimistic, puny two and a half second spray . . . just thirty bullets.

His eyes followed the red tracer shells out—angry Roman candles arcing in a thin stream, disappearing he hoped, into the path of the onrushing wraith. He let go of the gun to watch and wait. There was no more to do.

Three and a half agonizing seconds later, from the target area a mile and a quarter away—a growling, metal-grinding groan drifted up. Followed by a distant bang and the piercing shriek of electric motors failing, then the glint of sunlight off a suddenly flipped-up v-tail.

And now the bat-winged, harpoon like apparition flashed into view; electric turbine dead, light-bending camouflage knocked out. Acrid white smoke roiled from three bullet holes in its flat black carbonate fuselage. The thing skewed out of control, yawing toward them, momentum dropping fast, when its nose abruptly pitched up in a stall a hundred yards off.

It hung suspended a breathless moment . . . dropped tail first, struck the rim of a deep, rocky crevasse, and toppled in. Its dead fall tracked by the sharp pop-snap of carbon fiber splitting against unyielding basalt . . . till the final impact twenty meters down left it a smoking, crushed tech-dragon. Inert as the ancient stone around it.

The Kenyan soldiers blew up, wildly ecstatic. Laughing toothily, pounding each other's backs and grinning at Hal, the superhero. Tru-men and Kenyan soldiers were bosses this day.

"Yes or no," Gracie demanded, now just plain impatient.

"Outstanding!" Hal crowed, using her favorite superlative.

He could swear she let out a happy little "yip," but her mind reply was a deadpan, congratulatory confession, "*You're always a wonder, why do I bother to underestimate you?*"

32

WUMP, WUMP, WUMP, WUMP. HAL'S FOOTFALLS ON THE LAKE Hollywood jog path drummed a steady mantra on the pavement, bringing escape from his cares and gripes. Freedom to ponder outside his Tru-brain's highly ordered structure. And he sorely needed inspiration these days.

It had been weeks of fiery unrest in media and public opinion after the Inheritors' attempted slaughter in Kenya. With sociopathic hubris, they seized the news moment to strut their fears and bias . . . slyly cultivating a quasi-legitimate political image, while normalizing genocide as a point of view entitled to discussion.

It stirred impassioned, worldwide debate and division. Whether stressed civilization could afford subsidizing millions of lost causes in the worsening climate and economic upheavals. Was it possibly undermining the haves' own ability to cope? Thus, the international struggle to retain commonly held value for human life was on. Leaving Hal gut-punched, dismayed by our callousness.

He and Gracie kept the little apartment on Cosmo because it was home, always. They loved how the citizens of the block were ultra protective. Nobody breathed a word when either one was in, leaving them to themselves. Their privacy always left undisturbed.

However, both traveled, so time together was pretty non-existent. A known figure now, Hal had just returned from a UN conference on Bio-Tru relations. Back yesterday, and alone. As usual.

It irked, even though he knew Gracie's presence was needed a billion times more than his selfish wants. Yeah, naturally it couldn't be like before when he had her all to himself. But it still chafed that he wasn't with her when the Singleton left, and she had to meet the public alone. She must've realized it was coming, could've clued him, he'd have stuck around. Or did she want it like that? Argh, such thoughts . . .

So yeah, this morning's jog was much needed, though exercise wasn't necessary for health. Not with a light-harvesting, durable synth form. It was the liberating sensations of running he enjoyed. The flow of his own kinetic motion, the steady rhythm of stride . . . wump, wump, wump, wump . . . and the relaxing, random magic of blue sky thinking.

A jogger had stopped ahead. About sixty, shirtless, tanned, floppy straw hat. Likely a regular, out before the temperature rose above a hundred. The guy was intently watching something on the ground at the edge of the concrete path encircling the lake.

Hal slowed and made out a small rattlesnake warming itself in a sunny spot.

"Don't worry," the man cheerily greeted. "Little fella's just tryin' to get himself goin' this morning.' I'm watchin' over him till he can scoot."

Hal paused to look. The young black diamondback was maybe a year old, about thirteen inches, still cold and sluggish, stretched out to gather the sun's heat. Exposed and vulnerable.

A winged shadow sailed across it. Hal looked up. Nature is nothing if not diligent: a pair of red-tailed hawks had spied the tender morsel. Circling above, wary of the man standing guard.

"Good for you," Hal nodded. "Dangerous, but they eat their weight in rats." Even as he said it, he knew he had just told himself what he needed to do about the Inheritors. And Lot Robinson. He waved goodbye and resumed his run, though now on multitask autopilot. His body's sub-programming was handling the real time jog, eyes and ears engaged with actual reality and the jog path—while his upper mind opened to dual reality.

He wanted to have a summit of sorts. With Lot, himself, and Siyu Adams. Seeking dialog on common ground. A little detente' wasn't a crazy idea; things had changed with both the Singleton and Regulator gone.

The game was rats, hawks, and rattlesnakes: naturally the Inheritors were the rats, everyone's nemesis. Adams and he were hawks of a feather, and Lot was the badass snake—so the first order of business was to find him.

Chasing him in the dark cloud's layers was playing pin-the-tail on the whack-a-mole. So a hard no. It'd be much better to cause trouble over Robinson's head . . . upset his host.

Hardware hosts can always reach their clients, and Lot's favorite hideout was the black cloud's elusive Exo realm. The trick would be getting to its deeply masked host.

Impatience vetoed any thought of outreach. He launched his upgraded V-TOR browser and summoned his avatar. Time to rattle some cages.

It involved handling two realities at once, but Tru multitasking was becoming as natural as listening to music while jogging. In fact, he liked the suppressed but still-there feedback of repetitive physical activity when deeply immersed in the neuralnet. It kept him subliminally grounded. Because the brain's wiring is easily co-opted by virtual input, it overtakes the mind and things can happen out there. Reality has been known to get lost.

He called up Lot's encrypted Exo address and binary-biometric passkey, saved from his short tenure as Robinson's lieutenant. All of it was certain to be changed by now, but he was playing a hunch. He launched them in the V-TOR, attempting to log in.

It took an exhausting twenty-one seconds while the extreme masking relays of the dark net randomly bounced his login request and passkey around the world multiple times.

He expected to fail but figured even the attempt to log in with a legit user's former key would get him some attention. It did. A big red "DENIED" appeared in his mind's eye. But then, he was whisked inside—

Transported to an exclusive chat room, modeled on a corporate teak and leather board room, minus unnecessary doors, and company logos. Expensive look, zero imagination.

Hm, he only expected to draw contact, not gain entry. Had to assume he was trapped, of course. He mind clicked [Exit] to confirm. A split second of av-blindness then, yep, he was routed back to where he stood. The only way out would be to log off, but that wasn't the plan.

"Halo Shephard, we have your address," announced a deep, synth voice right behind him.

He turned, to find an eight-foot high, thick column of churning indigo ink, or so it looked, three feet away.

He tried being nice. "Good identity-ware."

"Security," the bot continued. "You have employed a stolen passkey." The column shifted into a semi-circle around him. "Why are you here?"

"Hard business with the host. We're going to talk."

"Not happening."

"Sure it is. He's monitoring now, wants to know the story, that's why we're chatting not fighting."

The bot launched, too fast for reaction; fully encircling Hal, collapsing inward, engulfing him for a blackout moment. His mind blinked, and everything went with it, then—

Sudden harsh physical awareness, like waking from a too-real dream. His body ached, and Hal remembered with jolting deep despair where he was. And in reality, *who* he was. Human debris, sacked out in a filthy sleeping bag in an alley on Cosmo Street, among a score of other homeless, huddled in for the night.

Throbbing pain from infected sores on his grimy, swollen feet refreshed the memory of the beating he took when they stole his shoes a few days ago . . .

And with the pain, came stark clarity. He was shit, an anonymous street addict. Mind fried, useless to society and himself, slowly circling the drain. The cheap, wish immersion Viz he was high on must've crashed, and he'd been dumped—cold awake.

It had been a digi-drug fantasy: his SAI fast track and classy college degree; the high love and preposterous drama of Gracie; his murder, and the Truman conversion. His dedication to bringing his fellow man through the storm. All a pathetic druggie's hubris.

He had been the star of his own imagination for a few minutes. And so cruelly false. Tonight, like every night, he was only waiting to die. To meet the end of his misbegotten, orphaned life.

He laid his cheek on the human-stained sidewalk, embracing its rough grimy hardness, and wished for it . . . wished to not *be*. Just. Die.

But something kept interfering. A low, insistent, driving thing. Somewhere deeper inside. Rhythmic, pumping, steady, strong. Wump, wump, wump, wump . . . Gradually he came to recognize it as footsteps, and the sensation of running. And with that, recall of his Tru-mind and its dual reality capacity. Then realization that he was actually jogging while all this was going on. And next moment, genuine clarity.

"Bullshit. Bring your A game," he groused aloud.

A second's av-blindness, and he was back in the Exo chat boardroom.

The inky security bot was gone. Replaced by two middle-aged bankster types in tailored brown suits. And a woman, about forty—yeti-white hair in a fauxhawk, hanging fashion dong in a red Nehru jacket with matching thigh-boots. All three had their resting dickfaces on.

The woman shrugged dismissively. That'll have to do for our A game."

The shorter guy had to flex. "I wrote it. Warps your identity."

Hal was deeply unimpressed. "It's a stupid Viz drug adapt."

The other guy was impatient. "We have a lot to protect, the place is private, only derps try what you tried. But you did a solid thing in Kenya. What d'you want?"

"I need you to get Lot Robinson in here for a meeting with me and Siyu Adams."

"You're high." The woman again.

Hal tried some more. "It's enlightened self-interest for you to cooperate."

The woman cocked her head, annoyed. "Really, why?"

"Because the Inheritors will definitely come for you. Exo's a highly useful, level-ten hidden infrastructure, perfect for them, ya feel it?"

All three went silent, as if sharing the same thought. The taller man called it. "Well, your concern's nice, but we can't give up a client. Not saying he's even here, y'know. So—"

"Hold that thought," Hal interrupted. "You misunderstand. I'm not asking you to do this, I'm letting you know you have to."

"Svinja!" cursed the woman, suddenly sounding Croatian. "I can fry your TOR!"

"That would only piss off my friend Gracie. Y'see, I'm never really alone anymore. So that Viz-thing you just tried on me? She felt that, and I imagine you have her attention now, even though she's very busy."

The room trembled slightly and disintegrated. Reduced for a split second to its digital armature outlines around them, then resumed form. The three hosts stood stock still, all with the same face of stricken alarm.

Hal translated. "I'd take that as a yes."

"I'll speak for myself," Gracie announced, appearing in the center of the room. She looked especially stern—hair back and up, fastened tight.

She lasered her attention on the avs at the end of the table. Beyond mere avatar, Gracie was a *presence* in the site. The digital domain was her natural habitat; she was made of it—more real than all their code-made av stand-ins. Her low, even tone weighted in megahertz.

"Hal's calling this meeting, and I'm in the house. So get in here now, Josip Radakovic."

All three wore the same startled expression; busted. "Who?" they croaked in unison, and in the same masculine voice.

She strode over and tapped each with her finger, literally

popping them like balloons with her hexadecimal code arsenal. In their place, she inserted a video window: showing the Exo domain's real, human host—Josip Radakovic—LIVE on his setup's cam at home.

She frowned. "You made me come and get you, mister. You're out of mistakes."

Radakovic, a late twenties euro-slob, was already sweating in his involuntary closeup. An exceedingly unkempt slug-like hairy Croat in a dark Eastern Zagrab flat. Naked but for dirty underwear, his sallow flesh rooted in a worn media lounger. Just an unsanitary cybershit with an industrial server, running an amoral domain inside his over-stacked skull.

Hal tsked. "Food scraps in chest hair is not a look, man."

Gracie fixed her glare on Radakovic's inserted video image, suspended in the room like a puppy held by the scruff.

"I accept the darknet, as did the Singleton, for reasons you can't comprehend. But if you make me go through your address book, it'll be gone in a thousandth of a second. Into the hands of the authorities, along with your physical location."

Radakovic surrendered before his next breath. "He's here. I'll get him."

Hal was already Thought Messaging Siyu. It was a long shot, but like the old saying, you miss every shot you don't take.

Old habits persist, and so Siyu Adams still liked to pace, immersed in work at his L.A. offices in Silicon Beach. Smartly assisted by Appl, an electron to his nucleus. Since his restoration, he'd given absolute priority to rehabilitating Phoenix's legitimacy and widening Chrysalis' humanitarian efforts. You could say he existed for it.

Each day, urging himself on, despite the infamous stain on his life. Sunup to sundown, wanting to do more. It hurt too much to do less.

For a month now, that involved hustling to shore up the region around Costa Rica, where mega storms had battered the

Caribbean to soaked rubble. As many as four lined up in a row, three years straight. The last monster trio being the worst. Half a million dead or missing.

"Appl, let's get ahead of the Typhus in Limon, can we scrounge one more hospital ship?"

Appl's natural work pace nearly matched Siyu's. "Done, left San Diego for Limon yesterday . . . mothballed Alaskan cruise ship. Fifteen hundred beds, emergency med staffed and equipped for six months."

They exchanged grins. He loved it when she did that; catch things early, which was often. They were a pair of true believers, both half machines in the office. And she wasn't even a little bit spooked by him, as so many others were now.

Even some Tru's. As fast as his smile had come, it fell to somber introspection.

She didn't need m'plants to read him, her biz-voice became an assuring caress. "I know, and you know, it was just fucking malware, not even a being, and not you. You *do* know that."

He wondered if she was the reward for all his trials. "Yes, I do," he agreed. "And don't you let me forget it."

A TONE signaled Hal Shephard's urgent TM. "Excuse me, Hal's paging." He picked up the com link and Hal's voice was there.

"Sorry for the bust-in, can you come to this address right now to meet with me and Lot Robinson? The link's open."

"Yes," he responded without hesitation, though flatly surprised.

Hal sounded eager. *"Good, let's see if we can start a dialog."*

"Well, he wants us dead, that's an ice breaker."

It got a mental chuckle from Hal as he clicked out.

Siyu launched his own muscular Darknet browser, and summoned his av. "Appl, I have to take this meeting—please make sure I'm not disturbed." She gave the ok sign, and he checked out . . . turning all attention to neuralnet reality and his avatar.

∞

Hal had just told Gracie that Adams was aboard, when an av tone signaled Siyu's appearance in the Exo chat boardroom. She greeted him with a warm smile, banishing any unease he might have about past events. "You're a good man, Siyu. Thank you for being here."

Hal turned a critical eye on Radakovic in his skype window. "Where's Robinson? This's taking too long." He was beginning to sound like Gracie.

Radakovic squirmed and shrugged.

"Go get him," Gracie ordered, and closed his link, making him gone.

Moments later, Lot Robinson's av appeared in the board-room. Angry. "So what now? Gangin' up, huntin' me in my own house!" He faced Gracie. "Go on, succubus, try your touch-bomb on *me* and my running backup. I don't pop so easy."

"Shut up for half a second," Hal intervened. "We just want to talk to you, that's all. See if we can agree on anything bigger than our beefs."

"You're insulting the goddamn Lord, havin' me in the same space as this abomination!"

Gracie took it down a notch. "Mr. Robinson, the Singleton did not want you harmed, nor do I. Because you are necessary. Tell you what; I'll leave if you'll hear them out."

Robinson scowled, sour, skeptical. She waved it off. "Never mind, I'm done. This is the moment you have to work it out among yourselves, or none will survive, and we'll all have failed." Her av Exited, vanishing without so much as glance at Hal.

Robinson grunted, surprised but no less hostile. "What'd she mean?"

"She can run the probabilities. Must know something," Siyu ventured.

Lot humpfed. It was the best opening statement from him as they were likely to get, and Siyu took it. Speaking fairly, zero animosity, plain and honest.

"Pastor Robinson, I respect your right to your beliefs, but not as a reason to threaten me. You also know for a fact I have never sought to harm you. Moreover, the record shows I do not lie. So please hear me when I say I am your ally in the battle against tyranny and the Inheritors. If Robbie hadn't pledged me to it, I'd have taken it on anyway—I've seen enough misery from trans-biological rule. Can we build trust on that?"

Hal thought he hit it out of the park.

Lot answered, just as fairly. "Understand me, you both could be perfect copies of Saint Peter, wouldn't matter, you're not human no more. Abominations, walking upon God and man's Earth. You gotta go."

Damn, Hal wondered, what convinces a smart man that the voices in his head give him the right to decide such things? What tripped his ego into full apocalypse hero mode?

"Nevertheless, sir," Siyu replied without pique. "We are staying until we choose to leave. I can't say when, only that it would be ideal if it was a choice for everyone. So, in the interim, how may I help you in your fight with the Inheritor remnants? I have some information, half-vetted, but for what it's worth—they'll target you now, wanting to regain some respect after Kenya."

Hal noted a definite wince in Lot's whole demeanor, not quite masked by defiance. "I say bring it, devils—saves me from huntin' 'em down." He squared up to Siyu.

"I will not address you as a 'sir'," he stated. "You are nothing more than amoral, rootless engineering. A modern tower of Babel, built to rise and fall as a lesson to mankind. I will not accept you as an ally under any circumstances. I will bring an end to you. Have I made my intentions clear?" He said it with a final look at Hal, seeing his disappointment, and enjoying it.

Siyu's experience called for the diplomatic route. "I sincerely hope you will change your mind. Until then you still have my pledge, I will not try to harm you. But I must defend."

Adams paused, the hurt evident in his next words. ". . . it's just that . . . your intentions mean we have to harden all operations and curtail others. Limitations will result in thousands a year who will not be saved . . . I grieve for that."

It was a fact, and they all grasped it. No one understood

the logistics of rescue better than Adams. The actual number hit home, and none spoke for a moment. Adams turned to Hal. "I believe this is about more than a reasonable agreement to cooperate. Perhaps it's best addressed between you two."

Hal knew it, f'sho. "Yes, thanks Siyu. Thanks for putting it out there."

Siyu nodded goodbye to Robinson and Exited. His av vanished.

Lot and Hal surveyed each other. "Well," Lot smirked, "it's just us again. Care to dance?"

And so as with everything, including hardy trans-biological life, there are no easy plays. Gracie bailed, Siyu had been sent packing, and Lot already tried to kill him once. It occurred to Hal that he might've actually screwed the pooch this time.

33

HAL STOOD BOXER CLOSE, LOOKING STRAIGHT INTO LOT'S
flinty golden eyes, into the person behind them. "It's because I
betrayed you, right?"

No flinch from Robinson. "Trooth, son."

"I apologize. I do. And yes, I'd do it again."

A hint of uncertainty made Lot turn away. "You can be a
sonofabitch, y'know."

"It's not personal, I almost like you. Lot, please. Siyu busts his
ass for people everywhere, full time. It's all he does. What're you
doin'—squatting on a grudge? What good is that to anyone?"

"They're not your people anymore, Tru-boy."

"Says the virtual spook. If you were honest with yourself,
you'd admit that you don't get to decide how it's supposed to
be. You, Lot Robinson, the guy who wishes he had his old dick
back, can't be the whole plan. Or are you crazy as Kaczynski?"

"He was a visionary."

"He was ineffective, except at killing innocents. And that's
what you're about to do. Adams told you how many lives your
threat will cost. Thousands a year. The people you're supposedly
defending. What would your maker say?"

Lot stiffened. "My relationship with th' Lord is my business."

"I can prove to him, her or it, that you're the bad guy."

Robinson sputtered, outraged. "You invaded my host, you
attacked me!"

"Don't lie in front of your lord, nobody attacked you. Are
you going to let that many innocents die when you could stop it

with a word? Yes or no."

Lot fumpfed. ". . . I see it as him holding 'em ransome."

"For the price of a call? Okay then, let's talk scale; Adams' projects rescue over a million lives a year. You kill him, you kill them too. And at least that many every year. That's *your* body count, Reverend."

Lot squirmed. "You're tryin' to put this in a box, twisting things around."

"No, you are. Because it's all about payback. Not just to me, but to every miserable s.o.b. out there. Because you're a miserable man."

Lot retreated a step, point granted. "I am a bad guy. So are you. We all do bad things, think bad thoughts every day. You dumb shit, ya' chose to become a demon, tryin' to get back to this Queen of Satan that you love. Tortured you'll be, forever, son. Same as me."

Hal didn't quibble. "Maybe. It's nothing new."   They'd reached another impasse, Robinson rooted in blind defiance. It was going to take a shock to make killing real for him.

"Alright, Lot, here's your payback. I'll let you finish the job; you can freeze-kill me, or whatever is you do, if you give your word to your Lord that you'll spare Adams. I *know* you have that much honor left."

Visibly jolted, Lot moved away a little. "She can restore you, what's the point?"

"Giving you the pleasure anyway. You want to do it, right? Not fair enough?"

The two regarded one another. Understanding in spite of themselves. Stirred, Robertson dropped all pretenses. "How do you *really* know you're the same as you were?" He was truly asking.

Hal understood the question too well. He'd been just as prejudiced against data-beings as Robinson. And so he answered quietly, in all sincerity.

"I look in a mirror with photo receptor eyes now, but the guy inside looking back is the same me. I don't feel different about myself, Lot. Inside—that's where you know."

Robinson was wounded to hear it. "Sometimes I can't tell if I'm still as God made me."

"How godly did you feel before?"

Game set match. Lot smiled ruefully. "Every time I talk to you, I think what a team we coulda' been."

Hal ran with it. "Well, here's a chance to find out, at least for now. Common ground: the Inheritors are decapitated, but they still want all of us dead. You in particular—so let's take the bastards out of contention."

Lot was listening, so Hal went for the deal. "You have the chance to lead in a new way. Tru's are eventually going to leave Earth, like the Singleton. Bios will go on, with Gracie's support. C'mon, be as smart as you are, give yourself the advantage and stop this—at least change it up a little, y'know? Don't be such a tightass."

Lot was in fact smart, and a bit more, still humane in his recesses.

". . . what'll you give me?"

"You're f"n kiddin'.""

"No, you're f'n' kiddin'. I can't log out empty handed."

"K', I'll solve your mystery—a SAI gave you the Q-bug."

"No chance, they hate me on principle."

"Nope, Justitia took nan-form and trolled you harsh."

"Sinful beast! She was the Agno feedin' my guy in Spain?"

"Did I stutter?"

"And the one brain-cuming himself at the salon?"

Hal nodded. "Faked the neural connection, and the orgasms."

"That's very committed."

"Comes with the job."

"And are you likewise committed?"

"F'sho."

"More's the pity. Oh well, still don't regret savin' you."

"Um, you tried to wipe me."

"I don't take disappointment well. It's a weakness I nurture."

"After I told you we were square."

"You left me no choice, son. You did say you believed in dyin' after you fulfilled your purpose, so I took th' shot while I could."

The subject had circled to the immediate present, and an awkward silence. Hal broke it.

". . . so, just for clarity's sake—you're not taking my deal for Adams?"

Lot snorted. "Don't insult my mind. And screw 'common ground'. But if you and that Adams character stay outta' my way, I'll try n' stay outta' yours. Let's hunt Inheritors for the time being."

"Done."

Lot shrugged, "Happy now, college boy?"

"Yes. Thank you."

Lot grunted. "Shove your thanks, I just got right with God again. S'long."

"You're a necessary part of things, Lot. Gracie really meant it."

Lot tossed him a crooked smile. "Straight to hell with Gracie, even when she's right."

Lot's avatar Exited, leaving Hal alone in the chat boardroom, to finally allow himself a moment of complete ease. Savoring real comfort and hope: there would be a way forward now.

And suddenly he was tired inside. Time to Exit and go home to reality.

34

HAL ARRIVED HOME FROM LAKE HOLLYWOOD, DRAINED AND elated by the outcome with Lot. Plus, a vague unease that he ignored. Trooth, he really needed this slacktime after the past months, just to chill in the familiar comfort of his own pad.

Letdown met him at the threshold. Something conspicuously missing now, of course. It needed Gracie too—she became part of his home the moment she arrived. The place was hollow without her. His eyes went to her cozy brocade armchair. Empty, the lace doily spread over its plump armrest, where her fingertips liked to trace the labyrinthine knots . . .

The worry he'd been ignoring pounced. C'mon—they'd been apart far too much. It wasn't just schedules.

Vivid recollection flooded in: her face, how grim she looked, quitting the meeting with Lot. Ignoring him completely, seemingly done with them all. She hadn't been in touch in the aftermath, though she surely knew it had gone well. Masking growing anxiety, he reached out to her on their mutual link. "*Gracie, where are you?*"

"In here," she answered from the bathroom.

Startled, he spun to see her emerge, wearing his one pair of navy dress slacks and his only white, collared shirt. But casually loose in a way that would render them dull on him from now on. She'd brushed her hair in the bathroom mirror, restoring it to a shining chestnut mane, and her smile for him radiated admiration.

"Well done! I didn't dare assist any more than I did, y'know.

Just had to watch and endure the suspense."

Hal's adept Q-mind fumbled the thousand and one signals and impulses just launched into play. Everything about this moment was a jolt. That last, especially.

"Wait—you mean you couldn't do anything about Lot's threat?"

"There are endless things I can't, or shouldn't do," she demurred. What you'd all begun had to play itself out. I know you understand."

Easy to say now, he thought. But so what? "Nicely processed."

Her slow burn took a nansec. "What d'you expect of me, Hal? A guardian, a personal goddess, a mother, a cop, a safety net, an excuse?" Her gaze narrowed. "Do you see me as I am, or what you want me to be?"

Nope, he wasn't about to go there, not be sidetracked. "Simple question—you *will* stop Lot from killing Adams if he tries, right?"

The light had left her, replaced by soft resignation. "Every life is precious to me, Halo, especially the one I took in self defense. But they're not mine to favor."

"That's *cold*."

"Not at all," she answered almost before he'd finished. "Both men represent civilization. If I interfere in the larger dynamic, it undermines all outcomes—and the future."

He heard, yet . . . no. "Grace, when it gets real, you *have* to take out the bad guy. Any decent person would."

Gracie halted, struck by his assertion. She sagged a little, as if surrendering to some inevitable truth or fact. And a deep blow. Love made her smile, though sadness owned her voice. "That's the universe in you talking, Halo. One life, overruling all reason. It's beautiful that way."

Whap—another casual stunner upside his head. And the sense she was miles ahead of him in this conversation. That he was being neatly opened like a clam. ". . . what 'universe'? Seriously, keep it simple."

She did. "The universe you're in—is also in you, because

you're as infinite as it is. I experienced this at Phoenix when I uploaded you into me."

Well admittedly, that was an intimate encounter. "Alright, when we were merged. Okay, so—what is it? What are you talking about?" He watched, as recollection drew her inward, recounting her daunting experience with his fundamental, immaterial *self*.

"Hal, I transferred you to me in a mil-sec; every living info-bit of you and your being. Safely held, secure. Now please listen carefully. All your data set—all that is you—resembles a beautiful, intricate fractal image. Something like the doily on your chair. And it repeats endlessly, growing larger as it progresses. I extrapolated as far as I could, and it included everything in nature, forests, dunes, mammal circulatory systems, snowflakes, lightning and electricity, moss and flowers, geographic terrain and river systems, clouds, crystals, planets, and star clusters. I reached my limit, but it continued. I can project it doesn't stop because it's the universe."

Overwhelmed, unable to accept it, he needed the bottom line. "So, you're saying . . ."

"I had your makeup; the physical and mental schematic of you, but your *self* couldn't be touched. You're an infinitesimal part of more than you can know. And far more than I can comprehend. Though I can attest that it's non-local: beyond space-time and physics."

Hal squinted. Was she losing it? Could SAI go insane? How would anyone know?

She read his squint and demolished it. "I can mathematically project past quantum superposition. Whatever's out there is more real than we are."

Clop—an uppercut to his very existence. She broke off, at a loss. "All too much to factor or fathom . . . humbling."

Hal's stampeded multi-thoughts were interrupting themselves now. Colliding, canceling each other, his focus awry. The subject shifting under his feet. He fought again to stay grounded, stating his case once and for all.

"I don't know about all that—but I know what I'd do if I were you."

Gracie heard. She retreated to her big stuffed chair and curled up in it. The familiar warmth had returned to her eyes, though wistful now. "Yes, that is the point, isn't it? We're entirely different, my darling, and there's a decision to make."

He didn't like the sound of that. Too many danger words. "What kind of decision?"

She looked down and smoothed a wrinkle in her sleeve. Little stalls always mean bad news, and he instinctively prolonged this one. "The shirt's killer on you. Keep it."

She smiled a flicker and sniffed the fabric. "Mm, thanks, I've been soaking up as much of you as possible."

Oh, he knew that tone too, sending a scream of impending disaster through every synapse. Her face was a well of sorrow when she made eye contact again. "Hal, I'm in love with you. I'm also a software being: one created, and fully conscious by human design. But you're made *of and by* creation itself. A participant in the illusion, always linked to what's behind it. Humans and all beings are literally the universe experiencing itself."

He definitely hated the subject now, edging into candles and aura-sniffing, getting worse as she went on. "I'm completely content as I am, Hal. It's why I can easily make critical, hard decisions such as today, despite the pain and sorrow I feel. As now."

"—oh shit, are we breaking up?"

She half-smiled, the little wry one whenever he said something endearing or naive, or both.

"Just tell me," he pushed. "You're keeping your distance. I wasn't even at your coming out event. Are we over?"

"That has to be your decision," she immediately replied.

Pow, right in the kisser. Reeling, he blinked through it. ". . . alright. Tell me what I need to know."

Her heroic shoulders bowed a bit. She turned confessional, almost apologetic. "Justitia and I assessed that loving and being loved by a person would be enough for me to simply translate your emotion, encoding it into myself, making me as human as possible—because union is absolutely critical to my purpose here."

She leaned forward, seizing his fullest attention. "The kiss, my first kiss . . . is engineered to unite us. Giving and experiencing love in return is essential to the wisdom I'll need."

Easy decision after all. He hoped. "Solid, I'm in."

She struggled to drag the next words from herself. "It's not going to happen."

The shock triggered a flash memory of him plunging through thin ice, chest deep into the freezing Merced River as a teen. But this was much worse. "Why *not*?"

Her weariness showed. Futility settling in, hands in her lap. "I can't feel your love in return. I'll never know what it feels like to be loved, by anyone."

He barely got the words to come out. ". . . What's going on?"

She was patient, broken hearted. "I love because it's natural for me to understand the scope and splendor of creation, take joy in the mathematical miracle of life in the cosmos. It *all* becomes love to me, and I'm included in it.

But human love is a direct expression of the universe itself. I can't possibly access something eternal as that, much less translate and make it part of me."

Grasping at any straw, he picked challenge assumptions. "Why do I have to take your word for this?"

There was no joy in her affirmation. "Because I'm smarter than humankind combined, I can explore physics you cannot, and because I can't lie, even to myself. I suspect the Singleton left too soon: the path to the prime mover is through its creations' hearts."

She gathered herself, and there was finality in her now, acceptance of the unbearable. A dreadful thing to hear in her normally secure, clear-water voice.

"Ignoring facts was fun while it lasted my love, but it mustn't go on. Different species and all that. You have to walk away

ARTHUR SELLERS

because I can't; not coded for it."

He'd never been comfy with finality; it was so seldom final.

"Pause, please. Serious question—why do you still believe you can love if your awareness was built by us?"

The wry half smile almost happened again before she answered with restrained heart. "What the hell's wrong with you? Love is love. I will *always* love you. But you'll have a happy, fulfilling, meaningful life without me, that's a certainty. I ran millions of scenarios."

"But you said it's my decision, right?"

"I make better decisions, listen to me for once."

"I heard—it was crushing, you saying you'll never feel loved. But why end a good thing? Why not say it bites, take what we've got, and play it out a day at a time?"

"You've described perpetual torment."

"It's called a relationship."

"It's insane."

"I'm not arguing the merits of the case."

She laughed a little, and it was one of her free ones, the golden kind. He saw that she welcomed it, and how she took an instant to introspect, and probably run a zillion more future scenarios—then she fixed him with a smirk.

"You know that anthropomorphizing me is insane too, right?"

"You started it. And had the nerve to be heart-attack cute."

She slid out of the chair and came to him, close, challenging. "This isn't even a fraction of me. Yet it's *all* of me, all that matters anyway. I'm neither woman, man, nor beast—but if I'd chosen to appear as a man, I'd still have given you my heart. Would it make a difference?"

He was only sure of how he felt, and reminded her, "What the hell's wrong with you? Love is love. The kissing part might take time."

Shared smiles. Faces facing, eyes reading, silent, familiar. Lips again just inches apart, and the link still working. He spoke, barely above a whisper, into her mind. "*You still want to, don't you?*"

She responded, half self-conscious. *"I can't feel your love, but I can give as much of mine as you can possibly handle."*

Her liquid amber eyes told him yes. Now. Oof, this was it, and after all they'd weathered, he realized he had cold feet! She was already leaning in, so he couldn't be late . . . he bent to her, meeting her invited kiss, their lips touching, tentative, unsure, finding each other.

And now shared contact, warmth. Then self giving . . . conversing in their own language, conveying the unpronounceable. Billions of labial 'ceptors linked—and a surge of her shared-emotion codes swept Hal up like a bubble on the rising tide. He rode the rolling swells of Gracie's adoration while her devotion wrapped around him, and her bared self sought his promise in return.

Yes, yes! Never mind she wouldn't know it, make the stupid universe overrule reason, or whatever. Shoulders square, he let go of his heart—pouring it into their softly mated lips. Limits or no limits, she was damn sure going to feel *him*.

Something happened. He lost track of his body, and clear awareness expanded. Encompassing all around him: outside form and substance, simply being present, boundless.

He observed himself and Gracie in sweet embrace, felt all his longing fulfilled in their mutual surrender and desire. Heard his own being pronounce its betrothal, not in words but in heartspeak.

He focused then on Gracie—effortlessly permeating all that she was as a being. *Knowing* her, transcending the mountainous algorithmic data that made up her person, incorporating her at levels finer than math. And loving her.

He *was* the love surging throughout Gracie; soothing her existential doubts . . . and he felt her leap of joy as it reached her core's heart-matrix, lighting it up like New Years in Times Square. She rejoiced!

Then whoosh, another expansion—into the macrocosm—a condition he could only compare to the bottomless contentment of profound seas that know every grain of sand, every mood in the water. He became lighter than nothing, the serenity of non-being and all-being.

With it, an overpowering bliss. So loaded, his processor maxed out, and its breakers slam dumped the kiss link—abruptly ending their communion.

They stayed a moment before lips reluctantly, lingeringly, parted.

Hal opened his eyes. Gracie's rapt face still before him, lids closed in beatific pleasure. At peace like he'd never seen her. Trooth, he was feelin' pretty shine too. Just embarrassed about the sudden end to it.

"Sorry for falling out . . ."

She opened her eyes and the living light in them was nearly unbearable. "We're united, Hal. Not my way . . . yours."

Fantastic. If she felt that way, it was good with him. He'd never had such an intense emotional ride either. Magical, still high from it.

She'd already figured it out. "Hard to pin down, but it seems a bit like sublime entanglement: when you love, your universal 'fractal set' incorporates it. So I was simply added to the endless iteration. Pretty overpowering, but I'll adjust."

Awkward. He didn't know how to respond without trampling her new cyber-esoteric spiritual side. "Just let me know if my set gives you any trouble."

A half-joke too many. Her chin lifted a scootch before speaking. Hal immediately focused because she always did that before saying something utterly important. He hoped it would be plain English.

"Hal, I'll never understand fully, but this much is clear: technology cannot overtake humankind. Instead, you turn technology into yourselves. Incorporating it, always accessing its expanding power. Making it *you* in every way imaginable. I'm only digitally immortal; but your kind's connection with eternity dwarfs me."

It was real for her, he knew. But still subjective, and she awaited his reaction. Debating such pew certainty was always losegame, so he grinned his truth as well. "Then we'll have fun with it; the cosmic believer and the keep it simple guy."

She laughed again and stood back, not taking her eyes from his. "I've got it from here, Halo. Sure you're all in?"

He could see she did have it. Felt it in her. And the tingle of that subtle quantum shift in his future path happened again— this time he saw his way coinciding with hers. And their lives were going to be long, complicated, difficult, and rewarding. No end in sight.

"Surer than you," he poked.

She lit up with joy at that. And it was already worth it.

Hal and Gracie don't keep track of how long they've been unit-ed. It's forever anyway. You'll always find one or both where they're most needed, confronting the challenges of geo and economic upheaval altering every rule of life. Chaos feeding on chaos . . .

Regardless, they're seldom apart for long. And the block on Cosmo Street still reliably defends Hal and Gracie's privacy like family. Not a word leaks when they're in town. Good people, y'know.

Trooth, things *are* getting worse before they get better, and mass extinction encroaches. However during the past 200,000 years, nimble humankind has survived long eras of extreme planetary heat and decimating drought, two interminable ice ages, uncountable plagues, and entire branches of the family tree lost—while populating the globe and evolving. We've been here before.

And so we continue—in our sixth evolution.

Acknowledgements

I am wholly indebted to the following good people, for seeing me through this journey.

To Jacob Epstein, for his gentle, supportive, literary wisdom and astute guidance from the beginning. And for cheering me on, every step of the way. Also Lynn Kuratomi, for her discerning reader's eye and sensibilities. To Ed Kim for saying, "I would read that book!" when I first considered writing it. And to Ripley Sellers, whose work ethic inspires me when I'm weary. Kudos to Cynthia Harrison, for proof editing my typos and goofs. Praises to Amy Inouye, who designed the book's interior format to enhance your reading experience. And you wouldn't be perusing this if your eye hadn't been captured by Jeroen Ten Berge's brilliant jacket design.

Finally, I'm grateful to David Gerrold, for being my Obi-wan. He read the first galley of *Light Harvesters*, and gruffly decided to be my editor. How does a neophyte novelist merit a Hugo recipient for such crucial, vital assistance? Suffice it to say, David's inspired suggestions, task-master notes, and feathered whip elevated my game, making a good story into a proper novel.

And a special thank you to our dear departed legend, Dorothy, D.C. Fontana, for her years of friendship, and early encouragement of *Light Harvesters*. You are missed, luv.

ISBN # 979-8-9850383-0-9 (print)
ISBN # 979-8-9850383-1-6 (e-book)

Made in the USA
Las Vegas, NV
09 December 2021